I0535469

I dedicate this novel to Yvette. It was your love, support, and patience that gave me the courage I needed to share my vision with the rest of the world.

Jonathan Rivera

The Dreamer: Origins

Jonathan Rivera

Act I

A Forgotten Past

Jonathan Rivera

I: Imprisoned

Beyond the rusted metal bars of his prison, John stared into the abyss of her eyes as he desperately searched for answers. Why was he being held prisoner? What had he done to deserve this? And more importantly, who was he? John had no memory of his past. All he had was the pain of the nightmares that haunted him each night without fail.

He saw nothing but pain and sorrow deep within her eyes, and he felt an excruciating migraine that tore his mind apart. He could stare no longer as his body began to numb and forced him to surrender his efforts to search for those answers.

She passed by his cell every evening as supper was thrown in; her visit was routinely accompanied by a conversation devoid of words. After she blinked her eyes once, she would often roll them into the back of her head as if to look upon the young prisoners behind her. She would often exhale a humph at John in disappointment. After one final gaze, she reveled in a wicked laugh that made him cringe.

She had earned the title of Ice Queen.

On this night, he attempted a desperate, final plea with her for his freedom, a plea that fell flat as he was unable to build up the courage to utter his words beyond a whisper.

"Can I please g-g-go?" The words vanished into thin air before they completed their flight to her ears, or so he thought.

She acknowledged his mumble and ceased her malevolent laughter. She turned around immediately and yelled beyond the worn teeth of her barely open mouth, "*What* did you say?"

Rumor had it among the young captives that her teeth were worn because she had eaten any child who attempted to flee, flesh and bone. A young prisoner nicknamed Delusional Dahlia swore that she had seen the wicked lady devour an eyeball that dangled from the tip of her ice arrow after an adrenaline-filled escape attempt.

John mumbled, "Nothing, Your M-Majesty."

Once again, she screamed through her teeth and almost shattered them with the sheer force of her words. "That's what I thought! You will *never* leave this place! Now go eat your liver porridge, you ungrateful little *pauper*!"

Unable to speak anymore, John retreated into the corner of his cell, which he had begun to rapidly outgrow. It was a mere six by six feet and only six feet tall. It hardly accommodated a growing eleven-year-old.

As was his routine every evening before he lay down on his rat-chewed mattress, he gazed beyond the gated window, barely two feet in diameter, situated in the center of the dungeon wall. John enjoyed the view of a beautiful landscape below, lush with foliage and abundant with life. He often imagined freedom beyond the thick stone walls and the rusted metal bars that he was imprisoned by. He was not alone; several other children, many of whom were two or three years his junior, shared the same hopeless fate.

To the east he had begun to hear the shrieks of the phoenix dragons, which had been dormant for the past several years. Over the past days, they were active during the late hours and were often confused for meteorites as they soared past the east wing and across the southern skies.

He could not see much to the west either, as the west wing of the dungeon protruded into his line of sight. All he could see was the weakening earth that broke apart in clusters from time to time. It covered the one-foot-thick stone walls that imprisoned countless young captives beneath the palace.

He often looked toward one of the cells in the west wing, in hopes that she would gaze upon the few stars that struggled to get noticed in the distance, beyond the ominous southern kingdom of Villanis. On this night she did. Her emerald eyes, which glistened during the hours of daylight, were not as noticeable against the stars. However, her radiant smile still managed to glow against her smooth caramel skin with hopes of finding freedom one day. She raised her heels from the ground and stood on her toes while she looked over to John's gated window. She waved to him. He panicked and released his grip from the bars. He jumped away and gasped as he leaned against the cold dungeon wall while his heart raced. She had frightened him. Tonight, however, he would finally build up the courage to return her wave. He approached the gated window deliberately as he hugged the wall. He peeked from its side, but she had already gone. He would no longer be able to admire Ivy's beauty on this evening.

He was not a courageous lad and was disappointed in himself once again. He returned his gaze toward the lush jungle several hundreds of feet below, in which villages were scattered, with torches that shifted throughout as the palace guards moved about during the evening hours of their patrol.

He turned his attention toward the south. Beyond the lush paradise, there was a desert, in which sandstorms gusted regularly and rarely allowed visibility during the late hours. Farther south was an expansive sea, which appeared calm, as was usual at this time of the day. Beyond the sea was Villanis, from which rose the Fire King's castle, veiled by the darkness of ever-present black storm clouds.

Freedom would be as likely as him soaring across the sky along with the phoenix dragons. John stepped away from the window and lay down. He pulled his blanket over himself and exposed his aching feet to the elements, thanks to the hungry rats that often passed by in the middle of the night and nibbled on his blanket for nourishment. It was a constant reminder of the chilly winter as the coldness of the stone dungeon grounds permeated his mattress, which was barely thicker than his blanket. As he curled into a fetal position in order to trap the heat, he often shivered uncontrollably. He was forced to rest his hands between his knees so they would not crash into each other continuously throughout the night.

His body often ached, and this day was no different, as the other young prisoners had just twice re-iced the entire hundred-chamber Ice Palace. Icing duties, which lasted from immediately after breakfast until just before supper, had become increasingly challenging over the past few days as icicles unshackled from the palace ceilings and fell upon the young workers beneath. This was one of the first signs that the impossibly cold winter finally was approaching its end.

Especially excruciating was the pain he'd felt in his left foot since the day prior, when an icicle penetrated his thick boot after it had fallen from the ceiling. Though the Ice Queen afforded most of the prisoners visibility, John was required to wear a blindfold within Her Majesty's master chamber. Still, she expected nothing short of perfection.

As the icicle pierced his foot, he stumbled directly into an antique porcelain doll, which had allegedly been stolen from the young princess of the lavish western kingdom of Buv're in a vicious crime of envy. This mishap triggered an unfortunate sequence of events. A large shard from the shattered doll broke free and collided with the icicle-laden ceiling. Her Majesty's royal bathtub brimmed to the top with a deep black substance that she bathed in daily. Perhaps she was attempting to darken her merciless soul further, but without success, as it could not become even one shade darker.

The massive icicle approached rapidly. The impact in the tub was so massive that the thick substance exploded throughout the chamber and left almost the entire space coated in black. John was not sure what had happened until he peeked from behind his blindfold. He immediately knew there would be consequences and feared that he would be consumed next. A collective gasp followed, and nervous screams soon echoed throughout the Ice Palace.

Just before the frozen door swiveled on its iced hinges, he quickly veiled his eyes once again. Her Majesty was at his feet, and the chilled and terrible smell of her breath permeated his nose. It forced his face to contort in anguish and gave him the appearance of wrinkles that seemed comparable to those residing within her frosted, middle-aged skin. Her long, deep black hair was pulled back into an unfashionable twist and remained unmoved as the chill that emanated from her body froze it into place; it juxtaposed against her pale skin.

"Do you realize what you've done?" she screamed.

"Um…no, Your M-Majesty," replied John deceitfully.

"Well…" She began to speak as she lifted her scepter and forced his body to bend at his knees, which were soon soaked by the oily substance. "You will scrub this chamber until only the chill of the ice remains…*tonight!* And you will *not* rest until you are finished!" She stormed off to her secondary resting chamber.

John scrubbed throughout the wintry night until he could scrub no longer. He took only one brief break before he completed the daunting task as several sets of eyes observed and judged his every movement. Guards had been on watch to ensure he finished by the break of dawn. He finally finished at the hour of sunrise, just in time for breakfast. He rested his eyes only briefly, however, during breakfast, and as a result, his face had swum in his bowl of liver porridge.

John snapped back to the frozen present after he reflected on the past days as he lay on his mattress. He overheard some chatter from the other cells. Whispers of his name barely broke the silence of the frigid night.

Finally one of the other children yelled out, "Nice job, Joe!"

He mumbled to himself, "It's…John."

A few extra torches were lit while the guards finished their final patrol of the night, not out of generosity but to prevent the young captives from becoming frozen in the dead of the night, which often dropped by at least twenty degrees in temperature. The illumination also forced the children to watch one another in despair, which added to the terror they already felt. Her Majesty needed to preserve her labor force, though she often threatened to worsen the conditions with the removal of the torches if they misbehaved.

The guards usually rushed their last patrol to expedite their after-hours activities, which included drinking mead over a raucous game of modinos, a game that confused many. It consisted of face cards, stone tiles, and a wooden board. Modinos often led to loud and obnoxious yells as flying fists rumbled throughout the halls of the dungeon. The ruckus routinely woke the young prisoners, who tried desperately to rest and regain their strength for the following day of unfair duties.

As John looked hopelessly at the dirt-filled gray dungeon floor, he observed every breath, each one visible due to the bone-bitingly cold temperatures of the night. The billows of his breaths began to break form around a hazy chocolate figure. The figure continued to approach him slowly, and it soon revealed itself. It was nothing more than a frail, aged rodent that was quite large for its kind. It coughed against John's unsavory breath and looked at him as they both groaned in pain.

John was famished as he had missed his opportunity to eat breakfast. His supper portion barely made a dent in his belly after the long day of labor followed another sleep-deprived night.

The liver porridge from the morning had been smothered into his blanket, as he'd used it to wipe himself. The unsavory odor brought him some welcome company this evening. With a desperate hunger of its own, the overgrown rodent approached cautiously. It looked at John with each step as if it were concerned that it would become dinner itself.

The silence was finally broken when John mumbled miserably, "Don't worry…I prefer liver in my porridge."

Upon hearing this, the furry little rodent raced toward the foot of John's chewed-up mattress and scoured the blanket for the dried porridge until none remained. The feast was finished, and the rodent was aware its welcome had come to an end. It looked upon John as it crept away. He realized the frailty of the rodent was actually a shiver, so he offered what little warmth remained under his blanket. The furry rodent raced once again and joined the young prisoner to share the isolated and minimal warmth.

The guards played modinos each night. They were about to commence their disorderly game, though this night seemed a bit more civilized, since no fights broke out before the game. Perhaps they had run out of mead. The yells became muffled and distant, as did the soft whispers of John's name from the other cells. His chilled breaths began to vanish, while the ominous, rustic gray that surrounded him on all sides subsided to the darkness.

The last sounds he heard before he faded into the darkness himself were, "Don't worry, John."

John was in a dark room illuminated only slightly by a few torches that flickered in a struggle for their lives. The flickers of light allowed for only brief visibility of his surroundings. As the last of the debris fell and settled in, he could see several partially burned scrolls among the rubble of a battle that appeared to have just reached its dramatic conclusion. With his head lowered, he searched desperately for anything that resembled some meaning. He found nothing.

He began to hear footsteps in the distance, increasingly amplified with each step as they approached. A red silhouette finally appeared around a figure before him, veiled predominantly by the darkness of the shadows. The dark figure was beastly, with crimson eyes on the verge of erupting. John cowered. The footsteps approached and became heavier and louder. The heat emitted by the beast began to warm his skin and soon created a mild burn. John did not have the courage to look up. He began to weep as he covered his ears, with his head sheltered between his knees. He sang a familiar lullaby: "Don't worry…It's going to be all right…"

The beast roared John's name repeatedly as he whimpered. He continued to hum the lullaby as his lips became paralyzed; he had lost his ability to sing aloud any longer. He still could not face the beast. Soon the voice transformed into a tone no different from that of a young boy, which calmed him; however, John's wrist suddenly seared as it was clenched by the firm grip of the beast. The tension that had subsided just a moment ago returned.

"John! Wake up!"

And he suddenly awoke.

"John, hurry up. You overslept again. She's going to eat us for breakfast if we don't hurry up!"

"Sorry, Jacob…Sorry, William," John replied as he wiped the sweat that had drenched his hair and face throughout the night yet again.

"Don't be sorry to us. The others despise you for what you did," said William.

Jacob added, "Don't worry, John. For most of them, this is their first winter in the Ice Palace. Spring is a few weeks early this year. We would need to re-ice the palace twice a day anyway." A mild relief reset John's apprehensions.

After he hastily dressed himself in his winter attire, John missed breakfast once again due to his tardiness. He nearly tripped over his own feet as he raced toward the queue of prisoners who were on their way into the great hall. He briefly looked back at his mattress and noticed a small, empty imprint from his company the night before. As he clutched his wrist in pain, he realized that he had a mild burn in the same place that he had been grabbed in his dream, something that had not happened before. The burning sensation was soon soothed by the coolness of the great hall.

II: An Attempt to Flee Thwarted

The young captives each had specific duties. Most were tasked to re-ice the walls of the massive Ice Palace. Several were required to make sure the palace was spotless, free of fallen debris, as the winter came to an end and unshackled icicles from great heights. They also needed to cleanse the frosty surfaces of the mud tracked into the palace by the guards.

Other captives were side by side as they chiseled the doorways and statues, among other furnishings, back into Her Majesty's desired moldings. The temperatures rose quickly as the season shifted from winter to spring, and labor would be most grueling during the summer months as the ambient temperatures blazed and fueled a massive melting process. This usually caused many of the frozen layers that blanketed the furniture and corridors to distort while the young workers struggled to keep pace. It was already on pace to become the hottest season over recent years. It was rumored that it was due to the recent awakening of two of the phoenix dragons in the East.

Still, some were forced to cook delicious meals for the palace guards who watched over the captives to ensure they did not sneak in an occasional bite. This was considered to be the cruelest duty and often reserved for those on punishment.

John was taking leave from the fifth chamber he had re-iced on the twenty-seventh floor this day, along with his bucket of freezing water that was needed to add an extra layer of ice to the walls and furniture. Before he closed the chamber door, he walked over to the rail and scanned several floors of the palace. It was just about time for the captives to move on to the next chamber.

He looked around for Ivy, as he normally did. He just wanted a glance, as he was too frightened to speak with her. He saw her walk a few floors below, alongside Pippy, whom she was paired with. They always giggled together, especially as they looked around at the boys and decided who was or was not cute. Rob always took the opportunity during chamber transitions to attempt to flirt with Ivy as he passed, along with his duty partner, Joey. She revealed an annoyed face to Pippy as Rob again failed miserably to court her. She was not enamored with the attraction of his blond hair and blue eyes, as he did not possess the personality to match his physical features. She glanced up toward John when she noticed him from the corner of her translucent emerald eyes. As her long, dark-brown hair flowed across her face, he dropped immediately behind the rail and hoped she had not seen him. He cowered away once again.

John slammed his hand against the frozen floor in frustration. Why could he not talk to her, let alone look at her? Perhaps it was because he did not have anyone to guide him. He was always alone in the palace. The Ice Queen did not provide him with a partner. She left him without his memories and did not even give him a chance to get to know anyone who could possibly help jog them forth. While the other captives occasionally congregated in the corridors when the palace guards were not looking, he worked alone on the twenty-seventh floor. There was not a moment that he did not feel lonely.

As he leaned against the solid wall of the rail with his short, scruffy, brown hair, he looked back at the chamber he had just re-iced. He had done an abysmal job. By midday, the hunger pains had begun to significantly affect his ability to carry out his duties properly. He could barely focus with the distraction of the piercing pain and thunderous screams his belly made in protest.

With no desire to displease the Ice Queen any further, John returned to the chamber and once again ascended the frozen ladder to reach the upper limits of the concave ceiling. Midway through his fourth thrust upward, he felt a tug at the bottom of his pants, which caused him to slip wildly and fall off; however, thanks to his quick reflexes, he managed to grab a hold of a step. He released his grip and dropped to the iced floor, and almost slipped again.

"Sorry, mate," said Norman. "Jacob and William have called for a meeting. The details are in this note."

However, the note lacked details. It simply stated in poor penmanship:

Two-Tone Tony, Heartthrob Rob, Wallaby Joey, Pippy the Piper, Freddie Fixer, Poison Ivy, Norman the Navigator, and John the Dreamer—Be at the thirteenth-floor restroom exactly at midday during the guards' shift change.

When John looked up to ask some questions, Norman was nowhere to be found. He had already rushed off and returned to his duties before the guards could take notice of his disappearance. Norman was quite nimble for his chubby stature.

Twenty-five minutes remained until midday. John re-iced the chamber properly and began to make his way to the meeting. He reached the thirteenth floor with haste as he maneuvered within the shadows and avoided the palace guardsmen. He reached it with fifteen minutes to spare; however, as he had been assigned to only the twenty-seventh floor, he was unfamiliar with the layout of most of the palace.

He looked at the dark, labyrinth-like halls with confusion and concern. However, this was precisely why Jacob and William had chosen it. The guardsmen rarely patrolled these halls because they would often get lost themselves.

After several right turns and even more lefts, John was lost. He whispered the names of the other kids, but it did not yield any replies. He removed the note from the inside of his boot and unfolded it. He whispered the words aloud, over and over again. It did not make any more sense, as the words did not change. The note made no mention of which direction he needed to head in.

In frustration, John ripped the hand-sized note into quarters and tossed it toward the ground. The torn note slowly made its descent toward the icy ground and faded into the darkness that engulfed it. As only a few minutes remained, John whimpered while he sat and ignored the numbness that set into his backside.

Suddenly there was a squeak. Another squeak followed shortly after. The rodent he had seen the night prior was once again before him. He knew it was the same rodent because of its distinctive chocolate color, which was a contrast to the usual shades of gray of the other rodents at the palace. The rodent dragged the torn quarters of the note toward John. It flipped them over and then pointed to the corner with its tail.

In frustrated relief, John hit his head against the wall behind him, a bit harder than he intended to. There was a small map on the flip side of the note, something Norman had failed to point out; perhaps it was just an oversight, but John could not believe he had missed it himself. The young lad was not detail oriented. With a brief glimpse, he noticed the restroom was on the far end of the floor. He stuffed the note back into his boot as he looked in the direction of the rodent, but once again, it had vanished. Perhaps he had finally lost his mind in this dreadful place.

As he sprinted around the corner in pain, only one minute remained with some corridors still to race down. He finally arrived at the X marked on the map, but only darkness awaited him. To worsen matters, it was already past the midday mark. John was spent of what little energy he had left.

He whispered their names as he gasped for air, just loud enough so only someone a few feet away could hear, but he was greeted only by the silence of the darkness. With his patience and mood deteriorated, at five minutes past midday, he heard a muffled whisper, "Password?"

He was perplexed as he whispered, "I don't know. No one told me."

Shortly after, he heard another whisper. "Norman, you idiot…Come in, John." A door that was hidden in the darkness now had a visible crack of light and grew wider as it opened slowly.

John entered the room and overheard voices in the distance. Ivy apologized on Norman's behalf and emphasized that he was a lousy communicator, not unlike John himself. He barely heard what she said. He was mesmerized by her alluring eyes and equally endearing smile set against her smooth caramel complexion. She stood a couple inches shorter than John, who was of average height himself.

Ivy giggled as she knocked him on the shoulder to bring him back to reality, "Come on, *Dreamer*. They're waiting in the back for us."

As the three of them passed the last stall, they saw Tony, Rob, Joey, Freddie, and Pippy as they all listened intently to Jacob and William, who barely noticed John's arrival.

John waited in the back of the group and attempted to go unnoticed, unlike Ivy and Norman, who made their way closer to be involved in the discussion. They stood side by side in heavy uniforms suitable for the palace, which consisted of a hefty winter coat, thick pants, and boots. Underneath were thin yet warm garments of varying earthy tones and shoes which themselves would be adequate to wear anywhere outside of the dreadful place they were confined to year round. The boys were forced to maintain hair of certain length; it could not fall below their ears. The palace barber, who was a grumpy, balding man, made certain the experience was as uncomfortable as possible for them. Girls, on the other hand, were not permitted to cut their hair, as Her Majesty demanded that they uphold a feminine appearance.

John had already made William and Jacob's acquaintance, but he was not familiar with the others, as he was a bit of an asocial lad. Even though he did not know them personally, he could tell who was who based on their nicknames, which they used to identify one another. Otherwise they possessed only first names, an unusual punishment imposed by the Ice Queen. It caused confusion among the captives who shared the same names.

The young prisoner of thirteen years, who stood taller than the others with his persistent but nonpermanent half-tan and half-pale face, was Two-Tone Tony. He was partially blind in his left eye, which was masked by its naturally gray hue that contrasted against his dark brown hair. Heartthrob Rob had the blondest hair and bluest eyes. Most of the girls had a crush on him, even though he was a smidgeon shorter than average height. He possessed an ability to charm his way in and out of almost any situation and often got the young female prisoners to do his duties with Joey while he napped. Next to him was a skinny kid, no more than three feet in height; he appeared older than his physique suggested. He possessed dirty blond hair and gray eyes, which allowed the usually shallow Rob to overlook his shortcomings. This must have been Wallaby Joey, who was often teased that he could fit into the pouch of a female wallaby in the lands far away; doubts of exaggeration were justified.

Freddie Fixer was often dirtier than the others, had rough hands, and possessed a lengthy nose that was surrounded by freckles. Sometimes it was a challenge to determine where the dirt on his face ended and his brown hair began. He was noticeably shorter than John, but he also possessed fewer years of age. He had lost his left ring finger during an accident when he created a specialty blade that responded only to his grip. He was popular among the captives for his inventions, not the least of which was hair product. He discovered that by wetting his hair with the freezing re-icing waters, he could shape it as desired and it would eventually stiffen into place. This created a trend among the prisoners, especially Rob, but some, including John, decided to stick with the naturally scruffy look.

Pippy the Piper possessed a whistle made from the bowls they ate from, which gave it a permanent and disgusting aroma of liver porridge. The whistle always dangled from her neck and gave her the uncanny ability to communicate with the rodents that dwelled beneath the palace. She did not have a favorable reputation for her hygiene and often challenged Freddie for the foulest smelling. She shared Freddie's age of nine years, along with his height, which was four inches shorter than John's.

The one who was tossing an icicle shard up and down was Poison Ivy. She juggled anything that she could lift; she also possessed pinpoint throwing accuracy. Her nickname was a puzzle, however. She did not appear poisonous with her features of beauty, which included impossibly long and lush dark-brown hair. Perhaps it was her emerald eyes, or rather because she was dangerous, a sign for him to continue to stay far away. As she looked over at him, he quickly looked away, yet again. None was shier than John.

Jacob and William did not have nicknames. Everyone knew who they were, not because they were the eldest, but because they looked after the others. Jacob stood almost as tall as Tony and possessed brown hair that he did not allow to grow more than a few inches. He tended to wear a face of concern and consistently appeared to be carrying a chip on his shoulder. Many attempted to figure out what it was, but without success. William shared John's height and hair color. Though they shared similar hairstyles, John's was noticeably scruffier.

And of course there was John. He was given the simple nickname of Dreamer because he always seemed to drift away to his dreams, a rare gift or curse none of the other kids were afforded, at least to his knowledge. He had no special abilities worthy of note other than his quick reflexes. His blue eyes were not typical of someone with his hair color. Perhaps this was one of the reasons Ivy sought his attention. He was otherwise average, physically, with no standout features.

"Nice of you to join us, John." William interrupted. "You're always running late."

"Sorry, guys," replied John.

Jacob commanded silence and pointed to each kid he addressed. "Don't worry, John. We have an escape plan and have already assigned duties. You're our watchman. OK, let's go over the plan again. We've got a tight schedule, so pay attention!

"Pippy, you're up first. You will communicate with the rats and prepare them to wreak havoc exactly at midday.

"Freddie, at one minute prior, you will disable the clock in the main tower. This will give us a fifteen-minute period of mass confusion.

"Rob will then run up to the lead guard and insist that the Ice Queen is furious. In the meantime, Joey will lift the dungeon key.

Rob will then persuade the guard to lead the next shift into the palace, which will leave minimal resistance in the dungeon. Once Ivy retrieves the key, she will open all the cells and free all the others.

"Norman will be with me and William. We'll access the underground, where we'll make our escape.

"Tony, you escort the kids.

"Norman will have already scouted and determined the best route. He will mark it clearly.

"John, you wait outside the Ice Queen's master chamber. Keep watch and make sure she doesn't come out until at least ten minutes past midday. By then, all the kids will already be outside the palace, and you can start making your way down. If she emerges, yell as loud as you can. I'm sorry, but you will be the closest, and this is the way it has to be. Besides, most of the kids despise you, so it's your chance for redemption. OK, everyone, get back to your duties, and make sure you have a solid night of rest. You're going to need it."

The group swiftly returned to their normal routines in their respective chambers and corridors.

It was John's second icing shift of the day in the Ice Queen's master chamber, which was required to be one of the coldest chambers of the palace, second only to her phoenix dragon's lair. John pondered the glory that the following day would bring him. He would be surrounded by all the young, liberated kids outside the palace, and they would cheer his name. "John!…John!…John!" The Ice Queen would be defeated. He would be king, and Ivy his queen.

But John's thoughts faded into the dream that had haunted him for the past several months. It was abruptly interrupted as he awoke to the aroma of seasoned pontaccio. He quickly lifted his blindfold and stared at the succulent leg of the cooked fowl-like bird, which looked delightfully appetizing. As he took a bite, he noticed the chocolate rodent in the corner of his eye; it stared intently at him.

As John took a second bite, the rodent opened its mouth and spoke in a masculine, elderly voice. "John, the darkest of times are

22

coming. We are all going to need you, more than you realize. You must believe in yourself, even when all others do not..."

John was in shock; he could not believe what he had just heard, let alone seen. He wiped his eyes to make sure he had not dreamed it, but he discovered that he had.

The rodent was no longer before him, and his belly was as empty as it had been just moments ago. John's dreams began to blend with reality. He dreamed his way into suppertime and soon noticed a guard who waited impatiently at his feet. He would not have supper this evening, as the Ice Queen would not return until it was the chilliest chamber possible.

John would once again go hungry. He was escorted down twenty-six iced flights of steps to the dungeon. They passed by Her Majesty along the way. The palace guard addressed her as he avoided direct eye contact. He explained that John had fallen asleep and also removed his blindfold, both of which were strictly forbidden within Her Majesty's master chamber. She expressed extreme displeasure and instructed the guard to escort the tentative little pauper down to the dungeon and make sure he suffered. She was clearly upset.

When they finally reached John's prison cell, the guard shoved him inside so hard that he tumbled over and scraped his forehead roughly on the dungeon ground. The guard turned his back because it was difficult to look at John as he wept and held himself in agony. Hungry and hurt, John limped over to his mattress as he wiped the blood from his forehead.

He decided to maintain his routine, even in pain. He looked beyond his gated window and gazed below at the lush jungle and then toward the west wing of the exposed dungeon. Ivy observed him from her own prison. He did not jump away as he normally did. He was in too much pain to have butterflies. He finally built up the courage to smile at her. It was not his best smile since the throb of his forehead burned. As he held it, blood dripped down his hand. She returned his smile, but it was not quite as radiant as he was used to.

Her hand leaned against one of the bars of her gated window as her smile subsided. A tear flowed down her smooth caramel cheek. She felt bad for him.

John would not have it. He would not be a pity case. He had already pitied himself enough. He did not need it from the others. He backed away from the window, and she slowly disappeared from his view. He kneeled and lay down as quickly as his aching body allowed. His hunger pains would deprive him of sleep. Eventually the guards would begin to shut down their patrol and prepare for another raucous game of modinos.

Eventually he became numb to the pains as his mind began to drift into the darkness. His nose suddenly went on alert and triggered a grumble in his belly. He felt a tug on his holey sock. As he looked over, he saw the chocolate rodent, which had hauled a piece of unseasoned but cooked pontaccio from the kitchen.

John snatched the pontaccio and devoured it, glad that it was unseasoned because the usually delightful aroma would have otherwise alerted the guards. As he took his last bite, John looked over to the rodent, but all that remained were the outlines of its oversized paw prints. His hunger pains subsided, and he once again began to ponder the glory that would come on the next day. He faded along with the night.

When the following morning arrived, John woke punctually. He consumed his liver porridge, tossed down his bowl, and then counted the seconds until they would be released into the Ice Palace. The kids gave one another looks of acknowledgment; fortunately, the guardsmen did not take notice. Most did not look at John, while those who did gave him dubious glances.

The kids marched into the Ice Palace as they masked their intentions. Room after room was re-iced, moldings reshaped, and debris collected until the clock tower rang and echoed an hour prior to midday. This prompted the youngest prisoners to be escorted back into their dungeon cells for their usual one-hour break, a break the elder prisoners were not afforded. By twenty minutes past the eleventh hour, the youngest waited impatiently in their prison cells for the escape plan to commence.

The plan was officially set into motion fifteen minutes prior to midday when Jacob coughed. It echoed throughout the Ice Palace and signaled the others to prepare for action. Pippy immediately began to communicate with the rodents that resided underground. They soon lined up into formation and prepared to wreak havoc precisely at midday. The first domino had fallen.

When one minute remained, Freddie deactivated the central clock in the main tower. His heart beat so hard that its rhythm provided him with a countdown toward midday. John began to make his way over to the Ice Queen's master chamber, where he had just left several moments prior after it had been re-iced. She had just begun her late-morning nap. After he avoided a few guards along the way, he would need to wait impatiently. All the kids knew it would soon be time; the anticipation built up to a feverish pitch when only ten silent ticks of the clock remained.

Five…four…three…two…one…silence.

Freddie was successful. Pippy blew into her whistle, and the rodents began their race into the palace. They ran amok as the young prisoners screamed out, "*Rats!*" This would soon echo throughout the first several floors of the palace and caused mass confusion among the guards. As the first shift of guards waited to be relieved by the next, they were instead greeted by thousands of rodents. The guards were mauled, while the captives raced untouched toward the dungeon for their escape.

Freddie began his sprint to the dungeon as well. He had a lot of ground to cover, as the central clock tower was the highest point in the Ice Palace. Time was of the essence if they were to pull off this plan before the Ice Queen realized what was happening.

Three minutes past midday, everything had begun to unfold just as planned. It was now showtime for Rob and Joey. They swiftly reached the lead guardsman and yelled frantically. He immediately dismissed Rob's claim, as the rats knew their place in the palace. Joey waited impatiently behind Rob and gave him a tug that he needed to hurry things along. Ivy needed the dungeon key soon, or the whole operation would be at risk.

"Look," said Rob, now calm after he caught his breath, "do you know what the Ice Queen will do to the person who has allowed this to happen? *Thousands of rats* are running rampant throughout *her* palace, mauling all the guards and pooping *everywhere*. She'll come straight to you, won't she?"

This caught the guard's attention and caused him to ponder the consequences. Joey knew this was his cue. He barely lowered himself as he maneuvered around the lead guard and lifted the key from his holster. The guard did not notice as he wondered whether or not the Ice Queen would force him to face her captive yet dangerous phoenix dragon or freeze him outright.

Joey dove into the shadows and passed the key to a rodent that eventually brought it to Ivy. Rob snapped the lead guard out of his trance and convinced him they had to move into the great hall immediately to sort out the disaster. Joey shadowed the guard toward the staircase, where both he and Rob broke away and raced down to the dungeon. The guardsman held his hands to his head in distress as he looked upon the rodents causing chaos.

John waited impatiently outside the Ice Queen's master chamber as his mark to sprint fast approached. He was about to take his first step toward the dungeon when he heard noises from within the chamber. He felt imminent danger in his bones.

Meanwhile, Ivy finally received the key and wasted no time as she opened the cells and freed the kids within. As soon as she unlocked one cell, she tossed the key into the opposite cell. It saved her valuable time and ensured all the captives would make it out. She raced up and down the east, central, and west wings of the U-shaped dungeon.

Tony arrived at the underground entrance where William and Jacob stood tall above an unconscious guard. Norman emerged and quickly explained the marked route toward the exit. Tony began to escort roughly half of the kids, along with William, who was tasked to open the gate at the far end. Meanwhile, Norman carried out one last sweep of the prison cells along the west and central wings to make sure every young captive had been accounted for.

John heard footsteps as they approached ahead of schedule. The door swung open and slammed into the wall as the Ice Queen emerged. He needed to alert the others immediately. Her Majesty passed John as she waved her scepter over his eyes. He finally felt a burst of courage and yelled his emergency signal; however, all he could provide was a muffled yell that barely broke the air around him. His mouth had been incapacitated along with the rest of his body. The Ice Queen moved on and waved her scepter in all directions. The rodents were immediately frozen and crashed, intact, against the chilled grounds of the palace as she descended toward the dungeon. Their souls were absorbed by the scepter.

Meanwhile, Tony finished his second escort along with Freddie, Rob, and Joey. Jacob, as the leader of the group, waited impatiently at the entrance for John, who was the only one from the core team who had not established contact with him. They needed to make their move soon, or else the entire operation would be compromised. Heavyheartedly, Jacob contemplated whether or not he would send a signal over to the far end where the others waited impatiently to flee outside the palace.

Norman returned from his final sweep, along with Ivy and the few captives who remained. Jacob nervously asked them if they had seen John.

Ivy replied nervously, "No. Please tell me you have!"

Norman replied, "I think I saw him go in with the last group."

Jacob questioned him. "I didn't see him. *Are you sure?*"

Norman nodded positively. Jacob immediately whistled, which signaled William to begin the escort outside the palace.

As they made their way over to the exit, Jacob noticed William and Tony had only just managed to open the lock and yelled, "What happened? You should have been outside by now!"

27

William replied, "It was trickier than I had expected. Come on, let's get out of here!"

The Ice Queen suddenly yelled above their voices, "You silly children, *you will never escape from here!*" All the kids suddenly became incapacitated. "You will stay here until you can no longer fit in your prisons. And once they can no longer accommodate you, you shall be forever frozen by Frostbite and placed in my lovely little collection. If you are lucky, you can be…shall we say *promoted*; you could begin training to eventually become one of my loyal palace guards. Now who is responsible for all of this?" She revealed John, who was being dragged behind her by a palace guard. "This little *pauper* wanted to say something as I passed, but he couldn't because he's a *coward!*"

John tried to defend himself. "It's not true! She put a spell—"

But the Ice Queen interjected, "*Silence!*" and he could speak no more.

The Ice Queen paced around and interrogated them individually on their involvement in the escape plot. She briefly removed her spell so they could concede. However, everyone knew that if they admitted involvement, it meant they had effectively surrendered and would be subject to a brutal punishment. They all insisted on firm denials.

The Ice Queen approached Norman and noticed the look of fear in his eyes, along with an eagerness to please. "Norman…or do you prefer Norman the Navigator, as your *friends* call you? Do you think they are your *friends*? *No, they aren't!* You have no past! Only a future with me! Oh, Norman…my little Norman…don't you want the rest of your days here to be happy? One day I will make you my king and give you great power. Norman…" She spoke with an uncharacteristic tenderness in her voice.

After some hesitation, Norman replied, "Jacob, William, Tony, Rob, Joey, Ivy, Freddie, Pippy…and John, it was *his* plan."

The Ice Queen lifted the spell from all of the mentioned kids and demanded, "What say you?"

Jacob stepped forward, prepared to accept responsibility and its consequences as he gave Norman a look of disgust and disappointment.

Norman yelled at him in protest, "It's all because of John that the plan failed. Everything was going perfectly until he messed it up. *It's all John's fault!*"

The Ice Queen was disappointed with this revelation and ordered for them to be dragged off to her private prison, where they would be frozen by Frostbite and their souls consumed by her scepter. They all had looks of terror on their faces.

As Norman stood next to the Ice Queen, relieved that he would be spared, she pushed him into the arms of the lead palace guard, Number Eleven. She yelled, "Take him as well. Frostbite loves big…tender…*rats!*"

"But…but I told you everything that you asked for! I want to be your king!" replied Norman, the nerves exposed in his voice.

The Ice Queen replied, "You told me because you are *weak*! You could *never* be my king! Now take them away. And lock the rest of the kids in this putrid place. That'll teach them how generous I really am. I provide them with so much…and they show no gratitude in return!"

III: Escaping the Ice Arrow

Imprisoned in ten individual cages and stripped of their winter clothing, the kids stared hopelessly at one another. William and Jacob attempted to communicate signals, but it was difficult because the Ice Queen was nearby. The key to their freedom dangled from the belt of an out-of-reach palace guard.

Her Majesty made final preparations for the feast. As Frostbite waited anxiously in its lair, the kids watched the Ice Queen sprinkle the final seasoning into the massive pot in which they believed they would be cooked. They had no choice but to accept their fate.

"Bring over the fat one!" yelled Her Majesty.

The guard unlocked Norman's cage and dragged him over. He lifted and lowered him slowly toward the pot, in which the seasoned, thick water boiled profusely.

Norman squirmed and screamed as he was lowered, "Aaaahhhhhh!" His feet became warmer as he approached the lavalike surface. The screams suddenly ceased, and he looked at the others with frightened confusion.

The Ice Queen yelled, "Did you think I would *boil* you into a premature death?" as she laughed uncontrollably. She finally regained her composure. "You will *not* be so lucky after what you've done! Frostbite will freeze you alive, and your soul will become part of my collection! Anyhow, it does *not* feed on children. It's rather partial to pontaccio. We have to raise *so* many to satisfy his appetite. Guard, bring over the pontaccios at once."

These words instigated further screams as Norman realized he would soon face the phoenix dragon. The guard removed Norman from the lift above the pot. He subsequently unbolted the gate that led into Frostbite's lair, shoved the young traitor in, and slammed the gate shut behind him. Frostbite's muffled shriek permeated the densely iced stone walls, in tandem with the screams of a little boy.

"*Get away from me!*" Norman ran for his life on the other side.

The Ice Queen screamed, "Now bring me Jacob!"

Feeling courageous, John spoke up. "Take me instead!"

Everyone was puzzled, except Ivy, who was impressed at his courage. John had a plan, a terrible one, but a plan nonetheless.

The Ice Queen abruptly turned around and whispered, "Oh," then yelled, "OK, bring the little pauper here, *now!*"

The guard released the lock on John's cage and began to drag him recklessly toward the lair. The young captive caught his balance and suddenly stomped the guard's toes, turned quickly, and kicked the guard where it hurt most. John escaped from the now-limp grip as the guard tumbled into the Ice Queen and knocked her scepter deep into the boiling pot. She reached in and desperately searched for it. She suffered excruciating pain, as she had become predominantly made of ice over the years.

In the confusion, John lifted the key from the palace guard, who was still cringing in pain on the ground. He unlocked Ivy's and Jacob's cages and then the remainder with haste. They were ready to make a run for it. However, he could not in good conscience abandon Norman, who was still screaming desperately on the other side of the wall. John unbolted the gate and entered Frostbite's lair, along with the others, while the Ice Queen screamed at them with her arm still at the bottom of the boiling pot as she tried to reach her scepter. She decided to pull her burned arm out and instructed the palace guard, who still was in dire pain, to kick over the pot. As he did, a sizzle spread along the floor of the chamber. She was finally able to retrieve her damaged scepter. Shortly after, the gate slammed shut behind the kids, along with a muffled shriek from the phoenix dragon that accompanied them.

"*Fools!* Now you will all be frozen over, and your souls will be mine!"

The kids spread out strategically and forced Frostbite backward in confusion. They effectively reduced the focus on Norman as he moved to a less dangerous distance. The towering phoenix dragon appeared to be in pain, as he was chained to the ground with iron shackles two feet thick. It cringed as it jolted forward, and a current from the chain sent a shock throughout its body. Frostbite began to breathe frosted flames throughout its lair, as it could not reach them. The kids ran for shelter. Ivy ran toward John as if he could protect her. Tony and Rob looked at John with envy; however, it was not John who approached her. His mystery intrigued her and naturally drew her to him.

She held his hand. "Please protect me, John."

John replied, "I can try, but..."

Tony ran over, past a blast of frozen flames, and grabbed her hand. "Come with me, Ivy. I'll protect you." She tried to let go of his hand, but his grip was too tight.

The phoenix dragon paced around its lair as the chains allowed while the kids moved from one rock of safety to the next. John watched as Tony protected Ivy. He had blown his chance. But it was no time to be melodramatic as Frostbite loomed around corners with heavy footsteps that crashed into the ground. They knew they could not defeat it as it shrieked and swiped at them wildly; however, Ivy noticed an exit chute directly behind it. The putrid smell suggested that it led deep down to the underground.

Jacob took the lead as he taunted and lured Frostbite away from the others. He gave them an opportunity to leap into the chute. One by one, they slid and tumbled down several spiral flights of iced stone that were littered with the flesh and bones of unfortunate pontaccios; eventually they crashed into a pile of them in the underground. Norman quickly scouted the area as the others waited impatiently for Jacob. However, Jacob would never make it down; only the echoes of his screams reached them.

William took over the leadership role and instructed Norman to take them toward the exit in order to regroup with the others, but the path had been closed off. They searched desperately for another exit, but it was a futile effort.

A gate rose at the far end. They heard the screams of the other kids and raced toward them quickly. They regrouped and attempted to reopen the exit that William had managed to open. They continued their attempts without success.

Another, heavier gate opened in the middle of the tunnel, and a chilled draft exuded throughout. It made the young captives shiver, especially the ones who had just escaped from the queen's private prison and did not have the warmth of heavy clothing.

Footsteps commenced from the opposite end, down a flight of steps, and approached quickly around the corners. A shriek echoed throughout, and the footsteps ceased. The guards parted in the middle as Her Majesty advanced toward the front, scepter in hand. The flesh on her arm had been burned off and exposed her frosted, stone-like bones.

"Not so fast!" she yelled as she looked left and right feverishly. "No Jacob, I see. He must be...*gone* by now!" she added with a sinister laugh reserved only for the cruelest of rulers. She continued to look around. "*Where's John?*"

Everyone was puzzled as they shifted their eyes back and forth. John was nowhere to be found. They all had the same thought: he must have escaped.

However, John had not escaped. He was no more than a few feet away, equally as confused. John was able to see everyone, though he was too nervous to move or speak; perhaps he was hidden in an adequately dark shadow. He glanced at his feet and saw the chocolate rodent. It had its paw extended and was somehow suspending the two of them in another dimension, invisible to everyone around them.

The rodent said to John, "It's OK. We can speak. They can't hear us from here."

John was speechless.

The rodent added, "Don't worry, John, you are not crazy. My name is Midwa. I am your...protector."

John whispered to himself, "Oh boy...I've finally lost it."

Midwa said, "I will explain everything later, but first we need to get out of here."

John seemed to accept what had happened and finally spoke up. "Can't you take us away from here with your magic?"

Midwa replied, "It's not that simple, but I can't explain at this time."

Perplexed, John asked, "OK, so what do we do now?"

Midwa replied, "We wait, just a bit longer."

The kids feared for their lives as the Ice Queen decided to freeze unsuspecting guards at random, while she commanded the others to carry them off to her secret chamber, where she had accumulated a terribly impressive collection. Their souls were absorbed by her scepter. She was humiliated and did not think clearly about the secret that she had just revealed.

The Ice Queen demanded with immediacy that all the kids be returned to the dungeon. They would be limited to one meal per day and forced to work through supper. They would suffer to their absolute limits. The Ice Queen would not be made a fool of without dire consequences. She stormed off, and the guards who remained followed in fear as they carried the frozen guards to her massive collection.

John was alone with Midwa and asked, "Now what?"

Midwa replied, "Follow me."

Midwa led John back to the pile of flesh and bones and pointed into the chute. John gazed into the darkness and then back down at Midwa. He expressed his concern that it was impossible, but Midwa had vanished once again.

John realized that he did not have a choice, so he grabbed on to every stone that protruded, and slipped several times. After nearly

34

an hour, he made it to the top of the chute, but he could not make his move just yet, as Frostbite was still excited and swiped anxiously at something. Its reach was limited by its shackles. It had given up its frosted flames as it gnawed away at the small cave and attempted to dig something out. The screams from inside suggested that Jacob was still alive and fought for his life.

Braver than usual, John built up the courage to enter the phoenix dragon's lair. He knew time had just about run out. Jacob would either be frozen by the terrifying beast or by the Ice Queen when she eventually returned. Either way his soul would be part of her collection. John knew he had to save him; Jacob was the only one who had shown him companionship.

John snuck around with footsteps as light as air. As he looked down, he noticed that his feet hovered above the ground. In amazement, John let out a gasp, loud enough for Frostbite to hear; the phoenix dragon turned its head toward him. But it saw nothing and returned to its attempts to dig the young leader out.

Jacob was losing energy rapidly as he desperately kicked Frostbite backward and tossed small stones toward it. The phoenix dragon showed no signs of fatigue. Suddenly Jacob saw John lurking behind the phoenix dragon with a massive boulder lifted above his head. Frostbite noticed the distraction in Jacob's expression and then saw the reflection in his eyes. It turned its head sharply, but it was immediately met with the boulder. The phoenix dragon let out a whimper before it collapsed to the ground; it was unconscious.

John grabbed Jacob's hand and inquired about his health. Jacob nodded that he was fine; however, John noticed a deep gash on the young leader's arm that was steadily losing blood. Thinking on his feet, he tore off the sleeve of his shirt and created a tourniquet.

Jacob gave him a puzzled look and finally spoke. "What...happened?"

John explained everything that had transpired, but soon the reality of his aching body returned. No longer did he float above the ground and possess great strength. Had he imagined what just happened? Had Midwa helped him? He had so many questions, but there was no time to ponder them because they needed to escape with haste.

Side by side they limped away from Frostbite, who was laid out on the ground. They both desperately needed rest, but they would not be afforded such a luxury. It would not be long before the phoenix dragon would awaken, and they knew it was just a matter of time before they once again crossed paths with the Ice Queen. However, they had no escape plan; the gate was still locked from the other side, and the chute John had descended earlier led to a dead end. In their search for a way out, they noticed a frozen furnace situated at the far end of the lair. Jacob said that he once overheard a guard claim the phoenix dragon breathed ice fire into the furnace and that was what kept the Ice Palace's surrounding climate so cold. It was the source of what kept the Ice Palace itself so frigid. It even gave Her Majesty the ability to control the weather.

Jacob looked at John and asked the obvious question. "How did you lift that rock over your head? You barely have enough energy to walk me over."

John, unsure of what to believe, replied, "I think you must have hit your head pretty hard, Jacob. The rock wasn't that big. I'm sure you could have lifted it yourself. I think we caught a break for a change."

Jacob replied, "Sure…That must be it."

They began to hear voices on the other side, and they became increasingly louder. They sought cover within the small cave that Jacob had cowered in moments ago. They passed the unconscious Frostbite along the way and tried not to disturb it. *Click, click*. The lock had been opened. Two of the guards brought in several pontaccios for Frostbite to feed on. The guards saw that the phoenix dragon was unconscious and tossed them near its snout. A hungry phoenix dragon could not resist the scent of the delicious pontaccio for long, even unconscious. It heightened the beast's senses and appetite.

As the guards nervously exited Frostbite's lair, they forgot to relock the gate as they spoke, a welcome break for John and Jacob.

Frostbite's breaths became heavier, however, which was not a good sign for them. They sprinted toward the gate and slowly opened it, which caused it to creak. They peeked out. There was no resistance in their path. They glanced back at Frostbite to make sure it was still in its slumber, but it had already regained consciousness thanks to the scent of the pontaccio and quickly recuperated. Frostbite took a deep breath and released a large flame of white frost, which rapidly froze the air in its periphery as it made its way toward them. In desperation, they leaped into the next room as the flame crashed into the gate, slammed, and froze it shut. It would be a while before anyone could enter Frostbite's lair again.

Jacob and John desperately needed a strategy. They were in the Ice Queen's private prison and knew there was only one possible direction: back into the great hall of the Ice Palace. They would need to race past the Ice Queen's master chamber and then descend twenty-six flights of frozen steps past the guards, who were now on high alert. They would then need to race through the dungeon and underground toward freedom.

Jacob and John once again committed to an attempt to flee. They limped across and looked upon the cages as well as the knocked-over stewing pot that John was responsible for. The stew no longer boiled and had frozen to the surface of the floor. It would be an unpleasant job for the young captives to clean up.

They soon emerged in the great hall and gave each other one final look before they began a cautious sprint. The reality of the bitingly cold temperatures of the Ice Palace set in. Their arms and legs were exposed and shook uncontrollably. John could not mask his pain well as he let out a grunt with each step on his left foot.

His grunts finally drew some unwanted attention. A guard yelled, "They're here!" which echoed throughout the palace and reached Her Majesty's master chamber. Her door swung open and crashed into the wall as she let out a shriek. John and Jacob were now in an all-out sprint, but they had several flights to race down. Their effort proved ineffective.

The Ice Queen emerged with her hunting bow. Their chances dwindled swiftly with each painful step. The guards quickly grew in numbers and soon blocked off each exit above the third floor as they closed in on them. Her Majesty prepped her bow and extended her right arm, now only iced bones. As she recited an ancient enchantment, she froze the surrounding air, and it slowly transformed into the shape of an arrow. Their fate was all but sealed.

She released the ice arrow, and it took flight. It maneuvered rapidly down the spiral steps toward them. John remembered what Midwa had said: "I am your protector."

With the arrow only one flight away from them, John grabbed Jacob's hand and yelled, "Jump!"

Without giving it a second thought, they leaped over the ledge. The arrow grazed and soothed the gash on Jacob's arm before it struck a nearby guard, who immediately froze in place; his soul did not race toward the scepter. It dissipated into a crimson vapor as a result of the chant Her Majesty had recited. They descended quickly as the guards and the Ice Queen looked on.

Everything appeared in silent slow motion as they saw a look of shock on the Ice Queen's face. The mute words *"Capture them!"* were thrust from her lips. The reality, however, was that the ground was fast approaching, and there was nothing they could do to stop the inevitable impact. John had put a lot of trust in Midwa, but why? He was not sure whether he was even real.

John imagined a cushion of soft air beneath them, but it did not work. With only a few flights between them and the rigid surface of the great hall below, John realized that the leap had been a terrible idea. Why had he been so stupid? But he then realized it did not matter; it was just a different means to the same end. Jacob and John were now two flights from their unfortunate fate…one floor…But no splat followed. They were suspended mere inches above the ground as their hearts raced. They shared the same terrified look across their faces.

The Ice Queen knew they could not be alone. "Midwaaaaaa!" she screamed incredibly loud and unshackled hundreds upon hundreds of sharp icicle shards from the palace ceiling. All the guards leaped out of the way, though many could not avoid being pierced. As they hovered, John and Jacob looked briefly at each other and then in front of them. Midwa was there. He stood on his hind legs and cast a spell upon them as he continued to recite the enchantment. Midwa finally lowered his paw, which prompted John and Jacob to fall on the ground and grunt upon impact.

"Let's get out of here!"

John and Jacob sprang to their feet and began to sprint along with Midwa. They passed through the dungeon, where the kids were once again imprisoned; they looked the worst John had ever seen them, completely demoralized. As they quickly treaded through the underground tunnels, John's foot was mildly relieved by the soothing waters that channeled down the middle. It was far more pleasant than the tunnel they discovered when they escaped from Frostbite's lair.

The exit gate was now in sight and had already been unlocked. It revealed a bright white light in the distance beyond the dark tunnels. As they approached, they noticed several shadowed figures near the exit.

Midwa yelled out, "Now run! Run far away from this place, until you are strong enough to return and free the rest!"

John pleaded, "Can't you come with us?"

Midwa replied, "Sorry, John, but I cannot. Now go before they arrive!"

The shadowed figures emerged from the underground, and the light revealed their company: William, Two-Tone Tony, Heartthrob Rob, Wallaby Joey, Freddie Fixer, Pippy the Piper, Poison Ivy, and Norman the Navigator. They were once again dressed in their winter clothes, and they tossed over a couple of winter outfits to John and Jacob before they emerged themselves.

They could barely see beyond a few feet in front of them. A blizzard was upon them, brought by the Ice Queen, who was determined to terminate their attempt to flee.

Midwa yelled, *"Run! She's here!* I'll hold her off as long as I can!"

They began their sprint away from the Ice Palace. They struggled to tread through the nearly two-foot-high snow that had already accumulated. Midwa slowed the guards with effective spells, but the Ice Queen deflected the magic with her scepter; he had not encountered a force such as hers.

The Ice Queen rested her scepter momentarily, though she still possessed some residual power from it. She extended her arm, and once again created an arrow from the surrounding air as she recited an enchantment. She nocked it in the bow, drew, and released it. The arrow maneuvered through the air as it evaded all of the spells Midwa cast upon it. It bolted past the chocolate rodent and headed directly for John. It shot past Norman and Freddie, William and Rob, and then Tony and Ivy. It passed by Joey and Pippy, who were just a few paces behind John, and made its final approach.

Everyone looked on in concern. *"John!"* they yelled.

And the ice arrow struck.

John was in a dark room illuminated only slightly by a few torches that flickered in a struggle for their lives. The flickers of light allowed for only brief visibility of his surroundings. As the last of the debris fell and settled in, he could see several partially burned scrolls among the rubble of a battle that appeared to have just reached its dramatic conclusion. With his head lowered, he searched desperately for anything that resembled some meaning. He found nothing.

He began to hear footsteps in the distance, but these were much lighter than the usual steps. Midwa revealed himself. He had a look of dire concern on his relatively large rodent face.

He approached John and explained, "I don't have much time, John. The key is the Fire King's ring. You must secure it to defeat the Ice Queen. We can only meet in your dreams from this point forward. You will understand in due time..." Midwa suddenly vanished.

The Dreamer: Origins

Heavy footsteps commenced in the distance, increasingly amplified with each step as they approached. A red silhouette finally appeared around a figure before him, veiled predominantly by the darkness of the shadows. The dark figure was beastly, with crimson eyes on the verge of erupting. John cowered. The footsteps approached and became heavier and louder. The heat emitted by the beast began to warm John's skin and soon created a mild burn. John did not have the courage to look up. He began to weep as he covered his ears, with his head sheltered between his knees. The tension was partially broken as he heard Midwa's voice.

"Don't worry, John. It's going to be all right."

The beast roared John's name repeatedly as he whimpered. He still struggled to look up. But he thought of what Midwa had said: "The key is the Fire King's ring." John was not fond of riddles, but he knew that he should heed the advice of the mysterious Midwa. He finally raised his head and looked at the Fire King's fingers, and gazed at the ring; it was difficult to miss as it spewed fire profusely. John raised his head further and looked directly into the eyes of the Fire King. But the young boy turned his head away almost immediately as his eyes began to burn from the intense heat of the Fire King's stare.

"John...John!"

And he woke. He was facedown in the snow, almost completely covered in white.

Surrounded by familiar faces, John looked around feverishly for the rodent. "Where's the chocolate...Midwa?"

But silence fell upon everyone. Jacob finally spoke up. "He's gone, John...He raced toward you once the arrow passed him, and leaped from twenty paces away. He attached himself to the ice arrow just as it was about to strike your heart. The arrow shattered past you...and he just vanished. The Ice Queen shrieked in pain and retreated after she commanded all the guards to follow her back into the Ice Palace. I don't know who this Midwa was or where he came from, but he was absolutely brilliant."

Midwa was brilliant indeed.

IV: A Journey Begins with a Stumble

With increasingly heavier snowfall and stronger winds brought about by the Ice Queen, the group was nearly blinded. They needed to stick close together. The need for shelter became imminent, as the dangers of exposure to the brutal elements would soon impose frostbite and hypothermia upon them.

As they struggled to tread through the snow, they needed to think quickly and take advantage of everyone's individual skills. Given his prowess, Norman was naturally assigned as navigator. Without much visibility, he decided to go with his gut.

He hesitated for a few moments as if he were in meditation and yelled above the howling winds, "I think we just came from *this* way…We need to head *that* way!" As most of them lacked their own directional intuition, they trusted Norman's.

They proceeded in a southerly direction and hoped it would lead to some much-needed shelter before they froze to death. As their sense of urgency kicked in, they trekked double time. With their fingers and toes numb, they were beginning to feel the preliminary effects of frostbite.

After several minutes of a near-impossible trek, William screamed. Everyone went on high alert, unsure of what had happened. William had stubbed his toe on a rock beneath the white that blanketed the ground. While painful, this was positive news because they realized that they must be close to a cavernous structure Jacob and William had once told them about. It gave them hope to find shelter soon.

Everyone gathered around William and followed the rock formations, which provided a definitive course. Before long, they headed southeast and eventually arrived at a large cluster of rocks exposed from the snow. The image of complete white had finally been broken up.

The Dreamer: Origins

As the initial effects of hypothermia finally hit Pippy, they were desperate to find shelter, at least until the storm had passed. They assumed the Ice Queen would not let up on the storm until she believed that they had frozen over. Any normal kid would have already diminished under these brutal conditions; however, these were not normal kids, as they had weathered the numbing temperatures of the Ice Palace for what seemed to be an eternity. But they would share a bitter-cold fate if they failed to find immediate shelter.

Suddenly John, Jacob, and Norman disappeared with screams that quickly grew faint and were followed by thumps. The others scrambled toward the echoes of the screams, which led them to a dark void in the white.

The kids stood above the darkness, unable to see anything as they were blinded by the brutal winds. However, they soon heard yells from deep within. Jacob instructed them to come down. They had stumbled upon shelter after all. As they climbed down, most of them tripped and tumbled. Some landed on their feet, while Ivy and Freddie landed on their backsides, but at least they did not land on their faces as Rob did. Rob threw a tantrum because he believed his perfect face was now ruined.

As they gathered in a huddle, they began to feel some warmth, much more bearable than the frigid temperatures that persisted outside. However, the conditions were far from ideal, and an extended period in this place would eventually be the end of them. Freddie was tasked to create a fire, which would buy them some time until the Ice Queen eased her efforts. He felt around and found some loose branches. He instructed everyone to gather as many as they could find. This proved to be a challenge the farther they delved into the darkness. They called out often to identify their positions and affirm their well-being. They grouped into twos for safety. Tony tried to grab Ivy's hand, but she pulled it away and sought John. Tony's desire to protect her annoyed her, as it was unwarranted.

After the better part of an hour, nearly all of them gathered in a huddle and emptied their pockets of the branches and twigs they had gathered. Freddie felt around and said with a sigh of disappointment, "This isn't enough."

However, from the distance, Norman soon yelled, "Hey, guys...I think I found something! It's a root, but I'm not sure how to remove it."

Freddie lit up and instructed the others, "Everyone, grab what we have here and follow Norman's voice!"

Freddie reached the proclaimed navigator and felt the root. He grinned so wide they could almost see the glimmer of his teeth. He tossed the branches from his pockets and asked the others to do the same.

"OK, empty your pockets."

However, all the kids had a puzzled look on their faces as they whispered to one another, "Huh?"

Freddie spoke again. "Just do it!"

William replied, "We've got nothing left in our pockets, Freddie."

Freddie replied, "Yes, you do! Dig out all the lint from the corners and hand it to me." So they dug away.

Freddie piled up the branches and twigs and placed the lint on top. He then grabbed two small stones he had found moments ago. He asked all of them to huddle over him to block any wind that may pass through. Freddie scraped the two stones together, but nothing happened. He made another attempt, but this yielded the same result. The third time created a small flicker, which appropriately gave everyone a spark of hope.

A few more attempts and just as many sparks later, Freddie finally created an ember that caught on to the lint. A tiny flame was born. They needed to incubate it, at least until they nursed it into a bigger flame. After a few moments, the flame finally spread to the branches. They began to feel some warmth as it emitted from beneath them, which had never felt so good. They cheered the flame in a whisper as they covered their mouths so that their chilled breath would not give the flame a premature demise.

The growing flame flirted with the root and attempted several times to latch on to it. Suddenly the root lit, and the flame then began to spread rapidly. The flame soon shot up the root, which extended far beyond what they had imagined. A deep cavern tunnel was revealed. The narrow tunnel could only accommodate one kid at a time and eventually splintered into several tunnels, almost equally as narrow. They knew at this point that the only option was to push forward.

The unknown was scary and was made no less frightening by the shadows that persisted below the illuminated root. But this was not the time to panic; they had already escaped the Ice Palace and the most brutal weather the Ice Queen could conjure. They decided to march forward and made sure to be no more than a few paces apart, at least until they reached wider ground.

The burning root ran above them throughout the tunnel. It grooved left and right with a hypnotizing effect. The flames struggled to jump from the root but could not escape its grasp. The kids were not at risk of lost visibility; however, the tunnel proved to be much longer than it had originally appeared. They barely advanced, no matter how many tough steps they took forward.

Progress was sluggish even after half an hour, which prompted some visual and audible signs of frustration. William yelled to the far end, "Hey, Norman! We haven't moved at all!" Everyone turned their heads sharply, all in shock.

"What the...?" exclaimed Jacob as he briefly noticed a pair of murky jade eyes glisten in the dark distance before they vanished. The others echoed the same.

"Jacob...what do we do now?" asked Rob, who was still disgruntled about his imperfect face. Tony echoed Rob's concern with less anxiety.

Pippy chimed in, almost as if she had whistled a call to the rodents. "Follow me...I can get us out of here."

Norman interrupted, "No, we follow Jacob's lead."

Pippy replied, annoyed, "Why? If it wasn't for John, we'd still be in that dreadful palace, probably dead!"

Rob joined in. "If it wasn't for John, we would have escaped as planned!"

John remained quiet. Joey added another jab. "John hasn't contributed anything. That *rat* helped us, and John got him killed!"

Jacob shouted, "*Enough!* Listen…obviously we're all frustrated. We're cold, hungry, and holding on to a thread of hope that's just about to snap. We need to think!"

John finally spoke. "Shhh…Listen." They couldn't hear anything, but the tremor that followed was undeniable.

They were situated near the beginning of the tunnel as they stared at the burning root, helpless against its hypnotizing effects. One by one they began to awaken from their trances, thanks to the tremor that endured. It had begun as an insignificant rumble and increased in force as each moment passed. They started to lose their balance; they stumbled and slammed into the walls of the narrow tunnel, violently, side to side. And then it suddenly stopped.

Jacob yelled, "Is everyone all right?"

William whimpered in a soft voice, "Yeah, I'm fine." He tried to stay strong in spite of his fear.

Tony followed. "I'm cool."

Rob replied, "No! My *face* isn't perfect anymore!"

Joey added, "Yep, it's a good thing I'm short. I can't sway back and forth much at my height!"

Freddie jumped in. "I sprained my finger, but I'll fix myself up."

Pippy spoke in pain. "I guess so, but I think I twisted my ankle!"

Ivy spoke calmly. "Just a few bruises, but I'll live."

Wow, beautiful and tough, John thought.

Always eager to please, Norman added, "Yes, sir."

John replied last. "Um, yeah, I think. Whoa...Whooooa..."

Everyone began to scream. The ground beneath them rumbled violently and soon began to part. Jacob noticed the pair of murky jade eyes glisten in the dark distance once again. The eyes slowly emerged, and an odd-looking creature that mumbled indiscernible words was revealed.

They scrambled to grab on to whatever crevices they found within the walls. This proved to be futile as the gap grew wider and wider, and one by one they began to fall into the darkness below. They screamed at the top of their lungs. As they could not see one another, their anxiety reached the absolute bearable limits.

And *splash*, a painful impact that could have been much worse. After several splashes, they emerged, and Jacob immediately called for name checks. As they treaded water, they quickly yelled out their names in succession. However, all but one name had been called.

Jacob shouted, "*Jooooooooohn!*" There was no reply. The others followed suit, but their calls did not yield a reply either.

"Shouldn't we go look for him?" yelled out Pippy, who was fond of John. She was fascinated by the fact that he seemed to be at the center of all of the events that had transpired until now.

Jacob replied, "I'm sorry, Pippy, but we don't know what's down there, and even if we did, we can't see anything."

Silence fell upon them.

A glimmer of two green slivers appeared in the distant darkness, and subsequently, four more did. The slivers began to expand from their centers and became huge, bulbous orbs. With a murky jade hue that illuminated the cavern far into the distance, they finally had visibility of their surroundings.

"Who disturbs my slumber?" echoed with a rumble throughout the cavern. They looked at one another as they fought the weight of their heavy clothing to stay afloat.

Jacob yelled, "Everyone, take off your coats. We need to lighten our weight as much as possible!"

"*Answer me!*" The massive cavern rumbled once again.

Pippy yelled out, "Hey, guys! Look below. Do you see what I'm seeing?"

There was a long pause before anyone answered, but one by one they affirmed. A bright blue illumination at least twenty feet below was becoming increasingly larger and brighter and appeared to be in the form of a bubble. They focused and realized that John was at the center, unconscious, as he was barely breathing.

John was beside himself as he looked upon everything that was transpiring. He watched the others above hastily remove their heavy coats and saw the fear in their eyes. He saw a creature in the distance, resting upon a rocky surface above the water. Bizarrely, he could also see himself within the bright blue field. Accompanied by the chocolate rodent Midwa, the two of them waded deep within the waters beside each other.

John spoke to Midwa. "Am I…dead?"

Midwa replied, "No, you are not."

John was confused. "How can I be here…and there? And I'm swimming…but *how?*"

"John, you know that you cannot swim." Midwa attempted to explain. "We're not here. You're in that protective field."

Even more perplexed, John answered, "But…"

Midwa continued his explanation. "John, do you remember when I told you that we would only be able to meet while you are dreaming?"

John's confusion continued. "Yeah, but…am I dreaming all of this?"

Midwa elaborated. "Everything around us is actually happening, but we are in one of your dreams."

John answered, "I don't understand. Does this mean you aren't real?"

Midwa clarified. "I am as real as you believe me to be."

John was no less confused. "But how is all of this—"

Midwa interrupted. "You took a hard fall into the water. The impact nearly knocked you unconscious, and the weight of your clothing dragged you below. You were about to give up."

John countered, "But you said it yourself: I *can't* swim."

Midwa spoke in a soft voice. "John. You are capable of much more than you realize, but you need to believe in yourself. You almost gave up on your friends, and most importantly, on yourself."

John was silent.

Midwa continued. "But deep within you, there is hope. I believe in you. That's why I chose to save you—because I believe you can realize your potential and save us all."

John's silence finally broke. "But…why me? I'm no one…just a talentless little…*pauper*." He said it as Her Majesty often did.

Midwa replied, "That's what the Ice Queen would have you believe, but that could not be further from the truth. She stole your memories so you would not remember who you really are. But we don't have time. *Look!*" He pointed into the distance.

In the distance, the creature began to rise. The rumble intensified throughout the cavern. Small clusters of rock fell from the ceiling and crashed into the water. The kids desperately waded from side to side as they tried to avoid the debris. The creature must have been at least fifty feet in height at its tallest point. More and more hues of murky jade began to appear, and soon they had a clear visual of this creature. They could see the outline of several claws made of solid rock, some larger than others. This was a creature born of myth, unlike anything they had ever seen. It was a bizarre spiderlike creature, made almost entirely of rock, with six huge, glowing eyes. It spoke in the kids' native tongue, though the words were not projected directly from its mouth. It was as if they could hear its thoughts.

The creature was fully extended when it grumbled, "Arachno will find you. And you will pay!" The creature spewed forth a neon-green acid-like substance. It began to tread backward and then appeared to levitate above the ground. However, its claws had grappled on to the uneven walls of the cavern, and it began its ascent. Several rocks fell in its wake; they crashed into the water as the kids attempted to evade them.

Arachno was directly above them. Suddenly, it came to a halt. A loud shriek produced a tremor that shook the cavern. More rocks fell, but this time Ivy and Norman would not be as lucky; they were both struck. Ivy was grazed on the foot, which hindered her attempts to wade. William and Tony grabbed on to Ivy before she was submerged. Norman wasn't as fortunate. A small rock collided with his head after it ricocheted off of a larger rock as it approached the water. It knocked him unconscious. His right foot, which he favored, was now caught beneath a fallen boulder that was more than half his size. Tony called upon Jacob and Rob to keep Ivy afloat as he dove down with William to save Norman. They were the two strongest swimmers and reached him within moments, but the boulder was too heavy to move. Norman slowly lost valuable air, as he was unconscious. William and Tony lost theirs much quicker as a result of their efforts.

Meanwhile, Arachno continued its raging shrieks and spewed forth acid wildly from above. As they constantly submerged and emerged from beneath the waters to avoid direct impact from the acid, the kids once again fought for their lives. The acid appeared to cool immediately upon impact with the water, which transformed it into warm, gelatinous ooze. The situation deteriorated, and time quickly began to run out, a familiar problem for them.

Far beneath the surface, John looked on, barely able to speak because he was in shock from what he saw. "Midwa, *what do I do?*"

Midwa replied, "You will soon wake, John. When you wake, you must remember that I am with you, at all times…"

Suddenly John's eyes opened. He felt weak as he regained consciousness, but he quickly gained his composure once he processed his surroundings. He looked beyond his brilliantly illuminated bubble and saw Norman trapped beneath the boulder as William and Tony tried helplessly to remove it. They had to ascend once again to the surface to catch their breath in order to make one final attempt to save Norman; otherwise, they would need to accept his unfortunate fate. As John watched them ascend, he noticed their arms and legs flail wildly as they avoided the air strikes of the rocks. He also saw the others, who maneuvered around the acid that had discharged everywhere.

Fully conscious, John whispered to himself, "OK, Midwa. I'm ready." The bright blue field rapidly became smaller and eventually became just an illuminated outline around his body. He swam swiftly over to Norman and lifted the boulder with relative ease, almost as if it were hollow. John grabbed him, as he was still unconscious and almost fully depleted of air. As soon as they reached the surface, he passed Norman over to Jacob, whom he trusted with his own life.

All the kids stared at John, who shone even more brightly above the surface. He instructed everyone to swim over to the platform from which Arachno had come. They swam as quickly as their depleted bodies allowed. They grouped into threes to bring over the wounded Ivy and Norman. Jacob, William, and Pippy gathered around Norman, whose weight made it a challenge. Meanwhile, Tony, Rob, and Freddie assisted Ivy. Joey followed in their wake.

Arachno stared intensely at John, who was unmoved by the treacherous conditions. The wrath ceased momentarily and provided the kids with some much-needed time to make their way over to the platform.

Furious, Arachno spoke to John. "You are not human! What are you?" Its eyes twitched wildly.

"My friends call me John," he said as he observed the others.

"Haaaahaaaahaaaa! Is that supposed to frighten me, boy? Haaaahaaaahaaaa!"

Looking over once again to the others, John saw that they finally had reached the platform and climbed up one by one.

"*Answer me!*" Arachno screamed, furious at the young boy's distraction and disrespect.

John emerged from the murky waters and soon levitated above. The kids watched in the distance, speechless. This surprised even Arachno, who backed up to reassess his strategy.

John was now suspended several feet above the murky waters. The bright-blue outline around his body slowly dimmed. It appeared as if his eyes had absorbed the energy as they became increasingly bluer and brighter. His heavy coat exploded into shreds from his body and afforded him mobility.

Arachno backed up farther. The creature prepared for the battle of its ancient life and released a war cry as it charged forward from above. It spewed forth acid profusely and imposed tremors on the cavern, which released hundreds of rocks to rain upon John. In the distance, the kids found nearby shelter and protected themselves as the debris fell. Meanwhile, John remained unmoved as the acid flew past him and the rocks came within inches of him.

Arachno was desperate. Over the thousands of years it had lived in this world, there was no one, not man nor creature, who had survived its wrath, except for one. Arachno dug its claws violently into the ceiling of the cavern and soon hurled a boulder toward John, a massive boulder thrice his size. The boulder should have crushed him in an instant. However, it suddenly halted in midair.

John was face-to-face with the boulder as the thick air brushed past him and ruffled his short, scruffy hair before it crashed into the water beneath him. It caused a large ripple effect that reached the platform where the kids remained hidden. With a motion of his hand, John lifted the boulder above his head, high enough so Arachno could see him.

John exclaimed, "My friends call me John…but *you* can call me *Midwa*!"

Arachno shouted back, "No…It can't be! The Fire King…he…he destroyed you!"

John spoke no more words. He cocked his arm and then shot the boulder forward at full speed. Arachno had barely enough time to let out a shriek. The cavern shook to its core from the impact, which caused hundreds upon hundreds of rocks to crash into the waters and raised the water level to within inches of the platform.

The greatest impact was imminent, as Arachno's final efforts to escape from behind the boulder would soon cease. The murky jade orbs faded and escaped from its dying body. The energy flew toward the ceiling of the cavern and was absorbed by a nearby creature that was in Jacob's sight for a brief moment. No one else noticed the creature. Perhaps he was the only one who could see it.

Arachno's claws went limp, and its dead weight proved too much. Arachno fell no differently than a meteor would crash into land. The rumble resounded throughout the cavern. The rocky, spiderlike creature crashed into the pile of fallen rocks below and created a mound high into the cavern. This raised the water level to the kids' chests, and even higher for Joey.

In the distance they saw John still hovering in the air; however, his eyes quickly dimmed. Seconds later, the bright blue illumination faded, and he fell limp and descended into the waters below. Jacob called upon William, and they swam as fast as they could toward the splash. They submerged far below the surface before they latched on to him. They returned to the surface, rested him upon nearby rocks, and called over the others from the now-submerged platform.

John was once again in a dark room.

V: Mourning Glory

John was in a dark room illuminated only slightly by a few torches that flickered in a struggle for their lives. The flickers of light allowed for only brief visibility of his surroundings. Midwa had collapsed on the ground in front of John. His eyes remained shut, and he barely took breaths.

John knelt down and spoke. "Midwa? Can you hear me? *Midwa?*" But there was no reply. John looked around frantically for something he could use to help the weak rodent, but he was barely able to see as the light flickered and caused Midwa to fade in and out.

Suddenly there was a cough. John immediately looked beneath him and saw that Midwa had opened his eyes. Though he struggled to open his mouth, the rodent uttered, "John…we don't have much time…The longer we meet here, the weaker I am becoming."

John replied with a voice filled with concern, "But you seemed so strong. I don't understand."

Midwa struggled to respond. "I do not know how many more times we can meet before I will…" He stopped himself before he could complete the sentence.

John's voice had transformed into one filled with desperation. "But I need you…We need you."

Midwa attempted to ease John's apprehensions. "No, John. It is I who needs you."

However, this remark perplexed John further. "But how? I'm not…"

John woke up to the sound of screams instigated by the tremors that had continued to rumble throughout the cavern for the past hour. As his eyes opened wider, the blur became more focused. He saw all the kids scramble. They carried rocks from the massive base of rubble toward its highest point. The higher they ascended, the narrower it became, which made it increasingly unstable. They did not have much time before the cavern collapsed.

Fully alert, John sprang to his feet. Although he was banged up badly, pain was the least of his concerns; the same went for the others. The brushes with death had become more frequent; however, it was still better than the alternative of imprisonment in the palace at Her Majesty's mercy. They needed to escape soon, and just as importantly, they needed to eat something that would provide them with enough nourishment to continue their journey. They were running on empty.

John began to contribute as he grabbed some sizable rocks from the base and carried them to the top. This gave them the additional height they needed to reach a ledge in the cavern ceiling and return into the primary corridor. The tremors became more frequent as they advanced further. They picked up their pace as they scaled the claws of Arachno.

As several feet remained from the ledge above, the rumble became constant as more rocks fell from the cavern ceiling. Tony was at the highest point, while the others were scattered throughout the mound they had constructed.

"We need to go now!" he yelled.

Jacob spoke up as well. "Come on! This place is about to fall apart!"

Everyone dropped the rocks they carried and began to sprint toward the top. They soon gathered around the highest point, still several feet shy of the ledge that led back to the corridor. They had built up just enough to give themselves a chance to escape. Tony, who was the tallest and strongest of the bunch, was up first. He jumped up, grabbed on to the rough ledge, and pulled himself up with relative ease. Jacob lifted Joey up toward Tony, who pulled him so strongly that he flew a few feet behind him. William and Rob followed next. This was good progress, but several still remained, and the mound had become increasingly unstable.

Jacob yelled out, "OK, everyone, we need to send two at a time now!"

William pulled up Freddie as Tony pulled up Ivy. Tony hoped to gain her favor by saving her life. Norman and Pippy were next. As Freddie pulled up Pippy, it took the collective effort of the others to lift Norman. Only Jacob and John remained below. The rumbles finally pushed the mound's stability past its breaking point, and it suddenly collapsed a few feet. John and Jacob jumped up, but they could not reach the ledge. It was simply too high, even when the kids above them extended their arms as far as they could.

The mound was on the verge of collapse. Freddie suggested that they lower him so they could grab on to his ankles and they could lift them together.

William yelled, "It's risky, but worth a try!"

Freddie cautiously extended his legs over the ledge as Tony tightened his grip around his hands. The others anchored Tony by forming a line behind him.

John encouraged Jacob to go ahead of him and grab on to Freddie's ankles because he believed that Midwa would protect him. However, Jacob, valiant as always, felt personally responsible to protect them and insisted that John go first.

"John, we don't have time to argue! Go ahead! I'll lift you. You grab on to Freddie's legs. I'll hold on to yours! They'll pull us both up. Now go! Trust me!"

Without giving it another thought, John climbed onto Jacob's shoulders and was lifted as high as Jacob could manage, barely reaching Freddie's ankles. Tony was ready to pull as the others anchored him in place. Once John had a firm grip, Jacob jumped up and latched on to John's still-drying pants.

As Jacob managed a firm grip, the mound collapsed beneath him. Most of the fallen rocks, along with Arachno, were now submerged. The rumbles echoed throughout. However, a bigger problem loomed. The cavern was about to collapse completely on itself. As space was limited at the end where they were attempting to pull up Jacob and John, William suggested that some of others head to safety. Otherwise, the weight would collapse the area they stood upon.

The weight of Jacob and John proved to be too much. Progress was stagnant, as Tony, William, Norman, and Rob could not pull up the weight of both John and Jacob.

Tony called over to the others, "Hey, guys! Come and help! We need all the strength we can muster before we all fall!"

William yelled, "But the extra weight!"

Tony was upset with William's lack of empathy. "We leave no one behind!"

The kids struggled in their efforts as they failed to manage the pace they needed. Time had begun to run out rapidly. The ground had begun to crack beneath them and part in the middle. Joey and Pippy were knocked off balance, and they stumbled off the side. Ivy and Norman were able to grab on to Pippy and pull her quickly back up. Joey managed to grab on to the ledge and pulled himself up. Unfortunately, this cost them valuable strength and time. John and Jacob were now a foot closer to their demise below as they stretched and strained the arms of the kids above.

The ground started to splinter further, forcing Ivy and Pippy to race to the opposite side of Tony and William, who suddenly held on to the total weight of Freddie, John, and Jacob.

John looked down at Jacob and yelled, "Try to climb ahead of me!"

As they struggled to maintain their grips, Jacob attempted to follow John's instructions and climb, but the wetness of John's pants prevented him. He looked up and yelled, "I can't! Your pants are too wet. I'm sorry, John, but both of us can't make it... You're our best chance. Promise me you'll take care of the others!"

John yelled again, "No, Jacob! You can't let go! I *can't* lead them! He whispered to himself, "Midwa, please…"

Tony yelled below, barely louder than the powerful rumbles, "This isn't working! You have to try to climb!"

Jacob stared into John's eyes as he spoke. "Don't worry, John. I believe in you." He released his grip and fell below. He descended and faded into the abyss.

John's scream echoed above the violent rumble that shook the cavern to its core: "Jaaaaacoooooooob!"

But Jacob had disappeared from their view.

The screams of the others also echoed throughout the cavern; however, there was no time to mourn Jacob's death because they were about to share the same fate if they did not get out immediately. With the weight of only John and Freddie, Tony and the others were able to lift him with just about everything they had left. As John reached the ledge, Tony turned around and instructed the others to run toward safe ground immediately. He did not need to tell them twice. They sprinted as they never had before.

John ran as fast and hard as he could. He quickly gained on the others, who were already close to safe ground. The ledge finally gave in under the extra body weight, triggering the remainder of the ground beneath him to collapse in his wake. Only moments remained before Ivy, Tony, and John reached the platform, where the others waited impatiently and cheered them on.

The ground splintered further and left just enough room for them to run single file. Ivy crossed first, with Tony almost immediately behind her. He held on to her and asked if she was OK. John's pace had slowed slightly as the disappearing ground flirted with his toes at each step. As he took his final step, the ground beneath him collapsed. Ivy pushed Tony back and raced toward John. He had just enough forward momentum to reach Ivy's extended arm. Ivy, with her lightning-quick reflexes, had reacted before anyone else noticed John would not reach. As he dangled over the edge, the others quickly gathered around and pulled him up to safety.

John did not shy away from eye contact with her this time. He was grateful, and she knew it, as she said, "You owe me one," with that endearing grin of hers. Tony's glance of jealousy did not go unnoticed by Pippy, who had always thought he was an odd character.

As the last of the rocks crashed down below, they realized that they were at the end of the corridor that they could not advance to earlier. The burning root extended far beyond the entrance, running throughout an entire network of tunnels. They needed to decide which tunnel they would enter.

It was critical that they find food quickly, or they would not last much longer. Fortunately, they were able to quench their thirst from the surprisingly fresh waters of the cavern before it had been taken over by the murky jade ooze of Arachno.

Before they moved forward, they all turned around and looked upon the collapsed cavern. Far below, their leader had fallen. They paid their respects as they remained silent for a few heartrending moments. Unfortunately, they did not have much time to linger and mourn the death of Jacob properly, as much as they wished to. The adrenaline began to subside, and the harsh reality of hunger once again dominated their thoughts.

"What do we do now?" asked Joey, the youngest of them all, as he desperately looked for leadership and guidance. Freddie and Ivy asked the same, followed by Norman and Rob.

Tony remained quiet, but William chimed in. "Jacob and I were the closest, and since I'm the eldest now, I should be the new leader."

Freddie jumped in. "That's not fair! You're only a month older than Tony. At least that's what he said."

"I suppose you think that *Tony* should be the leader?" William replied aggressively.

Freddie managed to overcome his intimidation. "You just can't claim leadership. You have to *earn* it!"

"Well, we should cast a vote. I vote for William," Norman, ever so eager to please, yelled out.

Rob jumped in. "Me too. I vote for William."

Tony joined in. "Sorry, William, but I don't trust you. I'm going to have to vote for *myself*."

William continued his aggressive demeanor. "Fine, I don't trust you either!"

"What has William contributed? Just because he was close with Jacob doesn't mean he can lead like Jacob. My vote is for Tony!" Ivy was now engaged in the discussion. She nervously looked over at John as she stood next to Tony.

It was a silly notion to think she would vote for me, John thought.

"Tony!" Freddie yelled out excitedly.

William's attitude persisted. "What about you, John?" He mumbled to himself, "Better not vote for yourself. We'll all end up like Jacob..."

John overheard William, but it did not matter because he was already overwhelmed with guilt, as he felt responsible for Jacob's demise. It was irrelevant that the fallen leader had insisted that John go first. He knew the others had reached the same conclusion: Jacob had died because of John's selfishness. And he was convinced of it as well.

He glanced at Ivy and replied after several silent seconds, "I vote for...Tony."

Tony was surprised but understood that if he voted for William, he basically admitted his guilt. John felt it was best to internalize his guilt for a while.

Joey followed the footsteps of Rob, as always. "I vote for William."

William looked over to the last voter. "What do you say, Pippy? Go ahead and make the *obvious* choice." He was clearly referring to himself, as his words were accompanied by an undercurrent of unsubtle pretentiousness. He knew that Pippy had a crush on Rob, so she would go to whichever side he had chosen. It was a no-brainer. In Jacob's absence, William seemed to have stepped from behind his shadow and proved to be arrogant.

The Dreamer: Origins

"John," Pippy whispered.

William yelled at Pippy, "You can't vote for John! You know what he's done! He's a *freak*! He'll get us all killed!"

Tony jumped in and shouted, "Shut up, William!" She can vote for whomever she wants! If she wants to vote for John, then she can vote for him!" Tony felt empowered as Ivy stood by his side, even if she did not look at him.

William shot back, "Well, OK, you two-tone idiot, that doesn't help us! That leaves us a split vote, with four votes each if you do the math. So no one wins, you two-tone bonehead!"

Tony was unmoved by these words. "Go ahead, make fun of me. The others may not remember their past, but I do. And so do you. So if you want me to stay quiet, then you sure as heck better…"

William could not gather any words together in response. An uncomfortable silence overcame everyone and lasted an unbearable minute.

Pippy broke the silence. "I…I…" But she was overwhelmed with the decision-making process and ran off into one of the tunnels, the dimmest one, as the burning root terminated at its entrance.

As he felt responsible for Pippy's fleeing, John immediately ran after her. Tony called over to the others to follow as well so they could stick together. Ivy and Freddie did not hesitate and ran after Pippy, John, and Tony.

Joey began to follow as well, but William shouted, "Hey! You're with *me*; you voted for *me*! If you go with them, don't bother to run back when they get themselves slain!"

Rob joined in. "Come on, Joey. This is our best chance."

Joey slowly returned with his head down, filled with shame of the weakness within his tiny frame. Worse still, he had a crush on Pippy. He was enamored with her quirks.

William commanded Rob, Joey, and Norman, "Follow me. This tunnel is the brightest. Those idiots won't last five minutes." They followed the burning root down the length of the tunnel. Along the way, they noticed an open hall illuminated in the distance, which gave them hope.

"Come on, guys! Hurry up!" William shouted.

As they reached the hall, they observed the elegant lighting on display, which highlighted a large dining table in the middle, fit for a king. Every seat was occupied by men and women who appeared to be enjoying a fantastic feast over engaging dialogue. One man laughed so hard that wine exploded from his nose. A figure with glistening, murky jade eyes faded into the shadows. It went unnoticed by the group.

William once again shouted to the others, "Come on!"

They sprinted toward the table, but as they approached, they realized that it was just an illusion that began to fade back to their harsh reality. No living being dined at the table. They appeared to have been deceased for several years, as cobwebs covered them almost in their entirety, along with the food they appeared to consume.

The kids looked at one another with concern but soon noticed in the middle of the table an enormous, freshly cooked pontaccio. This was quite a mysterious hall. They were overcome with the delightful aroma and did not hesitate to climb onto the table. They crawled hastily over and took several mouthfuls of pontaccio, as big as their young mouths could handle. They tore apart the large fowl animal, and within minutes, all that remained were the bones. They washed it down with some accompanying freshwater that had been laid out for them.

William said to the others as he chewed on the last piece of pontaccio that he'd wrestled away from Joey, "What did I tell you guys?" He spat on the others inadvertently as he sucked his teeth for remnants. "Stick with me, and you'll be OK. Do you think the others are eating this well? They're probably rotting somewhere, dying from starvation."

However, the others did not say a word. They silently questioned his arrogance. Nonetheless, their bellies were full, and they acknowledged his leadership.

It became eerily quiet when they stopped their dialogue. They looked beyond the dusty seats of the table as a sea of murky jade eyes slowly approached along with mild shrieks. The kids huddled to the center of the large table, where the lone spotlight highlighted their meal. Their screams of fear echoed throughout the tunnels of the cavern, though not far enough to reach the others, who were still in pursuit of Pippy.

Tony, John, Freddie, and Ivy followed the faint footsteps and whimpers of Pippy as they ran cautiously through the barely illuminated tunnel. They managed to keep up the pace until they suddenly heard a loud thump that echoed in the distance, followed by complete silence. Concern overcame them. They quickened their pursuit and crashed into a gate as they kicked up a cloud of dust that had just settled. They rubbed their arms and feet for the minor bruises that resulted from the impact. They knew Pippy must be on the other side, as there were no other paths that branched off from the tunnel until that point. John felt personally responsible for Pippy's safety, especially as Jacob's death had already begun to weigh heavily on him.

John began to strike his open palm repeatedly on the ancient gate. He was frustrated. A tear ran down his cheek.

Tony noticed the sniffle and spoke up to take the attention away from John. "OK, guys, there should be a lever around here somewhere."

Freddie responded, "Tony, I'm starving." Ivy echoed the same. John could not focus on his hunger because he was still distracted by the burdens he had allowed to overwhelm him.

Tony spoke. "We'll find food as soon as we find Pippy, OK?" They nodded hesitantly, barely able to see the outlines of one another's faces.

Tony began to feel around the shadows for a lever. The others did the same as they stuck their arms and hands everywhere they could reach.

Tony whispered to himself, "I remember it was around here somewhere…" This continued for several minutes, unsuccessfully. "I got it!" Tony yelled excitedly as he pulled the lever. But it had no effect.

Freddie whispered to the others, "Hey, there are flowers near the borders of the gate."

Intrigued, Ivy whispered back, "That's odd. No flora should be growing this far underground."

Tony added, "Nice job, Freddie! Those are morning glories. Everything is edible except for the seeds, which can be poisonous. *So do not eat the seeds!* It should hold us over until we find something more substantial."

The kids grabbed as much as they could find and ate most of it even though it was mildly unpleasant. They stored the rest for later.

Ivy, with her astute sense of hearing, started to pick up on some noise and whispered to the others, "Guys, I hear something from the other side of the gate. It sounds like a voice, but it's muffled, and I can't make it out clearly."

But as she finished her sentence, Freddie whispered, "Shhh…I hear footsteps. It sounds like they're coming from back over there." They fell silent and listened intently. But the sounds stopped. "I swear I heard footsteps!" repeated Freddie.

Ivy interrupted. "Shhh, I just heard them."

They again fell silent, but once again, there was no sound. They began to slowly step backward toward the gate as they remained in close proximity to one another. John, however, sat on the ground in the corner, his head rested on his knees. He was silent as he caressed a lone morning glory below that had grown in isolation.

The sounds recommenced, and soon faint shadows appeared on the walls. They originated from around the corner of the tunnel. The shadows shrank as they continued to lurk closer. They soon appeared to outline men. Before long, the figures revealed themselves. They seemed to be ancient soldiers, ghostly as their spirits faded in and out as if they were not quite there. Their murky jade eyes contrasted against the faint shadows. Dozens upon dozens of orbs began to blend together as the dark figures dominated what little light remained in the tunnel. The undead warriors approached unusually slowly, as if they were under a spell.

John finally looked up, speechless, as a final tear rolled down his adolescent face. His eyes were once again bright blue. They illuminated his surroundings and revealed the soldiers who appeared even more terrifying against the radiance of his light. John was empty of expression.

The ancient army continued their advance. The brilliance of John's eyes began to dim. The energy did not fade, however; it had begun to outline his body. His body was soon completely outlined, and the illumination began to flow outward, no different from when he was in the depths of the cavern waters. A field enveloped the kids, who were still frightened about the uncertainty of what was going to happen to them.

The ancient soldiers were now within striking distance. They unsheathed their swords, which possessed a hazy jade glow along their piercing edges. The warriors took their final steps, cocked back their swords, and swung directly at the kids, with the intent to thrash them. The long swords swung downward with the force of their ancient might and made even the usually calm Tony cringe in anguish. Ivy and Freddie squealed in anticipation of the strikes. John stood tall. The swords struck, and a loud impact echoed throughout the tunnels of the cavern.

Tony, Ivy, and Freddie looked up and realized they were still alive. The undead warriors appeared to actually be dead, as they were laid out on the ground, immobile; they had been thrown backward from the impact. They gawked in astonishment at John.

After a few moments, John finally broke the silence. "The undead cannot be killed, not here at least. The enchantment that controls them is too strong in these tunnels and will once again take effect. We don't have much time; we need to get to the other side of the gate before they wake up. I don't know how much longer Midwa can help us. Let's go!"

John turned his back to the undead warriors, who would lie immobile only momentarily. Facing the gate with the others, he slowly began to walk. They passed through the gate as if it were not there. Freddie was impressed by the mechanical inner workings of the ancient nine-foot-thick gate, which took them several seconds to walk all the way through. Ivy glimpsed behind and saw the soldiers once again rise to their feet and recommence their advance.

The darkness was soon broken by a blinding light as the kids emerged on the other side. They overheard the fiendish thrashes of swords against the gate. However, they knew they were safe; there was no way that even the might of their thrusts could breach the impenetrable gate. The field of energy slowly faded back into John's eyes and then faded away completely. He was again his normal self.

Tony's two-tone face was now masked with a huge grin. Ivy jumped at John and embraced him. She even gave him a peck on the cheek, which made his face flush with red. Tony looked on briefly with envy before he looked away at what was before them. All their eyes were wide open. As they regrouped with Pippy, they had finally gotten the break they desperately needed.

VI: Freedom, at Last

Never had they seen such vivid colors. They were accustomed to the shades of gray and white at the Ice Palace. Above them was the bluest sky with naught a cloud. Surrounded by a wealth of shrubbery and wildlife, they could not recall the last time they had seen such beauty from so close. They had been left to use their imaginations as they looked upon the lush jungle lands from the gated windows of their cells.

Freddie watched several dozen pontaccios feed on the vibrant green grass, their white feathers shining in the sunlight. Above them on the far end of the land, there was a waterfall that rushed to escape a channel cutting through the force field that protected the palace. The waterfall fed a vivid river that flowed into the vast jungle before them. Butterflies of countless colors swept across the flora.

A lovely lilac-breasted roller soared high up a tree to its nest. These trees were healthy, with light brown bark, lush green leaves, and ripe, low-hanging fruit. Fawns grazed alongside the channel that eventually flowed into the Larris River as the stags and doe rested on the soft grounds on either side. The kids had already become acclimated to the warmer temperatures. Their moods reflected the same. No longer were they fighting to survive from one minute to the next.

Hunger once again settled in as the temporary relief of the morning glories had worn off; however, they were surrounded by a plethora of options. They began to yell out their desires for dinner; unsurprisingly, there were no requests for liver porridge.

Tony took the lead and assigned individual tasks for dinner preparations. "John, gather as much fruit as you can carry. It should be easy since they're hanging low. Ivy, go and milk a cow or a goat, whichever you find first. Freddie, prepare a fire, with enough wood to last us through the night. Pippy, go and scout the area. Sprint back here if you see anything of interest, or yell out if you get into any sort of trouble. I'll catch and prepare a pontaccio."

Everyone was ecstatic with their newfound freedom. The kids ran off in all directions to prepare the dinner they had desired for so long. John ran directly toward the trees and bushes and picked some fresh mangoes, berries, and avocadoes. With his shirt packed with fruit, he ran back to the campsite, where Freddie had already begun to prepare a campfire. Freddie made good progress with his makeshift ax, which was crafted out of a slender tree trunk and a sharp-edged stone and was held together by a soft yet tough branch from a nearby mackelroy tree.

In the distance, Ivy attempted to coerce a goat to provide some milk, but the goat did not give it up easily. It hopped away each time she approached. Ivy displayed some frustration and soon tripped over herself, getting dirt in her mouth. As she looked up and spit the dirt out, she saw John laugh at her.

"Oh, so you"—she spat out the rest of the dirt—"think *that's* funny, huh?" She grabbed a nearby rock and tossed it way above him, toward the top of the tree.

"Ahahahahaha, I thought you had *good* aim, Ivy," John laughed as he dropped a few fruits from his shirt because his belly hurt from laughter.

"I don't like you anymore, *OK?*" she yelled.

John's laughs ceased, and he replied with nerves in his voice, "Wait…you like me?"

She smiled radiantly. "Sure, you have all those powers. Why *wouldn't* I?"

"Oh," he replied as his smile transformed into a frown.

"Hey, John…" Ivy looked at him with her irresistible smile.

"Yeah?" He still felt a bit down by her reply, as the powers were not his own.

She continued. "You should know…that I…*do have good aim!*"

Suddenly John heard a commotion. It sounded as if it originated above him. A vertical stampede of ripe somachis, tomato-like fruits that grew on trees rather than vines, fell on him. He tried to

68

run away but slipped on the splattered ones already on the ground. As he lay on his back, the rush lasted for several more seconds, until he was orange.

She ran over and offered him a hand. He reluctantly accepted, and she pulled him up. They both managed to stay upright, barely.

She said to him, "But you should know…that I do like you." She ran off as she giggled.

John had the biggest smile he'd ever had. He called for her attention as she ran off. She turned around as she continued to jog sideways. As he was about to yell back that he liked her too, one last somachi smashed against his head and oozed into his mouth. She giggled again and turned in the direction of the goat. John watched her continue her efforts to milk it. The tensions of the goat had eased, and eventually it let her milk it. Though she lacked a proper bucket, she had created drinking cups out of some overgrown apples by carving out the centers. A little ingenuity went a long way in the wild.

John finally turned his eyes away from Ivy, who glowed as he had not seen before. He began to wipe his clothes of the smashed somachis all over him. As he raised his head, he saw Tony stare at him. The older, taller kid did not look pleased. They broke eye contact, and Tony returned to his efforts to catch the elusive pontaccio. He ran left; they ran right. He ran right; they ran left. They scrambled between his legs when he stood upright and between his arms when he dove. The pontaccios were quick but not incredibly smart. They ran wildly within the same area, a peculiarity in their behavior, as pontaccios insisted on not being removed from their favorite feeding spots. Tony grew frustrated and grunted to show it. He was not upset with the pontaccios, as he knew he would eventually catch one. It was who he could not catch that was at the root of his frustrations.

Pippy weaved left and right past the trees of the forest. It was so lush with bush that she could not see its end. Eager to know where it would eventually end, however, she began to ascend the tallest tree in the area; it was nearly seventy-five feet in height. She found some strong and flexible branches of the curious mackelroy trees nearby. The branches felt almost like rope as they hung droopily. They would eventually fall off after several years, but no one understood why.

Pippy tied the flexible branch around its mother tree and then around her fist for a firm grip. She was endowed with great balance and determination. Within minutes she had scaled the tree, and what she saw was amazing, enough to cause her to gasp and fall silent. She looked in every direction, eyes wide open.

Pippy had made a discovery that the others needed to know about immediately. She quickly but cautiously descended the tree and sprinted back toward the camp. Pippy's sense of direction was second only to Norman's; she rarely got lost in surroundings that were even just barely familiar.

She returned to the camp, where Freddie already had started a fire, with plenty of reserve wood off to the side. John still had not sorted out all of the fruit; he was meticulous about these kinds of things. The setback was the forty-five minutes it had taken him to wash properly in the river to rid himself of the somachis that had found their way everywhere imaginable.

Pippy observed John. He watched Ivy relax as she lay down and tossed up her carved-apple cup, angled slightly so a few drops of fresh milk would fall into her mouth. These kinds of acts were so natural for Ivy she sometimes did not realize she had done them. Tony, meanwhile, plucked the last few feathers from the pontaccio he had finally caught.

Pippy finally yelled out at the foot of the camp, out of breath, "Hey, I have to show all of you something. You're not going to believe this!"

Tony asked her to relax because they would have plenty of time to see whatever it was she wanted to show them. For the moment, they would feast. Tony skewered the pontaccio and roasted it over the fire. He had even managed to find a few spices locally and added some seasoning. Pippy relaxed once the pontaccio was served. The feast was under way, and they soon forgot their problems.

Tony initiated a relaxed dialogue. "Hey, John, can you toss over a mango?" His tan had begun to subside ever so slightly, as he had not soaked in the sun during sunrise. The sun shone brightest against the east wing, and he often basked in its glory. His crush on Ivy was obvious, but no more obvious than that all of the other young boys who got butterflies from her presence. It was said that his tan was only on one side because he only looked to her window, which exposed the left side of his face for unhealthy periods of time.

John appeared distracted. "Sure, here you go. So…um…"

Tony interrupted. "Go ahead. What's on your mind, John?"

"Is anyone going to talk about Jacob?" Pippy jumped in.

Tony answered, obviously distraught, "He was…a great friend, a great leader…a brother to us *all*. It's a tragedy."

John was heavily impacted by the remarks and at a loss for words.

Tony continued. "I'm sorry, John. I know you are…We'll talk about this another time, when all of us are ready."

Ivy broke the awkwardness and unashamedly asked one of the questions that had been burning within her and no doubt the others. "What did you mean when you told William that he had better be quiet or else?"

Pippy and Freddie looked on as they each took a bite of pontaccio and waited eagerly for Tony to reply.

Tony hesitantly spoke up. "Well…Her Majesty erases the memories of all her captives. This is why you guys can't remember your past."

Ivy now appeared excited. "First of all, why do you keep saying 'Her Majesty,' and second of all, what do you mean 'you guys'?"

"Ivy, please calm down. I don't want you to…um…" He changed course from where he was about to take the dialogue. "Well, Jacob, William, and I were allowed to keep our memories."

Tony's reply did not do much to calm her. Ivy was becoming increasingly more anxious. "Calm down? No! I will *not* calm down! Why *you* and not *us*?" She was a firecracker. Once lit, it was only a matter of time before she exploded. And with a short fuse, it usually did not take long.

The others, with the exception of John, were curious as well and echoed, "Yeah, Tony, *why*?"

Tony answered, "I don't know…" before he looked away and avoided eye contact with them.

Ivy shot back, "Sure you do! There *must* be a reason, and you're going to tell us!"

Tony, now annoyed and frustrated, tossed down his mango and snapped back at Ivy, "Look, I don't know! OK? Just drop it."

Everyone fell silent.

Tony changed the subject. "So…Pippy, what did you see before?"

Pippy could not describe what she had seen with justice and replied, "Um…I think it's better to see it for yourself."

John, Freddie, and Ivy remained quiet for different reasons.

Tony displayed his frustration unsubtly and replied, "Well, the sun has just about set, so it'll have to wait until the morning. We need to get some rest."

They each retired in a corner of the camp, close enough to the fire to stay warm during the night hours. Each one lay on his or her back, quiet, as they gazed into the night sky, which was littered with stars that shone from far away.

John heard some light footsteps approach.

"Do you mind if I sit with you for a while? I'm not tired yet," Ivy whispered to him.

"Keep it down," Tony whispered as annoyance bled from his words.

John replied to her, "Of course not," and he sat up.

"I'm really sorry about Jacob," she began.

"It's OK…Well, it's not OK, but I guess it has to be…I just wish—"

Ivy interrupted. "Hey, it's not your fault. It's none of our fault. We tried. You tried."

He hesitantly replied, "Yeah, I just…You're right."

She changed the subject. "So, what do you make of Tony? What do you think he's hiding?"

"I have no idea, but whatever it is, it seems very sensitive."

"I've heard some things about him, but I don't know what to believe. There's a rumor that he was a palace guard, but I don't see how that is possible since they don't select kids for those positions. But what do I know? I can't remember anything. Few of us can. I don't remember if I was a hunter, if I enjoyed dancing, if I could horseback ride, or if I was a beggar. I don't know who my family is. I just have these instincts with no memories of ever using them before I got here. I don't know who most of the captives in the palace are, even if they have familiar faces. I don't even know if I had a boyfriend," Ivy said as she glanced at him and noticed him gulp.

"Maybe you were a horseback hunter who liked to dance as you shot your arrows. And maybe…Rob…was your boyfriend," John replied, the nerves exposed in his voice.

She replied excitedly, "Rob? Please! He's a jerk. He takes advantage of all the girls, making them do all of his duties while he does nothing. I would never! I prefer nice quiet boys who have superpowers and save the world," she said as she pushed him with her shoulder, nearly knocking him over.

John struggled to make eye contact with her and tried to change the subject. "Have you ever wondered how many stars there are in the sky?"

Ivy ignored his question and answered with a question of her own. "You know I don't bite, right?"

"Of course I know. Otherwise, you would…um, kill me with your poison…right?" he answered nervously.

"What are you talking about?"

"Well, don't they call you 'Poison Ivy'? So I could die with a bite, right?"

She giggled as she spoke. "No, silly! First of all, it's not *'Poison* Ivy;' it's *'Poisson* Ivy,' and I'm named after a wonderful and fancy fish native to the shores of the Buv're. I don't remember ever tasting it, but I smelled it one time in the kitchen, and there was a familiarity to the scent. I figured I *must* have tried it, right? Everyone misunderstands me because of my accent! I got tired of correcting everyone, so I just let them call me that, and it stuck. And secondly, I *do* bite!"

John was confused. He looked off to the side as he searched for an answer and replied, "But I thought you just said—ouch!"

Ivy had bitten him in his left hand and was running off toward Pippy, who was still up. He could see them giggle uncontrollably as they spoke to each other while looking in his direction. He grinned nervously in return before Tony spoke up again.

"Come on, guys. We need the rest!" He slammed his palm into the soft ground.

John lay back down as he watched Ivy and Pippy doing the same in the distance as they continued to gossip and giggle. He looked up into the stars and tried to tally them, as if it were possible. The more stars he counted, the more they began to outline the face of Ivy. But he would never be able to approach her, even if he saved the world. No one was shier than he was. She may as well have been as far as the stars were. As he stared into the stars, he slowly faded away.

John was once again in a dark room. Midwa waited for him. He was not at full strength. The chocolate rodent started to speak to him immediately, with an uncharacteristically nervous voice.

"John, I know I told you that dark times are coming. But they are here. The Ice Queen has received news of your survival, and she's preparing an army."

John continued to feel lost. "I don't understand. Why would she need to build up an army? She could have killed me a thousand times if she felt I was a threat."

Midwa spoke with a sense of haste. "You'll understand in due time, young one, but for now, you have to forge a fellowship with your friends. You will need one another to get to the Fire King's castle."

John yelled in protest, "But that's suicide!"

Midwa took a deep breath. He attempted to calm John, as well as himself. "John, you must remember…the key is his ring. You must rid this kingdom of the darkness that Agri…the Ice Queen casts upon it. You *must* save those children for the sake of the future generations who will suffer the same fate if you decide to do nothing about it."

John was unsure how to reply to such a loaded statement. "But…"

Midwa broke the silence. "I believe in you, John. Remember, I am with you. My powers are yours, but use them wisely."

Still confused, John replied again, "But…"

"John!" yelled Ivy, inches from John's ear. Morning had arrived, and the sun was already high in the sky.

"Not *again*," John whispered to himself.

"Come on, John. Pippy's going to show us what she saw yesterday!"

John jumped up to his feet and ran over for a brief breakfast. The others had consumed nearly all the remnants of the previous night's feast. His left foot felt as good as new.

They quickly gained ground on Pippy, Tony, and Freddie. They were once again at the tree where Pippy had made her discovery just a day earlier. The tree was strong enough to support two kids at a time. They scaled it in tandem, which allowed them to look after each other in case one of them slipped. Tony and Freddie got a head start and eventually reached the top after half an hour of cautious climbing. Freddie wanted to scale it at a quicker pace, which was facilitated by his curiosity about what could have impressed Pippy so much. It took John and Ivy a bit more time for preparation, as he was nervous to hold her hands for so long. She occasionally peeked from behind the tree and teased him by sticking out her tongue and making funny noises.

"Ivy, stop. That's dangerous!" he said to her.

"Oh, come on, John. Stop being such a square," she said and then suddenly slipped. John grabbed her hand almost instantly and pulled her back up. There was something extra behind her smile as she spoke. "My hero owed me one from the cavern. It seems he just repaid his debt." She began to shy away from eye contact suddenly. The only eyes she had shied away from until this point were the Ice Queen's.

They soon reached the top along with Tony and Freddie and were in awe, as if a veil had been lifted from their eyes. The Ice Palace was directly in front of John, with Ivy's face set against it. There was a dramatic contrast between her warmth and the frigidity of the palace. A huge storm was raging outside the palace, making it barely visible. It was enclosed by a field of energy, which gave the Ice Queen the ability to control the weather with incredibly concentrated force. John turned his head to the right and saw that the north did not end at the kingdom Belghan. It went beyond rather extensively.

He looked at Ivy to tell her to turn around to look at it, but she was mesmerized with what she saw. Her jaw remained dropped. He saw the reflection in her eyes and immediately turned around. He was mesmerized as well by the distant islands of the East, commonly referred to as the Islands of the Phoenix Dragons.

There were five caverns separated by just as many islands. Each was ruled by the phoenix dragon of its corresponding element: fire, ice, earth, wind, and water. He had seen the tamed phoenix dragon of ice in the lair that Her Majesty had constructed for him, but as he looked into the skies to the east, from afar, he saw the phoenix dragons of wind and water as they flew about.

Aeris, the phoenix dragon of wind, and Aquaris, phoenix dragon of water, had just completed their cycles of dormancy and were up in the air to reacquaint themselves with their respective elements. They flapped their wings tirelessly as they worked together to re-master them. As Aquaris exhaled a rush of streaming water, Aeris divided it into multiple streams and directed it back to the phoenix dragon of water, striking it from several directions simultaneously.

Not to be outdone, Aquaris took an even deeper breath and blasted Aeris with a constant stream of brutal water. The phoenix dragon that commanded the element of wind was unable to deflect the stream. It was too strong, and its lungs had begun to flood with the water. As Aquaris noticed that its sparring opponent had begun to weaken, it stopped its stream and inhaled all of it back. Aeris was overpowered this round and still had some weeks before it would reach full strength. It would be as strong as Aquaris, but as it lagged behind in its rebirth by days, it had to be patient and continue its practice. They both descended back toward their respective caverns to rest for the remainder of the day. They were known to be active during the late hours. Perhaps the day exercises were temporary until they returned to full form.

John turned his eyes to the west. Though his view was partially obstructed by the palace, he saw the fanciful kingdom of Buv're. It was the richest of the three known kingdoms. Even from this distance, the gold and silver glistened. The surrounding landscape even appeared to be sprinkled with gold. It appeared civilized compared to what they had just witnessed to the east.

His eyes took their attention above, toward the sky, which was filled with several planets of different colors and sizes far in the distance. As the sun erupted, it contrasted beautifully against the calmness of the blue skies.

Beneath the sky, he saw the edge of the jungle they were in, where the rushing channel became a powerful waterfall and descended a great distance into Lake Tarin, where the Ice Palace once was. The lake fed into the Larris River, which flowed from the far north to the southern perimeter of the lands of the jungle before it ceased to flow. As he had seen from the gated windows of his cell, the lush, forest-filled lands below accommodated several dozen villages. He had not seen them during the mid-morning hours, however, and was amazed by how vivid the jungles radiated and how active the wildlife was. He even saw a few leopards weave in and out of the trees as they hunted.

The villagers were out and about, and they went on with their daily routines. Gardens were tended to. Young kids played games as elders yelled at them to be careful where they threw their toys, which often ended up through their neighbors' windows. Folks greeted each other in the streets and spoke freely, unlike the Ice Palace, where they had to sneak away to speak to each other, or at least talk under their breaths. Those who spoke in the palace and were caught were punished with dreadful cooking duties. As Rob was a chatterbox, he often experienced the punishment, but unlike others, he was able to persuade the guards to let him sneak in a bite or two of pontaccio.

He looked farther up and beyond the jungle. A desert was situated past the green lands and was home to colossal giants that roamed endlessly, or at least it seemed that way. They were visible even from this great distance. They appeared to be made of the sands of the desert, but it was difficult to tell, as the sandstorms often obstructed visibility from outside the realm.

Beyond the desert, the hues transformed significantly into a deep blue sea that spanned the length of the horizon. The waters were ever calm and uneventful. If John were not so afraid of the sea, he would not mind a swim there—if he could swim, of course. The others would definitely enjoy it, however.

Farther beyond to the south, the vast castle of the Fire King rose, partially veiled behind darkness as balls of fire aggressively erupted through the ominous clouds of several shades of black and gray. He took one final look as Tony called for a meeting at the base of the tree.

They descended and regrouped in order to form a plan. As they engaged in a healthy debate, some argued in favor of an attempt to descend to the lands below, while others insisted they could survive in their newfound paradise. Ivy agreed with the latter and insisted the lands below were impossible to reach since there was no way to descend without the palace guards discovering them. Also, they had just been shut off from the Ice Palace, as the only way back was to encounter the undead army once again. Tony argued that they could not stay there indefinitely because the Ice Queen would eventually find them.

Ivy begged John to side with her, but he could not after what Midwa had told him in his dream. "We need to find a way down. We need to get to the Fire King's castle. It's the only way."

Tony jumped in. "That's suicide, John! How do you suppose we make it across? The only thing that awaits us over there is death!"

After a long silence, John responded, "Death awaits us in the Ice Palace, and death may await us in the lands below. And yes, death may wait for us at the Fire King's castle. But death also awaits us here in this supposed paradise. We have a choice. We can do nothing, here, and just survive for as long as we can at the expense of all those innocent children in the Ice Palace…or, we can do something about it. We can give some meaning, some purpose to our lives. At least we would know that we tried to make a difference."

Tony replied, "How do you suppose we do that?"

John displayed confidence in Midwa. "Midwa said the key is the Fire King's ring—"

Tony interrupted. "John, the rodent is gone! We need to work with what we can see, OK?"

It was a jab to his confidence, but John continued. "We need it to defeat the Ice Queen, but more importantly, we need to stick together. Or else we have no chance."

Tony was not convinced. "And you're sure we can do this?"

John now spoke with some uncertainty. "I...don't know. But we have to try."

Tony slowly approached John and stopped just short of him. He then looked to Ivy and then around at the others, who all shared a look of concern. He was slowly losing the tan that gave him his moniker, Two-Tone Tony. His eyes returned to John's, who was nervous with what was about to happen.

"OK, we break camp at dawn. Let us have one last day of peace." Tony then thrust John backward and yelled, "Tag! You're it!" as he ran off into the forest.

John looked at the others, confused. He then walked up to Ivy, who had a blank look on her face. "Um...tag, you're it!" And John quickly ran off into the forest as well as he held a smile for the longest he had in a while.

"Hey!" Ivy yelled out. She ran over to tag Pippy, but she and Freddie had already begun their sprint toward the forest.

It was not long before Ivy caught Freddie off guard and pushed him into and through a bush as she tagged him. Tony and John stood beside each other in silence as they attempted to hide behind a narrow mackelroy tree.

Tony broke the silence. "I'm sorry, John. There are ugly truths in this world that I don't wish any of you to know."

"But that's not for you to decide."

"Yeah, you're right...I'll try to explain everything if and when we reach the land below. We *should* be able to, but we are going to need to be careful. And one more thing...there are things you don't know about Ivy. Just...don't hurt her, OK?"

"What are you talking about?"

Tony answered cryptically, "Well, as I said, I'll explain everything when we reach below. For now, I think we should try to enjoy this moment."

"Agreed," Ivy replied. She had just snuck from behind them and heard only their last words.

"Whoa, where did *you* come from?" Tony yelled nervously, giving away their position to the others.

"I was trying to run away from Freddie"—she paused—"before he *tagged me*!"

The boys looked at each other, and John spoke. "Wait...what?"

"Tag! You're it!" she shouted as she pushed both of them simultaneously, knocked them both down, and ran away.

Ivy appeared to run away in slow motion in John's eyes.

"Hey! John!" Tony bellowed and finally snapped him back to the present. "So you have a thing for her, don't you?" he asked, grinning.

"Well, no, I mean...I guess..." John's words stumbled over one another.

"Well, everyone does," Tony said. "But be careful. Like I said, there are things about her..."

"Like what?" John asked even more inquisitively than the last time. "Like an extra toe?"

"No!" Tony laughed. "Like I said, we'll talk when the time is right. Oh, I forgot to tell you..."

"What?" John asked nervously.

But as soon as he asked the question, Tony pushed him to the ground. "You're it!" echoed as Tony ran away.

They went on to play for hours and occasionally broke for a snack. When they were not chasing one another on the forest ground, they chased one another up trees. None of them, with the exception of Tony, could recall such a feeling of excitement and genuine fun. They played and ate well until the sun began to set, which prompted one final feast before they embarked on their adventure.

VII: Falling Hard

John suddenly awoke as the ground he lay on began to tremble. He was confused. He looked around and watched the others fall after several attempts to stand. Fruit fell from the trees and crushed upon impact. All wildlife had also fallen to their knees, unable to maintain balance.

Tony yelled over to the others, "Is everyone OK?"

Able to hear Tony over the rumbles, everyone confirmed they were all right. The rumbles grew increasingly more powerful and rocked them until they ceased their efforts to get up. They lay there helpless with the rest of the animals and waited out the quake.

The rumbles suddenly stopped. They were finally able to get themselves up to their feet. An audible sigh of relief echoed; however, it would not last long. They began to feel a shift of the land, with their feet now at uneven heights. The shifts became more pronounced as the land swayed back and forth. The campfire wood rolled away and tumbled deep into the jungle. The wildlife continued to struggle and stumbled helplessly. The trees stood at sharp angles, with the large leaves of the hibich trees now diagonal, along with the droopy branches of the mackelroy trees. As they looked behind them, they noticed the land was no longer attached to the mass that housed the cavern.

The angle became steeper as Tony shouted, "Run to the nearest mackelroy tree and tie one of the branches around you!"

None skipped a beat as they ran immediately to the nearest cluster of mackelroy trees, of which there were several. The rumbles finally ceased as they made the final twists of their mackelroy knots.

The wind brushed against their faces at increasing speeds, as dynamically as the wind decided. They descended quickly while the gusts of wind flowed through their unkempt hair. Everyone looked at one another, terrified, as they were suspended above the ground. The branches of the mackelroy trees kept them from being swept away.

The jungle below approached quickly. They rapidly lost visibility of the sea in the distance, as only a faint view of the Fire King's castle remained through the thick dust storm that had developed in the desert. Even the colossal giants rapidly disappeared from their view. Within a hundred yards from the jungle, the land began to stabilize and no longer swayed back and forth as wildly as it had just moments earlier. After a soft impact, they were once again grounded.

Tony yelled over to the others, "Climb!"

They all looked at him. "Huh?"

Tony replied, "Just climb!"

They mounted the mackelroy trees with haste and ascended until they were hidden.

Tony whispered to the others, "Shhh…"

They acknowledged him with a nod as they fell silent. There was a commotion in the distance that became increasingly louder. It was soon clear that the voices belonged to obnoxious men.

They overheard one man yell, "Stupid cattle! Why do they still come to this part of the land? Don't they know better by now?" Nearby cattle mooed at him as if they understood the offensive words.

Another man yelled, "Ahhhh, I'll take one of these pontaccios. You'll make a great supper tonight, *won't you?*" followed by a yelp from the large fowl-like creature.

As the men approached, their voices became louder and even more obnoxious. The men were soon in sight below the kids. They were guards of the Ice Palace passing by. Their hefty armor made the impact of their steps echo. After a few guards passed, they began to hear voices of young boys, no older than six or seven. They were pleading to return to their families.

One of the guards, Number Forty-Seven, yelled to the others, "Her Majesty won't be pleased. They're getting younger and younger! Pretty soon we'll be capturing babies! Ahahahahaha!"

Another guard, Number Fifty-Two, added, "You're right. We only brought back five of the peasants this time."

Number Forty-Seven replied, "Well, we were instructed only to replace the five who got away. That other lot got caught. And they're going to be on double duty permanently, if they're lucky. If they're unlucky, they're going straight to Frostbite's lair. Ahahahahaha!"

The lead guard, Number Eleven, engaged in the dialogue. "We shouldn't get too comfortable back at the palace. The Ice Queen has put out a search party for the ones who got away. She's also commanding a claim on all able children. Something big is brewing!"

Soon their voices faded away into the distance. After a few moments of silence to make sure they had passed completely, Tony whispered to the others, "Climb down now!"

They descended the trees until they were close to the ground and jumped off as they followed Tony's lead. He signaled to the others to run as fast as they could. They were roughly thirty feet from the edge when the ground began to rumble once again. The ascent back into the sky would soon commence.

Tony leaped off first as the mass of land they were standing on began to break apart from the earth beneath it. Ivy and Freddie leaped almost immediately after. John was about to leap but stopped in his tracks just a few feet short of the edge. He had overheard a grunt from behind. Pippy had tripped and fallen over, and she was in tears as she held her ankle that she had twisted in the cavern.

The ascent had begun, but John still had an opportunity to leap off, since it was a drop of only a few feet. However, the guilt he still carried from Jacob's death overcame him again. Also, as they almost lost Pippy earlier, the guilt compounded. She was several yards inland, and the ascent began to accelerate. Soon any jump at the increasing height meant certain demise.

Pippy was hysterical as she clutched her ankle. He sprinted back toward her, extended his arm, and grabbed on to her hand. She could barely walk and had already lost valuable time. As they hobbled toward the edge, John looked above and behind and could see that the mass of earth where the Ice Palace rose fast approached. It floated in the sky as if it were in a world of its own. He could see the clear water rush out of the channel that flowed from the force field, even more wildly than before. He realized the water must be the exhaust for the ice that melted; otherwise the palace grounds would have become a globe of freezing waters, an impossible habitat for anyone to live, perhaps even for the Ice Queen herself.

Tony, Ivy, and Freddie watched impatiently to see if John and Pippy would emerge. However, even if they did, there was no way to reach them. They would need to wait until the next descent; even then it would be full of guards, and they would need to defend themselves.

John and Pippy now stood at the edge of the rapidly ascending land. They could once again see above the desert, and beyond they saw the calm sea. John stared at the Fire King's castle with the intent to reach it.

He then looked at Pippy and said, "Trust me." As John lifted Pippy onto his back, he whispered, "Hold on as tight as you can."

Tony and the others waited impatiently below, unable to see John and Pippy along the ledge. However, they soon noticed a bright blue illumination leap beyond the edge. It quickly descended. John and Pippy fell fast and hard. They appeared to break everything in their path as a thunderous sound tore through the sky.

The illumination became increasingly larger. Tony and the others were once again nervous. Although they had heard the story of John and Jacob jumping down several flights in the Ice Palace, they had not seen anything like this before. The descent became faster and louder, and soon they heard a muffled scream: "Ruuuuuuuunnn!"

Tony and the others ran for cover, but they could not manage to take more than a few steps, as a destructive impact forced itself upon the ground and created winds that lifted them off their feet. Fortunately, Tony, Ivy, and Freddie were on soft ground, so the impact caused only minor cuts and bruises.

The bright blue illumination had vanished. All that remained was a large cloud of dust. The kids rushed to the site and coughed as they breathed in the dust-filled air. Nothing was visible within the impact radius, and it became almost impossible to breathe. Tony suggested that they wait, and the others agreed. After a short while, the dust began to settle and provided an outline of John and Pippy as they lay on the ground.

Amazingly, John and Pippy both still breathed, though they had been knocked unconscious by the impact. The others carried them away from the dust, toward fresher air. Shortly after, Pippy regained consciousness and immediately grabbed her ankle.

Tony asked her if she was OK, and she replied, "Yeah, it's just my ankle. I think I twisted it again, even worse. What happened?"

Tony told her, "John saved your life. Both of you just…fell down here." They were now all looking down upon John, who was still unconscious and barely breathing.

John was once again in a dark room.

Midwa looked exhausted as he spoke. "John, I am proud of you."

John was unsure of what was going on. "What…what happened?"

Midwa explained, "You saved Pippy's life. You can let go of the guilt that has weighed so heavily on you. You *must* persuade the others to go to the Fire King's castle. Do not delay any further. The Ice Queen will chase you down if you remain in her kingdom. Remember, I am with you always."

"Wait!" John yelled desperately. But his dream faded. His eyes slowly opened as he coughed up some dust and provided the others with some much-needed relief.

Pippy handed him an apple to replenish some energy as she whispered, "Thank you, John. Thank you for saving my life."

VIII: A Fellowship Forged

As John and Pippy regained full consciousness, they knew they had to decide where to go before more guards eventually passed by. The crater that John had created would be unavoidable, and the report of their whereabouts was inevitable. While most could not recollect which villages they called home, Tony vaguely remembered and would be their guide.

Tony began to lead them on a southwesterly path because he recalled that it led to the first of several small villages. When they arrived, they would be able to stock up on the supplies they needed for their difficult journey. With the sun already high, they knew they did not have the cover of darkness to sneak around, so they stayed on the main road only when it was clear and quiet. They avoided any passersby, namely the palace guards.

A short time later, after they trekked quietly, they overheard footsteps in the distance, just out of sight. They immediately leaped into a nearby bush just on the side of the road. Out of plain sight, they hid. The heavy footsteps and muffled voices became louder. Another group of guards was about to pass with even more captured kids, who begged for their families no differently than the others they had just seen.

Tony, John, and the others looked at one another in concern. They were concerned for themselves, but even more for the young captives who would not survive under the working conditions of the Ice Palace.

The guards were now close enough to understand.

"I heard those kids are dropping like flies in the palace," said the first guard, Number Twenty-Six.

"Her Majesty has big plans. She has commanded the capture of all able children. If they can lift a chisel, they will work in the Ice Palace," responded another guard, Number Twenty-Eight.

"Shut up, you little runt," yelled another guard, Number Twenty-Four, who squeezed a boy's arm so tightly that his face cringed and was beet red.

Pippy whispered, "We have to do something!"

The lead guard of the group, Number Twenty-One, stopped immediately and commanded the others to do the same. "Did you hear that?"

One of the guards, Number Twenty-Nine, clearly not the brightest, responded, "Um…do you mean…our footsteps?" as his eyes crossed permanently.

Number Twenty-One yelled back, "No, you twit! How did you make it into our bracket? There was a *voice*…a young voice…and *not* in excruciating pain! Look in the bushes. We may be lucky after all and find a runaway. Do you know what the reward is for catching one? *Now look!*"

The kids were nervous, especially Pippy, who had drawn their attention. They counted seven guards, with twice as many children in shackles. The palace guards began to scour both sides of the road as they prodded the bushes with their aged, dull-edged swords. Dim-witted Number Twenty-Nine slowly approached their bush and stopped just shy of it as he began to prod. The sword just missed Ivy's head and Freddie's forearm, but it grazed Pippy's ear, and she did all she could not to make any sounds. Three attempts proved to be enough. The guard moved along.

The leaves beneath them began to rustle past Ivy and then Tony before they finally ceased in front of Freddie's feet. The amalgam of old and new leaves was displaced as green, scaly skin emerged. The reptilian skin was accompanied by two large round eyes with vertical slits, and two large fangs. A gasp escaped from Pippy's mouth, which Ivy's hand immediately covered.

The dim-witted guard yelled over to the others, "Hey! I think I…I think I heard something over here!"

They hurried over to check it out. The snake stared into Pippy's eyes and then turned its intense gaze toward John as it continued to hiss. Its eyes shuttered, and it swiftly raced away. John felt good about his intimidation, especially as his eyes were not illuminated. He looked at the others, expecting them to be impressed, especially Ivy; however, they returned looks of unease. John was puzzled by the looks, but as he slowly turned around, he realized it was not he who had scared off the usually intrepid poisonous snake.

John stared directly into the eyes of a Tiberian leopard with one eye blinded from a fierce battle. Its head was thrice the size of John's. Fearful silence overcame them. Pippy whimpered because they were suddenly surrounded by a Tiberian leopard on one side and the guards of the Ice Queen on the other.

John's eyes began to illuminate, and this instigated a snarl from the Tiberian leopard. John remained unmoved, however, unlike the others, who rustled the leaves beneath them.

The guards were now on high alert; they recognized this snarl and immediately backed away.

John continued his stare and whispered, but with a voice that was not his own, "Sandriver…it's Midwa. We need your help."

Sandriver leaped from behind the bush and into the road. The guards yelled, "It's Sandriver! Run!"

They scrambled away as the Tiberian leopard stood tall in the middle of the road and released a growl that caused some guards to trip over one another. Sandriver was no ordinary feline. He stood as tall as the guards, with a body frame that could not be challenged by any other. The leopard growled once more to display his dominance as the warrior king of the jungle.

John, Tony, Ivy, Pippy, and Freddie all emerged from the bush. The young captives were still shackled, and many cried for their parents, but at least they would not be imprisoned in the Ice Palace and forced to become slaves of the Ice Queen.

John walked over to Sandriver and looked him in his good eye. He thanked him and understood that the warrior king had heeded Midwa's call. From the near distance, Ivy yelled excitedly that she had located the key that would unshackle the young captives.

John looked over only briefly, but by the time he turned back around, Sandriver had already begun to run off through the thick leaves of the jungle.

Ivy freed the children one by one and suggested they follow the young captives to their villages so they could be reunited with their own families.

Tony hesitated before he replied. "You...you won't remember who your family is."

Ivy replied, "Maybe they'll remember us. I guess it doesn't matter for you since *you* still have your memories."

Tony had no more words and proceeded to walk ahead. He signaled the others to follow along.

Almost an hour later, they reached a simple village filled with modest homes framed with logs and sheltered by large hibich leaves. Each property accommodated a small garden, which was home to an abundance of wildlife. Frogs and swallows made their ways from one garden to the next. Pippy looked upon the freed kids as they went to their homes to reunite with their parents and siblings, who were too weak to wield chisels and other tools of the palace just yet. This was a moving moment for them to watch, but also a reminder that they may never see their families again.

A young mother emerged from her home in the distance and gasped in their direction. John, Ivy, Freddie, and Pippy looked at one another nervously.

Tony put his hand on Pippy's shoulder. "Go on. She is your mother."

Pippy glanced at Tony and then at the lady who raced hastily toward her. With her eyes filled with tears, she yelled hysterically, "Oh, my baby Pippy!" She embraced her with a mother's love.

As Pippy walked away with her family, she looked back at the others and whispered, "I remember!" Her grin disappeared, though, when her eyes locked with Tony's, who struggled to look back at her.

John looked at Tony. "Well, that brings us down to four."

Tony replied, "It may be just three of us by the time we pass through the villages."

They continued on to the next village as Tony explained that they needed to pass through just a few more before they would reach the town center. Along the way, Freddie's name was yelled, which prompted them all to turn around. Freddie ran over to the woman who had called after him. She was clearly his mother, as she shared the same long nose.

John, Tony, and Ivy watched the reunion from a distance. Freddie sprinted back to them, out of breath, but soon caught it once again. "Mother insists you join us for supper! We have to eat in the basement since the guards will have another search sweep this evening, but it'll be fun!"

Ivy immediately accepted the invitation, since she had built up an appetite. Tony kindly rejected it. He claimed that he was not hungry.

John echoed the same. "I'm not that hungry either. I'll go with Tony. He can help me find my parents." Tony fell silent.

With a beaming smile, Freddie said, "It's amazing! My memories came back as soon as I hugged my mother!"

Ivy spoke up excitedly. "I'm starving! I'm going with Freddie. I'll find my parents after."

Tony remained silent as Ivy and Freddie ran off for supper. He looked at John. "I guess it's just the two of us now. Let's go and get something to eat."

John looked confused. "I thought you said you weren't hungry."

Tony's face became straight as he replied, "I had to say that. Look, John, there are things you don't know…and you may not understand."

John's apprehensions began to build up once again. "Why aren't *you* looking for your parents?"

Tony was able to defer the discussion by answering, "We should talk about it over some grub."

John followed Tony into the town center. Several shops stretched from one end to the other, with a few pubs and inns scattered throughout. There were a few elders who walked along the roads as they chose among the few run-down pubs that remained after the fanciful saloon did not take them in.

The sun began to set as Tony led John to the fanciful Palace Pardons. John stopped short of the entrance. "Tony, I don't think we're allowed to enter."

Tony replied, "It's OK, mate. Don't worry. They know me here. Anyhow, they serve juice and milk as well."

As they entered the saloon, it was already rowdy. Fists flew in all corners. Retired guards of the Ice Palace frequented the establishment because the mead flowed from the tap. Tony did not believe his presence would be a concern with the guards' inebriated state. It was likely that they would not have yet heard of his escape, as they were preoccupied predominantly with mead. The owner of the establishment, an elder gentleman named Wilbur, struggled to keep pace with the palace guards. He could not pour the drinks quickly enough to keep up with the demand.

John overheard them speak behind the bar.

"That'll be one silver, thank you," Wilbur said as another palace guard had already yelled another order into his ear.

"Here you go!" the obnoxious palace guard yelled as he tossed over a piece of shoe leather. "One *sliver* for the pint. Ahahahahaha!"

"I said one *silver* for the—" Wilbur began to speak, but the drunk palace guard cut him short as he grabbed him by the shirt and pulled him down hard onto the wooden bar. He cut his chin on some nearby shattered glass that had landed there as a result from a brawl that ensued off to the side.

"Well, that is definitely going to leave a mark!" the obnoxious palace guard yelled as he laughed. "Eat that sliver of my boot *now!*"

"I'll get sick!" Wilbur pleaded desperately to be let go of.

"Now!" the palace guard demanded, and Wilbur soon extended his tongue to eat the leather sliver and further humiliate himself.

"You idiot!" a voice yelled, and the palace guard was struck from the side with a bar stool and knocked unconscious as he released Wilbur from his humiliation and fell to the floor.

"If he gets sick, who will serve us?" the voice of another palace guard said. "I guess he won't be answering my question tonight. Ahahahahaha! Now, Wilbur, get me four pints! And I would like to pay in slivers as well! Ahahahahaha!"

Wilbur's humiliation would not end anytime soon. As he went to the tap to pour the pints, he looked up and noticed a distorted but familiar face. A guard on active search duty followed Wilbur's eyes to the young fugitives.

Tony suggested they leave immediately. "I think I've been recognized by the wrong people. We need to go now."

"But I thought you said—"

Tony interrupted. "*Now!*"

The saloon teemed with guards on active duty who sought them out. Tony covered his face and began to retreat. "I know another place just down the road."

They quickly exited the pub, but not before one of the guards who had noticed Wilbur's gaze caught a glimpse of Tony's distinctive face.

"Hey!" the guard yelled, but they could not hear it over the racket.

Tony and John arrived at a small, cozy pub named Pint-accio at the far corner of the road; it was basically barren, with only a few regulars. It served the best combination of mead and pontaccio; that was its reputation, at least.

The pub's owner, an elderly man who walked with a limp from one end of the bar to the other, mumbled under his breath, "Darn Wilbur, taking all my business, he's just giving away his mead over at that Palace Pardons…" From the corner of his eye, he noticed the boys walk in and spoke up. "You look a bit young. I won't be serving any mead to either of you. I'll have to see if I have any milk left."

Tony replied, "Come on, Gavin. How about some of the world-famous pontaccio?"

Gavin grinned as he decided to engage in the dialogue. "Sure…if you have coin, that is! Hahaha. Wait. How'd you know my name…Tony? Tony, is that you?"

Tony now wore a huge grin himself. "It's me, Grandpa!"

Gavin's grin subsided slightly. "What…what in the world happened to you? Did *Her Travesty* do this to you?"

But before Tony was able to answer, Gavin looked behind the boys and fell silent. John and Tony looked behind as well.

A rough voice grumbled, "Oooh, Tony's been a bad boy…just like his father! How does it feel, Tony? Your father fled the palace knowing you'd have to take his place and capture all those innocent little children yourself. I guess you couldn't take the cries any more either, eh? You're weak *just* like your father. You've been caught, boy, and you'll pay with your soul just like he did. Your exiled family will never see you again. I can't wait to see the look on Her Majesty's face."

John jumped in nervously. "Leave him alone…"

The guard looked at John. "What are you going to do, *boy*? Hey, Gavin, get this boy a glass of milk!"

Gavin was frozen in place.

"Go on, Gavin! Get this boy some milk! *Are you deaf?*"

Gavin apologized. "I'm sorry, milord. I'll get some right away."

Tony interrupted. "No, Grandpa. John, do something!"

The guard stared at John, who stood there unassumingly. "Who do you think you are, *boy?*"

John spoke no words as his eyes illuminated bright blue and reflected against his clothes.

The palace guard quickly transitioned from arrogant to confused, and then settled in at frightened. "You…you're the one that Her Majesty speaks of," he said as he sprinted over to the front door. However, before he could reach it, John slammed it shut with a motion of his hands. The guard began to tremble as he attempted with all his might to open the door, an act of futility. The guard then ran toward a nearby window to jump through, but the shutters slammed shut as well.

"You're not going to tell anyone that you saw us, OK?" John yelled out.

The guard cowered in the corner as he pleaded for his life and avoided eye contact. With a gesture of his left hand, John grabbed the guard by his collar and pulled him closer as he suspended him in midair. He slowly tightened his grip and cocked back his right hand, which was now illuminated bright blue as well. The guard continued his plea. He swore that he would not say anything, but the blue-lit boy did not loosen his grip because there was no sincerity in his words.

Tony yelled from behind, "Come on, John! Knock him out! You can't trust him!"

John stood still as he stared into the guard's terrified eyes, conflicted and unable to deliver a final blow.

"I…I can't…" John mumbled. But as soon as he said this, Tony came out of nowhere and slammed a glass mug into the guard's head and knocked him unconscious. A loud thump on the pub floor followed.

"Come on, John. We have to go now! It won't be long before he wakes up and alerts the other guards!"

John and Tony rushed out of Pint-accio and out of sight into the nearby bushes, where they waited impatiently. They whispered to each other and tried to determine what their next move would be. They knew they would need to regroup in order to have any chance to make it across to the Fire King's castle. However, this was not going to be easy, since Pippy and Freddie had already been reunited with their families.

John whispered inquisitively in spite of the desperate situation that had developed around them. "Tony…what happened to us? Where's my family?" These were questions he needed to have answered.

Tony whispered in reply, "Well…for the past several years or so, every year, all villages must offer three children, and just as many men, to the Ice Queen; she only chooses one of each. The men will be palace guards, and the children slaves of the palace. The young are eligible at seven years of age, while the men must have already fathered at least one child. Children remain in the palace until they are of age or have outgrown their cells, usually around thirteen years. At that point they are sent away to the lands outside of the three kingdoms to act as spies for the queen. They are not suspected of their true activities because they appear as unassuming paupers. They must report everything of note back to Her Majesty throughout the various spy channels at their disposal, whether it's through their own kind or through the animal kingdom. She has spies everywhere. Each one of us has a role in Her Majesty's ambitious plans. She is aware of almost everything that transpires in the world. Some are able to return after their tour, but some are stationed outside the kingdom permanently, especially if they have become particularly skilled in the art of spying.

"I have heard of people from afar with different cultures, skin and hair colors, eye shapes, languages, accents, you name it. Maybe one day we will see them for ourselves. It is rumored that many, including Manny Petty and Messy Jesse, are from other lands, even Norman as well with his ginger hair. There have been several rumored instances of children being born afar when the spies come of age and fall in love. However, this occurs out of wedlock because of the laws of our kingdom. The bastard children are kept secret and then eventually smuggled back into the kingdom when their parents are summoned to become normal citizens of Belghan.

"She steals specific memories of the chosen ones because she doesn't want anyone to work for her that is still attached to their past. The silver lining is that it becomes easier to live such a life when you're detached from everything and everyone you've ever known and loved. The year my father was chosen, the Ice Queen decided not to put a memory loss spell on him."

John asked, "Why would she do such a thing?"

Tony went on to explain in detail, "She did it out of spite…didn't like the way my father spoke *back* to her as she sat obnoxiously in her frozen throne. He humiliated her in front of all the guards and captives. My father wasn't afraid like most of the others. The same went for Jacob's and William's fathers, who were best friends. She made examples of them all and assigned them to claim children from the villages each year. Over the years, however, she's become supremely ruthless and now demands the capture of any child who is able to do any sort of meaningful work around the palace. Most guards couldn't remember their fellow villagers, but our fathers could.

"The three of them would occasionally sneak away to see their families during their village visits, while the other guards got smashed properly at the Palace Pardons. My father taught us how to hunt and survive, and we'd even find time to play sometimes.

"The first several years were fine, but then it started to hit my father: within a year, I would be eligible to be offered. My father couldn't accept that. He persuaded Jacob's and William's fathers to form a plot together. They would flee with their families to the West before we could be claimed. They agreed to the plot…but they got caught. Their punishment was to watch their sons serve as guards, while their families were exiled. We had to claim children until the Ice Queen was no longer amused. Our fathers were then frozen for eternity by Frostbite…and we were thrown into prison along with the children we had helped capture for the queen. I hated myself almost as much as I hated her. William and Jacob blamed me at first since it was my father's idea. Jacob eventually forgave me when we became best friends; however, William never did. He's always held a grudge against me, especially as he lost his best friend to me. Everyone wanted to be friends with Jacob.

"I would stare into the sun for hours on end. I nearly blinded my left eye. I tried hard to stay unrecognizable in case the kids got back their memories somehow. I did not want them to know that I had helped put so many of them there. I've tried to hide my shame, but now my face is returning to normal because I haven't been soaking in the sun for the past days. Soon everyone will be able to recognize me and that has me worried. Jacob and William bottled up their guilt in other ways. Jacob tried to make all the kids feel better any way he could. He looked after them. As for William, I don't know…He hardly spoke. He harbored all of his hatred internally and nursed it over time. I think that's why he looked at Jacob the way he did—"

John interrupted. "Shhh, there goes the guard."

The guard whom Tony had knocked unconscious had just stumbled out of Pint-accio and sprinted over to the Palace Pardons—after he fell over a few times.

Tony said with a sense of haste, "We have to go now, John."

John was insistent. "Wait, we need to get the others first. Midwa said so."

Tony was not confident in this plan. "We can try to convince them, but it'll be tough, especially since Pippy and Freddie remember everything now."

John asked with concern, "What about Ivy?"

Tony replied, "Ivy…well, she won't be able to remember."

John's inquisitive mind continued to get the best of him, even during this pressing time. "Why's that?"

Tony explained as swiftly as his lips allowed. "Her mom put up a fight when they tried to take her. And when she did…when she did, they burned down their house…with the whole family inside except Ivy. But that's not the worst part. The Ice Queen has a sick sense of humor; she assigns each palace guard to his own house if he has a child to be offered. Poor Ivy, she had to watch as her father forced her pleading mother back into the house with her younger brothers and sisters. Ivy's mom…she just screamed at him. She begged him to remember that they were his family, that they loved him. And the little ones…they never did find the bodies of her family… There is some hope. Perhaps they returned to the West, from which they came. I was there that night. They told me to keep her from running back to her family. She was strong, but I was stronger. That's why I feel such a need to protect her. I don't want anyone to hurt her again. She doesn't deserve any more than she's already been through. I think that's why I lo…I'm sorry…I can't talk about it anymore."

John felt terrible for Ivy. "I…I don't know what to say. I would never hurt her."

Tony's eyes appeared to be welling up with tears. "Yeah, I know. I hope she never remembers her past."

John attempted one final question as time pressed. "What about my past…my family?"

But the doors of the Palace Pardons flew open before Tony could answer. The guards flooded into the streets; many of them stumbled over one another and passed out as they fell to the ground.

Tony whispered, "Sorry, John, another time. We have to move *now*. They're about to search every house for us, from the basement to the attic. If they see the others, they will take them away to the queen."

Tony and John needed to stay out of sight, so they treaded carefully in the bushes behind the pubs. They watched as the guards stormed recklessly into each home. They kicked most doors open and pushed aside the elders who tried to block them. The houses did not take long to search because they were so small.

The guards were only a few houses away from Freddie's home, where he, along with Ivy and his family, still dined in the basement. Tony and John knew they had to rush, so they needed to risk a sprint out in the open road. They emerged from the bush and maneuvered between the shadows, just as they had done at the Ice Palace.

John and Tony were able to sneak past the guards as they searched the house before Freddie's. Tony gave the secret knock that they had used for their secret meeting; Ivy and Freddie immediately knew it was a friendly knock. Freddie signaled his mother that it was OK to open the door. She closed the door as soon as the kids had entered. Freddie and Ivy were hidden in the shadows of the attic, where the lights had been turned off. They had been moved there immediately after they were alerted by the commotion outside.

Tony whispered to them, "Hey, guys, we have to go now and get Pippy!"

Freddie and Ivy raced down the steps from the attic; however, just as they reached the bottom, there was a loud, obnoxious knock on the front door.

"Let us in now! We know you're harboring one of Her Majesty's children!" yelled the guard as he continued his obnoxious knocks.

Freddie whispered to the others, "Come on. There's a window in the back we can escape from. Just be careful not to rile up the pontaccios."

They sprinted as light-footedly as they could as Freddie's mother approached the front door. Freddie was the first out the window to make sure the grounds were clear of any pontaccios that roamed, as they possessed many. He gave the signal to the others that it was clear, and Ivy jumped out next.

Freddie's mother opened the door to an anxious, belligerent, drunken palace guard, who nearly shoved her out of the way, but she pushed him back. She was a feisty one. But she needed to be at this moment, as she needed to buy the kids a few more precious seconds to escape.

John jumped out next and landed on his feet, but he let out a small grunt. Unfortunately, the sound traveled to the front of the house, where Freddie's mother argued with the guard as a diversion. The faint grunt caught the guard's attention, and he looked toward the back, which fortunately was partitioned off from the living area.

The guard grumbled, "What was *that?*" as he pushed her out of the way and rushed toward the back of the home.

As Tony overheard this, he leaped out of the window; however, he lost his footing, slipped on the windowsill, and began a plunge face-first toward the ground.

Tony's face had a grimace as if it had already hit the ground. But it had not. He was suspended a few inches above the ground, while John's left arm extended toward him with his palm faced upward, as if it were holding Tony up. John's eyes were once again illuminated. His right arm was arched backward, and his elbow pointed forward.

The guard ran over to the window and looked outside as the kids knelt on the ground, nervous. The guard saw nothing. He scratched his head and mumbled to himself, "I better stop drinking so much," and he stormed out of the front door and on to the next home to continue the search.

The kids looked over to John, who was no longer in a trance. He released Tony, who felt a small, unexpected impact from the drop. "I think I'm getting the hang of this. I put up an invisible shield around us so no one could see us. It's as if Midwa is treating me as an apprentice from within."

Freddie replied, "Pretty soon, you won't even need Midwa!"

"I don't know about that, Freddie. But it's like he's giving me more control each time."

Tony interrupted. "That's amazing, guys…but we *really* have to go after Pippy before it's too late!"

They ran off and maneuvered through the shadows of the dirt paved roads. They eventually reached Pippy's house, but they were too late. The guards had already begun to drag her away; it was the second time her mother had to bear witness to the horrific scene.

Freddie whispered to the others, "We have to do something. John, you have to do something!"

John was silent.

Tony spoke up. "Freddie, there's nothing we can do now, not without alarming all the guards. I'm sorry."

Freddie was now silent.

John broke his own silence. "Freddie, don't worry. We'll get Pippy back. We'll get all of them back, but we'll have to work together, OK?" He looked at Tony, then Ivy, and finally Freddie. "We stick together, OK? We can't do this without each other. We're already down one. We can't afford to lose anyone else."

John extended his hand and whispered, "A fellowship forged."

Tony, Ivy, and Freddie each followed suit and took an oath of fellowship. It was official. A fellowship had been forged. They were bound by their word, and their loyalty could not be broken, even under the direst circumstances. They were beyond the point of no return.

John looked at them and spoke the final words of the evening. "We depart at dawn for the desert. Nothing will stop us. We do this for the greater good, for all the children imprisoned at the Ice Palace, for Pippy…for Jacob."

IX: Sandstorms

Dawn finally broke. John woke the others, who were still fast asleep on their haystacks. He could barely sleep throughout the night, and for the few moments that he could, there were no dreams, just empty darkness. The kids figured it would be safest to sleep in a nearby barn, since several guards remained in the villages to patrol throughout the night.

Tony noticed the shadow of a guard pass beneath the barn's front entrance, so he suggested they go out back where they could find a suitable path through the bushes. Since they could not risk having a proper breakfast, they grabbed various fruits that had fallen from the trees as they entered the jungle.

Eventually they reached a safe distance from the villages and could speak freely. Freddie requested a break because his feet ached. The others welcomed a break as well, and soon they were resting on large rocks nearby.

Ivy spoke first. "I'm disappointed. I didn't get to see my family. Maybe when we return…"

Freddie added with a smile, "I'm sure you will, Ivy. At least you have something to look forward to!"

John and Tony looked at each other, silent. It was obvious that Freddie did not know the truth about Ivy's family. Freddie had been far away, hunting with his father and sister, at the time her home was lit ablaze, so he was unaware of what happened in the village on the night that changed Ivy's life forever.

Freddie gave a wicked looked at Tony. "So…anything you'd like to tell us?"

John jumped in. "Freddie, we need to focus on getting to the desert."

Freddie suppressed his frustration and simply replied, "Fine."

Ivy spoke up. "I can't believe we have to go all the way over there. Are you sure about this, John?"

He replied, "Yes. I wish it were closer too."

Tony finally joined in. "We're at least a two-day hike from the desert."

Freddie suddenly became distracted and ran off. Tony immediately yelled at him to come back. They saw him in the distance petting a Tiberian leopard cub, barely a third of his size but larger than a normal cub. Freddie forgot for a moment that he was upset with Tony as the cub purred and rubbed its head against his leg.

Tony warned him, "Freddie, step away. Wherever there is a cub, there is a…" But before Tony could finish his sentence, the bushes that surrounded them began to rustle.

A large male leopard emerged from the bush beside Freddie and approached him. More leopards emerged and slowly formed a perimeter around them. A larger leopard emerged in front of Freddie. It let out a growl, the kind a mother releases when her cub is in danger.

Tony again urged Freddie, "Step away slowly, Freddie. No sudden movements."

The leopard, as tall as Freddie, continued to approach the cub as it stared at Freddie.

"John, *do* something," Tony pleaded with a sense of urgency.

"OK, but I need everyone to come toward me, slowly. I'll block us off."

The kids listened, and it didn't take long before they were together, with the exception of Freddie, who had run far off.

"I don't know if I can make it, guys," Freddie said nervously as the leopard continued its slow approach.

Tony yelled as they inched toward Freddie, "You have to come to us, *now!*"

As soon as Tony finished his sentence, an adolescent male leopard pounced toward Freddie. But as soon as it was airborne, a Tiberian leopard, twice the mass of the leopard, emerged from the bush and knocked the adolescent away and quieted the others.

It was Sandriver. The large male Tiberian leopard paced back and forth for what seemed like an eternity as it snarled continuously. He eventually approached John and became silent himself as he halted within a foot of him. The leopard sniffed him and began an intense stare down; both refused to back down. John calmed and illuminated his irises just enough so only Sandriver would take notice. The leopard began to stretch his jaws and revealed his dangerously long fangs as he snarled. He then did something unexpected: he licked John's face and then stepped away. He growled at the others. Three of the larger leopards that surrounded the kids broke formation and paced toward Sandriver and lined up. The leopards knelt down.

By a motion of his head, Sandriver signaled the kids to mount them. With the exception of Tony, the kids lacked experience. They had never mounted any animals before, especially as most of the horses had fled several years ago. But they did not dare to refuse. Tony had never ridden a Tiberian leopard, however, so he did not know exactly what to expect, but he knew that they would need to secure themselves. He ran over to a mackelroy tree and grabbed several branches from their bases. They would use these branches as reins in order to avoid being thrown from the leopards.

Tony, Ivy, and Freddie stood tall on their leopards. John stood alone on the ground, but not for long, as Sandriver knelt down himself and signaled with a snarl to mount him. John had trouble because the leopard was incredibly high above the ground, but he eventually managed and soon stood tall above the rest atop the warrior king of the jungle.

Sandriver's roar echoed throughout the jungle as they raced through. The leopards of the leap that remained growled continuously as they grew smaller in the distance. The leopards weaved left and right of the trees as the kids gripped their mackelroy reins tightly. Freddie whimpered for the duration of their race through the jungle. These felines were strong, fast, and unrelenting. The kids were on pace to clear the jungle within an hour and gain ample time they had lost.

The jungle began to show signs of its end as the density of foliage rapidly declined. They soon emerged from the thinning forest and sprinted on open flatlands. They could see in front of them the Desert Realm they had viewed from high in the sky. It was much larger than it appeared originally, and the wind gusts were even more extreme. The hisses of the winds became louder and higher in pitch as they approached. The lands had quickly faded from lush to barren.

Sandriver halted at the outer reaches of the desert where the land began to become comprised of sand. He looked back at John as if saying, "I hope you are prepared." John looked behind at the jungle and then above into the distance at the Ice Palace, which was suspended high in the sky. It seemed so far away; he knew that meant that they had already come so far. He turned back around and signaled to Sandriver that he was ready.

As they commenced their passage toward the Desert Realm, the elevation dropped significantly. However, the winds were not strong just yet and allowed them to maintain communication.

Tony yelled over to John, "What's the plan?"

John yelled back, "They will lead us to the other side!"

Tony was not confident. "I don't know, John. It looks like it's getting pretty rough up there!"

Freddie was now complaining. "The sand is getting in my eyes!"

Tony suggested, "Take your shirt off and wrap it around your head! That should help!"

Freddie's tension with Tony eased temporarily as he yelled back, "OK, thanks!"

Ivy added her two cents. "I guess I'll just be closing my eyes!"

John was not worried. "Don't worry! Just keep your head down. They'll take us where we need to go!"

Ivy barely understood what John said because the wind was starting to pick up. A sandstorm approached. Without further delay, Tony and Freddie wrapped their shirts around their heads to keep their eyes protected from the damaging sands. Ivy closed her eyes, while John shielded his eyes at will, as they were lit blue. Their bodies could afford to take the beating of the sandstorm.

The wind became brutal, but there was no other way to cross. They all kept their heads lowered against the backs of the leopards, which also experienced trouble and had to close their eyes in order to protect them. The nimble leopards opened them occasionally to ensure they were heading in the correct direction. Their traversal of the border of the Desert Realm slowed since the wind beat against them violently from all directions; Sandriver, who was born of the desert, was the exception.

Almost an hour later, they scaled a massive sand dune, and the winds eased significantly, but it was still forceful. Sandriver halted at the edge of the dune and prompted the others to do the same. It was blazingly hot because the sun was at its peak. As the wind continued to ease, their eyes were no longer at risk of damage.

John advised the others to unveil their eyes. His and Ivy's jaws dropped in awe when they looked beyond the edge of the dune. Freddie's and Tony's did as well as soon as they removed their shirts from their heads. They looked upon the colossal giants they had seen from the sky. The giants were much larger than they had appeared previously.

The giants looked ancient and were made entirely from sand. Most stood at least three hundred feet tall, large even in the distance. Some were taller and more agile than others. Their movements were sluggish, and they screeched as they walked about, but because of their gigantic size, they were able to cover large distances across the desert with each step.

The eyes of all the giants glowed crimson. Several giants roamed the desert, searching its floor. Many appeared to be warriors of a once-glorious army, while others were in the form of animals, both leopards and horses alike. Still some soared above them. Legend had it that one of the dark lords cast all traitors of the Forsaken Realm into exile here. Some considered them as gifts to the keeper of the Desert Realm, Desacles.

John realized that there was a reason Sandriver had stopped; the leopards could not proceed farther. Moreover, he had to protect his leap from the forces of the North. Beyond the edge was a steep drop of at least one hundred feet. Even the mighty Sandriver would not be able to survive such a fall. He knelt down and cued the young boy to dismount. The other leopards followed suit. The fellowship would be alone from this point forward. They would need to figure out a way to cross the desert themselves.

The leopards did not leave immediately, however; they waited until John signaled to the warrior king of the jungle that they would be all right. John knew they could not turn back; they had come too far already. Everyone was counting on them, whether they knew it or not. This was a heavy burden to place on their youthful shoulders, but at least Midwa would share it. John gave the signal to Sandriver, and the leopards hurried back to the jungle.

Another sandstorm approached, and the winds picked up. John yelled, "We need to eat something now! We won't have another chance for a while!"

The others hastily grabbed pieces of pontaccio from their sacks made from large hibich leaves. They ate swiftly, since the sandstorm was almost upon them.

Tony spoke up. "Bring us to the bottom, John! You can put a protective field around us until we reach the other side!" He had begun to believe in the powers of the rodent since John had created the invisible shield in Freddie's backyard.

Ivy and Freddie agreed.

The winds continued to pick up, so they raised their voices.

John yelled, "Guys, I don't think I can hold a protective field for that long! If I lose power, we'll be crushed!"

Tony yelled even louder, "What do you suggest then?"

John raised his voice further. "I think we should let the giants take us across!"

The hisses of the gusts broke up their words.

Tony shouted to the point that his throat began to hurt, "Sorry, I thought…said…go…them?"

John screamed, "Yeah! We…them…to…oss!"

Tony could not understand what John said, as he could barely hear his own voice now. "What?"

"We wait…of…close…sprint…" John said in vain. Everyone was confused, as the winds captured his words.

John attempted again. "Look! *Now!*"

The others could barely make out what he said, but none misinterpreted his eyes, which illuminated that familiar bright blue. He pointed toward a giant in the form of an ancient warrior. Its eyes glowed crimson, and it approached quickly.

John had begun to lose his voice. "Stay…close!"

He ran off the edge of the massive dune. The others hesitated briefly but soon saw a bright blue trail he created in his wake as he extended his arms fully behind him. They realized what he had planned, and all soon ran along the trail suspended high above the desert floor. John was still unaware of his limits, so he only made his wake roughly thirty feet. The runway maintained its length. The back end faded away while he continued to create the path forward.

The others sprinted as fast as they could in order to keep up with him. Freddie fell behind and was frequently within a few feet of the terrifying fall to the depths of the desert below, but his adrenaline kept him ahead of the edge. They quickly approached the giant, but it took an unexpected deviation in its path. It seemed to react to the blue trail of light that approached it and began to change its direction.

John yelled back at the others, *"Faster!"*

None of them could hear him, as the gusts of wind stole his words away into the desert, but there was no mistake that his pace had quickened. They were approximately fifty feet away from a ledge on the giant, which appeared to be the handle of a battle-ax. John looked behind him and saw that Freddie was once again close to the edge, so he extended his wake by several feet. This put a strain on him, and he felt his energy slowly fade away. The wake began to flicker in and out, but he knew he needed to hold on a bit longer.

John's nose began to bleed. He felt overwhelmed by the pressure to give up as it clashed against his will to go on. He was within a few feet of the ledge and leaped forward. He twisted his body so he could face the others while he maintained the runway for as long as he could. He had lost energy rapidly, and the integrity of the trail had begun to deteriorate as a result.

Ivy and Tony leaped safely toward the ledge where John continued his struggle. Freddie was now at the edge of the trail as it flickered. He fought not to lose any more steps and even tossed his sack into the desert winds to improve his odds.

Tony looked at John and noticed he was about to pass out. Blood dripped from both of his nostrils; his eyes flickered in and out just as the trail did.

Tony yelled over to Freddie, "Jump!" as he held out his arm.

John passed out almost immediately after Tony yelled. The illuminated trail vanished as Freddie took a leap. His arms flailed, while his face was filled with fear. Tony had serious doubts that he could clear the distance as the winds gusted between them.

John was once again in a dark room. He looked around anxiously for Midwa in the light of the torches as they flickered. John finally found him, but it was not a sight he welcomed. Midwa barely breathed as blood dripped from both nostrils.

Midwa struggled to speak. "John…"

John replied with concern in his voice, "I'm sorry. I thought I could…"

Midwa continued to struggle. "It's OK, John. You did what needed to be done."

John could not shake his concern. "But it almost killed you."

Midwa coughed uncontrollably. "That's…true…and you almost…killed yourself…as well…"

John was once again perplexed.

Midwa replied, "But you did not. Great rewards are born from great risks taken. However, a choice needs to be made before it's too late."

John was now even more perplexed. "What choice?"

However, John did not receive an answer to his question because he woke abruptly from his brief dream. He looked around nervously to make sure they had all made it. Tony was there, and so was Ivy, but he did not see Freddie.

John feared for the worst and looked at Tony. "Where's Freddie?"

Tony leaned backward and revealed the young lad behind him.

Freddie spoke up. "I'm OK…but boy, that was *close*!" You were out for at least half an hour, John. It's scary. What happens when you are…dreaming?"

John was still perplexed. "I…I'm really not sure."

As John's eyes began to wander and he got lost in his apprehensions, Tony brought him back. "We seem to be going in circles. We're never going to make it across to the other end of the desert."

Ivy approached John with concern. "Are you OK? You don't look so great."

John felt inadequate. "Do I really look *that* bad?"

"Well, right now you do…but normally, you're not *that* bad," she said with her infectious smile, which made him break from his depressed mood and smile. She continued. "Come on. Let's not allow every moment to be miserable, OK?"

John replied, "How can I not? Jacob is gone because of me. I couldn't save Pippy. I barely got us here. What if *I'm* the problem? What if *I'm* not enough?"

Ivy replied, "Look, John. You did get us here. That's what matters. You did save Pippy, once. We'll save her again, together. And Jacob…I know. Don't be so hard on yourself. We did everything we could. And lastly, it is enough. You are enough, for us…for me…We'll get through this together, OK?"

She had a way to make John feel better, whether it was with her words, radiant smile, or beaming emerald eyes. She looked over at the others, who had begun to eavesdrop. Tony appeared to show some jealousy, even though he attempted to be coy about it. It was no secret that many of the kids had a crush on her, Tony not excluded. However, she did not care for the distraction of the games that boys played even at their young ages. She was one of the few girls who did not fall for the charms of the self-proclaimed Heartthrob Rob.

The gusts of wind had slowed, at least enough so they could hear one another and plan their next move. As John wiped the blood from his nose, the mystery of what Midwa had said began to consume him.

"What choice?" he repeatedly asked himself. However, he did not have much time to dwell on what the answer to this question might be because another sandstorm began to approach.

As they swayed back and forth to the rhythm of the giant's sluggish walk, Ivy patted John on the back to grab his attention and then yelled out, "I think we can reach the next giant from here! It seems to be going in the right direction!"

Tony immediately looked at John. "What do you think? Do you have it in you?"

John could not speak with confidence. "I don't know. That last one took everything out of me. I think we need to rest for a while."

Tony did not agree. "We can't rest here, John. The sandstorms will sweep us away in our sleep."

Ivy pointed into the distance. "Look! I think we can rest there!"

The others looked in the same direction. It appeared to be a puncture in the upper leg of the warrior giant they had mounted, likely a battle wound.

Tony yelled to the others, "I think we can make it if we time it just right!"

The others agreed that it was worth a try. They needed to get off the handle of the battle-ax as soon as possible; otherwise, the sandstorm would take them to the depths of the desert.

"OK, I'll let you know when to jump!" yelled Tony. He then looked over to John. "Do you think you can give them a little nudge into that opening on their way down?"

John replied, "I think I can manage that," though he showed obvious signs of exhaustion.

Tony yelled to the others, "I'll jump first!" as he looked back at John and reminded him with a nod that they were counting on him for backup. As it turned out, Tony would not need John's assistance. He timed his jump perfectly and landed directly in the open wound softly. They noticed Tony's clothing was no longer flowing wildly, a sign that the winds did not make their way into the cavity that now fortified him.

Ivy waited for Tony's signal to jump as she stood anxiously near the edge as it swayed. Fortunately for her, the pace of the giant slowed, making the jump a bit less of a challenge.

"Now!" yelled Tony, and without hesitation, Ivy jumped.

Ivy screamed the entire way down as she prayed she would align with Tony by the time she made contact; otherwise, she would slam into a wall of sand and fall to her demise below. However, the jump was timed perfectly, and she landed directly in Tony's arms.

After they toppled over, Tony spoke with a smile. "I told you I had you."

Ivy replied with some zest in her voice, "You will *never* have me." His smile disappeared as he let her go.

John was relieved because he had been able to conserve what little power that remained for a bit longer. He looked over to Freddie and told him, "You're up next!"

Freddie was frightened, especially since Ivy had screamed the whole way down. He inched toward the edge, but he immediately backed away once he looked down and yelled to John, "I can't do it!"

"Come on, Freddie! You can do it! I have your back! We need to hurry; the winds are picking up. It won't be long before the next sandstorm is here!"

Freddie acknowledged what he said and crept back toward the edge and waited for Tony's signal. Ivy looked on anxiously.

"Now!" yelled Tony, which prompted Freddie to jump. He whimpered but didn't scream as Ivy had. He kept his eyes closed to control his fear. That was, until Tony began to scream for John's help. The timing was fine, but the giant had changed direction slightly. Freddie opened his eyes wide and soon screamed as loud as he could, even louder than Ivy, as he watched the wall of sand approaching quickly.

"John!" Tony yelled again, and this time John heard. His eyes illuminated, and with a motion of his hand, he gave Freddie a nudge into the cavity where Tony and Ivy waited. Freddie flew directly into Tony, which softened the impact.

It was now John's turn, but the sandstorm was at his figurative doorstep. The winds once again gusted brutally against his skin. He had to use what little energy remained to protect his eyes. He could not spare any to give himself a nudge. John's eyes were barely illuminated. They flickered in and out as he walked up to the swaying ledge and waited for Tony's signal. He could barely see anything as the powerful sandstorm blinded his view. No signal would come.

Though exhausted, John was reinvigorated with confidence and trusted his instincts, especially as he knew that Ivy was waiting for him on the other side. Midwa had not failed him yet. He decided to proceed on a leap of faith. After he took a few steps backward, he sprinted forward and lunged from the ledge, through the air.

The others slowly came into view. He saw them yell and wave to him to nudge himself to his left. He sacrificed his vision for a moment and gave himself the small nudge he needed. It worked; his alignment was fixed. He approached rapidly as the cheers were swallowed by the howls of the desert winds.

A violent gust of wind passed through at that very moment, however, and greeted him before he could reach the others. The cheers were short-lived and replaced by concern and tears, especially by Ivy, as John was suddenly swept away into the depths of the desert. Suddenly Tony, Ivy, and Freddie were stranded with little food. Still worse, they had just lost the one person who could save them.

Jonathan Rivera

Act II
A Dark Past Revealed

Jonathan Rivera

X: Meanwhile, Back at the Ice Palace

"Bring them to me...*now!*" screamed Her Majesty as her heavy footsteps collided with the frigid ground while she approached the throne. Several teeth shattered as the raging force of her words crashed into them. William, Rob, Joey, and Norman were dragged forward and thrown to the ground. They raised their heads to an utterly displeased queen.

She looked at Rob as he caressed his face, which he'd once again landed on; his looks had begun to deteriorate fast. She then looked to the others.

"On your feet!" she screamed from the comfort of her frozen throne, obviously annoyed as she pulled away her arm that a guard was chiseling back into shape. She was unable to do it herself while her scepter was in the process of reparation by the tamed phoenix dragon, Frostbite. As the boys rose to their feet, she rose to her own and began to pace before them.

"*Where are they?*" The fury of her words echoed beyond the great hall and instilled fear throughout.

"My sweet Norman, where are they?" Her Majesty spoke with a deceptively soft tone.

Norman was nervous. "You...you sent me to Frostbite."

Her Majesty once again assumed her moniker of Ice Queen and yelled, "*I don't have time for games!* It seems the *fat rat* wants to play with Frostbite again. Guard, take him to the lair at once!"

Norman pleaded with desperation, "But...Your Majesty...I didn't mean any offense! Apologies, Your Majesty! *Please!*"

She raised her voice again. "Remove him from my presence at once!" The frigid queen turned to the others. "I hope we have *all* learned a lesson here. Now...*Where are they?*"

William spoke up. "They abandoned us, Your Majesty."

She directed her attention to William. "I see you've smartened up, *peasant*. Did they *mention* where they were heading?"

William replied, "No, Your Majesty. They left us to die nearly two days ago...after they pushed Jacob to his death."

The others looked at each other discreetly as they wondered what he was up to. Their glances did not go unnoticed, as the Ice Queen's eyes shifted toward them while she addressed William. "Go on. Explain yourself." She always seemed as if her head were about to explode.

William continued. "John is getting stronger, Your Majesty, and he seeks more power."

She was visibly impatient, though intrigued. "What *kind* of power?"

William replied nervously, "I'm not sure, Your Majesty. I think it was all the rat's doing." He went on to tell her a twisted version of what had happened and wrapped up the false tale with "And they left us behind."

"Oh...the *rat*," she said aloud before whispering to herself, "What are you up to, *Midwa?*"

She cringed whenever she spoke his name. Her yells recommenced.

"You are to bring them to me at once! They must not reach Villanis!" She turned to the lead guard and yelled, "Fetch the young one," and then shifted her eyes toward William.

The lead guard dragged forward a young girl in shackles, much younger than the others. She possessed long brown hair that flowed down to the middle of her back, along with bangs that covered her small forehead. She shared the same color of William's eyes, brown.

The young girl whimpered, "Willie! Please help me!"

"*Penelope!*" William yelled to the young girl and then turned to the Ice Queen. "Please, Your Majesty, she's only five!"

The queen spoke with malice. "*Oh*, so you *do* remember her?" An undercurrent of sarcasm flowed through the words that followed. "Of course you do. You remember what I *allow* you to! If you do not persuade those *peasants* to return at once and submit themselves to me, then I will take the memories of your little sister from you and force you to toss her in with Frostbite *yourself*. Now swear it to me!" She was clearly in agonizing pain due to her flesh being still exposed.

William answered nervously, "Your Majesty, I'm truly sorry, but they will not listen to us after what we…what *they* did. *Please* just let her go."

The queen appeared to calm down. "OK, well, I *guess* I should believe you after all you've done for me…and *to* me," she said as she raised her arm in front of his face and the foul smell of her bones permeated his nose. "I guess we won't need the young one after all. Guard! Take her just outside of Frostbite's lair and toss her into a cage immediately. I shall decide later whether it will freeze the young one or the fat one first! Ahahahahaha!"

William yelled, "Wait!"

"Oh, do you have something you would like to *tell* me?" the Ice Queen asked sarcastically.

"We'll find them. Just don't hurt my baby sister, please…" William added, unnerved by the fear in Penelope's eyes.

The Ice Queen yelled in reply, "Of course you will! You will do as I tell you! Now *listen* to me. You will stop them and bring them back to me at once. They will stand trial for what they've...*done*. You will leave midday tomorrow, accompanied by my finest guards." Her lips trembled as her words ceased.

William spoke. "I don't think—"

The Ice Queen interrupted. "*Enough!* Just bring them back here if you ever want to see your sister alive again. Guard! Take them away! I'm disgusted just by looking at them." She reclaimed her seat and turned her head away violently. She signaled the guard to continue to work on her arm with a wave of her hand as she rolled her eyes.

William whispered to Penelope, "Don't worry, baby sister, I'll..." but the lead palace guard, Number Eleven, grabbed his arm and violently dragged him away. The other prisoners were secured and followed along. All of the guards who remained returned to their patrol duties.

Day's end approached as the guards crudely escorted them to the dungeon. Along the way, the returning captives lured several displeased gazes from the other prisoners, who never stood a chance to escape. William observed the eldest as they attempted to comfort the recently captured ones.

As William, Rob, and Joey reached the dungeon, they looked upon the young prisoners, who had never looked more demoralized. They were forced to work under the new dismal conditions declared by the Ice Queen. They were fed once daily at sunrise without any breaks until the torches were relieved at night. Several were forced to share cells, as there was no longer enough capacity to afford each one his or her own. The heat felt scarcer now since it needed to warm nearly twice as many, a figure that continued to grow.

"Get over there, boy!" a guard yelled as he threw William into a cell already occupied by one of the more unpredictable kids, who spoke with an uncontrollable twitch in his neck and often made the others feel uncomfortable. The kid stood slightly shorter than William. He possessed black hair that was not typical of those born within the kingdom of Belghan. Also, he spoke with an accent that was not native to these lands, which somehow made him sound more sophisticated than the others.

William spoke. "Hey, Twitch…I mean Mitch, sorry."

Mitch replied, "Oh, so ya think it's funny, don'cha? 'There once was a boy with an itch; distracted he fell in a ditch. With a permanent twitch and a voice out of pitch, they call him Mitch the Twitch.' Thanks for that, mate! I tell you, if it wasn't for Dahlia, I'd be normal. I haven't been the same since she arrived. I think we have a connection. It must be love. She just doesn't know it yet."

William replied, "You're ten! You can barely read, and you can't even tie your boots. How can you *possibly* know what love is?"

Mitch yelled back, "I don't know what my past was, but I guess it wasn't as *fortunate* as yours, mate! You probably had all of the newest books and new clothes, eh? And stop making make fun of me! What if I made fun of you, huh? William has a big fat head, round as round can be. All wonder why he just doesn't float away. They call him William!"

William was puzzled by the comeback. "That doesn't make *any* sense, and it doesn't even rhyme."

Mitch yelled back, "Shut it, William! You left us all here to die! We were supposed to escape together!"

A nervous plea for help nearby broke the tension as Mitch began to lean in. "William…help…" Joey whimpered as Delusional Dahlia taunted him. She mumbled gibberish that no one understood as she twirled and shook her brown, scruffy locks that protruded from her hat, which was handmade with materials from unused garments she found. She spoke with a fancy accent that regularly incorporated phlegm. It was an accent rarely heard around the kingdom of Belghan. It really stood out.

Whimpers from Rob also reached him as he was intimidated by Messy Jesse and Stingy Salina. Jesse's chocolate skin juxtaposed against Salina's paleness. While she was obviously a native Belghan, he was not. However, they could not determine where he was from. Not even he could, since he lacked memories of his past. In the background, several others heckled them. The voices belonged to Manny Petty, the olive-skin boy who spoke with a lisp, and Scary Carrie, who spoke only on occasion and painted the edges of her eyes with an oily black substance that sporadically dripped from the queen herself. She also streaked her light brown hair with the substance, giving herself a bizarre appearance. The scary-looking girl carried around strange straw dolls that she molded in the shapes of the other prisoners. She attempted to give them away to the ones they resembled, but no one would accept them out of fear; except for Nameless and Aimless Amos, the dim-witted identical twins, who gladly accepted any gifts. Their short curly brown hair fit well with their pudgy build. They had a habit of shaking their heads in all directions during dialogue, making it distracting and near impossible to determine whom they were addressing. They were the most gullible of the kids in the palace. Passive Paul stood quietly in the background as if nothing had happened. Much happened in front of his eyes, and he rarely thought twice about reacting to any of it, even when the raucous games of modinos unfolded into complete mayhem. With his average physical features, including the typically Belghan brown hair, he also went by unnoticed by the others most of the time.

William began a nervous plea. "Wait, Mitch! It…it wasn't *our* fault!"

Mitch backed down slightly as his teeth nearly ground together. "Then *whose* fault was it?"

William responded, "It was the *others*. John, Tony, Ivy, Freddie, and Pippy."

Mitch's voice became noticeably more tense. "And what about *Jacob*? He never came back for us *either*."

William replied, "He's…he's gone…" as a genuine tear welled up in his eye.

Mitch's tough demeanor suddenly subsided. "Oh no…" Jacob was like an older brother to all of them. "What…what happened?" he asked, as any vulnerable young boy would.

William hesitated. His recount of what had transpired needed to remain consistent with the one already provided to Her Majesty. "It was John…" He felt the inner conflict. He had just declared John an enemy to all, but he felt he had no choice. His thoughts were dominated by Penelope's well-being. He needed to make sure none of them sympathized with John and the others so they would not attempt to help them when they eventually returned. "He's been given great powers by that rat."

The kids in the other cells looked on with doubt, as they had not yet seen John's impressive display of powers. All they had seen was him flee with the others as an overgrown rat fled with them.

Mitch interrupted. "Stop with the nonsense already, William!" He was cheered on by the others, who breathed down the necks of Rob and Joey. More nervous yelps followed.

William continued. "Wait, wait, wait…OK, he told Jacob that *he* was going to take over as the new leader of the group. But Jacob claimed John was too naïve, and so he refused. So John just pushed him over a ledge. When Norman, Rob, Joey, and I confronted him about it—and you should know that we were much more upset than the others—he told us to shut up, or we would be next. The others…they were weak. They couldn't say no, not with the powers the rat had endowed him with. But we were stronger than them and refused just as Jacob did. He stared us down and just walked away. He commanded the others to follow his lead…and then he um…trapped us in that cavern. His last words before running off with the others were 'Go back and rot with the others in that dreadful palace. *That's* where you all belong.'"

Mitch was perplexed. "I can't believe it…How could they? *We trusted them!*"

All William could think about was that he needed to save Penelope. It gave him the strength to abandon John and the others. He then yelled, "It's true! Ask the others!"

Mitch looked away from William and yelled out to the cell across from them, "Hey, Rob! Is William telling the truth, mate? Did those *cowards* really leave you behind…and *push* Jacob to his death?"

Rob whimpered, "It's true! It's true!"

Joey echoed the same.

Mitch then spoke with hatred in his voice as he wished the worst upon the ones who had left them behind. "So, I guess that's that. What's the plan then?"

William replied, "Well, Her Majesty has ordered the three of us to find them, stop them, and bring them back to stand trial. I really don't know how we are going to do that, though."

Mitch responded, "Bringing them to her would be an injustice. They deserve a *worse* punishment. Make sure you bring them to us first."

William replied nervously, "But you don't understand, Mitch. John has—"

But Mitch cut him off. "*I don't care* what he has! He's going to pay for what he did to us and *especially* for what he did to Jacob." He then turned his back and walked over to his rat-chewed mattress. He spoke his final words of the evening. "You take the floor. And you better not snore. How's *that* for rhyming, mate?"

William grew quiet as he lay down on the filthy dungeon floor, forced to use his coat as a blanket. He was inches from the rusted iron bars as he held himself tightly. He tried his best to stay warm, as most of the torches had just been smothered until they were no longer lit.

The guards were reckless as they dragged the table and chairs along the floor. They scraped and screeched roughly against the dungeon surface—to their delight, as they knew it would awaken the young prisoners. They then sloppily placed down the board upon which the playing cards and tiles would be slammed. As William looked beyond the rusted bars, he observed the guards as they prepared for another raucous evening of modinos.

The most obnoxious of the three guards, Number Thirty-One, pushed the other guards away to claim his favorite spot against the dungeon wall, where the shadows were prevalent. He began to speak with an arrogant laugh. "Hey! Set it up and fetch me some mead!"

Number Thirty-Three replied, "Listen, Thirty-One, I got the barrel last time! It's your turn!"

Number Thirty-One grumbled, "Yeah, you did…but I don't care! I *ain't* getting it! Hey, Thirty-Seven, you're pulling the least rank here. Go fetch us some mead! And hurry up! I'm thirsty!"

Number Thirty-Seven, who was relatively new to the palace and about to experience his first game of modinos, replied, "Sure, Thirty-One, I'll get it right away."

Number Thirty-Three interrupted. "Sure, picking on the new guy, huh? You're no good, Number Thirty-One. Do you know that?"

Number Thirty-One stood up as he shuffled the deck of cards and slammed them against the board. He yelled, "Why, you…Well, of course I do, thank you! Ahahahahaha! I didn't realize you were going to shower me with compliments on this perfectly dreadful evening. Ahahahahaha!"

Number Thirty-Three replied, "My pleasure! But don't get too cocky, huh? One day when I outrank you, you will be getting a boot to your arse daily. Ahahahahaha!"

Number Thirty-One shot back, "Oh really? Ahahahahaha!" His grumble suddenly became serious. "Well, then…we'll just see how long you will keep that nice-looking boot of yours. *Where is Number Thirty-Seven?* I need some mead! Thirty-Seven! Hurry up!"

Number Thirty-Seven noticed the flushed, chilled faces of the young captives as he rolled the barrel of mead down the dungeon corridor. William looked especially distraught. The palace guard felt bad, but he was helpless, at the mercy of the Ice Queen just as William was.

"*Thirty-Seven!*" yelled Number Thirty-One.

"Sorry, boss, it's a full one. It's quite heavy," Number Thirty-Seven answered nervously.

"Don't worry, Thirty-Seven. You'll get used to all of this," Number Thirty-Three said as he waved his arms around to point at the entire dungeon.

Number Thirty-One interrupted impolitely. "*This?*" He pointed toward all of the cells. "They've got it made! If it was up to me, they would be suffering! I'd take away their coats and blankets."

Number Thirty-Seven replied, "But…it looks like they are suffering."

Number Thirty-One jumped up in protest. "Whose side are you on, huh? If you ain't on Her Majesty's team, then a…*demotion* is in your future. And when I say demotion, I mean—"

Number Thirty-Three cut him off. "We get it, Thirty-One. Now, are you ready to get your arse *handed* to you?"

Number Thirty-Seven began to pour the mead in healthy doses. Number Thirty-One took a big gulp, and a game of modinos was finally under way.

Number Thirty-Seven was an older fellow, a recent and admittedly desperate addition to the Palace Guard who filled in for the previous Thirty-Seven, who had been relieved of his duties due to an act of insubordination.

He spoke up. "Well, I've never played before. Can you explain the rules?"

Number Thirty-One had just finished his first mug of mead when he burped. It had been only a few seconds after he took his first gulp. "Look…" he began to say as he burped again and continued to grumble. "It don't matter. You'll lose anyway! I am the modinos champion!" He stood up and began to gloat about his glorious victories over the years.

Number Thirty-Seven began to ask nervously, "But, how am I…"

Number Thirty-One was anxious with frustration as he cued Number Thirty-Three to give a brief explanation of the rules while he crashed his rump back into his seat.

Number Thirty-Three explained, "OK, you get six face cards and six tiles. You shuffle your cards, and that is the order you must play them. You flip a card, which is numbered, and also a tile, which is marked with an arrow. You move your avatar that many places in the direction shown from your starting corner. You can overtake, reverse—"

"Blah…blah…*blah*!" yelled out Number Thirty-One obnoxiously as he grabbed hold of a second full mug of mead. "Are we going to start this game *anytime tonight*? He'll learn as we go along. Let's just get *on* with it already!"

"Sure, you big meathead," Number Thirty-Three mumbled under his breath.

"What did you say, *Thirty-Three*?" Number Thirty-One demanded.

"Nothing, let's just get on with this," he said and continued to whisper to himself.

Within a few minutes, there was no more laughter, just yells and slams that kept nearly all of the young captives awake. They would be deprived of some much-needed rest in advance of yet another long day at the Ice Palace. The mead flowed heavily and quickly increased the tension along with the volume of their voices.

Roughly an hour had passed, and the tension was as thick as it had ever been.

Number Thirty-One yelled out, "*There! I win!* Ahahahahaha! Where did you guys learn how to play…Pint-accio? All the pros play at the Palace Pardons! I was champion last year, you know?"

Number Thirty-Three was sick of Thirty-One by now. "Yes, we know. You've told us one hundred times already! But that's only because you *cheated*! You're a *cheat*, just like you cheated *tonight*!"

Number Thirty-Seven was anxious. "Come on, guys. Let's relax, please."

"Relax?" Number Thirty-One grumbled loudly. "How dare he accuse *me*! *I* am the *champion*." He stood up abruptly, which triggered three tiles and just as many face cards to fall from his sleeve.

Number Thirty-Three screamed as he stood up himself, "I knew it! *You're a cheat!*"

Number Thirty-One felt threatened and quickly grabbed a hold of the wooden modinos board. He flipped it upward, which caused all of the stone tiles to fly in every direction, one hitting Number Thirty-Seven painfully in the eye. It cued a loud scream from the newly appointed palace guard, who did not wish to be grouped with these two.

A brawl commenced among the guards, and they once again threw fists at each other, often with terrible accuracy courtesy of the mead. They soon rumbled throughout the dungeon. They smashed each other into the walls as Number Thirty-Seven escaped the quarrel and watched on from as far away as possible. Number Thirty-Three was eventually lit ablaze before he raced into the great hall, where the frigid temperatures would help extinguish him as he rolled about.

William continued to look on, unfazed, as this was a routine occurrence, coupled with the distraction that Penelope would be hurt if he did not return with John and the others. He would need to keep the others convinced of the story he'd recounted to them.

He would venture out the following morning and lead the hunt for John. William was yet to learn of Pippy's recapture and her potential to foil his scheme upon her delayed arrival due the next morning. In the meantime, he would fade into the darkness along with everyone else.

XI: Desert Demons

The void slowly revealed a hazy light at its epicenter, a glimmer that struggled to coexist. With its courageous efforts to expand, it began to steadily overcome the darkness. Before long, the black had subsided, and the veil that had covered his eyes was lifted.

John stared into the hazy sky above the sweltering desert, his vision still blurry and his body aching. He had been dreamless for roughly an hour. He was overwhelmed with uneasiness over whether or not he was still able to dream and meet with Midwa. Perhaps he was incapable because his dreams had finally become his reality. He quickly shook off the notion.

Suddenly the darkness that was once prevalent returned above him. *What's going on?* he thought nervously as the sky dimmed significantly. He looked around from his back and realized it was the massive foot of a passing giant that fast approached.

He crawled hastily on his back away from the shadow and rolled over. He lifted himself to his feet and sprinted as hard as he could, but soon realized that his effort would not be enough. John would be crushed unless he called upon the powers of Midwa from deep within. His eyes finally illuminated, and he blazed across the desert floor and leaped from harm's way.

John felt stronger, even though he had not dreamed of the chocolate rodent. The strength deep within him grew, and he had begun to become more confident. He began to believe that he could overcome this challenging journey. However, he knew he could not do it alone. He needed the others.

Relieved as he toned down his energy, he brought himself to his feet and observed the colossal giant as it passed. He felt insignificant next to its gargantuan frame. Before he turned away, he realized that it was the same one that he had fallen from; he identified it by its signature wound. He immediately thought about Ivy, Tony, and Freddie and hoped they were still alive.

As he illuminated, John was about to fly toward the giant demon made from the sands of the desert. However, a familiar growl grew louder as another shadow loomed over his shoulder. He was afraid to turn around, but he could not leave himself exposed.

He slowly turned his head. A Sultarian leopard made entirely of the desert sands stood tall before him. It was small in contrast to the colossal warrior that had just passed, but it was no less terrifying as its eyes burned crimson. It was clearly well battled, as it featured several battle scars along its sandy frame. It had once belonged to a rival clan that opposed Sandriver's leap.

The Sultarian leopard growled above the winds as sand exploded from its massive jaws. John lit up and backed away in preparation for battle. The Sultarian leopard became silent after its thunderous growl.

John waited patiently for the demon leopard to reveal its intentions. Neither of them budged for several moments. John finally grew impatient and lowered his arms. He left himself exposed. At this sudden movement, the leopard immediately stretched its claw and released a powerful swipe. The strike approached swiftly. John had become more capable with each battle and escaped unscathed. He lifted himself to eye level with the desert demon.

John knew that he could not afford to linger while the others remained in danger elsewhere. He would need to eliminate the sandy demon leopard with haste. He retreated cautiously as he began to illuminate brighter. It did not take long for him to notice a vulnerability. The demon leopard leaped toward him, with claws fully extended, and attempted to tear him to shreds. John catapulted himself forward, through the wide-open jaw. At the center of its leaping body, he released an enormous explosion of energy. This shattered the demon into countless sand particles and scattered it into the desert air.

John rested on the desert floor. He was exhausted. He watched while the winds swept away the demon's remnants, and they brushed against his face. It was time to begin his search for the others. He focused into the distance and noticed a few colossal desert demons, but none that bore the signature wound.

Several gazes lacked just as many results. He finally noticed the familiar giant once again as it loomed. As he prepared himself to race toward the giant, the desert winds began to pick up and gust around him. A sandstorm had spawned out of nowhere and beat into his skin unmercifully. He protected his eyes so he could see what was happening.

The sand gusted persistently. Something had begun to take form. It was vague at first, but after several moments, it possessed definition and shortly after took its final form. The sand no longer beat against his skin. The last of it was absorbed by what was once again the Sultarian leopard; he recognized the distinctive battle scars. It was furious, with its sandy fangs completely bare.

John was perplexed but thoroughly impressed with the enchantments of the Desert Realm. As he bided his time to develop a more favorable strategy, he catapulted himself repeatedly through the desert demon. It scattered repeatedly. Ultimately, however, it was an act of futility, as each time merely delayed the inevitable unless he could figure out what he needed to do to rid himself of this nuisance.

I need your help, Midwa, he thought, but he received no reply.

As the sand settled back into an even more furious leopard, its crimson eyes erupted in frustration. In his periphery, he noticed a

135

region nearby where the surrounding sands were pulled in relentlessly, unable to escape its grasp. Perhaps if he could lure the leopard into it, it would be enough to contain it.

John put some distance between the two of them as he reassessed his strategy. The leopard was reckless. If he could provoke a careless flurry of attacks, then he would have an opportunity. It was a risky strategy, as he could be engulfed as well, but he saw no other way.

He began to taunt it as he attempted to provoke it into a reckless flurry without regard for its direction. His long-distance hollers did not yield any reactions. An up-close-and-personal approach was needed if he was to be successful.

He slowly approached as the tension persisted. It appeared to be prepared to make an attack. John's blue eyes locked with those that bled crimson. He continued his cautious approach. Suddenly the leopard lowered into a pounce position. John's moment was about to arrive.

The demon leaped forward and took a violent swipe at him, but it missed. John began to lure the leopard toward the pit as it indulged in its own recklessness. He remained close and gradually changed direction as it took swipe after violent swipe. He was near the edge as the sands beat against him just before they were pulled into the pit behind him. He then illuminated to a blinding level, even to himself.

The leopard lacked visibility, but it knew John was ahead of him. It continued to swipe violently and then pounced once more in spite of the blinding light. The faint growl grew louder and gave away the leopard's position. John proved to be the more agile of the two and removed himself from the deadly path.

He dimmed himself to observe what would transpire. The leopard regained its visibility and realized that it had swiped in vain, as the blue-lit boy had already fled. It attempted to slow itself midair, but the effort proved to be useless. Its crimson eyes no longer overflowed. They appeared tame and filled with fear.

It soon made contact with an entrance to the Forsaken Realm, the grasp of which would be permanent. The rear limbs of the desert creature were consumed by the pit. It flailed its front limbs and clawed the desert in a desperate attempt to escape the magnetic grasp. Within moments, it was engulfed completely and no longer existed within the Desert Realm. John could now focus on his search efforts for the others.

He could no longer see the colossal warrior through the thickening desert air. As he mulled over where he should begin his search, he heard a trio of familiar growls. He turned around slowly. Three Sultarian leopards formed by the sands of the desert stared at him with determined fury.

XII: The Hunt Begins

"Hey, William, wake up!" yelled Mitch as he shook him awake.

"The day hasn't even broken yet," countered William as he struggled to open his eyes.

Mitch replied, "I know. That leaves plenty of time for us to talk. You're going to tell us *exactly* what happened."

William's eyes were suddenly wide open. He was surrounded by Mitch the Twitch, Stingy Salina, Aimless Amos and Nameless, and Delusional Dahlia. They were eager for answers.

"How did all of you get in here?" asked William. He was now fully alert. He looked around nervously but realized that their voices did not alarm any guards. Only Number Thirty-One remained nearby, and he had passed out and had been snoring relentlessly for the past hour. Not even his large frame could manage his excessive consumption of mead.

Mitch answered, "Don't worry about that. You have your ways to have secret meetings, and we have ours."

William asked, "So, what do you want to know?"

With a twitch in his neck, Mitch replied, "Everything, from the beginning."

William began to explain, "OK, well, here goes…"

He went on to tell them everything that had transpired, from the moment they fled from the Ice Palace, to when John was endowed with mystical powers, to the confrontation with Arachno, and up until when John and Jacob faced off in their alleged heated debate over group leadership.

William continued. "The cavern was collapsing, and we were screaming for John to pull him up while we waited on the other side. But he demanded that Jacob step down first as leader. When he refused, John made him step down, literally, stomping on each hand as he looked deviously into his eyes. He fell from the ledge, into the shadows of the rubble below. John then sprinted over to us and threatened us. He warned us that if we didn't acknowledge him as our leader, then we would fall just as Jacob did. When the four of us refused, he collapsed the tunnel between us and trapped us."

Mitch interrupted. "Wait…I thought you said he *pushed* him off?"

William replied nervously as he continued to weave a tangled web of lies. "No…he, um…stomped him off…" He appeared to be searching the dungeon floor for the words he needed.

"We thought we found some solace when we found a dining hall, where we ate and drank. It was really mysterious, and the comfort didn't last long. An army of ghostly…undead warriors surrounded us while we huddled in the center of the wide table. Their eyes glowed green. Before long, we heard a mumble from above. It was a curious-looking creature with glistening dull-green eyes. It lowered a chandelier for us to grab a hold of and then raised us up. Those…things kept thrashing their swords against us. It wasn't until we reached the top that we felt safe. But even then, we had no idea where we were or *what* that creature was.

"We waited for nearly two days as those ghostly warriors just stood below us, fading in and out. They appeared dormant on their feet. I've never seen anything like it. I think they were waiting for us to come back down. The table below us kept replenishing the pontaccio and freshwater every so often, and the odd-looking creature went down occasionally to get it for us. We couldn't understand its mumbles.

"We thought we caught a break once those ghost warriors began to retreat. They slowly cleared out of the dining hall. Once their footsteps faded to silence, we made our way back down, and that creature led us away from there. We paced ourselves slowly in order to avoid alerting anyone or anything. Within an hour, we were approaching an exit from the underground. We arrived at a blinding light, but as soon as our eyes adjusted to the brightness, several silhouettes were above us. And once they focused in on us, we realized it was too late. They were guards of the Ice Palace. And the odd creature that had led us there was nowhere to be seen. It vanished back into the shadows."

Mitch spoke after several moments of silence. "Wow…well, then I guess the Ice Queen won't let us have a go at them after all. You need to convince her to let us come along."

William replied, "She won't go for that. She may, however, agree to allow a couple of you to replace the others, who have been crying for the past two days to come back to the Ice Palace."

Mitch replied hesitantly, "OK, I'm definitely in. That leaves one spot open."

Stingy Salina yelled excitedly, "Me! Pick me!"

Mitch was annoyed. "No, Salina! We won't survive with you taking all of our food and supplies!"

Nameless spoke up. "That spot only has one name written all over it…and that's mine!"

Mitch replied with a sarcastic tone, "It can't be you, dimwit. How are we supposed to call you?"

Nameless was confused. "By calling out my name?"

Mitch yelled back, "No, you dimwit, *what* are we supposed to call you? Hey, No First Name, come here. That's just silly!"

He replied, "But, my name is Nameless…isn't it?"

All the kids shook their heads, except for his brother, Aimless Amos, who finally spoke up. "There's no way you're going to pick him over me!"

Mitch assumed Amos had addressed him, though it was difficult to determine, as his eyes were permanently crossed, and he looked at Dahlia as he spoke.

Mitch had a reason for not including anyone he was not fond of. "You couldn't hit a target if it was taped to your finger. How do you think you got your nickname, eh?"

Amos replied, "Oh…well, you're probably right…" He lowered his head and tried to touch his right thumb with his left hand unsuccessfully.

"Should call you hopeless…" Mitch had a twitch in his neck while he rolled his eyes. "Dahlia, what do you say?" He smiled at her, as she occasionally gave him jitters.

Delusional Dahlia seemed to be in a place all her own. "Stay…back…"

Mitch raised his voice. "Hey, *Dahlia*, snap out of it!" He began to get those familiar jitters again.

Dahlia awoke. "Oh, sorry…sometimes I just…Sorry…what was the question?"

Mitch answered, after he returned back to normal and twitched no more, "Do you want to be part of the hunting party?"

She twirled one of her scruffy locks. "Well, I don't really care for hunting. I've never really been fond of swords, bows, and arrows…OK, count me in!"

Mitch replied, "Just please try not to do that…*thing* you do, OK? Don't make me regret it. Well, it's not like I have much of a great choice with this lot to begin with. So…William, speak with Rob and Joey tomorrow morning and explain the situation to them. Then you're going to convince the Ice Queen that we need to replace them because they aren't up for it, those cowards."

William nodded his head in silence as he took a gulp of anxiety. His tale had been settled, and he needed to convince Her Majesty to make the swap. He would need to employ the conviction of Rob and Joey to have any chance. William fell into a trance, unable to hear any of the voices around him. He was overwhelmed as he blocked everything out.

"Prepare for your liver porridge, pauper!" said an obnoxious guard as William woke from his trance.

Day had broken, and he had not managed to get any rest. It was going to be a long day ahead of him. He looked over at all of the captives who had just woken and quickly turned around in worry that the others had been caught. But only Mitch lay there, and he had just awakened himself. Had he imagined the meeting with Mitch and the others? He felt as if he had finally begun to lose his mind, as John had lost his. But he'd never dreamed before. Perhaps he would be granted powers as well.

Two bowls of liver porridge were tossed into their cell. As William grabbed one of the bowls, it felt lighter than usual. The guards had begun to ration the porridge to accommodate the increase in number of mouths to feed; yet, there was no shortage of pontaccio served to the guards amid supper. The delightful aroma often reached the dungeon and caused the young bellies to grumble. William quickly consumed the porridge with a few gulps. It tasted disgusting after he had been spoiled with pontaccio in the cavern.

William turned to Mitch and asked him, "Um…we did have a meeting earlier, right?"

Mitch replied, "What meeting, mate?" with a twitch, followed by a wink.

William was hopeful that he had imagined the whole situation, but he had to acknowledge the reality of the daunting task ahead of him. Even if he caught up with John and the others, how was he supposed to persuade them to return to the Ice Palace and surrender willingly, especially after what had actually transpired within the cavern?

It was time to meet with the queen to try to convince her of the swap. William addressed the guard just before they were released from the dungeon. "We're supposed to meet with Her Majesty this morning. We need to explain to her that we need to make a swap."

Number Twenty-Three replied, "Oh no, you're not! Her Majesty mentioned nothing of you having a meeting with her this morning. You're coming with us, and we're going to follow you and make sure you do as you've been told!"

William spoke nervously. "But you don't understand. Norman's been thrown in with Frostbite! And Rob and Joey can't make it! They're...sick!"

Number Twenty-Three replied with uncertainty in his voice, "Rob and Joey...Rob and Joey...not ringing any bells, boy."

William answered, "Well, Joey is the really small one. They call him Wallaby Joey because he can supposedly fit in the pouch of a—"

"Wallaby!" yelled out the guard excitedly. "Ah yes! I know him. And who was the other one again?"

William replied, "Rob. Heartthrob R—"

"Rob, yes, Rob...I know which one you speak of. I don't like that boy! Always flirting with the girls and never doing any work, thanks to them. I'm going to tell Her Majesty one of these days, you know?" The guard looked over in the distance and cued another guard to drag the boys over. "They don't look sick to me, boy! Are you trying to pull a fast one on me?"

William spoke up as the kids were almost upon them. "They are, I swear. Just watch." He then called over to Rob and Joey, "Hey, guys…aren't you *sick?*"

Rob was relieved at the idea of staying in the Ice Palace after what he had seen looming outside. "Yeah…" He overacted his cough. "I don't feel so good. I shouldn't be going *anywhere.*" He then continued his coughing act. However, his conviction faded along with his confidence. With the rapid deterioration of his physical appearance, he had quickly lost his self-proclaimed nickname that he so cherished. Some of the kids had begun to call him Throbbing Rob since his face was beet red and seemed to throb half the time.

Joey jumped in, in agreement, with genuine fear in his eyes and small frame. "I'm sick…and I'm really, really scared, milord…"

The guard was ultimately convinced. "Fine, you *cowards,* but you're going to need two replacements. Her Majesty will *not* be pleased! Which ones will they be?" he asked as he looked at the horde of kids as they prepared to be sent off into the palace to work.

William first pointed to Mitch, who walked over shortly after and gained approval from the guard.

Mitch pointed to Dahlia, which was her cue to walk over. She was in a silent trance. She often drifted away during daylight hours.

Stingy Salina could be seen as she made one last plea. She whispered quietly over to Mitch with the intention that he would read her lips, "Me…pick me, please…" She featured her best guilt-inducing eyes in hopes that she would win him over.

Mitch whispered back, annoyed, "Quiet, Salina! We went over this already."

He turned his attention back to Number Twenty-Three. "It should be Dahlia and me. Right, Dahlia? Dahlia? *Dahlia?*"

Mitch finally broke her trance, and she spoke. "Sorry, Mitch, I just, uh...Yes, count me in!" She skipped over, and her scruffy hair bounced merrily.

Mitch shook his head, wondering if she was a good choice after all. But he could have done much worse, and he knew it.

Number Twenty-Three spoke to them. "OK, peasants, now hurry along. The RPG will be leaving punctually at midday from the main gate!"

Mitch whispered over to William, "The RPG?"

William answered, "The Royal Palace Guard. They're the best of the best, the top ten ranked guards of the palace. There are only ten spots available, and the competition can be fierce. As the palace guards approach the teen rankings, they tend to sober up from their days when they were ranked in the twenties and thirties. They're even worse when they are ranked higher, as they are still becoming accustomed to their memory-less selves. Her Majesty convinces them that the mead will help bring back their memories. But it is a cruel trick. It just makes them more gullible and willing to carry out her evil will."

Mitch replied, "How do you know all of this?"

William was caught off guard. "I...um...It was a rumor I heard."

Number Twenty-Three led them through the great hall to the main gate, where they waited impatiently for the RPG to arrive. "You do *not* keep the RPG waiting!"

William, Mitch, and Dahlia lined up at the gate and waited for some hours as the young prisoners gave them dirty gazes.

Some even tossed chunks of ice that they had chiseled from the moldings. The chunks were usually carted off by the captives on transport duty. They were tasked to transport the excess ice and toss it down one of the several conduits in the walls that led to the lair of Frostbite. As the phoenix dragon ate the chunks of ice, it curbed its appetite to consume the ice that surrounded it. It made Frostbite even colder and allowed it to exhaust its chill through a special vent that led to Her Majesty's secret chamber, which had to be the coldest of the palace.

Why would the Ice Queen require so many hands? William thought.

As they waited, he noticed Pippy had been dragged in through the front gate along with some new captives. William released a gasp as he gazed at her. They stared each other down in silence. Pippy had never looked as upset as she hobbled on her twisted ankle. There was no time for him to mull the consequences of her return.

The RPG arrived promptly at midday, and the kids were turned over to them. They did not waste any time and departed immediately. The Chief humiliated Number Five in front of the others because he was five seconds late. This was about to become a long trip.

As they exited the palace through the main gate, they immediately noticed that the blizzard had come to an end. This allowed the sunshine to pass through and warm their faces. The snow had melted rapidly after the queen's efforts outside of the palace all but ceased. Only remnants of the blizzard remained as she refocused her efforts internally.

What is she up to? William worried to himself.

The lush foliage was once again visible, and a sense of familiarity struck them. What was unfamiliar was the false sense of freedom that temporarily struck them as they were outside of the palace.

Guard Number One, also known simply as the Chief, finally spoke. "Forward, march!"

Royal palace guards numbered two through five began to march, shoving the kids forward to make sure they kept pace. Five royal guards remained on reserve at the palace, available at a moment's notice if needed.

They arrived at the cavern entrance, which was now visible, as the warm climate finally allowed it to be. The odd-looking creature that William had seen in the cavern the day prior awaited them. Barely exposed from the shadows, there was enough light to give them a clear view. The creature was slightly taller than they were, but much smaller than the royal guards. With a lanky frame, khaki complexion, and murky jade eyes, it was rather hideous to look at. One could only wonder what kind of life this creature had been subject to from a young age.

The Chief addressed the creature. "Well done, Pug." And it was then clear: Pug was employed by Her Majesty. But it hardly seemed like a glorious place to work. Perhaps just like the rest, it was subject to her slavery.

As it led them through the cavern, Pug shifted the corridors and walls with waves of its hands as its eyes illuminated a hue of murky jade. It made the once-labyrinth-like network of tunnels one continuous tunnel straight to the other end. They paced behind Pug as it mumbled to itself. They passed several chambers with the ghostlike soldiers that faded in and out. William, Mitch, and Dahlia all latched on to the royal guards, who did not openly offer comfort.

Number Five began to explain the origins of the goblin-like creature. "Don't worry. For some reason they fear Pug. It has some kind of enchantment that pushes them back. It's ancient magic. Pug is neither male nor female. *It* is not from around here, as you can imagine. Pug is from a land far, far away. It was helpless when we found it, but Her Majesty showed great benevolence when she took it in and allowed it to dwell in the tunnels in exchange for its loyal services."

The Chief raised his voice. "I think you've said too much already, Number Five. Keep moving ahead." He looked at William with a sense of familiarity, but looked away just as quickly. His face returned to its usual emotionless state.

They were soon at the impenetrable gate that John and the others had walked through when the ghostlike army attempted to claim them.

William spoke up. "I remember...Isn't the...lever somewhere here?"

The Chief answered, "So you do remember, huh? No one can say with certainty if Her Majesty's memory enchantment is a gift or a curse. Only few have seen both sides of it."

William was intrigued. "So...is it a gift or a curse?"

The Chief replied hesitantly, "I..." He cleared his throat before he continued. "Ahem...there are no more levers. Her Majesty upgraded the security to voice commands. Paloo Mala Tokai."

And suddenly the ancient gate lifted. It revealed a sight that few kids could recall. William felt a sense of regret that he had not gone with the others. He thought, *Where are they?*

The Chief spoke up as they walked to the far end of the jungle, which gave them oversight of the lands ahead of them. "Secure the mackelroy branches around you. *Hup!*"

The wildlife of the forest began to scatter and sprint for safety and shelter. This seemed curious to the kids, with the exception of William, who knew what was about to occur. He had briefly been a young palace guard, along with Jacob and Tony, due to the sins of their fathers. He showed the others how to tie themselves with the mackelroy branches, and they soon began their rough descent.

As they were suspended midair and swayed back and forth, William looked into the distance. He noticed something beyond the jungle lands and through the gusts of desert winds but was unsure what it was. After he focused further, he realized what he was looking at. There was an incredibly bright blue flash of light that raced across the desert sands.

XIII: When Demons Collide

A blue trail blazed along the desert floor in concert with three desert demons in the form of Sultarian leopards, which left sandy trails themselves. The image blurred against the backdrop from a distance.

John weaved left, and right, but the leopards weaved just the same. He looked back over his shoulder and realized the gap between them had diminished. They were within leaping distance and attempted to strike. John maneuvered around each swipe as they advanced closer.

As they raced past several desert demons, none bore the familiar battle-ax or signature wound he desperately searched for. Between swipes, he realized they were all traveling south. He changed to a southerly direction in hopes they would lead him to his fellowship.

He screamed as the demon grazed him and threw him violently from his feet. He crashed into the desert floor and landed on his chest. He quickly turned around to face the three leopards as they began to surround him and stare him down. His eyes flickered as he dug deep down within himself and pleaded with Midwa to give him the power he needed. He heard no voice in reply, but he did feel the energy build up rapidly. He soon illuminated and raised himself to his feet.

The demon leopards began to approach cautiously. Between two of them, he noticed a giant, taller than the rest, framed against the blue skies and slightly blurred by the strengthening desert winds. It bore the signature wound he sought.

He determined the best tactic was to approach it and outmaneuver the leopards between the giant's expansive steps. John thrust himself forward as he avoided two vicious attempts to end his young life. He hastened his pace toward the colossal desert warrior.

John reached its right foot as it cocked backward. The leopards trailed only by a few paces as the foot thrust forward. With his small frame, he edged himself past it while one of the leopards breathed heavily down his neck. The leopard would not be able to edge past, however. It was kicked with a destructive force that disintegrated it upon impact, an unexpected relief for the young apprentice.

It appeared that only the power of the desert could defeat those that dwelled within. It appeared to be permanent, as the demon did not reform as the first one had. Two leopards remained as he looked over his shoulder once more. One tripped over the other after a sharp turn, but both quickly regained their composure and appeared ferocious as the crimson bled from their eyes.

John had a sizable gap after he outmaneuvered the desert leopards between the giant's steps. However, he knew that he would eventually exhaust himself with a chase in the open desert; there was a precedent.

He turned sharply to his right and began an arc that would lead them back toward the colossal warrior; however, the leopards did not falter and did not allow John to utilize the giant once again. He attempted a sharp left, but the determination of the demon leopards did not waver. The distance from the giant had grown considerably, and his once-favorable odds slipped away.

As he felt the exhaustion settle in, John was greeted by a familiar, calm voice. Midwa had finally awakened from within and was prepared to offer counsel. He did not waste time with formalities as he immediately advised John to turn around and launch himself directly through the leopards. He had tried this tactic on the first demon leopard, but because now two attempted to strike him down, it was too risky. However, it would be an unexpected strategy. There were yet some tricks Midwa would show John.

The young apprentice sped up considerably and created a large gap. He suddenly halted and turned around. He began to sprint directly toward the two demons, who were perplexed by the tactic, yet eager, as they were both filled with rage.

A collision was imminent, and John worried if Midwa was wise in his counsel. Midwa yelled, *"Now jump toward them!"*

Without regard for safety, John heeded the instruction and leaped directly toward them. Time slowed down considerably. He noticed the particles of sand dissipate wildly from their large frames as the harsh winds beat against them. The crimson eruptions from their eyes burned the sand that surrounded them. The muscles flexed on their sandy frames as each step crashed into the desert floor beneath them.

Both leopards leaped simultaneously toward him and swiped ferociously. He reached within a few feet of their sharp claws and suddenly vanished. Time sped up once more. Because he was invisible to them, the leopards stumbled through the air and landed, disoriented, and crashed into each other.

They looked around hastily for the young, blue-lit boy ahead of them. As they turned around, they witnessed him reappear. A huge gap now separated them, and he gained momentum toward the giant as the demon leopards struggled to regain their composure. They slipped wildly against each other and even struck each other in frustration.

As they finally regained their footing, the leopards gawked at the blue blaze from a distance and wasted no time in resuming their chase. Reinvigorated, they began to close the gap swiftly. John's fatigue did not contribute to his purpose.

Midwa yelled, "Run directly into the giant's foot!"

John replied, "But how will—"

Midwa interrupted. "*Just do it!*"

John adjusted his path directly toward the giant's left foot as it cocked back. He catapulted himself toward it as it thrust forward. He once again began to feel insignificant in the shadow of the looming foot, which appeared just as it had when he first woke in the desert. The leopards trailed him and gained nearly all of the ground they had lost.

A moment away from impact, John vanished. The leopards could not conjure such magic and one was shattered by the devastating impact of the massive foot. The leopard blended with the winds of the desert. The final leopard managed to escape; however, it was in excruciating pain, as its tail had been torn from its body.

John reappeared beyond the giant's foot. The leopard took immediate notice. Although in great pain, it would have its vengeance. The human boy was responsible for the death of three of its Sultarian brothers.

The giant lost its balance after the impact and began to tumble sluggishly backward into John's path. The demon leopard had no regard for its life at this point, as it was filled only with a desire for vengeance. It began its final pursuit toward John. It knew well what the consequences were, but it would make sure to take the boy down with it. The colossal demon attempted to regain its balance, which slowed its descent, but its fall and massive collision was inevitable. Even at full speed, John and the leopard would not be able outrun the giant as gravity demanded that it reside on the desert floor.

Midwa yelled to John within his head, over the deafening gusts of wind, "John, your fellowship is nearby. You must find them and protect them. Follow their voices!"

John yelled back, "There's no time!"

Midwa yelled even louder, *"Focus on their voices!"*

Midwa's echoes were swallowed by the winds. The screams he heard faded as the winds howled louder. The giant had almost completed its descent. John vanished just before impact and reappeared in the familiar wound where his fellowship attempted to hold on to one another for their dear lives. He grabbed on to Ivy and Tony, who both held on to Freddie, and illuminated himself. He enveloped all of them a moment before impact with the ground.

There was an enormous crash against the desert floor that reverberated far and wide. John looked around at the others, who were all accounted for. Ivy, Tony, and Freddie all wore faces of shock and exhaustion. Meanwhile, the last leopard pursued him no more, as it was crushed beneath them.

"You sure know how to make an entrance and save lives, John!" Ivy yelled as she gave him a hug.

They would not have a fellowship reunion just yet, however, as John's view faded. He was once again greeted by a veil of darkness.

XIV: A King and His Heir

Remnants from the great impact of the fallen giant traveled far and wide. The winds carried the unsettled sands across the grasslands, past the forest, and through the villages. William, Mitch, and Dahlia shielded their eyes while the royal palace guards remained unmoved by the brush of sand against their faces.

Villagers dashed to their homes and locked the doors. Struck with fear, they were barely hidden as they peeked from behind curtains. They watched as the royal palace guards pushed the kids along. None of the villagers dared to instigate trouble with Her Majesty's most elite force. There were tales among the common folk that the queen had summoned half of their souls with her scepter and kept them captive in a secret chamber within the palace. It explained why they lacked empathy toward those they hurt.

They arrived at the Palace Pardons. The RPG tied the kids over in a nearby stable no longer occupied by equines, as they had fled the kingdom many years ago when it took a turn for the worse.

The royal guards entered the infamous saloon, curious to some, as they did not embrace mead. They were always primed for combat with their uncompromised discipline. The purpose of their visit was to interrogate the inebriated saloon dwellers who had the unenviable reputation of being a truth seeker's best friend. They usually could not recall what truths they had willingly offered.

Even though midday had not yet broken, the saloon was not without some regulars, most of whom were guards of the palace who slacked off. Some had just woken from the previous night's romp. The Chief scanned the large space and turned his attention to Wilbur, the owner of the Palace Pardons. He was often submissive to the will of the palace guards, especially those of the RPG.

Wilbur was in a daze himself, miserable from yet another raucous night without satisfactory compensation. He did not hear the shutters creak open and the heavy footsteps that followed. He reflected on what had gone wrong that left him in this undesirable situation.

Several years had passed since he and Gavin called each other best friends. They were once business partners at Pint-accio. Business was steady for ages, but depressingly underwhelming for his own ambitions.

One day Wilbur noticed a flier on a nearby husky hibich tree that a fanciful new saloon named the Palace Pardons would be opening at the town center, with full support from Her Majesty. Wilbur had built up a desire for more coin and fame over the years, so it was only natural for him to apply for the newly announced appointment.

He was awarded the position, and business immediately boomed. He accumulated more coin than he could have ever hoped for as he earned a portion of silver from each pint and pontaccio served. But it was not enough; he wanted more. He advertised his business around all the villages within the kingdom. He posted countless fliers everywhere and even sabotaged those that belonged to others, replacing them with his own. When he added gambling and other gaming activities, many of the smaller pubs were run out of business. The mighty power of coin stripped him of his morality.

The villagers and the palace guards got along for several years, for the most part, and often shared tables at the thriving saloon. Wilbur was blinded by greed as his desires for more coin continued to grow. No amount of coin was ever enough. He eventually accumulated enough to purchase the saloon outright from the kingdom and call it his own. Few pubs were able to survive in the new order of mead distribution. One of the few exceptions was Pint-accio, still run by his former best mate. Wilbur had all but monopolized the business, and his ambitions ultimately left Gavin in his wake. They had been separated by a bitter rivalry ever since.

When darkness swept across the land, nothing was left untouched. Wilbur and his business were no exceptions. The villagers were no longer able to congregate and enjoy pints of mead at the Palace Pardons when the guards began to refuse them entry. The palace guards had been stripped of moral conscience. They became rude and obnoxious. The villagers suddenly possessed limited options of where to drink as the guards claimed the drinking spaces of all but a few remaining pubs. Most villagers sobered up and quit mead entirely. Some protesters who found it too difficult to forfeit their vice frequented the street and demanded equal rights to drink. Some were courageous enough to run in, but were often sent back through the door shutters and crashed hard into the ground after their short flight.

The guards started to refuse to pay Wilbur. His fortunes quickly dwindled, though he was still required to provide the service of food, mead, and gaming to the guards; when he refused, he was threatened that he would have to explain himself directly to Her Majesty.

Before long, Wilbur had served so much mead without remuneration that he was driven to bankruptcy. With no more coin to purchase supplies, he often had to steal from his fellow villagers and visit the black markets at the far west end of the kingdom to procure illegal mead, which had been stolen, unnoticed, from the rich kingdom of Buv're, which overflowed with luxuries.

The disruptive sounds the palace guards created as they stumbled into the bar stools snapped Wilbur from his reflection. The lowly guards attempted to regain their composure. They did not wish their irresponsible activities to be reported to Her Majesty. As one guard slyly tried to sneak from the pub unnoticed, the Chief grabbed him by the shoulder and pulled him back in. The palace guard, ranked in the upper forties, still saw double, but quickly sobered as the stare of the Chief nearly pierced through him.

The Chief was tall and stocky, well weathered from several battles over years past. He had a diagonal scar across his forehead, deliberate and self-inflicted.

"Where did they go?" the Chief asked calmly while he looked at his hands and removed his thick, silver-sequined gloves, which coordinated well with the fancy garb he and the other royal guards wore.

The palace guard stuttered his comprehension, "I...I don't know...I..."

But before he could finish his reply, the Chief covered the guard's mouth and spoke. "Silence. You shall finish your explanation to Her Majesty." The Chief appeared to lack possession of a soul.

Two royal guards grabbed the inferior palace guard, whose struggle was even more futile given his persistent inebriated state. He was swept from his feet by the long sword of one of the royal guards, who flipped the sword and smashed the handle into the sternum of the lowly guard. After a brief suspension in midair, he crashed down into the wooden floor beneath him. All wind escaped him.

The Chief unsheathed and drew his own silver-laced sword and paced over to the fireplace. He extended it deep within in order to scald its razor-sharp edge. He returned to the squirming guard, whose screams were filled terror.

"I will *not* tolerate incompetence," the Chief said as he placed the point of his sword on the tip of the guard's knee, which triggered a cry of agony. The kids heard the cry from outside and cringed at the thought of what was transpiring. Wilbur looked on anxiously and did not dare to interrupt.

The Chief signaled the others to pin him down. An X was seared into the palace guard's forehead. The marking stretched from the borders of his hairline to the outer corners of his bushy brows. One could almost hear the screams of his tears as they raced from his eyes in an attempt to escape the pain that spread throughout his body. The guard finally forfeited his struggle. He had been given the mark that sentenced him to an unpleasant end.

"Lock him up until we return," said the ever-calm Chief as he meticulously put his gloves back on.

Number Four escorted the condemned palace guard to the basement, which had been remodeled in the fashion of a dungeon. As the palace guards often refused to part from their flowing mead in order to arrest a villager in rebellion, prisoners often waited overnight before they would be taken to the Ice Palace to stand trial before Her Majesty.

The Chief addressed Wilbur in his usual monotone voice. "Where did they go?"

Wilbur replied as he struggled to maintain eye contact, "I…I don't know."

The Chief instructed his fellow RPGs, "Hold him down."

Wilbur's nerves unintentionally raised his voice along with his hands. "OK, OK, OK…I heard they went to Pint-accio." He looked away in shame.

The Chief had no patience for dishonest men. "Hold him down."

Wilbur begged for his life. "Please! I swear, that's all I know!"

The Chief replied, "You are fortunate that we are in a rush and need someone to attend our prisoner. Now be a good puppet and look after him in our absence. But let me be clear. We will be back for you. Company, order! Proceed to Pint-accio." Her Majesty had not burdened them with empathy.

The royal guards marched over to Pint-accio at the far corner of the town center. The pub was barren as usual, with the exception of a few regulars who enjoyed an early lunch. The Chief paced calmly toward Gavin as he removed his gloves slowly once again. The elderly owner continued to wipe down the bar and placed some mugs atop in order to serve the new customers. However, he did not make eye contact, which was a punishable crime as per the newly written law. The three customers who dined nearby fell silent and looked down at their table as they attempted to not draw any attention.

The Chief asked ever so calmly, "You know it's a punishable offense to not acknowledge the presence of the RPG, *right?*"

Gavin paid them no mind as he continued to wipe down the bar top.

"So that's how you want to go about this, eh? Where did they go, old man?" The Chief asked, clearly annoyed.

Gavin continued to ignore them.

"I asked you, where did they—" the Chief began to ask again as he slammed his fist sideways on the bar before he was interrupted.

"I heard what you said, *Chief*, but you have me mistaken with a *rat*. Make your way over to the Palace Pardons, and you will have a *magnificent* selection!" Gavin replied. "Since you're here, I'd like to put in a complaint to your supervisor, that frigid—"

The Chief had had enough. His grip around Gavin's neck left him almost speechless—almost, but not quite.

"Would...you..."—he coughed as he struggled to breathe,—
"like...s...some...mead?" Gavin grabbed a full mug of mead nearby
that he had placed purposefully when they entered and smashed it
over the Chief's head.

Several shatters and screams echoed in the following
moments. The Royal Palace Guard soon emerged from Pint-accio
and dragged Gavin along the dirt road toward the Palace Pardons.
His head was lowered, and his arms were limp.

William was able to recognize him. He was horrified, as
Gavin looked to be in terrible pain in his frail frame. The familiar X
had been seared into his forehead. For all of his differences with
Tony, William was fond of the elder man, impressed by the glorious
tales that Tony often spoke of when they reminisced.

The Chief instructed Number Five to escort Gavin to the
dungeon of the saloon to join the condemned palace guard already
there until they would return to escort them to the palace. William
feared for his fate, but he had a glimmer of hope, as he would be
looked after by Wilbur. Perhaps they could rekindle their friendship
of years past.

The royal guard shoved Gavin through the shutter doors, but
not before he managed a glimpse of the kids who were tied up in the
nearby stable. As Gavin was dragged past the bar, he glared at Wilbur
with angry eyes, furious that he had given him up so easily, regardless
of their rivalry. Wilbur had no sense of honor. Gavin was coerced
down the steps into the dungeon and pushed against the wall
alongside the palace guard who would suffer the same fate. The
shackles would soon limit the energetic old man. They would both be
Wilbur's prisoners to look after.

Conflicted, William yelled out to the Chief, "Sir, please spare
his life. I know him...and...I know where the others are."

The Chief entertained the outburst. "Oh really? Where are they?"

William hesitated. "I saw John in the desert when we descended. The others must be with him."

The Chief answered, "Very well. To the desert we go. Company, gather up rations!"

William spoke. "So, you are going to let him go, *right?*"

The Chief replied, "He will suffer the consequences of his insults about Her Majesty."

William yelled back, "But he's old! Just let him live his remaining days in peace!"

The Chief raised his voice. "I shall afford him no such luxury. Now hold your tongue, boy, or you will suffer the same fate. And if you ever withhold valuable information from me again, you *most certainly will.*"

There would be no further words shared on the matter. The royal guards proceeded to gather rations. They took what they required from the nearby shops as well as the homes of the villagers. No one attempted to stop them.

Once they had full rations for their impending journey to the desert, they untied the kids from the stable and began to escort them toward the jungle. Many onlookers had expressions of concern, as well as confusion. Why would the RPG bring along these kids? However, none dared to question their authority.

Villages faded from view, and they were soon surrounded by several shades of green and brown. Wildlife scattered throughout the lush foliage, away from the group, as the RPG cut down everything that blocked their path.

Once they had a clear path, silence was prevalent with the exception of the chirps of the birds, calls of the monkeys, and croaks of the toads. Snakes and insects went about their normal ways of life. Such tranquility did not extend to the young tummies of the kids, however, as they had not eaten for hours. Hunger was no stranger to them, but that did not make it any less unpleasant.

Dahlia's delusions began to act up, the trigger of which was still a mystery. Mitch shook her by the shoulder, but it did not help.

She began to speak in an ominous tone. "Don't come…any closer…"

The ramblings caught the attention of one of the royal guards, who turned around and glared at Dahlia and Mitch. Silence was clearly in order. Mitch's nerves began to act up. They usually did when Dahlia began her delusional ramblings. He was soon twitching uncontrollably as mumbled words fled his mouth. William was worried that the royal guards may declare them a burden and he would forfeit his chance to save Penelope.

Dahlia continued her ramblings. "Don't let her take you…"

The Chief was not entertained and commanded a royal guard to silence both of them immediately. Mitch was pinned down, but the royal guard shook along with him. Dahlia's delusions finally ceased once the royal guard placed his oversized hand against her mouth. She raised her hand and pointed into the near distance.

All eyes shifted to the direction she pointed. There was a large cub in isolation as it played with a mackelroy branch on the bed of the forest.

The Chief commanded a guard, "Grab the cub. Her Majesty will make good use of it."

Number Four approached the playful cub slowly and then snatched it from the ground. As he paced quickly back to the group,

163

he stopped in his tracks midway to the sound of a growl behind him. A female leopard had emerged from the bush. Her cub had wandered off, yet again. A few adolescent leopards from her leap followed. The leopard's growl became louder as the guard refused to forfeit the catch. Maternal instincts escalated, and she soon approached the royal guard.

"What shall I do, Chief?"

The Chief commanded two royal guards to approach and protect their brother-in-arms and put down the leopard if it came any closer. The royal guards, approaching cautiously, stepped ahead by two lengthy paces. The leopard would be unable to breach their firm line.

The female leopard's patience finally broke as she leaped toward the guards in desperation to protect her cub. The other leopards stayed back impatiently, wary of the RPGs' elite reputation. The swift leap of the leopard was met with a swifter blade. She was struck down. The mortal wound produced a growl of agony that echoed throughout the jungle. The leopards that remained retreated into the bush with haste.

The guards returned to the Chief as victors and handed over the large cub for inspection.

"Oh yes. Yes, indeed. Her Majesty will be most pleased. This is the offspring of Sandriver. It shares the same spotted coat," the Chief said calmly, though his eyes appeared to be filled with excitement. "Bring the cub back to the palace at once. Stop and retrieve the two prisoners along the way."

However, before the Chief was able to release the cub, heavy footsteps began to trample the ground from a distance. They echoed and became increasingly louder. Soon, Sandriver emerged and leaped from the bush. His massive paws crashed into the ground. Several leopards followed behind his long, thick tail.

Sandriver sprinted toward the fallen leopard. He slowed his steps as he approached but did not remove his line of sight from the royal guards. He finally looked down. He licked the leopard's face desperately in hopes that life still remained, but only a few short fleeting breaths did. The mother of his heir had been slain. Once the final breath escaped from her lifeless body, Sandriver looked up in his huge frame with ferocity. He growled so that all within the jungle were aware of his presence.

His growls grew more ferocious as he noticed his heir in the criminal arms of the RPG. He paced toward them fearlessly. The Chief unsheathed his long sword, well aware of Sandriver's reputation. He placed it against the neck of the large cub, whose large eyes were filled with fear as he looked at its father for help.

The guards paced backward slowly, certain not to take any missteps. The Chief spoke. "One step closer and you will no longer have an heir. I know you can understand me, *Sandriver*."

The warrior king of the jungle could not protect his cub and in frustration growled once more. The echoes reached the villages, both near and far. He could not attack without risking his heir's life; however, he knew the guards would not end the cub's life, as it was much too valuable. The cub was still yet impressionable and could be raised by Her Majesty to fulfill some of her less honorable duties. Sandriver would need to wait until an opportune moment presented itself.

The guards continued their backpedaling until the leopards were eventually out of sight. The Chief spoke again, with some uncharacteristic nerves exposed within his voice. "We continue south and carry the cub with us. It's our only leverage. Keep watch of the bush. No one knows the jungle better than the leopards."

XV: Once Best Friends

A few hours and several pints of mead later, Wilbur stumbled down the steps to the small dungeon to tend to the prisoners of the Palace Pardons. It was the first time he had drunk on the job since occasionally sneaking in a drink or two during his days at Pint-accio. The owner of the fanciful saloon, he was forbidden to drink as long as he had the sponsorship of Her Majesty. But on this day, he needed to drown himself in mead if he was to face Gavin.

He brought some of his fine mead along with two well-cooked meals. He stocked nothing but the best quality ingredients in his establishment; the palace guards demanded so. He offered some to the palace guard, who accepted immediately and consumed it like the glutton he was. As he moved on and approached Gavin, each step exposed increasingly more shame. He extended his hands, one with mead and the other with a plate of rice, beans, and pontaccio as he avoided eye contact.

Gavin spoke up. "You can't even look me in the eye, eh?"

Wilbur could not bring himself to speak, let alone lock eyes.

Gavin spoke again. "I suppose not. You've turned into a coward, driven by material things that don't matter."

Wilbur held his tongue, but not for long after Gavin knocked away his hands and caused the mead and food to scatter in the direction of the palace guard. The guard had already consumed his own portion, but he wasted no time to pick the mashed food from the chilled, muddy stone ground. He even slurped the small puddles of mead that made its way between the cracks.

Wilbur spoke up. "Hey! You ungrateful—"

Gavin interrupted. "*Ungrateful?* After all I did for you? How dare you!" He trembled as he raised his voice. "You were a *peasant.* I took you in even when *Her Travesty* would not because of your bum knee. I made you a partner. I made you my *brother.* And this is how you repay me? You had already taken nearly everything away from me! *How could you?*" Gavin looked away in disgust.

Wilbur fell silent.

The palace guard broke the silence. "Are you going to eat that dead rat near the pontaccio?" he said as he licked his lips, the pig he was.

Wilbur was bothered and, in frustration, stormed upstairs, only to return shortly with two full plates of food. He laid them out in front of the insatiable guard and then went into the corner of the dungeon to retrieve a barrel of mead. He rolled it over to the guard as quickly as his faulty knee allowed.

"So you're still hungry…and *thirsty*, are ya?" Wilbur yelled. "Well, eat up! Drink up!" He started to force the food and mead into the guard's mouth until the guard could consume no more.

"That'll"—he hiccupped before he continued—"be all…thank you." The words managed to maneuver around the barely chewed food.

"No, that will *not* be all! You palace guards come into my establishment every day, consuming, commanding, and rarely relieving yourselves of coin! And who can I report this unjustness to? No one! And if I *do* complain, I get threatened with an unpleasant death! So you *are* going to consume until you pass out, ya hear?"

The palace guard had begun to burst at the seams but was physically unable to resist. He had all but passed out as Wilbur continued to top off his mouth with food and mead until none would go down anymore.

Gavin yelled, "*Stop!* What's gotten into you?"

Wilbur ceased and tossed the mug of mead into the wall; it shattered. He kicked away the keg, which spilled into the corners of the basement. He held his knee in pain and then leaned his back against the wall and slowly slid down until his rear was on the ground next to the unconscious palace guard. The guard's face was sideways in a puddle of his own vomit.

"I…I don't know," he finally replied. "What *has* gotten into me?"

"I'll tell you. Ya got greedy! Nothing was ever enough. More, more, and more! You became obsessed with *things*, things that don't matter. You wanted fame for all the wrong reasons. You became a slave of *Her Travesty* and didn't even realize it."

After a long pause, Wilbur replied, "You're right…" followed by another long pause. "I don't know how to fix it. The palace guards force me to accommodate them! It's my fault that Pint-accio has almost run out of business on several occasions. And worst of all, you're in this mess because of me. But I can't fix *any* of it because it's too late."

Gavin's frustration fled, and he suddenly spoke in a soft tone, as if he were speaking to the Wilbur of several years prior, before their falling-out. "It's never too late, old friend. You can still fix this. We can fix this, together. We just need to come up with a plan."

"What do you have in mind?" Wilbur asked.

Gavin answered, "Well, first things first. You need to get me out of these wretched shackles. Then we can start talking strategy."

Wilbur confidently answered as he reached for the key, "I'm sure we'll come up with *something*, just like the good old days. The mischief we caused, eh? So what did you say about Her M…sorry, *Travesty*, anyway?"

Gavin smirked. "Well, I called her all sorts of inappropriate names and then told the Chief that she really ought to take a look in her mirror and figure out how her arse ended up on her shoulders!" He broke out in hysterical laughter. "You should have seen their faces, ahahahahaha! They…couldn't believe an old fool…ahahahahaha …would dare say…such a thing, ahahahahaha!" He forced the words out as he was overwhelmed with laughter.

Wilbur joined in the laughter as he unlocked the first shackle. He coughed and choked as it got the best of him as well.

Wilbur added, "Oh man, I wish I could have been there! Though I would have been marked as well." A brief silence followed.

"OK, let's think now," Gavin said. "Maybe we can pull another Pantaloons Popper!"

Wilbur replied, "Wait, how about going back even further. We can do Thunder Blunder again, ahahahahaha!"

Gavin joined in the laughter. "Ahahahahaha! I don't think the RPG would fall for those again, but maybe, just maybe, they would fall for Misty Mayhem! Yes, I think we can pull it off before they sever our heads, ahahahahaha!"

Wilbur nodded as he once again lost control of his laughter and snorted loudly. "Now there are *two* pigs in the room, ahahahaha!"

As they wiped away their tears of laughter, they came to their senses and their voices began to return their normal tone. Wilbur unlocked the second shackle as Gavin spoke.

"They've got William and a couple kids I did not recognize. One of them was a girl. It looked like she was talking to someone, but she wasn't looking at any of them. The other…I'm not sure. I barely got a look."

Wilbur's face showed no signs that he had been laughing so hard for the past several minutes. "We have to free those kids. Let's give them some Misty Mayhem! You can finally give one of the royal guards that kick you've been meaning to give them for so long!"

"Yes! OK, we need to be getting on our way before this one wakes up."

Wilbur replied, "Yes, and you need to cover up that mark. You don't want to be drawing any unnecessary attention. Take this hood. Let's start preparing for our glorious final act, old friend."

Gavin was freed from his shackles. Barely clothed as a prisoner, he was physically fitter than fellows who shared the same age. They each extended their hands and shook each other's as they did several years ago. Wilbur no longer felt the burden of disgrace that had weighed him down for so long. He was finally able to look Gavin in the eyes. Once again, they were best friends.

XVI: A Fellowship Reunited

John was in a dark room. It had been a while since he had his last dream. Midwa was in a diminished posture as he looked upon John with anxious eyes and spoke.

"We cannot afford further delay. You must cross the sea with haste. I do not know how much longer I can assist. The Fire King has learned of your journey and will bring the sea to life in ways you have never imagined. It will greet you with rage, but you *will* overcome it. The fellowship *must* work as one, but I must warn you. This journey will require sacrifice."

Before John could question Midwa on his meaning, the darkness was lifted. His frustrations dissipated at the sight of the familiar faces of Ivy, Tony, and Freddie. They looked upon him as if he was a hero. They all appeared to be well, at least physically.

Distraction, however, once again set in as he pondered Midwa's final words: "I must warn you. This journey will require sacrifice." John's face contorted into one of caution and fear. He could not bear more sacrifice, not since the burden of Jacob's death had already been weighing heavily on him, as well as the loss of Pippy back to the palace.

He forced his focus on the present and spoke practically. "How's our stock of rations?"

Tony replied, "We're low, but we should have enough until we make it to the sea. Then we'll need to catch a few fish. Have you got anything left?"

John replied, "Not much, maybe enough for a meal or two."

"That won't make it any easier, but we'll manage." Tony paused before he spoke again. "So what happened to you?"

John detailed his encounters with the Sultarian demon leopards of the desert from the moment he woke. Their eyes lit up with wonder as they listened intently. He recounted how he flew through the first leopard and made it explode, and how it pulled itself back together. They were amazed how he outran and outmaneuvered the subsequent leopards between the colossal warrior's steps. He could not, however, bring himself to speak of Midwa's ominous message, as it would cause a disturbance among the group. He returned the same question.

Freddie was excited for John's encounter, but maybe even more so for their own. His words stumbled over one another. "John, you should have seen! There were giants everywhere! Some even larger than ours! It was like…whoa, and then it did this thing like…whoa!"

Tony laughed as he interrupted. "He's still excited. I'll explain. After we lost you, it seemed like we were roaming forever. We couldn't see beyond the sandstorms, but they eventually eased. When they did, wow. There were giants everywhere, John. They were meeting around a central figure. It was the largest of the giants, and it definitely looked like it commanded the most respect. Unlike the others, its eyes erupted with crimson. It was like lava."

John had a sense of uneasiness when Tony mentioned the eyes that erupted crimson. It sounded all too familiar to him.

Tony continued. "We slowed and stopped. It was nice not to sway, especially as Ivy got sick and had to hurl over the edge."

Ivy spoke up. "Jeez, Tony, you don't have to go into *every* detail! I'm fine now, by the way. Thanks for asking." She could be snippy at times.

"I'm sorry, Ivy. I didn't mean it like that," Tony said, but she had already given him the cold shoulder. He never could figure her out.

He decided to continue the story. "OK, so where was I? Oh yeah…several other giants were congregating, with even more approaching. There were dozens of colossal warriors made up of sand meeting up. I've heard tales that they are ruled by the keeper of the desert, Desacles, who can send them back to the Forsaken Realm where they came from. So, yeah…one was even taller than ours. It grazed us as it passed, and it rocked us back and forth. Our hearts were racing. We thought for sure that we were going down.

"Then the leader began to grumble. They stood there listening for a long time. It seemed like it was giving them commands, but we couldn't understand the language. Once it was finished, all of the giants began to return to their posts. When one group left, others approached to get their own commands. As our warrior walked away, the stomps of the others faded until they stopped. So it must have been fairly far from here.

"Our pace had purpose. We figured it was searching for you. We knew you were exposed in the open desert, so it would only be a matter of time before we saw you again. And there you were, a blue trail blazing with those leopards in your pursuit. Our pace quickened. And well, you know the rest. Here we are. We couldn't see you maneuver beneath us, but everything we *did* see was amazing. I wasn't a believer in that rodent, but I am now, I must admit."

John spoke. "Wow…I never thought we'd be going through all of this."

Freddie replied, "Yeah, tell me about it!" He had been mostly positive recently, with the exception of cut-off discussions that attempted to allude to Tony's dishonorable past. Perhaps it was because he had already been reunited with his mother and he felt complete once more with his memories.

John added, "Midwa advised that we need to make haste to the sea."

"Did he say how?" Tony asked.

John paused. "No, he just said that we must work as one."

Tony answered, "OK, we are in this together, so let's figure something out. I saw the sea at one point, but sandstorms stole our visibility shortly after. We should be able to determine the direction, at least, once the storms clear and I can get a good look at the sky. William showed me how to read the stars. He's an expert. The hard part, though, will be actually getting there."

John replied, "Unfortunately, this giant warrior is of no more use to us. It seems the desert no longer has a hold over it. Unless we can think of something that would bring it to its feet once more, we need to start thinking of something else."

Freddie spoke up. "Not even *I* can fix this one."

Ivy yelled in frustration, perhaps still annoyed that Tony told John about her vomit, "*What does it matter?* Even if we got this giant to its feet, we have no way of controlling its direction. And even if we *did*, we wouldn't know where to steer it. We can't see *through* the sandstorms!"

Freddie once again became excited. "Of course we can't see *through* the sandstorms. But if we could somehow get *above* them!"

Tony jumped in. "Of course, Freddie! John, do you think you can get us up there?"

John remained silent in thought. "Midwa, what would you have me do? I need some guidance. I can't bring all of them above the sandstorm with me. I'm not that strong."

Tony urged John to agree or come up with a plan of his own, but John seemed clueless, hidden in his thoughts.

"Midwa, please." But he received no reply.

Ivy yelled, but this time absent frustration, "Look! Up there!"

John broke free from his thoughts and looked above as the sandstorms weakened slightly. "*Of course!* Well done, Ivy. I forgot about the *eagles!*"

Ivy's keen eye gave them their way out; however, it was pointless if they could not lure the eagles to descend toward them. They needed to come up with a plan.

Freddie spoke. "Tell me everything we have left in the hibich leaves."

Tony listed his remaining items first. "I've got a piece of pontaccio, an apple, and a mackelroy branch."

Ivy followed. "I've got the same." They had split the rations equally.

Tony then addressed Freddie. "What can you come up with, Mr. Fixer?"

Freddie spoke to himself as he pulled out his lucky pocketknife. His eyes attempted to peek at the mad plan his mind drew up. He counted his fingers and pointed in random directions. This continued for some time. He worked out the problem as if it were an equation with a definitive answer. Tony's patience wore thin, as did Ivy's.

John pondered what Midwa meant: "I must warn you. This journey will require sacrifice." He thought, *Who needs to be sacrificed? How can we work as one if one needs to be* sacrificed? It did not make any sense to him.

"I've got it!" Freddie broke John from his trance and triggered sighs of relief from both Tony and Ivy.

Tony asked, "What do you have in mind?"

Freddie answered with his eyes wide open as his signature pointed smile showed how proud he was of himself. "OK, OK, OK. So, we use the food to attract the attention of the eagles. We group up in twos, John with Ivy, and I will go with Tony. Then, when an eagle descends and gets close, each group lassos the mackelroy branch around the eagle's talon. It will drag us with it and swing us toward its neck, where we'll ride and use the branches to steer its wings!"

Ivy replied, "Great idea, but it's impossible!"

Tony joined in. "Yeah, Freddie. It sounds great, but it's too long of a shot. The branches aren't long enough. And why can't I partner with Ivy? I work better with her than John does."

Ivy spoke up. "No, you don't. You work better with Freddie." Absent of the sun's intensity, the dark tone of Tony's face continued to fade and began to blend into one consistent tone. He appeared more attractive to her as the days passed, which made it more difficult for her to push him away.

Tony looked down in disappointment.

Freddie did not lose his excitement and spoke up again. "OK, OK, OK. So, we'll actually need the food for ourselves. And who knows if it will actually attract the attention of the eagle, right? They are made of sand, after all. So, what *will* attract its attention? John! We use John as bait as he illuminates. We tie the mackelroy branches together and then ourselves to each other. When the eagle dives down, Ivy can lasso the branch around John. Then we will all be attached to the eagle when he's grabbed! And from there, well, that's as far as I've thought it out."

John thought of what Midwa said once again and realized this must be the sacrifice he spoke of. "It's perfect!" he shouted. "I'll take it from there."

The sandstorm eased up. John stood at the edge of the cavity and illuminated; however, no eagles took notice.

"We need to get higher!" he yelled. "Attach yourself to me. I'll take us topside, to the head of the giant, where we should definitely get noticed."

Ivy, as accurate as ever, lassoed the noosed end of the mackelroy branch over John's arms as she whispered with a smile, "Gotcha!"

John returned her smile. The lasso tightened around his waist. His eyes dimmed slightly as his body grew brighter. He was soon airborne, and shortly after, so were the others, as they were attached to him. The weight dragged him, but he still made it to the sandy head of the colossal giant, which appeared even more battled from up close. It was nearly the size of the dungeon at the Ice Palace.

As John untied himself, the others readied themselves for the trap. However, there would not be much time for preparation, as an eagle from above had already spotted them and shrieked as it began its rapid descent. Short on time, they needed to think quickly. Ivy noticed a cavity nearby; it was the giant's nostril.

She yelled, "John, illuminate yourself at the end of the nose's bridge! We'll wait inside its nostril—yuck—until just before it grabs you, and then I'll lasso us around you!"

"We need to move *now*!" Tony said with a sense of urgency.

Everyone sprinted into position as the eagle approached. Ivy and Freddie stumbled over each other as they made their final steps and tripped into the giant's nose; thankfully, it was not functional, but it was no less disgusting to think about. Simultaneously, John was at the end of the nose's fractured bridge.

John was anxious. "Get ready!"

The eagle had made its descent quicker than anticipated and readied its talons to grab him.

John yelled again, "*Now!*"

Ivy's nerves got the best of her as she attempted to untangle the mackelroy branch after their stumble. She finally managed to untangle it and quickly readied it for lassoing. As the eagle grabbed John, Ivy looked upon him with determination in her eyes. She released the branch with precision. It quickly approached John through the calming desert winds as the eagle was at the cusp of its descent and about to regain altitude. The end of the branch reached the tips of John's fingers, which fumbled over one another as they tried to grasp it. But a tug from the eagle as it entered its ascent caused what little branch he could grab to slip away into the winds and back down toward the others.

Not again, John thought. "Not again!" he then yelled. Infuriated and unwilling to accept failure once again, his eyes lit with determination. He thought back to how Midwa had helped him reverse the pursuit with the desert leopards. He needed to take control of the situation and turn this eagle around.

The winds picked up as the ascent prolonged; however, his determination would not waver. He illuminated brighter and was visible to the others even through the strengthening sandstorm. The others looked on with anxious eyes, especially Ivy.

John vanished along with the eagle. He was engulfed in the sands as they gusted. Once again, he was lost to the desert winds.

Freddie ran to Tony with his head down as he cried, "Not again!"

Tony reiterated the same sentiments, as his words lost more hope with each one, a perfect reflection of how Ivy felt as well.

A loud shriek echoed from within the sandstorm and became louder. Soon the desert eagle emerged, and at its neck was a bright blue illumination. Two illuminated ropes flowed toward each side of its sandy beak. The eagle descended directly toward them and rekindled a glimmer of hope.

Tony yelled, "Everyone, run to the bridge of the nose, *now*!"

They wasted no time. Ivy was prepared this time as she spun the lasso in circles above her head. She honed in on the eagle's talon. They braced themselves as John and the eagle approached.

Ivy tossed the lassoed mackelroy branch. It was a perfect toss. A brief moment of tranquility was followed by a sudden jerk from the end of the bridge. They flew wildly through the gusting winds, which were strengthening. They were yanked from one side to the other, into one another, unable to hold on to one another to ease the violent and abrupt motions. They had trouble breathing because the mackelroy branches squeezed them tightly. They were unable to hear one another over the howling winds and were unsure of how much more they could take.

At the helm, John attempted to steer the wild desert eagle toward the sky, which proved challenging as the sands beat against his hands violently. The ascent was unpredictable. As his right hand was beat, the eagle jerked to the right. As his left hand was beat, there was a violent shake to the left. The volatile winds pushed them in every direction.

John redirected one of his illuminated ropes and extended it toward one of the eagle's titanic talons that the others hung from. The kids hesitated to release their grip as they swayed back and forth wildly. The movements were too erratic, even more so than when they leaped toward the colossal giant.

At last, Tony took the lead and persuaded the others to focus and swing toward the blue-lit rope John had harnessed. It would take their combined effort, and they needed to shift their weight in tandem. As the sways subsided momentarily, Tony began to shift his weight toward the rope. The others followed suit. Soon they swung together toward the blue-lit rope, which swayed itself while John attempted to steer the eagle simultaneously. They swung with their full weight when the winds began to pick up again. Freddie was close enough, and his hand was pulled in by the magnetic force of the illuminated rope.

The other end of the connected mackelroy branches was still attached to the eagle's talon. Tony pulled himself up past Ivy. It was a challenge to ascend the rope, but with help from the others, they shifted their weight toward the talon, and he was able to reach the noose and loosen it. He fell freely for a moment before he jolted and swung toward Freddie, who was secured to the blue-lit rope. Soon he was secured along with Ivy.

The heavy winds attempted to pry them away from the powerful force of the rope, unsuccessfully. Though their pace was slow, they eventually reached the eagle's neck, where Ivy was able to secure the group to John with the mackelroy branches that still held them together. Able to free his hand, John whipped the harnessed rope back to the other side of the desert eagle's beak, which allowed him to steer it properly.

However, John knew it was just a matter of time. The storms could not follow him to the skies. And he was right. The violent sandstorm came to an abrupt end as they were suddenly against the backdrop of a setting sun, along with constellations far above and massive planets that had never appeared so close.

The last of the sand scattered from their clothes and descended to the brutal sandstorm that still took place below in the desert. It was isolated, focused on their location. A force controlled this madness and from a distance, and John was able to see what it was.

The giant Tony had described was now visible to him as it towered above several others below and off into the distance. The general shrieked at its army; they fled from the position shortly after. There were far more giants than they had seen before as they approached the southern end of the Desert Realm. The general looked above and honed in on their position, which was given away by John's bright blue illumination. The sandstorm below weakened, and within moments, it was all but gone. The desert soon calmed.

Freddie yelled out, "They're giving up!"

His words were followed by further shrieks. However, these did not come from the desert below. They were much closer, and much sharper.

Ivy yelled out, "Guys…it's coming from *behind* us!"

Several desert eagles were in pursuit of them. The demons were consumed by ferocity in those familiar crimson eyes and began to pick up their pace.

John spoke to the demon eagle they had mounted. "Come on. Let's see what you're made of…"

XVII: Delusions

William gazed at the horizon until the sun no longer peeked from behind it and then turned his eyes toward the sky. He was familiar with the constellations, as his father had taught him about them when he was Penelope's age. His memories were all that had comforted him over the years in the Ice Palace, even though they were accompanied by the pain of the loss of his father. Since the capture of his younger sister, however, he found it increasingly difficult to find comfort in them. They were a painful reminder of how his father could not protect his family. Now William felt the same burden as he could not protect Penelope. He needed an escape from his memories. He was afforded a brief distraction when he noticed what appeared to be a shooting star soaring across the sky.

William tapped Mitch on the shoulder and pointed it out.

Mitch whispered, "Whoa, a shooting—"

William interrupted. "That's not a shooting star. That's John." He recognized the signature blue illumination. He looked over to Dahlia, whose eyes had already been drawn to the skies as she whispered to herself.

Mitch spoke. "What…but how is that even possible?"

William answered, "Like I told you, he has all kinds of powers now. There's no telling what he'll do next. We've got to stop him and bring him back." While deceit flavored his words, his primary concern was Penelope. He needed the others to believe that John was a threat to them so they would help him persuade John to return voluntarily and, in turn, save his little sister. He went so far as to tell Mitch that John planned to destroy the entire northern kingdom of Belghan.

William continued to speak just above a whisper. "We've got to let the RPG know immediately."

Mitch looked upon the Chief as he sharpened his blade and deliberated with the guards. The image sizzled just beyond the fire pit. They'd determined that they would need to wait out the leopards until the following evening, and then two of them would return to the palace with the heir while the others moved on in the search for the kids. The large cub they had captured had been shackled near the fiery red pit, which contrasted against the backdrop of the Larris River in the distance.

The Chief turned his back and looked at them. "Let us know *what?*"

William spoke up. "We saw—"

Dahlia stood up and yelled, "Stay…back! Don't come…any closer!"

Puzzled, the Chief looked at her.

She repeated herself. "Stay…back! Don't come…any closer! Don't let her take you back again!"

The Chief became annoyed and locked eyes with Mitch. "Her Majesty *will* take possession of the heir. Why does your friend speak such nonsense?"

Mitch began to twitch, stuttering his reply as a result. "I…I…I…I d-don't kn-know."

The Chief, in his sizzled image, spoke. "I do not have the patience for this nonsense. Hold him down."

One of the royal guards questioned the instruction. "But Chief…he's only a kid."

The Chief finally showed some mild anger in his usually calm voice. "*Hold him down.* Or you shall receive the mark in his place."

183

The royal guard replied, with his nerves apparent, "Yes, Chief."

As the guards approached Mitch, who twitched uncontrollably, Dahlia spoke up again as she remained in a trance. "Stay…back. Don't come…any closer. Don't let her take you back again. Run…*Run!*"

One of the royal guards spoke up. "I prefer to mark this one, Chief. Maybe it'll shut her up. Her Majesty will not have any use for her once we return with the other lot."

The Chief did not hesitate. "Very well, they shall both bear the mark."

Mitch was swept from his feet as the Chief unsheathed his blade, placed it in the fire pit, and scalded its edge. Mitch twitched uncontrollably on the ground as Dahlia continued to recite the same words over and over. Mitch was out of breath and shook as he was pinned down by two royal guards. One of the other royal guards urinated in a nearby bush.

Number Three secured Dahlia as he yelled, "Hurry up, Number Five! I warned you not to drink so much." He then looked at her as he gripped her shoulder yet tighter. "Don't worry. You shall receive your mark soon too."

Dahlia's face was no longer contorted as she snapped from her trance. "You are mistaken. Your friend is the one who shall receive the mark. And so shall you."

The guard returned the gaze and began to chuckle uncharacteristically as he tightened his grip. "I'm going to enjoy this."

A sudden scream followed, "Aaaahhhhhh!" All ears followed the scream to a nearby bush that dripped with yellow. Number Five was jolted into the yellow bush.

"Form an AD perimeter around the fire pit and secure the heir!" yelled the Chief.

The royal guards let go of Dahlia, as well as Mitch, who struggled to recapture his breath as his twitches subsided. The four royal guards formed an all-defensive perimeter around the pit. The heir was secured.

The Chief added, "Unsheathe your long swords and scald the edges in the fire. It will slice through any that approach. Light up the bushes. We will burn them all!"

Dahlia sprinted toward Mitch and yelled over to William, "Come here! Hold him up from the other side. We need to bring him farther away from the fire pit. He can't breathe with the smoke so close." William ran over and helped her carry Mitch away.

The Chief commanded the royal guards, "Swords ready. Light up the bushes now!"

A scream raced toward them from the bush, and the Chief demanded that they halt their efforts at once. He heard a prolonged scream from one of his own. It grew louder as the royal guard emerged from the bush and sprinted toward the fire, where he saw the other guards had just reformed their perimeter. Their fellow RPG looked upon them in shock as his face bore a large X, engraved into the four quadrants of his face. The mark was thick and looked brutally painful, engraved by the rugged claw of a Tiberian leopard. He passed out at their feet.

A loud growl broke the silence of the typically tranquil forest. Sandriver emerged from the bush as the other leopards of the leap followed in his wake. He paced slowly toward the royal guards as he stared at his heir. Sandriver turned his attention toward Dahlia and the others. He snarled briefly and nodded subtly.

Dahlia instructed William and Mitch, "We must help them secure the heir from the royal guards. The leopards will then take care of them for us."

William spoke frantically. "What do you mean? *Take care* of them?"

"They will rid us of our problem. John *must* succeed." Dahlia was anxious herself.

William answered back, "No! John must be captured and brought before Her Majesty. We *need* the royal guards for that!"

Dahlia shouted, "On which side do your loyalties lie?"

William shot back, "My sister's!"

"If you want Penelope to live, then John must succeed. He must return with the ring worn by the Fire King. It's the *only* way." Dahlia had lost her patience.

William replied, "You *are* crazy! *Who are you?*"

Dahlia's voice was filled with desperation, "Time escapes us! I will explain it to you, but first we must secure the heir!"

"I will *not* let you risk my baby sister's life! Her Majesty will keep her promise. I must protect *Penelope*. Nothing else matters." William then yelled toward the royal guards, "They mean to capture the heir!" He retreated toward the guards as he addressed Mitch and Dahlia. "We *must* capture John. If you will not help, then leave us *now!*"

Sandriver appeared confused, as he believed the young captive's loyalty lay on the same side, but this was apparently not so. William stood between the royal guards and Sandriver. The warrior king of the jungle growled as he paced toward them. William shook with nerves but held his ground as the large leopard approached.

Fear filled William's eyes and was apparent to Sandriver, but his courage commanded respect. The warrior king turned his head toward Dahlia and then back toward William, followed by a huff of frustration. He then looked at his cub and growled loudly before he retreated. The leopards followed him back into the lush bush. Another opportunity had been exhausted, and there was no guarantee that another one would present itself. Once the rustles of leaves faded, silence once again overtook the jungle. The leopards were no longer present.

The Chief approached William as they forfeited the AD perimeter. "Well done. Your father would be proud. You may yet find redemption and restore honor to your family name. From this moment on, we will treat you as one of us." The Chief then addressed the royal guards loudly. "Round up the captives!"

William spoke up. "Maybe they will come around..."

The Chief looked down at him. "You are one of us now. We cannot trust them after what they've just done."

William replied, "But *Mitch* tried to help."

The Chief replied, "He has a funny way of helping. Every time that girl speaks her nonsense, he goes into some kind of seizure. I am not buying it. They are working together. They will stand trial for obstruction of justice when we return."

William began to speak. "But—"

The Chief interrupted him. "This is not a debate. Her Majesty will determine their fate. Now tell me what you began to say before."

William hesitated but realized his chances were now much greater as he was aligned directly with the Chief himself. He was an unofficial member of the Royal Palace Guard. Many would have given up everything to achieve what he just did. And he had. He had abandoned his friendships with all he knew. It was the price of loyalty to his sister. He was obligated to protect Penelope. He admitted to the Chief that he had seen John flying in the night sky. He recounted what Dahlia mentioned about the Fire King's ring. The Chief turned pale and appeared shaken up.

The Chief replied, "Her Majesty *must* know of this at once. They must *not* return with the ring."

He went on to summon an Astoric eagle from the night sky. The eagle approached rapidly as the Chief wrote out a brief note addressed to Her Majesty. As soon as it was written, the eagle swooped down, and he attached the note to its talon. It flew north toward the palace.

The Chief addressed William. "Help us capture John, and you shall bear the official mark of the Royal Palace Guard. That will be enough to sway Her Majesty to allow your younger sister to live, free of shackles. But you must know…you will need to live and breathe the rest of your life as a member of the RPG. You shall keep your memories, but your existence will be wiped from your family's memories, as if you never existed. But they will be safe, even in exile."

William hesitated. "That's all that matters now."

XVIII: A Raging Sea

Far above the desert floor, dark clouds gradually became prevalent. The demon eagles were in pursuit of a blue blaze that soared across the sky. As the clouds continued to accumulate, they edged along the seams of them. Soon they were unable to avoid them no matter how well they maneuvered, and began to crash through. This generated an enormous eruption of precipitation and saturated the skies.

As they attempted to evade the eagles, Ivy squinted beyond her shoulder and realized that their efforts continued to prove ineffective. The precipitation became heavier and their view increasingly obstructed. Their hair became drenched along with their clothing as they struggled to block their eyes from the torrential downpour.

The eagles flirted with disaster as well while they approached the upper limits of the Desert Realm. Desacles's domination did not extend beyond. His powers over them began to weaken as they grazed the edges.

If they breached the Aerial Realm, the eagles would cease to exist. The realm was ruled by the phoenix dragons of the East. However, their activity had been limited over the past several years, as two had been tamed and held captive for much of the period. Two had just been awakened after a long dormancy that spanned over two generations, which began before evil was cast upon the world. It would still be a while until they would be strong enough to participate in the dark war that had been waged in the world. Until then, they honed their powers in the East. Still one phoenix dragon lay dormant and would for several more years. Their dormancy cycles rarely aligned, but when they did, the world was at their mercy.

The sandy frames of the eagles were weighed down by the precipitous climate and slowly began to break apart. This forced them to lower their altitude. A rumble echoed from the distance as they descended from the upper limits of the realm. As they fled from the clutch of the storm, the showers scattered and quickly evaporated. They approached the heart of the Desert Realm as the eagles heeded the rumbled call. John's effort was met with opposition, and he was soon overpowered. As he lost control, his focus was channeled to secure the others.

Moderate sandstorms were strewn throughout the realm. Their destination became apparent. There were several colossal warriors lined up in formation. One towered above the rest. It must have been the general that Tony had spoken of. Its arm extended as it waited for the wounded eagles to perch upon it. The blinding rains were replaced by the irritating and equally frustrating sandstorms as they blazed through.

"John, we need to do something!" Tony was anxious.

John yelled in return, "The wings are breaking apart, but they're drying. Use Freddy's knife to create a crack!"

He redirected one of his harnessed blue-lit ropes, which allowed the others to secure themselves. Ivy took the lead and untied the end of the mackelroy branch from John's torso. She ran cautiously as Tony and Freddie followed in her footsteps. They reached the cusp of the wing.

Tony shouted over to Ivy, "There's a large tear over there!"

Ivy replied, "Yeah, but it's healing too quickly!"

Freddie pointed. "Over there! It's struggling to heal!"

Ivy stressed the importance of caution. "OK, watch your steps!"

They sprinted toward the tear, which had caused the wing to flap awkwardly and made it even more dangerous as the winds continued to gust past them.

Tony yelled, "Dig your feet in!" and then addressed Freddie. "Give me your knife!"

Freddie hesitated. "But it's my lucky knife. *I* need to do it!"

Tony insisted, "*Just give it to me!* We don't have time to argue!"

Freddie handed over the knife to Tony, who immediately began hacking away at the wing. But nothing happened.

"What's wrong with this knife?" yelled Tony.

"*I told you*, it's my lucky knife. It only works with *my* grip!" Freddie grabbed it back.

Tony was concerned. "We don't have time for this! I hope you're strong enough!"

Freddie started to strike the tear with the blade now extended. But progress was sluggish, as he did not have the brute strength that Tony possessed.

"There's no time!" Tony raised his voice as he hacked away with Freddie's hand firmly in his own grip.

"Almost…got it…*There we go!*" Tony said in relief as the tear expanded along the crease. It stunted the healing process and rapidly pried the wing apart from rest of the eagle. Moments before they perched on the general's extended arm, the eagle initiated its brakes and shrieked in agony. The pressure of the gusty winds took advantage of the wing's exposed position and broke it off entirely. The relentless gravity of a sandpit below pulled it in.

Broken, the eagle jolted hard to the right and flapped its right wing wildly in a futile attempt to regain control. The eagles in their trail turned sharply and commenced a new pursuit. John began to tug the eagle's beak to the left in order to ease the flap of its right wing. It appeared to work, as the descent slowed. He continued to tug the beak of the eagle. It stabilized somewhat, but the eagles approached hastily, almost as rapidly as the desert floor did.

Ivy noticed relief as she pointed beyond the realm and shouted, "We're almost at the sea!" They advanced to the shoreline but were almost out of altitude to maneuver in.

Tony yelled, "I don't think they will follow us to the sea. They can't handle the water!"

The shoreline appeared gradually larger. They felt the freedom just beyond the desert. The eagles finally forfeited their chase and began a swift retreat. The kids cheered wildly, but the eagle they'd mounted would also try to remain in its native realm.

The eagle tugged in one direction while John yanked hard in the opposite. After a tug-of-war, he eventually forced it to depart the Desert Realm. It swiftly dissipated into the Sea Realm, taken prisoner by the strong winds. The kids would not be airborne for long and soon struck the soft sands of the shoreline.

Mentally and physically exhausted, John faded into the darkness. He woke up in a dark room illuminated only slightly by a few torches that flickered as they struggled in a fight for their lives. The flickers allowed for only brief visibility of his surroundings.

Midwa advanced hastily from the shadows with intense eyes and even sharper words. "Well done, John. But there is still much to overcome. While you cross the sea toward the Forsaken Fortress, the queen of the north remains unrelenting. She is forcing the young captives to do unfathomable things in order to help her bring life to an evil plan that will threaten those closest to you."

John was silent.

Midwa continued. "There is much you do not yet know. Your past resides in the shadows of the darkness, but in due time, all will be revealed. You *must* channel your efforts to the present." Midwa was uncharacteristically desperate in his words. The image of the rodent began to flicker in and out.

John spoke up. "*Wait*, please…please just…just let me know. *Who am I?*"

Midwa hesitated before replying swiftly, "I am sorry, John. You are not ready yet…You must focus on the sea and the great challenge it will present. A powerful force rules this realm and will push you to your absolute limits. Do not retreat. Do not surrender. Stare into the eye of fear and *destroy* it!"

Emotional, John yelled, "I need to know what I am fighting for!"

As he flickered and faded, Midwa regained his signature calmness and spoke his next words softly. "You must not fight for your past. You must fight for your future. Fight for those whom you love and for those who…love you…" There was a look of vulnerability in his eyes as he spoke, as if he wanted to tell John something but could not. Midwa quickly changed the focus to the clear and present dangers. "When the sea rages on, you must take the fight to the skies. *Exercise patience.* Know where and when to strike before you take flight."

As the flickers of the torches finally ceased, the room was engulfed by the shadows, and Midwa was no longer there. However, his final words found their way through the darkness: "Do not allow the sea to fill you with its fear. Turn the tide and fill *it* with fear…"

John woke up to a motion that rocked him back and forth. He had an uneasy feeling in his belly that he could not determine whether it was from the sea or from his ominous dialogue with Midwa. He looked around and noticed Freddie in the center of several floating pieces of wood that were tied together by some mackelroy branches. He was eating what seemed to be the last of the pontaccio. Meanwhile, Tony and Ivy rowed the makeshift raft with two awkward-looking oars. They must have built them from one of the out-of-place trees dispersed not far from the shoreline. He noticed a young felled mackelroy tree near the shore, which suggested that was the case.

His sudden movements alerted Freddie, who yelled over to the others joyfully, "He's awake!" He turned to John. "I'm never sure if you are going to wake up again. It's scary." He dug into a nearby hibich leaf and pulled out what was the final piece of pontaccio and tossed it over to John. "Here, you're going to need it. You've been out since last night."

Ivy then spoke up as she plowed through all of the hibich leaves. "That's it. No more food." She looked over to John with her radiant smile. "I hope your fishing skills are as good as your others. I have *no* doubts that they are."

John replied almost shamefully, "I don't know how to fish. I can't even swim…"

Tony jumped in. "It doesn't matter. You have those powers. You can do *anything*!" He knew that he could not compete with John for Ivy's affection, not without powers of his own.

John then whispered under his breath, "I can't do anything without Midwa. Maybe he can catch us some fish."

Tony overheard and replied, "Look, John. Whatever the reason, Midwa chose *you*. Not *me*, not *Ivy*, not *Freddie…you*. Do you *need* a reason?"

John, still deflated, answered, "Yes…I do need one. Why me? Why am I so special? I don't even know who I am. Do you know who I am, Tony? Come on, you still owe me an answer!"

Tony was nervous in his reply. "I…I don't really know…" He paused before he continued. "You kind of just showed up. No one actually knows where you came from, not even the palace guards. There were rumors, but they all sounded farfetched. All I knew was that the Ice Queen loathed you, so you couldn't have been so bad."

John replied nervously, "What kind of rumors?"

Tony answered, "Well…there was one that you were raised by the leopards. Another was that you were born of another world. Still another was that you were created from the fire pits within the Fire King's Forsaken Fortress. There was even another one that you were actually part dragon. How was I supposed to know which one to believe? I didn't choose any. I figured the time would come that we would figure out the truth. But I have to be honest. After seeing what you're capable of, I'd probably believe just about anything."

John fell silent as he thought, *Midwa, why won't you just tell me?*

Freddie, in his small frame, then spoke up. "John, maybe you're better off. What if you find out and don't like it?"

John replied sharply, "Well, at least I'll—"

His words were swallowed by the sudden thunder. A bolt of lightning had just flashed in the distance as the thunder echoed across the skies. Clouds once again began to accumulate and made way for more intense thunder and lightning. As the lightning lit up the sky, the thunder reverberated and bullied the surface of the sea. Potent waves quickly formed and strengthened as they aggressively rocked the makeshift raft back and forth violently.

The unrelenting force caused Freddie to lose his balance. He fell overboard. Well aware of John's fears of the open water, Tony instructed Ivy to reach in for Freddie while he and John anchored her to the raft. Tony's grip on the raft did not waver, but while he carried the weight of both John and Ivy as they swayed wildly back and forth, it proved too much, and he struggled. He had already expended his energy.

Ivy lost her balance and tumbled off the other side. She began to drift away in a different direction from Freddie.

As the waves swelled well beyond a few feet and continued to rise still further, Tony looked at John with concern. "I can't save them both! You *have* to do something!"

John thought back to what Midwa had said: "When the sea rages on, you must take the fight to the skies. Exercise patience.

Know where and when to strike before you take flight." Unsure of where or when to strike, he proceeded to illuminate nevertheless. As he glowed brighter, he noticed the lightning bolts in the sky became more active while the thunderous sounds crashed continuously into his eardrums.

There was no time to figure out the answer to this riddle. Ivy and Freddie were struggling to stay afloat as the surface of the sea fluctuated rapidly.

John yelled over to Tony, "Go get Freddie! I'll get Ivy and then come for you guys!"

Concerned, Tony replied, "But John, are you *sure?* The sea—"

John interrupted. "Don't worry. I'll be fine."

Though Tony noticed the doubt in John's eyes, he could not mull over it any longer, as Freddie would not last long by himself in these raging waters. He dove in and swam as swift as he could through the fierce waters.

As John illuminated increasingly brighter, the lightning bolts became more focused around him. "I'm coming, Ivy! Hang in there!"

As his brightness peaked, several lightning bolts struck him directly and triggered a blinding light. An explosive force of energy broke the raft apart into several pieces and scattered them throughout the vicinity.

John was nearly unconscious as he lay on a large section of the raft's broken base. As the thunder and lightning slowed, the others swam quickly toward the safety of the floating sections of the raft's base that had just flown their way. His senses were restrained by blurred vision and a deafening silence while he looked upon the others as they flailed around and struggled to maintain their grips.

As his surroundings came into focus, John was perplexed as he recalled Midwa's words once more: "When the sea rages on, you must take the fight to the skies. Exercise patience. Know where and when to strike before you take flight." He could not dwell on this for too long because the others depended on him. He analyzed the sky as various ideas raced through his mind. His eyes scanned left, then quickly right, up and down. He even turned around, but he saw nothing as the rains began to beat against his face.

He illuminated his eyes and scanned the sky a second time. He noticed a region of the sky that shone brighter than the rest. A distinctive crimson originated from a particular cloud, which could very well be the *where* of Midwa's advice. But *when* should he strike? If he could avoid drawing the attention of the lightning until he was high enough in the sky, he could get close enough to combine the power of the strikes with his own.

"*John, help!*" Ivy screamed in desperation.

His strategy would need to be deferred for a few moments longer. He needed to go after her. John limited his illumination as he channeled the power of Midwa toward his hands and formed oars of blue light. Tony had already retrieved Freddie, and they were both secured to a broken section of the raft base.

He turned his search to Ivy and finally saw her in the distance. She rose and fell along with the waves repeatedly, at times hidden behind larger ones that did not discriminate against whom it tossed around violently. He rowed rapidly toward her. The blue-lit oars caught the attention of Tony and Freddie, who were safe with each other. They swam toward the lights along with the wreckage they were holding on to as they found the strength within to make their way over.

John eventually reached Ivy, who was nearly out of breath. She had been submerged for almost as much time as she had spent above the sea's surface. She exhaled her last breath. He reached out as she began to slip off and pulled her in closer, along with the wreckage. Tony and Freddie joined them shortly after and were tasked to reform the raft base with the mackelroy branches that hung off the edges. The young branches were torn, as they had not yet matured.

"She's not breathing, guys! What do I do?" John yelled desperately.

Tony had experience in this situation, but he could not be in both places at once, especially as John could not swim and was not strong enough to risk it. He yelled as the unremitting movement of the sea made it incredibly difficult to maintain stability and tie the sections together, "OK, first you have to make sure there's no water or debris in her mouth!"

John checked her mouth and noticed no debris, but there was some water. "Her mouth has some water in it! What do I do?"

"Turn her to her side and let it drain! But be careful with her neck!" Tony shouted as he struggled to keep his balance.

John followed Tony's instructions. "OK, there's none left. Now what do I do?"

Tony replied, "You need to open her airway now. She might have a neck injury, so be gentle and try not to move it. Place the fingers of both your hands on her jaw, just below her ears, and jut it forward! Place your ear close to her nose and listen for breathing and watch for any chest movement!"

John attempted to follow the instructions. "I'm trying, Tony, but I can barely hear anything above the crashing of the waves! And I can't tell if her chest is moving!" He was clearly frustrated. It was his fault that he'd decided to illuminate. She would not be in this position if it were not for him.

Tony raised his voice above the sounds of crashing waves, "OK, pinch her nose shut and seal your mouth over hers. Jut her jaw and blow hard enough until you see her chest rise. Repeat after two seconds and make sure you have a good seal over her mouth!"

Freddie dropped into the sea to gain the advantage of tying from a lower angle as Tony did his best to keep the sections together while John attempted to revive Ivy.

John was frightened at the thought of his mouth against hers, but not nearly as much as at the thought that he would lose her, especially as they had finally begun to bond. He sealed her mouth with his own and blew hard. Her chest rose. Two seconds passed, and he repeated. Her chest rose again.

Tony noticed the rise in her chest as they swayed. "Now compress her chest at least one hundred times per minute, and then breathe hard into her mouth again! Keep at it! We're making progress over here!"

John followed the instruction and began to compress quickly as he whispered, "Please, Ivy. Not you. I can't do this without you. Why couldn't he tell me that it was you who would be sacrificed? I never would've brought you along! Please…" He began to weep. "Please, Ivy, please…Jacob's loss is my fault…I can't have your loss on my hands too…please. He told me to fight for those I love and for those who love me. You have to believe that I'm trying, Ivy…I'm trying. *Please!*"

Tony and Freddie reformed the makeshift raft and were soon at John's side.

"John, I'll take it from here. Take care of this storm!" Tony yelled as he lowered himself and continued the breaths and compressions on Ivy.

John stepped back reluctantly. "Please, Tony, you have to save her…for me, please."

Tony replied with concern in his voice, "I'll do my best, John…Now please take care of this storm."

John spoke as he wiped the tears from his cheek. "I know what I must do."

As John began to illuminate again, Tony yelled out, "You tried this already! I don't think—"

The desperate scream from John's mouth cut Tony's words short. The lightning became more frequent as he shone steadily brighter. It was the storm that took Ivy away from him. He began a hasty ascent toward the vehement skies above as he screamed above the winds. As he approached the crimson heart of the storm, he boomed sonically and burned progressively brighter, directly proportional to the activity in the sky.

He entered the clouds and disappeared from view. Tony tried desperately to revive Ivy while Freddie searched helplessly for John in the sky. He was not out of view for long. He peaked and was visible through the rains and dark clouds. What struck almost immediately after was the power of one hundred lightning bolts that filled the sky with a blinding flash, coupled with a deafening bang of thunder. Tony and Freddie cringed as they barely managed to cover their ears.

Within moments, the flash faded and gave way to a sky that had begun to clear rapidly. The clouds dissipated and revealed the blue skies beyond. John was also now visible. However, their disbelief brought them silence as he fell from the sky, pale and limp. The remnants of rain that had been released late by the storm fell along with him. The deafening silence ended abruptly as a nearby crash left them drenched from the seawater.

Tony jumped in the water immediately in search of John. His hunt was short-lived, however, as the young apprentice soon swam toward him underwater. He was not breathing when he emerged with his shirt in the clutches of a friendly porpoise's jaws. Several porpoises followed, and soon an entire school revealed itself. Tony emerged with them. He grabbed John and lifted him onto the raft. Freddie then laid him out on the raft adjacent to Ivy.

With a clear sky, the sun shone brightly and dried them quickly. But it was not enough to brighten their moods as John and Ivy both lay there breathless.

John was in a dark room.

"Midwa?" he yelled. "*Midwa?*"

There was only silence.

"John?" asked a young girl's voice.

Another voice echoed, "Don't let her take you back again…"

"*John?*" asked the young girl's voice again.

The other voice echoed again, "Run…*Run!*"

"I can't see anything. Ivy, is that you?" he replied.

"Yes, it's me. Please stay with me. I'm scared," the young girl replied with a frightened voice.

The other voice echoed yet again, "Run…*Run!*"

"Of course I'll stay with you...*always*," he said softly.

"I know...I saw everything before it got dark. I saw what you did. I heard what you said," Ivy replied. "Where are we? Why can't I see you? Why is everything black? There are only our voices. I thought...I...Why is it getting so warm in here? What's that red? John...why...I don't....*Aaaahhhhh!*"

John replied in desperation, "Ivy? *Ivy?*"

The other voice echoed yet again, "Run...*Run!*"

"John!" Ivy's screeching voice became faint.

John ran as the other voice instructed and pursued Ivy's voice as it screamed among the darkness.

"Ivy! Wait!" he yelled desperately. He channeled the power of Midwa, but instead of being illuminated bright blue himself, everything around him was lit blue. He looked at himself and saw only a shadow, a void among the empty blue space. He looked up and saw that another shadow broke up the blue oblivion. It ran off into the distance as it carried Ivy's voice along with it. He sprinted as fast as he could.

"Ivy! Wait!" John shouted, but her screams grew fainter.

"She's mine!" grumbled a hoarse voice behind him.

John began to feel the heat as well as he ran. He stopped in his tracks and turned around slowly. What he saw frightened him. The black shadow towered above him in the distance and revealed its crimson eyes. *This is what she saw*, he thought. The crimson eyes were familiar. It was the same pair of eyes he had seen throughout the desert and within his dreams. John looked at Ivy's shadow once again as it fled before he turned back around. The crimson hue that lined the towering shadow's borders began to spread and overtake the blue that lit the rest of the space.

"Who...are you?" John asked as the burning terror permeated his being.

The shadow replied in an ominous tone, "I am the one whom all fear. I have seen your dream...John. I have seen *all* through the crimson eyes of my puppets. *She* will not return. Her journey ends *here!*"

Burning fire filled John's voided body. He became hotter with each moment that he stood near the shadowed figure as it loomed closer. His will to go on fled him, and he found it increasingly more difficult to move. He turned around sluggishly and looked at Ivy's shadow once more. The towering black figure stomped past him and began to hasten its pursuit toward the shadow that carried Ivy's voice.

He reached deep down within himself and channeled the power of Midwa. "It…will…not…end…*here!*" He was overcome with power and cooled the burning hold that took over his being. He blazed across the space toward Ivy as it transformed from brilliant blue to crimson. He raced past the shadowed figure, which erupted pure evil from its eyes. John flashed across the space and closed in on the fleeing shadow. "Ivy! Stop running! It's me!"

The shadow stopped, and he reached it shortly after.

"Ivy, it's me, John! Don't worry! Ivy!"

"Oh, John! I'm so scared!" she yelled back as she hugged him for comfort. They turned toward the crimson eyes that loomed closer.

"We can't run forever. I'm sorry I couldn't protect you, Ivy," John said.

She replied, "Hey, it's not your fault. It's neither of ours. We tried. You tried."

They both put their heads down as they hugged each other. The shadowed figure loomed even closer and would soon be upon them.

John raised his head and spoke. "No, that's not good enough." He turned toward the shadow as it drew closer and screamed, "No! You will *not* have her! *Take me instead!*"

The figure was moments away from them when it shrieked, "Nooooooo!"

"John, you're fading!" Ivy yelled with concern.

"So are you! I don't know w—"

A tremendous force suddenly ripped their shadowed existences from this empty space. They had begun to fade.

"John, I'm scared!" Ivy yelled.

"Don't worry, Ivy. I'll always be with you!"

The figure with crimson eyes swiped ferociously where the shadows had been just a moment ago.

"Freddie, she's breathing! Quick, get me some freshwater!" Tony said excitedly.

"Sure! Wait…so is John!" Freddie yelled with relief.

John's eyes opened, and he jolted forward. "*Ivy!*"

Tony addressed John. "She's over here, John. She's going to be OK."

Ivy had just vomited, and her lungs were now clear of the seawater. She looked weak, but she would be all right.

John nervously leaned over. "Ivy, are you…"

Ivy covered his mouth with her finger. Her radiant smile was hidden behind the pain she was still in, but she said simply, "Always…" Her eyes said the rest.

XIX: Misty Mayhem

Torches irradiated the roads as wax candles illuminated the humble homes of the village. Darkness had fallen. Gavin and Wilbur assembled the last of their essential equipment and prepared to transform the jungle into Misty Mayhem. Under the veil of night, they began to make their way through the village in disguise. Even after all these years filled with bitter rivalry, they'd kept their inconspicuous cloaks hidden away from the sticky hands of the palace guards. They were a reminder of the glory days. They easily sneaked past the palace guards who were scattered throughout.

The elderly men followed the shadows into the forest. It had been several years since they hiked together. By now they had both developed a limp. Wilbur had carried the limp since he was much younger from a hunting accident; Gavin's was from the gift of age. They reviewed the details of their simple yet effective plan countless times as they walked the trails of the jungle and along the Larris River.

They limped their way a few miles until they had a visual of the RPG, who sat around a campfire and laughed uncharacteristically. To their surprise, William nervously chuckled along with them. On the ground, they noticed a royal guard resting on the ground with a bandage over his head, filled with blood.

The elders looked off to the side and noticed Mitch and Dahlia tied to a nearby pikmee tree. Unlike Gavin, they did not bear the mark of the X; however, they were gagged thanks to Dahlia's ramblings. She continued to ramble as she mumbled sounds through the thick rag wedged into her mouth.

Fully aware of their surroundings, Gavin and Wilbur signaled each other and determined it was time to initiate Misty Mayhem. They walked around the perimeter and positioned themselves in a spot that only Dahlia and Mitch could see. They discreetly sent signals and were able to get their attention. The young captives understood their instructions to distract the royal guards while the pair of elders made their way around to the campfire.

Muffled screams found their way through Dahlia's gag, which unsuccessfully attempted to block the indiscernible words. Meanwhile, Mitch's twitch became more intense. This captured the attention of the Chief, who commanded a royal guard to go over and cease their cries. Number Three proceeded to make his way over. He passed by Mitch in order to deal with Dahlia and her ramblings first. The guard removed the gag from her mouth, and suddenly the screams transformed into whispers.

The guard asked, "I warned you the last time you tried this, didn't I? Now *what* are you saying, girl?"

Dahlia continued to whisper.

The guard grew impatient and yanked her closer. "What are you saying, *girl?*"

She leaned in and whispered again, but the guard still could not hear her.

He clearly lost his patience as he pulled her in even closer. Their noses were now pressed against each other's. It was an obvious attempt to intimidate her, as he raised his voice even further.

"*What are y—*"

But before the guard could finish his question, Dahlia leaned in as if she were going to whisper her mumblings directly into his ear. With a vicious bite to the ear, the guard screamed in pain. She followed up with a double stomp to both feet. With her shoulder, she shoved the guard into Mitch's unintentionally extended feet. The guard tumbled backward and hit his head with a great impact on the ground. He was unconscious.

This caught the attention of the other royal guards, which included the Chief, who stood up immediately and paced over toward the anxious kids. William followed, nervous of what the RPG would do to them. Halfway across, the Chief turned around and instructed him to stay behind and look after Sandriver's heir beside the campfire while they disciplined the others. William hesitated but ultimately returned to the campfire in order to stay in his good graces.

As he sat uncomfortably on a jagged rock, William watched with apprehension. He caught a sudden movement in his periphery and heard the rustle of some leaves nearby. He quickly turned his head and noticed two shadows hastily limp just beyond the bushes that bordered the campfire. He thought it may have been a leopard as it paced the perimeter, but after a moment, he recognized the familiar limp. The Chief needed to know, so he began a speedy jog toward him.

Number Four pinned Dahlia against the ground. Her physique was more advanced than the average eleven-year-old girl's, but it was because she was the most rambunctious captive ever caught that he had so much trouble with her. Mitch was subdued by Number Two, who shook along with the young boy.

William approached the Chief, who was caught off guard and turned his head anxiously as he raised his voice. "I *thought* I told you to look after the heir."

"I'm sorry," said William, "but there's something I need to tell—"

The Chief pushed him to the side and yelled, "*Get them!*"

The two hooded figures had emerged and hastily limped back into the bushes. After a grunt of pain followed by a stumble, William knew with certainty that it was Wilbur and Gavin who had run off. The royal guards raced anxiously toward the campfire in the direction of the cloaked figures. Number Two unshackled the heir of the warrior king of the jungle and held the cub tightly as he awakened.

As the guards passed the campfire, there were some muffled explosions. Few in number but powerful, they released a fog into the environment and grew denser with time. Two of the royal guards stumbled away from the explosions due to their force, into the bushes ahead of them. Only three royal guards remained, as two were out of commission. Number Three had just been knocked unconscious, and Number Five was still in deep rest beneath his bandaged head, thanks to the numbing medicine he'd ingested.

Within moments, it was completely foggy, and neither the RPG nor the kids could see more than a few feet in any direction. The only way to traverse the jungle was to listen intently and feel their way around. Even the experience of the royal guards did not afford them any material advantage.

Moments later, there was a loud explosion from the Larris River nearby. The explosion carried a thick mist toward the fog, which trapped it. Misty Mayhem was born.

The Chief whispered to the others and instructed them to track the heat back to the campfire. They took short, silent steps in a reduced AD perimeter, as they were two royal guards short of a complete formation. They slowly made their way back and placed their long blades into the fire until the edges scalded and could cut through flesh effortlessly.

The experience of the elders allowed them to make their way back around the camp swiftly. They reached Mitch and Dahlia and began to release them from the shackles that bound them to an aged pikmee tree. They needed to hurry and regroup at a secure location.

"Who are you?" said a young voice in the distance.

"Shhh!" an elderly voice nervously replied. "We're here to help."

This caught the attention of the Chief, who yelled, "Over there!"

They quickly followed the fading echo to the origin of the voice. They were no longer required to remain in formation, as they knew where the bandits were. With quick steps, their scalded iron blades burned brightly and lit a path through the thick mist, which gave them a hazy molten hue.

Number Four took the lead and reached the pikmee stump first. He reached down and spoke nervously to the Chief. "They're gone."

"Psst…" a mysterious voice whispered a few feet away.

"Who goes there? *Reveal yourself at once!*" yelled the guard in return.

"Oh…I'm just a little old man. Please don't hurt me. I'm already hurt badly. Oh…ouch, my back…"

"Reveal yourself, old man. I won't hurt you." The guard lowered his sword.

"My name is…" whispered the voice as it drew closer. He slowly revealed his wrinkled face, which projected the words, "The *Groin Ranger,*" followed by a wicked kick to the groin that relieved the royal guard of his long sword.

As Gavin made a move to escape, the guard hunched over by instinct and latched on to the frail man's shoulder. "You're…going to pay for that… old man!" the guard grumbled as his face contorted in anguish.

"Who are you calling *old man?*" yelled another voice to the side.

The guard turned his attention to the next mysterious voice, unable to see the figure in the thick fog. As the guard squinted, the image of a shovel quickly grew larger. It flattened his nose and knocked him out cold.

"Let's go, Gavin! We need to get back to the kids and get out of here!" yelled Wilbur as he dropped the shovel to the ground and grabbed the fallen blade of the royal guard.

Their footsteps raced away and faded quickly. The guards were unable to get a clear direction on where they were heading. Number Three regained his consciousness and followed the voice of the Chief to rejoin the diminished group. Their molten-edged blades had already begun to dim from exposure to the misty air. This was good news for Wilbur, as they were no longer able to track him beyond several feet.

A few feet away in the thick of the murky mist, another voice spoke up. "I overheard them. They said they will be going to the river and following it south toward the desert until morning. The hooded figures were no strangers. It was Wilbur…and…"

"And who?" asked the Chief.

"And Gavin," William finally answered as he walked forward and removed himself partially from the veil of the mist.

"Well done, William. You are proving your worth, and your sister will be proud of you when she learns of your loyalty toward Her Majesty. She may yet be freed."

William's countenance was still barely visible through the fog. He hung his head low and spoke, conflicted. "Yes, sir."

"To the river!" commanded the Chief.

As they ran, a familiar snarl broke the silence of their voices and forced them to cease in their tracks.

"Whoa, whoa, whoa," the Chief whispered. A leopard was nearby. Soon more snarls echoed. The Chief instructed them to maintain silence as they walked light on their feet in single file toward the river.

They continued on light feet until the snarls finally prompted a whimper from Sandriver's heir. Their position in the jungle had been given away. Still worse, the illumination that powered their blades had all but dimmed, and soon they became their natural color of pure iron and silver. The fog once again dominated their path.

They acknowledged that they had been compromised, and with their path difficult to see through, they quickened their pace in hopes they would find safety soon. William followed the guard who ran in front of the line, Number Three, while the other two paced behind. The jungle faded to silence and triggered concern among the guards.

"AD perim—" the Chief began to command, but a leopard leaped from the right, directly in front of William and into Number Three. The royal guard was suddenly knocked from his feet and was airborne. He faded into the darkness off to the side. After a scream by the guard, silence followed. He had been marked with an X by the claw of a Tiberian leopard. Dahlia was accurate in her prediction.

There was another growl. William sprinted forward recklessly and eventually tumbled over several rocks. A splash echoed; he had reached the Larris River. The two royal guards who remained heard the welcome sound and hastened their pace desperately. They soon leaped into the Larris River for safety themselves.

"Swim north!" yelled the Chief.

Number Two replied, "But Chief, they are heading south."

The Chief replied, "Our primary mission may be a lost cause, but we have the heir of Sandriver. This may well be a victory for the kingdom."

Though the fog was still thick, it slowly dissipated. William and the royal guards swam against the current as they headed north toward the palace. Their pace was deliberate, as it allowed the fog to dispel along the way. North was the only direction toward safe ground for them.

As the fog cleared, they noticed silhouettes pace slowly along the Larris River. The farther they advanced, the clearer it was that the profiles belonged to the leopards of the jungle. Several walked along the banks of the river, and even more ran wildly in frustration as they leaped and weaved through the jungle on either side. They usually did not appear in such numbers, as they were naturally solitary creatures and had a tendency to group in two or three.

Heavy footsteps approached the clearing river. William became nervous as Sandriver paced along with intense breaths and a stare that was even more so. They would not get away with his heir this time, and they would pay for the slaying of his queen.

The Chief yelled, "Don't slow down! We'll soon be at safe ground where they won't be able to follow."

William was young, but he was a strong swimmer, as he had regularly swum in the Larris River when he was younger, before he was condemned for life at the Ice Palace.

Eventually they reached a large bank at the base of a village, which marked the beginning of their path back to the palace. The leopards suddenly halted in their tracks; however, the RPG, along with William, continued on and eventually reached the edge of the bank. They pulled themselves up and out of the river.

They looked back at two dozen leopards that were staring at them ferociously, their eyes filled with frustration. The Chief turned his back to the leopards and walked away from them, through an army of palace guards who waited patiently for them. The palace guards created a path down the middle as they stepped aside. The Chief walked with William at his side, followed by Number Two, who held the heir of Sandriver. Most of the eyes of the palace guards looked at William with amazement. None of them could ever hope to achieve what he had just achieved.

Once they reached the center of the palace guards, a perimeter was formed for protection. There were at least fifty palace guards present, several newly recruited; this accounted for most of the palace's force. They knew that the leopards would not attack while heavily outnumbered. As they began to make their way through the villages, they paced quickly toward the lift that would return them to the safety of the Ice Palace.

However, they did not know the pain that cut through Sandriver's heavy heart. He huffed and whimpered for a brief, vulnerable moment and then shook off all sentiment. He composed himself as the warrior king of the jungle that reflected his reputation. He growled to the other leopards. They lined up and commenced a deliberate forward march. The palace guards tensed up at the perimeter and sent a warning to the Chief. Nervous of what may follow, they hastened their pace.

As Sandriver's focus was forward, he snarled. Four leopards on the far ends of their line formation scattered out of sight. He snarled again, and several more leopards ran off and disappeared into the shadows. An aggressive growl followed. Sandriver and the leopards that remained hastened their advance as they burned with the desire for revenge. Justice would be served. The royal guards would surrender his heir.

The fast trot of the leopards soon hastened to an all-out sprint. They headed directly toward the palace guards, who stumbled over one another. The Chief commanded the palace guards to clear a path so they could advance toward the front, as far away from Sandriver as possible.

Sandriver breached the rear perimeter. He swiped at the palace guards and tossed them out of the way. He left them injured as he progressed through the ranks. The Chief became nervous as the leopards advanced quickly toward the center of the pack. Screams were heard from the south end of the perimeter and swiftly approached the center.

The screams from the southern end were joined by several from both the east and west as more leopards suddenly reappeared and breached their respective sides of the perimeter. Though unable to break the ranks of palace guards as handily as Sandriver, the smaller but strong and agile leopards were effective. They created mass confusion among the dim-witted guards, who began to stumble over one another and knocked one another out inadvertently.

As the Chief approached the front of the pack, he realized that his perimeter had closed on him rapidly. Time was about to run out, and they needed to reach the lift as soon as possible. They sprinted recklessly through the last village. The villagers looked on with fear from the safety of their homes as the leopards leaped over their fences, deflected off of the roofs of their homes, and attacked the palace guards by air. The dominant numbers of the palace guards had quickly dwindled, and the once-significant advantage had vanished.

The Chief, Number Two, and William approached the lift surrounded by only a handful of palace guards. Suddenly, four leopards appeared from both sides of the lift and ran directly into their path. Sandriver and the leopards of various allied leaps closed in quickly from all angles.

The last of the palace guards continued to swipe at the leopards effectively with their dull swords. One leopard leaped past two palace guards and approached the heir, but the Chief grabbed one of the palace guards from in front of him, tossed him into the leopard's direct path, and tripped it up.

The palace guards succeeded. They held off the leopards just long enough for them to reach the lift. They boarded, and it broke away from the earth immediately and began its hasty ascent toward the Ice Palace. They would reach safety after all.

Sandriver was forced to cease his valiant pursuit. Though able to make the leap, it would be too risky for him to enter the palace. Her Majesty would have indulged in his death, and the leap would be without a formidable leader, both present and future.

Sandriver growled loudly as he commanded two of his more nimble leopards to continue the pursuit. They recovered their missteps and managed to leap onto the edge of the lift as it accelerated. The stronger of the two pulled itself up from the ledge and then assisted the other. The leopards assumed they were safe because the royal guards had not expected them to attempt the leap. The leopards would need to track down the heir and rescue him. Unable to attack the guards without setting off an alarm, they would need to remain hidden high up in the mackelroy trees, at least until they could take advantage of the shadows that lay beyond.

XX: Unleashed by the Sea

John had calmed the sea so the porpoises could live their quiet lives once again. In gratitude, they had tossed over several small fish onto the raft earlier, and the kids feasted. Ivy slowly regained her strength, helped by the poisson brought from the western region of the sea. It was a welcome break from the pontaccio and fruit they had consumed for the past days.

The friendly mammals lapped the raft several times as they performed a plethora of tricks and provided some much-needed light entertainment. The kids consumed the poisson as they watched and gasped at the more impressive flips.

John assisted Ivy as she ate, as she was still too weak to manage it herself. With their tummies satisfied, they leaned back and relaxed, absent of dialogue. They enjoyed the serenity of the sea, which no longer raged violently.

Hours later, the sun was still high, and the tranquility persisted. The silence was occasionally broken by the sound of a porpoise that surfaced in the distance or by their own stress-free movements. A portrait of the universe had never been painted so beautifully. The blue sky contrasted against the bright sun and planets, both nearby and distant. As they gazed above, it was hard to imagine that the world they lived in was filled with evil.

Ivy finally spoke up. "What a view, huh?"

"It sure is," John said as he gazed upon her beauty.

She continued. "I especially like the one that starts from the…Hey! You're not even looking!"

"Oh, sorry…which one were you pointing to?" he said as he looked beyond the smooth tips of her fingers.

Tony looked on and huffed as he deliberated whether he would ever be enough for her.

"Ivy, are you OK?" John asked with sincere concern.

"Yeah, I'm fine, thanks," she replied as she lifted herself to sit up. She was no longer pale, and her radiant smile had returned. She had never looked at John with such impression. He was her hero.

Tony was relieved by her well-being, even if she did not have eyes for him. He was pessimistic, however, as they had been drawn closer to the southern kingdom of Villanis, where the Fire King resided. "I didn't realize it was so vast."

Freddie jumped in. "Yes, but think about what we've accomplished so far. *Nothing* can stop us!"

John finally took his eyes off of Ivy and sat up. "Freddie, maybe you're right about what you said before. Perhaps it's for the best that I don't know my past. I may be better off not knowing. Midwa told me that my past lies in the darkness of the shadows. I don't think I would able to accept such a dark past."

Tony spoke up. "I don't need to know your past, John. You're already like a brother. Both of you are, and Ivy's like a…sister. I mean, Freddie's right. Look at what we've been through together." They all looked at one another in silent agreement.

They planned to relax until dawn broke the following morning. At first light, they would begin to row in shifts until they reached the shores of the Fire King's Forsaken Fortress.

John recovered as he lay back and heard the whisper of a familiar voice. "It's only just begun…" He was unsettled, as the words were not spoken by Midwa.

The sun set, preparing them for a clear and starry night. As Freddie tossed his blade in the air repeatedly, he had never felt as relaxed. His blade reflected the rays of light from the distant stars. Tony lay in a corner unto himself as he looked at the waters. John and Ivy lay next to each another mesmerized by the beautiful portrait above them. But they knew this bliss could not last forever.

The silence was broken in the distance as a porpoise emerged from the sea. However, this splash was more disturbed than the previous ones. More porpoises suddenly broke the surface. The splashes were continual and became more disruptive as they passed the raft. There was a sense of urgency in them as they yelped with concern. The kids became tense and alert.

A rumble beneath vibrated their salvaged raft as it disrupted the calmness of the sea. They gathered toward the center of it as they waited anxiously to find out what situation they were involved in. The vibration suddenly ceased.

Curious as ever, Freddie crawled to the edge of the raft and looked beneath the waters. He began to squint. "I think I see something."

Tony replied, "What do you see?"

Freddie had no words in reply as he lowered his head closer to the surface of the sea. Then he whispered, "I...I..." and fell silent.

Tony lunged toward Freddie and pulled him back as something had begun to emerge slowly from the sea on the opposite side. A thick tentacle rose several feet above the surface and began to lean in toward them as it assessed its surroundings. A tentacle also rose from where Freddie had been looking. Soon, directly above them, fluid oozed from many of its orifices. As the fluid dripped on them, Freddie made a sound that reflected his nervousness. The tentacle tensed and retreated several feet as its orifices wheezed.

Several more tentacles emerged from the sea and surrounded the raft. The pace quickened, and soon dozens more tentacles erupted simultaneously and wheezed desperately. The raft was rocked back and forth as the kids gripped it tightly.

Suddenly a large mass emerged in the distance and revealed a creature several times the size of Arachno. John thought briefly about the rock-made creature, which would always be a reminder of when they lost Jacob.

A much larger battleground surrounded them as the bizarre creature created a perimeter around them with dozens upon dozens of its hundred-foot-long tentacles. The kids were trapped and unable to row away. They looked at one another as their salvaged raft continued to sway.

John recalled Midwa's guidance: "A powerful force rules this realm and will push you to your absolute limits. Do not retreat. Do not surrender. Stare into the eye of fear and *destroy it*." However, he possessed an uncertainty, as the creature was rather unorthodox, especially in the deep blue sea.

He huddled with the others and explained that he would attempt to lead the creature away from them toward the shore; however, as he spoke, one hundred more tentacles emerged high above the sea and formed an enclosure. It no longer permitted any light from the starry sky to enter. In the cover of darkness, they could not see. John hastily illuminated their huddle, as his back was turned toward the massive creature's central figure. The slimy textures of the tentacles radiated as they intermittently dripped with ooze.

The waters ahead reflected crimson, a hue that appeared even brighter against their faces. John turned around nervously. A large crimson eye revealed itself as its pupil dilated rapidly. It was situated above a large orifice filled with massive serrated teeth.

John recalled Midwa's advice and began to levitate. He prepared for an attack on the unusually large eye, but he needed to avoid the nearby orifice. He was caught off guard as he focused ahead. Ooze spewed forth from the tentacles behind him unexpectedly and crashed into him. He flew across the waters from its incredibly strong pressure.

Being tangled in a mesh of ooze significantly hindered his mobility. Though the low density of the fluid kept him afloat, his efforts to escape were ineffective. He had trouble as he tried to breathe because the seawater sporadically found its way into his mouth. His struggles were made no easier as his limbs flailed apprehensively. His attempts to illuminate consisted of false flickers as the sea filled him with fear. Nothing had filled him with more terror, not even the Fire King.

John yelled to the others repeatedly, "Help me! Help!"

The others knew they could not stand a chance against this creature without him, so they leaped into the sea in an attempt to release him from the ooze. As they approached, however, a few tentacles broke formation from above. The oozing appendages raced toward the kids and seized them within their firm grips. They were all prisoners.

The tentacles swayed back and forth as they attempted to break free without success. Freddie managed to puncture the tentacle with his blade, but it only aggravated the creature further. He was subsequently slammed repeatedly into the water, which left him submerged for several seconds at a time.

Tony yelled over to Freddie as he desperately tried to free himself and save the youngest of the fellowship. However, his voice distorted as it traveled through the thickening waters before it reached Freddie's ears. Tony then yelled over to John, who was still struggling to release himself from the ooze.

John had all but lost hope, as it was not possible for the situation to deteriorate much further. He whispered to himself, "Please, Midwa. Help me. Guide me." But the words once again echoed in his head without a reply.

A familiar feeling had begun to overcome him as he felt an uncontrollable chill within his body. It was as if he had returned to the Ice Palace, once again imprisoned in his undersized dungeon cell and unable to move around much. He reflected on the long hours that he was disciplined. The chill of his thoughts channeled throughout his core. The scars of the Ice Palace ran deep. They would never truly heal no matter how far away he fled. Even outside the palace, he never stopped being a prisoner. Fears of the impossibly cold heart of the Ice Queen offered no comfort. As reality once again set in, the fog of his thoughts fled from his mind and returned to the painful compartment he had created long ago.

The ambient temperature that surrounded him had dropped considerably. The ooze that kept him prisoner had hardened. He began to focus once again on the unbearably cold temperatures of the Ice Palace. Soon the ooze was frozen and began to crack. It was followed by an explosion that shattered it.

John emerged with a crystallized texture that covered the surface of his skin. As he was filled with an arctic anger, his reflection made him appear to shine brighter than before. The creature made a sudden move with Freddie in its grip. Its tentacle raced toward its razor-sharp teeth. John reacted immediately and flew fast toward Freddie. He crashed into the tentacle and wrestled it. Freddie dangled in front of the ten-foot-long serrated teeth as the creature's foul breath permeated his nose. John continued to channel his scarring memories of the Ice Palace. The tentacle quickly froze, and within moments, he was able to shatter it with a blow. Freddie fell into the waters below.

The creature's shriek echoed within the enclosure it had created. Its crimson eye dilated increasingly more rapidly. The others were released into the sea, and large splashes followed.

John commanded the creature's undivided attention. The young boy would suffer for what he had done. Absent of fear as he hovered high above the sea, John was filled with a newfound confidence. He stared directly into the large crimson eye of this creature that had been unleashed by the sea. What he had not realized, however, was that the sea had just unleashed something even more powerful in him.

He knew that he did not have time to engage all of the tentacles individually, but at least he had a proven tactic he could employ. As they looked on from the surface below, John appeared insignificant, but only in size. His courage was tremendous.

Another shriek followed, and the creature thrust a tentacle toward John, who remained unmoved. He allowed the creature to wrap its tentacle around him and cringed from the unexpectedly tight grip. He then channeled the unimaginable chill of the Ice Palace as he thought of all the cold nights when his knees had crashed into each other as the palace guards looked on in amusement. Anxiety built up feverishly within the creature as its tentacle was frozen. It thrust several more toward John and squeezed him even tighter. He was soon concealed from everyone's visibility. The kids looked on with concern as they made their way over to the salvaged raft to wait anxiously.

An evaporated chill began to exude from the interior of the tentacles. An explosion shattered them in every direction and forced them to jump off the raft and maneuver around the water as chunks of the tentacles flew everywhere. This led to an ear-piercing shriek as the creature completely broke formation of its tentacles and once again revealed the open water and starry night.

John yelled his instructions to the others. "Get to shore quickly!" He knew that he needed to end this battle as soon as possible. No matter how determined he was, it was only a matter of time before the powers that he channeled would subside.

As the others lifted themselves back onto the raft, they began to row with a few shattered pieces of the iced tentacles. Tony was suddenly grabbed from behind, once again in the firm grip of the creature. The tentacle jolted toward the wide-open orifice. John shot forward in pursuit of Tony, but as the tentacle hastened its pace, he would not reach him in time. Tony was tossed just past the serrated teeth as they closed, and into the dark orifice. John crashed into the tentacle and broke it apart before he crashed directly into one of the teeth. He shattered it upon impact.

John made his way into the creature's dark and slimy interior. He illuminated himself as he desperately searched in all directions for Tony. After several glances, he noticed Tony in a pool of fluid at the far end of the cavity. He was slowly pulled in by the creature's tongue. John rushed toward him but was grabbed midair himself by its secondary tongue. The muscle escalated its heat levels in order to offset the chill of John and left him incapable of dropping his body temperature further.

John calmed his nerves and returned to normal. He permitted the tongue to transport him to the far end, along with Tony, who continued to yell desperately for help before he was suddenly out of sight. John followed the path and was suddenly released into a warm tubular conduit that the creature filled with fluids to flush them along.

Tony was within sight once again. He attempted to slow himself from the rushing descent, but without success. John accelerated and maneuvered around the debris and began to quickly close the gap. Tony remained out of reach as he tumbled over a cliff and fell toward a bay of molten lava, on which ancient skeletons floated.

John tumbled off shortly after and quickly reoriented himself. He illuminated himself and dashed toward Tony, who screamed and flailed as he approached the boiling belly of the sea creature. Tony was sweating profusely just above the surface when John grabbed his arm and stopped his descent.

As he began to cook just above the boiling surface, Tony stared down with a realization of the impossible odds. He looked up with concern as he watched the conduit close behind them. They were trapped, but John spoke with conviction.

"I'll get us out of here." The boiling fluids of the beast's belly began to swallow his words as they warmed his chilled face.

Tony was not comforted by the words. "But there's *no* way back up!"

John reassured him, "I'll make one! Come on. We don't have much time!"

Tony nodded. "OK! Let's get out of here!"

John began to channel all his energy from the coldest, darkest place he could manage, a coldness not even the boiling fluids of the creature's belly could hope to overcome. The texture of his skin became frosted again, while smoke exuded and collided with the intense heat that surrounded him.

Tony yelled nervously to John, above the molten sounds below them, "You're getting cold! Are you *sure* this is a good idea? My arm is numb!"

John turned toward Tony and revealed his crystallized eyes against the icy texture of his face. "I'm going to get very, *very* cold soon, and I'll need to let you go, or else you will be frozen."

Tony's eyes dilated in shock. "*What?*"

John yelled with unwavering conviction, "I'm going to freeze *every…last…breath* of life from it!"

He tossed Tony above him, low enough so that he would not break any bones upon the impact of his fall. John's arm quickly appeared the same as the rest of his frosted body. He channeled the ice-cold core of his pain as his thoughts were dominated by the Ice Queen and all the suffering she brought upon everyone. Every cell in his body burned with hatred, and soon the chill spewed from his entire body.

He raced toward the boiling surface. The collision of ice and fire created a crackling sizzle. The surface quickly froze over; it was no match for the power of John's burning hatred of the Ice Queen. It grew more extreme with each moment that passed. Tony fell as his limbs flailed. He attempted to correct his footing; however, he landed awkwardly and sprained his ankle on the frozen lava.

With a sense of haste Tony had never witnessed before, John flew throughout the belly of the beast. He overwhelmed the intensely hot temperatures and almost instantly froze the areas as he passed over them. Within minutes, the entire belly had been frozen over permanently. No heat remained. The Ice Queen would be at home here.

His efforts had just begun. As Tony watched, John flew up toward the conduit where they'd entered the belly. He screamed as he approached it and crashed through it. A trail of frosted air followed in his wake. The creature's agonizing scream rumbled the iced cavern Tony stood in.

John ascended through the digestive conduit as it froze over along with the fluids that once flushed down. He made his way back into the creature's mouth as the rest of its body already felt the chill of death and began to seize. The orifice would consume no more.

John shattered the creature's body recklessly as he searched for its heart, which was still beating. He crashed through organ after frozen organ until he finally reached it. It had slowed along with the rest of its dying body. It fought for its life in vain. Life fled it, and it would never recover. The young apprentice would make sure of it.

He finally located the heart and extended his hands. He placed them on the surface, which was twice his size. With a firm grip, he channeled all of the cold hatred within him into it as he screamed to release his pain. It slowed to its final beat and then arrested. It was entirely frozen over. John screamed one last time as he shattered it with a powerful blow that contained all of his pain.

It was finished. But he had never felt so empty. As he stole the life from this creature, he thought, *What have I become? What am I?* As his adrenaline began to subside, he suddenly felt very weak. He needed to return to Tony and then search for the others.

John made his way back down the digestive conduit toward the shattered entrance to the belly, but he continued to weaken rapidly. He was suddenly visible to Tony, who yelled over to him. However, at this moment, John's heart arrested, and he crashed into the edge of the shattered entrance. He fell limp uncontrollably.

Tony anticipated where he would land and raced toward him. He had forgotten about his sprained ankle as he lunged toward John and grappled him midair. He stunted what would have otherwise been far too great of an impact to survive. They tumbled several times before they stopped and rolled away from each other. Tony limped over to John and checked for vital signs. He was not breathing.

A rumble began to shake them across the frozen surface. Tony lifted John over his shoulder as he looked for a way out. He once again felt the pain of his sprained ankle, but he was tough.

Tony lacked the necessary equipment to climb the ice. He stood there puzzled, unsure of how to escape as everything around them had begun to collapse. He wished he had the collective creativity of the fellowship.

A loud and continuous flush came from above and soon became visible. The creature began to sink. Without life to regulate the flow of the sea, it had begun to flood. The seawater rapidly filled the frozen belly.

Tony held on to him as the water level rose. He was a strong swimmer, unlike John. Even with a sprained ankle, he would be able to carry them both to the surface and find the others. He stayed afloat until they could exit through the massive, serrated tooth John had destroyed and reenter the open sea.

Ivy and Freddie had not made it far. They knew they could not go on without Tony and John, so they decided not to row. They waited impatiently, but the longer they waited, the farther away hope fled.

Ivy attempted to console Freddie. "They'll come."

Freddie replied with frustration, "But it's been almost an hour!"

Ivy tried to maintain her composure, even though she was frightened at the thought that she and Freddie would be in the middle of the sea alone, without John and Tony. "All of the tentacles are gone, and it stopped moving. Maybe they got it good."

Freddie answered pessimistically, "Maybe it just isn't—"

But Freddie's words were interrupted by the sound of a splash in the near distance. Though it was dark, it was clear that Tony was swimming with John at his side. Freddie and Ivy grabbed the fragmented iced tentacles and began to row toward them. Eventually they reached each other. Tony lifted John as Ivy and Freddie pulled him aboard.

Freddie spoke. "I'm so glad to see both of you! Is John resting?"

With a grim voice, Tony replied, "He's not breathing."

They all stood above John with concern, as it would not be long before they would arrive at the Forsaken Fortress. Though they had seen him go through this many times already, they were never sure if he would wake.

XXI: A Dark Past Revealed

Settled in the south end of the Larris River, Gavin and Wilbur became acquainted with Mitch and Dahlia. The young boy was full of apologies, as the guilt weighed heavily on him. He had allowed himself to be manipulated by William.

"I'm sorry. I didn't really mean to hurt anyone. My emotions got the best of me. I was just so angry that no one came back for us," he said as he stared at the ground, filled with shame. He reflected on how he'd helped encourage all the young captives to blame John for everything.

Gavin replied, "It's OK, laddie. It's never too late. You have plenty of years in you yet to do some good. We all do." When he finished, he looked over to Wilbur, who had a look of agreement as he reflected upon his own actions of the past several hours against the past several years.

Mitch was comforted by his words.

Gavin moved along and asked, "So what happened to William? He was a good lad once. He opposed *Her Travesty*. It appears he is now working on her behalf."

Mitch replied, "She's got Penelope. William was threatened that he would be forced to toss her in to Frostbite himself if he doesn't cooperate."

Wilbur gasped. "Oh my…we need to get them both back somehow. We need to get all of those poor kids back from that dreadful place. They are innocent. How can she be so *bitter*? It's peculiar. I have memories of my past, but many are foggy. I tell you, *Her Travesty* put a curse over these lands…*a curse, I say*! That *frigid*…"

"Stay…back. Don't come…any closer…" Dahlia was in her own world again as her eyes rolled toward the back of her head.

Mitch suddenly started to twitch uncontrollably. He dropped to the jungle floor. Another seizure had grabbed a hold of him.

Wilbur dropped the sword he'd stolen from the RPG and rushed over and tried to calm him, but their efforts were not successful.

Wilbur called over to Dahlia, but she was still in a trance as she continued to ramble. "Don't let her take you back again…" He limped over to her and gave her a good shake. Dahlia was with them again. She looked around and noticed Mitch as he shook on the ground. She rushed over to him.

"I'm sorry, Mitch, but it's the only way." She then began to sing in a language that was foreign to their ears. She attempted to soothe his nerves by singing a lullaby her mother serenaded her with when she was frightened as a little girl.

Gavin and Wilbur both looked upon Dahlia with intrigue.

Gavin spoke up. "You're not from around here, are you? From where did you come?"

Dahlia continued to sing in her foreign tongue as she ignored his questions.

Wilbur added, "*Who* are you?"

Dahlia finally looked up and ceased her song. Mitch was suddenly calm and no longer at the mercy of the seizure that had grabbed an unpitying hold on him. Dahlia removed her mask of delusion.

"I'm from the Far West. I have fourteen years in this world, not eleven as I suggested. My grandmother is Annabel the Second, good and just queen of Buv're, younger sister of Agribel, queen of Belghan. You know Agribel as the Ice Queen.

"My grandfather, Heras, former king of Buv're, perished in a great battle at the Fire King's castle in the South. His soul was damned by the Fire King and cast to the Forsaken Realm to serve its dark lord for an eternity. It's a damned realm that became the place of choice for exiling the souls of those who attempted to overthrow him. Most of them were courageous men along with their loyal creatures. My grandfather's leopard was injured during their great battle and fell over. He was trapped beneath.

"The castle began to crumble under the will of the weakened and desperate Fire King. My grandfather's best friend, who was a middle-aged wizard, attempted to save him, but nothing he conjured could stop the debris as it fell—" Her eyes rolled to the back of her head, and she continued to speak while she fell into a dream sequence. Mitch caught her before she fell to the ground, and along with the elders, he listened intently. She appeared to be having a flashback as if she had been present during those years prior to her birth. She had a gift for clairvoyance and channeling the past, present, and future, though she did not have great control over her abilities.

A tear ran down her cheek. Nerves and desperation were apparent in her youthful voice. "Midwa, please help my grandpa!" Dahlia's plea fell on deaf ears because she had no actual presence in the flashback. She was merely a spectator. Her grandfather was trapped permanently, and there was nothing she could do to change this fact. After the unsuccessful attempt to save him, Midwa barely managed to escape the debris as he rode away on the back of the greatest leopard warrior king to ever live, Sandriver.

Dahlia followed along in the adventures with her clairvoyance throughout various scenes. Her words paraphrased the actions and recited the dialogue, which were related to Wilbur, Gavin, and Mitch, who listened with intrigue. They found it difficult to follow along at times as she went through the sequences in quick succession.

Midwa and Sandriver returned to the western kingdom of Buv're. He was the bearer of the most unfortunate news. "I'm sorry, Your Majesty. The king has perished." The queen of Buv're could not come to grips and immediately blamed the wizard for not protecting the king, her husband.

Dahlia looked upon herself as a baby. Not even a year of age at the time, she was unable to understand the gravity of the situation. Princess Sonya the Fourth, her mother, could only speak indiscernible words during her attempt to comfort her. Dahlia's father had also perished in battle previously, and her grandfather was suddenly gone as well. Two years of deep depression followed.

After a year of grievance and consolation from Midwa, who continued to carry the burden of allowing the king to perish, the princess had eased her hatred for the man of magic. Though no royalty ran through his bloodline, Midwa was an honorable man and would not have let Heras perish without trying all he could. She accepted that the king was ambitious and also naïve to expect that he could overthrow the Fire King after so many of his predecessors had failed. The king of Buv're thought that with his swift sword and the staff of the powerful wizard, he would be successful and claim eternal glory.

Dahlia's mother fell in love with the noble wizard even though he was well beyond her years. She gained the favor of the widowed queen Annabel the Second to support her decision. However, before they wed, the princess would soon bear another fruit, the love child of Midwa. They would name him John, after the wizard's father. Since he was not a pure Buv'rean, Dahlia refused to study with him. She was able to convince their mother, the queen, that it was to their benefit to have him tutored by a Belghan refugee who had fled from his native land a few years prior when Queen Agribel became an unjust ruler in the North. John could play the role of ambassador between the two kingdoms as the sister queens refused direct communication. To the common person, he would not be recognized as a rightful citizen of Buv're, as he carried a Belghan accent. For this reason he did not carry the same Buv'rean accent as his sister. Dahlia often looked at him as her bastard brother and forced him to play alone. Sporadically they played together near Omnus River, where she secretly hoped he would fall in and be swept away to Lake Magil, which bordered an abandoned village that went by the same name. It was the most ominous place in the entire kingdom of Buv're, said to be filled with monsters and evil spirits, and forbidden for any citizens to visit. One day John tripped while they were playing near Omnus River and fell in. Dahlia immediately regretted her malicious wishes and jumped in after him as he was being swept away by the strong current. He was only five years of age at the time and did not have any experience in the water because no one had taught him how to swim. Eventually she caught up to him and held onto him with a firm grip. The waters were too powerful for them to swim to the banks on either side. The current carried them one mile away to Lake Magil, where the waters were dark and murky. Dahlia swore she had seen spirits beneath them; however, John refused to look below. He pleaded with her to take him out from the lake immediately. Within a few minutes they were able to emerge and step on dry land. There was something strange and special about the experience at Lake Magil that changed the both of them forever, though she still did not accept him as her brother. She made him promise to never speak of the experience to anyone and to never revisit the forbidden place.

Midwa vowed revenge in honor of Heras, even at the queen's opposition. Her daughter Sonya the Fourth and Dahlia were already fatherless and could not bear the burden of another heavy loss. But deep in her heart, the queen longed for her late king to be avenged, so she allowed it. He was to return soon, and they set a date in the following six months so they could finally wed. It was long overdue because they had already borne a child, much to the displeasure of the queen. Invitations were sent far and wide to distant lands outside the realms of the three kingdoms.

Following one month of intense preparations, Midwa once again set sail across the Bellanis Sea. From the west, it was possible to avoid the great creature that resided beneath, as it could not dwell within the shallow waters that were strewn through the western parts of the sea. He knew the quickest and safest route. With favorable winds, he reached the southern island country within a day.

Midwa entered the fortress along with Sandriver. They slashed and thrust their way through the ranks of warriors who were tasked to keep the castle impenetrable. In less than an hour, they reached the castle gate. Midwa instructed Sandriver to wait for him in the great hall. He insisted that it was a battle he alone needed to triumph in. He was a proud wizard; however, pride did not favor the victor in these lands.

Midwa once again met the Fire King, staff versus sword. He planned to retrieve the ring that erupted with crimson as it resided on the black finger of the fire king. He could not destroy it, but he would return it to the Islands of the Phoenix Dragons for safekeeping.

A great and brutal battle commenced. The shadows on the walls clashed among themselves as the hues of blue and crimson aggressed without restraint. Screams echoed and blood flowed over the next hour as the two made rubble of the castle while they attempted to overpower each other. Windows shattered along with the dense walls as they tossed each other with great might.

Midwa had almost relieved the hulking Fire King of his ring as he knocked him from his feet. He kicked his sword away and blasted it with magic that destroyed it beyond repair. He tried his best to conceal the anguish apparent on his own face. However, Midwa was soon overwhelmed by the power of the Fire King's ring. The hand of the king of the South rose above his head as he looked above. Midwa looked up immediately and saw a grand chandelier falling quickly toward them. He could not raise his staff in time. He leaped out of the way, and his staff was shattered.

In the near distance, the staff-less Midwa lay exhausted, with cautious relief that the Fire King had once and for all been dethroned, as he was crushed underneath the rubble. But hope would be short-lived. The shattered chandelier slowly elevated above the ground and revealed the Fire King. The debris crashed into the walls in every direction. Midwa lowered his head and managed to avoid the flying iron and glass.

He needed to escape, or he would leave the princess to grieve once more. He lifted himself to his feet and hastened his steps toward the main gate at the castle entrance. The crimson king rose from the ground as he burned furiously.

Midwa reached the great hall and mounted Sandriver, who waited for him impatiently. They fled toward the closing castle gate. As freedom drew near, the desperate king directed a large section of fallen debris toward Midwa. Outside of his periphery, he could not see it as it approached, but he felt it sharply. It knocked him off of Sandriver and into a nearby suit of knight's armor, directly into its sharpened blade.

The Dreamer: Origins

Life fled from his body. He focused deep within his innermost being and projected his soul outward. Within moments, his soul would dissipate and be drawn away from the realm of the living. The world around him slowly faded and transformed into a hue of crimson as the Fire King recited his enchantment of soul exile. Shadowed figures appeared and reached toward him to claim his soul. He looked around desperately. He would be able to escape exile if he could project himself into a living being in close proximity. There was but one—a rat, an overgrown chocolate rat.

Desperate, Midwa proceeded to project himself forward into his new physical form. Hardly graceful, he would at least live to see another day among the living. He stumbled as he sprinted in his new form toward the gate that had just closed after Sandriver, barely and inadvertently, escaped without him.

The Fire King observed the lifeless body of Midwa against the long sword and retreated to his master chamber. Before he retired for the evening, however, he needed to deal with the dead soldiers who lay motionless on his fortress grounds. They had failed him. He split each of their souls in two and forsook them; half was banished to the kingdom of Belghan, beneath the palace, and the other half in the labyrinth he would create in the forward garden of the castle grounds. Their souls were tormented, as they belonged neither to the realm of the living nor the realm of the dead. Until their fate would be determined, the damned place that surrounded the castle adopted the moniker of the Forsaken Fortress.

Over the years, life dwindled in the South, as the only living beings that remained were the servants, who had no choice but to serve their king. They did not desire to suffer the same fate as the others. They chose to live in terror rather than be tormented for eternity. They hoped the king would provide them with a merciful death.

Midwa found a small crevice in the castle wall and squeezed his new boneless frame back outside to the fortress grounds. Sandriver grieved nearby. Midwa approached hastily to let the warrior king know that he was all right; however, as he got closer, the large leopard noticed the aged chocolate rodent and growled. It was a clear signal that if he approached any closer, he would be crushed.

He realized what he must have appeared as to Sandriver and spoke up. "It's me, old friend."

Sandriver looked on with confusion, but soon realized it actually was Midwa and not some trickery of the Fire King.

Midwa continued. "I know. I wish I'd found something more suitable, more attractive, for Sonya's sake…I don't know how I'm going to explain this one to her."

Sandriver extended his lengthy leg and allowed Midwa to race up and mount him. As the rodent dug his claws into the thick skin of the feline, the warrior king did not flinch.

Midwa added, "I don't think I can get used to this, but I guess I have no choice. I wish it were as easy as projecting my soul into another person, but that would be too complicated for someone with moral obligations. I would overtake that person's being within days."

Midwa delayed his return to Buv're by several days, as he was ashamed of his new appearance as well as his failure. He eventually presented himself to the queen of Buv're and then to Dahlia's mother. The princess declared herself crazy among her housemaids, as she could not believe what she was seeing. But after the housemaids admitted to seeing the same, and after multiple explanations from the chocolate rodent, she finally believed this nightmare was her new reality. However, she would not accept Midwa. She would rather her son be raised by housemaids than by an aged, overgrown, discolored rat. At the request of the princess, the queen sentenced Midwa to exile, never to be spoken of again, on the counts of having allowed the king to perish, as well as having seduced the princess into having a child out of wedlock as a play for power.

Forbidden to visit Sandriver, Midwa roamed the corners of the world for several months. He learned to master his meditation and magical prowess and no longer required a staff to conjure magnificent effects. Depression would, however, settle in intermittently within him. He attempted to blend in with the other rodents and learn their ways so he would go unnoticed and fade into obscurity. He no longer had the will to live and finally accepted that he had forever lost his best friend, the love of his life, and his only child.

Within a year he had all but given up hope. Until one day. News traveled throughout the rodent network, as he referred to it, that the Fire King had courted Agribel, good and just queen of the kingdom of Belghan. The king assured her of safe passage across the Bellanis Sea, and she was invited to a fancy dinner to meet the often-misunderstood king of Villanis.

The king removed his ring before her arrival, and the castle was returned to its former glorious state. It was a magnificently aged castle, though with obvious restoration apparent on the exterior. The castle gate creaked as it opened and slowly revealed an even more impressive interior, lined with servants who would wait at her beck and call. She was escorted into the main dining hall and seated at the far end of the expansive table.

Footsteps echoed as the servants waited on her. They became louder as they descended the several flights of a spiraling staircase. A graceful man entered the hall and was most pleasant to the northern queen's eyes. Her heart nearly melted at the sweetness of his soft-spoken words, which convinced her that all the rumors that he was a monster were false. Her heart convinced her of his sincerity. She was in love.

Unbeknownst to her, however, an ulterior motive was at play. An ally was needed in the North. The king of Villanis was hungry for power, and his ambitions would require no less than complete dominance of all three kingdoms and beyond. He would need to control the North and South along with the roads and sea between. With an ally in the North, he could then plan to dominate the West before he would be strong enough in numbers to overtake the Islands of the Phoenix Dragons in the East, which remained his only true challenge before he could claim dominance. He had chosen his ally, and she had not even realized it.

For three days the king of Villanis wined and dined the queen of the North, who continued to age and lacked a husband. She was also desperate to bear a child. While far from hideous, Agribel had lost many potential suitors over the years to her younger and decidedly more attractive sister, Annabel, who discarded them until she found one that satisfied her tastes, Heras. But Agribel's moment to command the desire of a suitor had finally arrived, and a king no less.

Over dinner on the third evening, the innocent and warmhearted queen sat gracefully at the far end of the long table in the great dining hall. She giggled at the king's witty jokes and was impressed by his grand tales of conquests in lands far beyond. She needed a brief break from giggling and gasping so much, so she proceeded to commence supper. She first took a sip of the delightfully fine wine, followed by a bite of the devilishly delicious pontaccio. She suddenly passed out. Her meal had been seasoned with a mild dose of poison, enough to leave her temporarily unconscious. The king's servants dragged her away while he finished his dinner in solitude.

The queen woke, bound and chilled, with her temperature continuing to drop. As she regained consciousness, she scanned the chamber desperately. She was alone. She looked down at her hands and saw they were bound by shackles; she was secured to the chamber wall. She looked closer and noticed that something exuded continuously from her hands. She followed the white smoke up her arms and then came to the realization that it emanated from all areas of her skin, even her face.

She noticed something off to the side that rested on top of an immaculately structured bureau. It was surrounded with the same smokelike substance. It was an elegant glass container lined with innumerable diamonds. It enclosed a heart that beat as if it were alive. She immediately looked down at herself. She noticed no marks or bruises, but realized at that moment that she felt no heart beat beneath her bosom.

She began to cry uncontrollably, with no discernible words.

The king of Villanis entered the room, with his ring removed, and looked as handsome yet devious as ever.

She screamed at him, "What have you done to me!"

He was heartless in his reply. "Don't worry, my queen, we are going to take over the world. But in order to do so, we cannot carry the burden of having a heart; I rid myself of mine long ago. You shall become ruthless like me. I will control the element of fire. You shall command the element of ice. No one will be able to stop us, not even the phoenix dragons, even if they can harness the elements naturally at will. The ring you see here in my palm was forged by the phoenix dragon of fire Pyro. I lost all my men as they attempted to bind him *just* so I could retrieve a link from the chain around its neck. Just one link would give me the pure power of its fire. As my men distracted the dragon, I managed to slash and separate a link from its chain. After I grabbed a hold of it, the phoenix dragon immediately turned its attention toward me and spit its fierce flames directly at me. I didn't perish as my men did. As I held the link, I became empowered. The chain link reduced to the size of a ring and allowed me to wear it at will.

"Unbeknownst to me, however, its fire was filled with pure evil, pure darkness. I have served *him* ever since. I have served the one all fear. Each time I wore it, a portion of my soul fled me permanently, until none remained. I am but a puppet of *his*. A leading puppet is still a puppet nonetheless. *He* has afforded me some indulgences, however. There is a reason why the phoenix dragons reside on faraway islands that are riddled with dangers once you make landfall. Within each of them resides a terribly powerful force that is ruled by one of the five elemental lords. They have commanded the attention of ambitious men throughout the lands, far and wide, for ages. While they lie dormant, they remain vulnerable. I retrieved one, as it had just awakened and was not at full strength. Once I wore the ring, it was mine to control. I've had recent success with obtaining another, which you shall soon hold and rule by my side. In time, there will be no opposition left. And you will not miss that beating heart of yours. As long as it beats, you shall suffer. I possess the key to your freedom, though I must warn you, it's a freedom you shall never have again. You shall do as I command. You are *my* puppet now."

He flashed his ring and placed it on his finger. He appeared as the monster he was alleged to be. He consumed the light in the room, which left her surrounded by nothing but darkness. He suddenly burst into flames and lit the room with a hue a deep crimson. Agribel screamed in agony as the heat began to melt her frosted skin.

The Fire King turned his back and began to walk away. Several servants entered the room as he spoke his final words. "Don't worry. Soon you will return north. You shall live as long as I have your loyalty, but you shall suffer just as long."

He disappeared from view as his servants emerged from the darkness with a large frozen cage on iron wheels. They surrounded, unshackled, and tossed her into the frozen prison. Having locked her in the cage, the servants began to wheel her off, away from the steaming temperatures of the king's castle, which were almost unbearable while his ring was worn.

As the queen of Belghan was carted off farther away, she observed the faint beat of her heart slow with each moment that passed. She finally broke her silence and began to scream. She could not be heard beyond her prison, as the thick glass was soundproof. She hit her palm against the glass repeatedly with her still-hardening skin. The drop in her temperature accelerated within the frozen prison.

She began to lose her will to fight and dropped to the floor. She noticed a scepter on the floor and crawled toward it slowly. She grabbed it with curiosity. Her desire to resist suddenly ceased entirely. The scepter had been fused by the freezing breath of the phoenix dragon of ice, Frostbite, and began to fuse to her soul. A sinister laugh soon thrust from her mouth uncontrollably. Tears were brought to her eyes; however, they froze almost immediately. Agribel's transformation was complete.

Several years passed. The powers that controlled the scepter had completely overtaken the queen and in turn the kingdom of

Belghan. Much changed throughout the lands of the North. With the assistance of a new ally that dwelled underground as it illuminated a hue of murky green from its eyes, she lifted her palace high in the sky, where the air was cooler and much easier to freeze. It also gave her distance from the lowly villagers who complained and submitted luxurious requests, as she thought them to be, such as food and shelter.

She became increasingly colder, not just physically but also toward the people of her kingdom. She created new laws that legalized child labor. She also controlled the memories of those who resided in her kingdom. She wiped away their happy memories. They would not remember life before the new world order. There were to be no memories of the once-good times that preceded her new reign of terror.

Child labor became prevalent over the years, as she needed to keep her palace as cold as possible to maintain her power but warm enough to keep the children able-bodied. The children's memories were much easier to manipulate, though not permanent, as a hug filled with a parent's love could break the spell. Eventually she built a force field around the palace grounds to ensure the coldness could not escape. The power of the sun, however, could not be contained so easily and managed to melt the ice continuously, though at a slower pace. She created an exhaust for the melted ice, which is the waterfall that flows from the sky and into the Larris River below. The river channels through the villages until the far end of the lush jungle lands.

With the power of her scepter, she tamed the phoenix dragon of ice. She captured it during its dormancy cycle as the Fire King taught her. She first froze over the palace and then transported over the phoenix dragon. It was a natural fit to her frozen palace, and she made sure it was as cold as possible to accommodate them both. Frostbite woke from its slumber in chains it was unable to free itself from. She must heed caution, however. Two other phoenix dragons had broken dormancy and will search for the others when they have built up their strength.

Agribel developed a nickname over time, the Ice Queen. She actually liked it, and it stuck, though she was initially taken aback and froze the offenders who whispered the treason-filled words. She stored them in her secret chamber, where their bodies rested as their souls were absorbed by her scepter and continued to give it more power.

She approached her middle ages, childless, and always had the burning desire for a son to succeed her one day as king of Belghan. She arranged for the kidnapping of a young prince from Buv're. A young prince who lacks the title because he is a bastard is a prince nonetheless. With her own memories distorted by the hatred that had been nursed within her heartless being, she kidnapped the child who was born of a princess and a great wizard who almost defeated the Fire King. She did not realize she had kidnapped the child who was destined to lead the war that would end in her demise.

Dahlia finally snapped from her trance, and her clairvoyant flashes ceased. Her eyes returned to normal. She gazed upon the others, whose mouths were wide open but filled with silence.

Act III
A New
Beginning

Jonathan Rivera

XXII: On the Brink of War

Its irritated eyes began to soothe as the winds slowed. It remained frightened, however, as these were unfamiliar grounds. The mass of land had ascended and reached the palace grounds. It left the cub far away from home, but not without friendly paws nearby.

The nimble leopards removed their claws from the depths of the mackelroy trees they had clung to for the duration of their ascension. It was time to move. The leopards quickly descended the sturdy trees and weaved quietly throughout the jungle that was native to the lift. They tracked the royal guards to the far end. The Chief stopped at the impenetrable gate and spoke the command. It began to rise and revealed a dark, lengthy tunnel.

The Chief entered the shadowed tunnel and retrieved an unlit torch just a few paces farther. He lit it and instructed William and Number Two to stay close behind as they made their way through the labyrinth of tunnels. As they began to walk, the gate behind them started to close and left little opportunity for the leopards. They raced quietly on their padded paws and managed to squeeze through as their tails brushed between the gate and rocky surface beneath.

The leopards hid among the shadows and made sure to move and breathe cautiously in order to maintain their silence. The Chief slowed his pace, as did the others. Ahead of them was a congregation of forsaken soldiers stuck between realms as they faded and flickered.

"Halt," whispered the Chief to the others. Their steps ceased almost immediately. "We must wait for the goblin."

The Chief gazed upon the ghostlike beings, which were unusually active. They normally gathered in small groups in isolated sectors of the underground network. As they flickered less frequently, it was clear that they were attempting to rejoin the world of the living. They had begun to draw in the remainder of their souls from the Forsaken Fortress as they reanimated and walked about frantically. William had been spooked since they attempted to claim his life. The Chief afforded him no comfort as he stood next to him.

"*What* is Her Majesty up to?" whispered the Chief apprehensively.

The leopards halted in their tracks as one of them slipped on a loose rock. The Chief's head turned swiftly. He stared into the darkness and saw a pair of glistening eyes suspended above the ground. One of the leopards must not have closed its eyes in time. It had been spotted. Or so it thought.

Pug emerged from the darkness, made its way past the leopards on either side, and stopped at the feet of the Chief. After Pug bowed awkwardly before him, it whispered to the Chief in an odd voice that trembled.

The Chief replied as he looked toward the rear of the tunnel, "OK, then. We shall not keep Her Majesty waiting any longer."

Pug limped several paces as the others remained in place, and started to glow a hue of murky jade. He rambled in a tongue unknown to the others. A rumble followed the foreign words, and the tunnels began to shift. William lost his balance during the sudden shift and was knocked unconscious as his head hit the ground.

William's clouded eyes opened.

A glimmer of two green slivers appeared in the distant darkness, and subsequently four more would. The slivers began to expand from their centers and became huge, bulbous orbs. With a murky jade hue that illuminated the cavern far into the distance, they finally had visibility of their surroundings.

"Who disturbs my slumber?" echoed with a rumble throughout the cavern.

William looked at the others. They struggled to remain afloat as he fought the weight of his own heavy clothing.

Jacob yelled, "Everyone, take off your coats! We need to lighten our weight as much as possible!"

"*Answer me!*" The massive cavern rumbled once again.

Pippy yelled out, "Hey, guys! Look below. Do you see what I'm seeing?"

There was a long pause before anyone answered, but one by one, they affirmed. There was a bright blue illumination about twenty feet below that became increasingly larger and brighter and appeared to be in the form of a bubble. After he focused, William realized that John was at the center, unconscious as he barely breathed.

"What's…ahhhhhh!" William cringed as he suffered from a sharp headache.

The headache subsided, and he opened his eyes again.

John was suspended several feet above the murky waters. The bright blue outline around his body slowly faded. It appeared as if his eyes had absorbed the energy as they became increasingly bluer and brighter. His heavy coat exploded into shreds from his body and afforded him mobility.

Arachno backed up farther. The creature prepared for the battle of its ancient life and released a war cry. It charged forward from above. It spewed forth acid profusely and imposed tremors on the cavern, which released hundreds of rocks to rain upon John. In the distance, the kids raced into a nearby shelter and protected themselves as the debris fell. Meanwhile, John remained unmoved as the acid flew past him and the rocks came within inches of him.

Arachno was desperate. Over the thousands of years that it had lived in this world, there was no one, not man nor creature who had survived its wrath, except for one. Arachno dug its claws violently into the ceiling of the cavern and soon hurled a boulder toward John, a massive boulder thrice his size. The boulder should have crushed him in an instant. However, it suddenly halted in midair.

John was face-to-face with the boulder as the thick air brushed past him and ruffled his short, scruffy hair before it crashed into the water beneath him. It caused a large ripple effect that reached the platform where the kids remained hidden. With a motion of his hand, John lifted the boulder above his head, high enough so Arachno could see him.

John exclaimed, "My friends call me John…But *you* can call me Midwa!"

Arachno shouted back, "No…It can't be! The Fire King…he…he destroyed you!"

John spoke no more words. He cocked his arm and then shot the boulder forward at full speed. Arachno had barely enough time to let out a shriek. The cavern shook to its core from the impact, which caused hundreds upon hundreds of rocks to crash into the waters and raised the water level to within inches of the platform.

The greatest impact was imminent, as Arachno's final efforts to escape from behind the boulder would soon cease. The murky jade orbs faded and escaped from its dying body. The energy flew to the ceiling of the cavern and was absorbed by a nearby creature.

"Wait, what was *that?*" William whispered to himself. He saw that Jacob had seen it, but he did not warn the others of what he had just seen.

Arachno's claws went limp, and its dead weight proved too much. Arachno fell no differently than a meteor would crash into land. The rumble resounded throughout the cavern. The rocky spiderlike creature crashed into the pile of fallen rocks below and created a mound high into the cavern. This raised the water level up to the kids' chest and even higher for Joey.

In the distance, William saw John still hovering in the air; however, his eyes quickly dimmed. Seconds later, the bright blue illumination faded, and he fell limp and descended into the waters below.

"William! Come and give me a hand! We have to dive below and get John!"

"OK, Jacob, I'm coming!"

They swam as fast as they could toward the splash. They submerged far below the surface before they latched on to John. William noticed a pair of murky jade eyes that glowed at the bottom of the cavern waters.

"Ahhhhhh!" William cringed again as he suffered from another, even sharper headache.

It suddenly stopped, and his eyes opened.

Jacob yelled out, "OK, everyone, we need to send two at a time!"

William pulled up Freddie as Tony pulled up Ivy. Tony hoped to gain her favor as he saved her life. Norman and Pippy were next. As Freddie pulled up Pippy, it took the collective effort of the others to lift Norman. Only Jacob and John remained below. John jumped up and barely reached the ledge. Tony pulled him up. The rumble finally pushed the mound's stability past its breaking point, and it suddenly collapsed a few feet. Jacob hung by the hand of John, who was unable to lift him even with Tony's assistance behind him.

"Wait...this isn't what happened..." William said as he began to back up.

"Help me!" Jacob yelled again.

William continued to back up but was stopped as he bumped into the group of the others, who blocked his path as the cavern was about to collapse.

Tony stood and turned around. He left John to struggle as he spoke. "What *did* happen, William?" As he faced him, his eyes began to glow murky jade. He recognized the glow.

"What's going on?" William said with a petrified voice.

As he turned around, the entire group stood in his path. Their eyes began to glow murky jade as well.

"Let me out of here!" he yelled to them as he tried to push his way through, but they pushed him back to the edge with Tony and John.

John then turned around as he struggled to lift Jacob. "I saved your life, William! I tried to save Jacob. I really did!" His eyes had a glow of murky jade as well. Something was wrong, as his eyes usually illuminated bright blue.

Tony then spoke. "Did you try *your* best, William? We know you hated Jacob. We knew you could never forgive him for what his father did to you and yours. So, tell me, William. Did you try your best to save Jacob? Or did you want him to—"

"Let me go! Please, I'll do anything!" he yelled desperately as he interrupted Tony.

"Anything?" Tony asked with the glow in his eyes.

"Yes, *anything!*" William replied in desperation.

Tony pushed him over the edge.

"Aaaahhhhhh!" William's yell echoed, but his fall was stunted. Jacob managed to grab his hand as he hung from John's hand with the other. All the others looked down on them with their glowing eyes as the cavern continued to rumble.

Jacob spoke. "It seems we have swapped positions, William. Why did *you* not pull when the others did? Why did *you* let me die? I trusted you more than the others. We were like brothers! You must speak the truth, or your precious Penelope will suffer a terrible fate."

William yelled, "But I didn't! I—"

"Stop lying to yourself!" grumbled Jacob in a frustrated voice that did not belong to him. His eyes and his mouth opened wide and became voids as a distant voice spoke.

"Good will prevail. The weak shall—"

"No, please, no…please…No, no, no…" William spoke desperately.

"Fall!" the voice said as Jacob released his grip from William's hand.

The descent was quick. The others above faded.

Impact was imminent.

"Ahhhhhh!" William cringed again as he suffered from a severe pain in his head for the duration of his fall.

Everything faded to black.

"Are you OK?" asked the Chief nervously as he shook William anxiously. "You hit your head hard."

William opened his eyes. "I don't know…I think so." He looked up and saw Pug, who looked directly into his eyes. The murky jade glow in his eyes suddenly dimmed.

Pug escorted them along the tunnels. It was not the direct path they expected, but the Chief assumed it was because of the dangers of the forsaken army, which had begun to restore and could be unpredictable.

"We're almost there." The Chief spoke. "Watch your step. There was an accident along this tunnel just days ago. Pug restored it as best he could so we can cross it."

As they walked along the bridge, William realized immediately that it had been the cavern where the battle with Arachno had taken place. But more importantly to him, it had been the place where Jacob had fallen into the darkness below.

Maybe I could have done more, William thought. *I tried my best. I struggled to lift them. They just wouldn't budge! That's how I remember it at least.* He looked below into the darkness beyond the rocky frame of Arachno among the rubble. As he scanned the shadows below, he noticed the glimmers of two eyes. After he blinked his own, the glimmers were no longer there. He no longer knew what to believe as reality. The mysteries of this place tormented him. He needed to get out of there as soon as possible.

There was a noticeable drop in heat as they emerged from the cavern, and it sent a shock to their bodies. It was not long ago when they had to tread through the deep snow. It had not appeared so cold from the jungle below, but the cover of the previous night shrouded the frozen temperatures.

They hastily made their way to the stairway that led to the main entrance of the palace. Before Pug moved to return to the depths of the underground, the leopards made their move and snuck to either side of them and out of view. They trailed the royal guards as the hiss of the wind masked the faint crunches of their soft steps in the snow.

The main gate of the palace opened. Her Majesty welcomed the cold winds. Moments later the door slammed, but not before the leopards could sneak in unseen as all of the attention had already been turned toward her private prison chamber above, from which shrieks had echoed for the past hour. The leopards ran off to either side and into the shadows.

The palace lacked a sufficient count of dim-witted but watchful guards. A significant majority of them had been scattered throughout the villages below. They either nursed injuries or were unconscious.

As the Chief advanced, he arrived at an empty throne. The Ice Queen was absent and preoccupied. The Chief commanded one of the inferior guards to request Her Majesty's presence. The palace guard mumbled to himself as he nervously went to retrieve the queen. He raced up the steps to her private prison chamber.

A loud screech echoed throughout the Ice Palace, followed by the slam of a heavy gate. Her Majesty emerged from her chamber and began to storm down the stairs as she stared at the Chief. She noticed they were light in company, with only William and Number Two by his side. She expected bad news, as they had returned too soon.

The Ice Queen's heavy steps clashed against the chilled palace floor as she approached her throne. With a grimace on her face, she spoke no words. She stared at her scepter and then each of them individually. Her gaze nearly pierced them.

No one was able to return eye contact for more than a brief moment. She looked worse than ever, as she no longer appeared to resemble a living being. She truly lived up to her moniker, the Ice Queen. She was entirely composed of ice, with the exception of her black eyes, which were the only remnants of her former self.

"Where are they?" She spoke softly as she rolled her eyes.

"Your Majesty, they…" The Chief began to speak; however, his hesitation revealed his intentions to offer excuses.

"*Where are they?*" She abruptly interrupted.

"The leopards overpowered us…"

"I did not ask about the leopards! I sent almost the entire army of palace guards to your aid. *Why are those peasants not captured?*" yelled the Ice Queen.

Suddenly there was another screech from her private chamber above. This caught the attention of all in the room, and their eyes shifted immediately toward the piercing sound, with the exception of the Ice Queen. She appeared physically drained and noticeably older as life fled her.

She screamed, "*Answer me!*"

The Chief replied, "We lost them, but…"

She clearly lost her patience from their incompetence and interrupted yet again. "*But what?* What could you possibly tell me that will not make me want to—" She paused unexpectedly. "William, come forward." Her voice once again seemed calm. "It appears you will have your…*reunion* with your younger sister after all."

The Chief nervously raised his voice. "Your Majesty, please. We have the heir of Sandriver." He instructed the royal guard to reveal the large cub.

This intrigued the Ice Queen. Her cold eyes opened wide as she turned toward the royal guard. He slowly revealed the cub, which at the sight of her, began to whimper. So empty were her eyes that it cast no reflection of the cub as she gazed upon it.

"Well…it appears you are not a complete waste of my time." The queen addressed the group. "I shall raise him alongside…the *other* one. Well done."

"Your Majesty, what of the others? It appears John may have crossed the desert, and possibly the sea as well," the Chief replied.

Taking a deep breath, the queen looked at them, speaking in a calm voice. "Your incompetence matters no more. *It* is almost complete. We will soon have an army that cannot be defeated, and under *my* control. *All* will fall before me, even the dark lords."

In the background, the leopards looked on. They looked at one another nervously, as they knew their moment of opportunity was about to pass. They signaled a strategy to one another, indicating the tall statues positioned behind the Ice Queen's throne. If they could knock it over onto her without being seen, they would eliminate her and make easy work of the guards, who were low in numbers.

"Guards, I think we have waited long enough. Reveal the trespassers!" the Chief said.

The leopards were anxious as Number Two once again concealed the heir of Sandriver. Opportunity had almost dissipated entirely. They set in motion their risky plan and prepared to take swift steps along the shadows. But their throats were met with blades before they could take even just one. They had been so focused on the heir that they did not pay attention to the royal guard reserves that had snuck behind them from the shadows as they awaited their cue.

They poked the leopards with the dull edge of their blades and forced them forward toward the throne. The leopards growled with frustration as they looked aggressively back at the royal guards.

The Chief spoke. "Pug tipped us off, Your Majesty. They have been trailing us for some time. As if they could actually—"

Suddenly one of the leopards sprang off to the side. It lost some steps from the frosted ground but managed its way around the rear of the statue. The young male leopard lacked the strength to push over the tall statue itself. This gave the Ice Queen enough time to remove herself from her throne. She was clearly upset and free of patience, though no one could recall when she had not been.

The Ice Queen looked at the Chief. "Take care of this now. Or must I do *everything*? Where is the other one?"

The female leopard had slipped away, as all the guards were distracted and had not paid attention to her. Unbeknownst to them, she had already made her way around to the rear of the statue to assist the male leopard. She signaled that the queen was no longer on the throne. They adjusted the angle toward the queen, and the statue began to plunge. The female leopard quickly ran around to the opposite end and suddenly emerged with a growl to capture all attention. It worked. They all stared at the leopard as she raced toward the queen.

"Stop it now!" yelled the Ice Queen.

A royal guard jumped between them with his blade extended, and the female leopard changed directions sharply and ran through a gap. However, as all the attention was on the female leopard, the male suddenly emerged from behind the queen and leaped with his jaws open wide. She would pay for her unfathomable crimes; however, not on this day. The queen looked behind as she heard the heavy breath and extended her scepter. A burst of frost exploded from its end toward the young male leopard midleap, but not before it absorbed his soul. He was frozen instantly and crashed against the chilled ground intact.

All of the guards turned their attention toward the queen and yelled, "Your Majesty!"

William looked on with anxious eyes. The fate of Penelope rested with the queen. But it was too late. The statue crashed down directly onto her extended arm. It sliced her forearm off cleanly. She did not yell in pain, as she could not feel any. No blood flowed from where the limb was once connected. It shattered among the rubble of the statue as she stood there.

She looked at the others and screamed, "What are you looking at? *Get the other one!*"

There was a yelp of grievance from the female leopard as she witnessed the demise of her younger brother. The guards tried to chase her, but they did not move well either on the frosted surface. The leopard continued to slip as she weaved throughout the various statues of the great hall. She caused the guards, both royal and inferior, to slip as well and break formation. There was a doorway in the distance. It appeared to descend into darkness, but she determined there was no way she could fare worse there.

The Ice Queen recovered her scepter as the leopard quickly changed direction and raced toward and through the palace guards. She sprinted toward the dark spiral stairwell. The Ice Queen yelled in frustration. She lifted her scepter with her less favorable arm and pointed it toward the stairwell, aiming for the leopard. She had never used the scepter with this arm.

She projected a burst of frost from her scepter as she had to the other leopard. A slight delay caused it to miss its mark. As the leopard stumbled down the stairway into the darkness, the frost exploded on the large group of palace guards who were in pursuit. They all froze immediately and slid into the stairway with their momentum. The guards created a loud crash as they made impact with the cold dungeon walls and steps. Their souls were absorbed by the scepter.

The Ice Queen spoke, emotionless. "Well, that's one way of doing it, I suppose. I hope it enjoys what it finds down there. Chief, bring the heir to my private chamber. It can rest with that *wretched* little girl. *What are you all staring at?*"

The few palace guards who remained looked away, uncertain of what to do. She pointed to the Chief with her incomplete arm. The frozen air that surrounded it suddenly orbited it and rapidly transformed it back into a complete arm of ice.

"Report to my chamber at one hour past the break of dawn, and not one minute later!" she yelled.

The path to the dungeon was blocked off. The female leopard was able to get to firm footing at the base of the spiral stairway. She noticed torches in the distance that lit up the area as she approached cautiously. She was free of the palace guards; however, she was among others at the far end.

The female leopard overheard a young voice beyond the several swaying silhouettes but was unable to determine its origin. It became more passionate as it continued. The figures that surrounded it began to return chants of "Yeah!" The energetic interaction continued for several moments.

"She must pay for what she's done to all of us! She must pay for what she's done to our families!" The young one looked at Rob and Joey. "William must pay for the lies he's told! He is responsible too!"

Several chants echoed throughout the dungeon: "William must pay," "John must prevail," and "The Ice Queen must fall! Melt her! Melt her! Melt her!"

The young captive once again had her memories and remembered all of the evil stories her parents had told her about the wicked queen. She shared them with all of the young captives. Her speech inspired them to prepare for a rebellion.

The huddle broke, and she began to walk through the center of the crowd and eventually emerged from the other end. It was one of the youngest prisoners, Pippy. Fired up, she convinced the others that it was time to fight back.

They had an advantage. The guards were scarce, as most had been sent to the lands below and were no longer serviceable to Her Majesty. As she continued to walk down the aisle of the dungeon, she encouraged the others, Stingy Salina, Manny Petty, Messy Jesse, and Nameless and Aimless included. Pippy stopped in her tracks as she saw two glistening eyes in the shadows.

She continued to stare at the shadows. The orbs began to approach and slowly revealed themselves along with their surrounding frame. Pippy stood her ground. She felt courageous. Her mother had filled her with love, and the fellowship had filled her with hope. The leopard revealed itself and continued to walk toward Pippy as the kids behind her took a few paces backward.

The leopard was at Pippy's feet. She was one of the smaller kids, but so was the leopard. With tension in the air, the kids did not know what to anticipate from the leopard, as none of them had ever encountered one. The leopard sniffed her as she circled, and eventually stopped after two revolutions. She looked up at her and purred. She even licked her hand. The leopard knew she could not save the heir herself, but perhaps they could work together.

Pippy stroked the leopard, which purred in return. She'd always had the gift of communication with animals. As she leaned in, Pippy began to speak to the leopard. The others could not understand what she said, as she spoke barely beyond a whisper. They could, however, hear the purr of the leopard. Her words appeared to comfort the feline.

Pippy turned around toward the others, who looked at her in astonishment. She proceeded to walk along with the leopard. The young prisoners backed away as they passed through. After they reached the end, Pippy turned around.

"This is Katina, proud member of the Northern Leap. She has just lost her brother in the great hall in an attempt to rescue the heir of Sandriver, future warrior king of the jungle and one of the protectors of the seven realms. We must help save the heir. In return, we will have the loyalty of the Northern Leap."

The kids roared with cheers. Morale was high.

XXIII: Forsaken Fortress

"He's still not breathing!" yelled a nervous voice.

"Check for his heartbeat!" another said.

"We've just made landfall. We need him back now!" said the final desperate voice.

"What's happening?" asked a voice from above the group of desperate kids surrounding the motionless body.

An elderly voice replied, "You are stuck in the plane that links the living and the dead. You have yet to cross. But you must project yourself back into your body soon before it's too late."

"Show me how," the young voice responded to Midwa.

"It will be dangerous, John. There is no guarantee which one of us will take over your body. If you are not strong enough, you will be stuck here while I alone take over your being. It may be too risky. Are you strong enough, young one?"

"My friends need me. Everyone needs me. I must stop *her*. Yes, I'm strong enough."

"OK. Focus on your friends, on your love for them, and on their love for you. Allow the positive energy to overwhelm you."

"Wait...you will join me, won't you?" John spoke with doubt.

Midwa answered, "I will try my best. If you do not cross, I will carry on for you, but your friends will not recognize you. They will see you, but your body will merely be a vessel for me. We must enter together at precisely the same time. Are you sure you are ready?"

John took a deep breath. "Yes." He began to focus on his friends. He thought about how much he had been through with them, how much love they had for him, how much love he had for them. Then he focused on none other than Ivy. He was suddenly surrounded by an unfamiliar energy, the energy of love. It was a powerful force. He felt himself fade alongside Midwa.

"Midwa...*Midwa?*" he yelled, but his voice grew increasingly faint as it echoed.

"He's breathing!" yelled an anxious voice.

John's eyes opened suddenly as he gasped for more air. Two more voices blended in relief.

"You scared us!"

Ivy hit him in the shoulder as she wept. "Don't you *ever* do that again to me, *OK?*" She then gave him a big hug. He was overwhelmed by the passion of it as the others joined in.

The spark of hope for the fellowship had been rekindled. They knew the journey ahead would not get any easier. The others knew that they would not be able to complete it without John, but they did not realize that he would need them even more.

Concerned for their safety as he looked upon the fortress just beyond the shore, John said to the others, "It's going to be really difficult, guys. Maybe you should wait out here for me."

Freddie yelled, "No way! We're in this together!"

Tony and Ivy echoed the same sentiments.

Still scared for the others, John replied, "OK, but once we get to the main gate, I need you to wait outside. I need to do this alone. I can't risk any of you...dying. I can't carry that burden again."

Tony replied, "No, mate. United we stand. Divided we fall."

John felt reinvigorated and agreed.

They looked upon the castle beyond the great wall that stretched far left and far right. There was no way around it. They would have to scale it in order to enter the Forsaken Fortress. As they approached the wall, John looked back to see how far he had come from the Ice Palace. But he could barely see anything beyond the black smoke that surrounded almost the entire fortress. It had never appeared so dark. They were afforded an occasional peek when the fiery lava breached the smoke.

John scanned the large stone wall but could not locate a path to scale it, not wide nor narrow. The large stones appeared to be scalable themselves with enough caution; however, it seemed to be simpler if he just elevated them up to the top himself. The others concurred.

"Hold on tight," John said as he illuminated.

They began to levitate and ascended toward the upper limit of the wall. They were soon able to see beyond it. As they drew closer to the solid stone, a large boulder that erupted crimson was launched in their direction and approached quickly. John panicked and lost his illumination. It caused the others to drop as he swung Ivy toward the wall away from the crimson. His focus on her left him and the others to fall. Tony was able to grab on to the ledge of the wall. He was strong enough to support Freddie, who barely clung on to the crevices of the large stones.

"Hurry up and climb up before I lose my grip!" Tony yelled to Freddie.

As John's eyes flickered during his fall, Ivy sprinted over to Tony, and she watched the flaming boulder strike the sea. John illuminated once again and halted his fall. He flashed toward the top of the wall to assist the others, but as he reached the top, another flaming boulder was launched at him. He dove out of the way, away from the others. However, yet another crimson boulder flew toward him.

"Power down, John!" Tony yelled as Ivy relieved Freddie from his grip.

John listened to the advice and powered down as he barely escaped a boulder that managed to warm his feet. It worked. The projectiles ceased.

The defenses of the Forsaken Fortress had been upgraded since the last battle with Midwa. John would need to limit his illumination, as it seemed to instigate the crimson boulders. He would need to leave himself exposed as the others were. He looked below at the labyrinth before him. He was not confident that they would make it through the labyrinth powerless.

They stared into the barren labyrinth. Faint shrieks of damned souls echoed throughout. Tony had serious doubts, and the others felt no different. But they had no choice. They had to push forward.

Tony spoke up as he looked around. "There are bow-and-arrows reserves everywhere. This is an archer's hold."

Ivy had already claimed a set herself. Freddie did as well, but it was too large for his small frame. They began to scale the sturdy wooden beams that protruded from the stone wall. The steps had been destroyed.

They reached the ground level. It was clear which direction they needed to proceed. There was only one entrance. However, it appeared to divide farther down the corridor. Tony instructed Freddie to ascend back to the top to see if he could determine the best route.

Freddie ascended the creaky steps hastily and was soon at the top. He created a mental map of the route. It appeared simple enough. Proceed down the corridor, right turn, right, straight, left, left, straight, right, straight, left turn. He recited it once more as a precaution to ensure he had memorized it.

"Proceed down the corridor, right turn, right, straight, right…Wait…it was just…Hold on. Let me start again. Down the corridor, right turn, left…what? This can't be! It keeps changing."

He yelled down to the others, but his yells rattled something that lurked below within the labyrinth. Louder shrieks followed. Freddie hurriedly descended the wooden beams.

He reached the bottom and whispered to the others, "It's impossible. The path keeps changing!"

"What are we supposed to do?" Tony was perplexed.

John answered, "Hang on." He illuminated his eyes dimly and was able to see beyond the stone walls that shifted within the labyrinth. "There is a faint trail of light guiding the path through. It's changing along with the wall, but at least we'll be able to see it from within."

"I can guide you from above," Freddie suggested.

Tony replied, "No. We stick *together*."

A loud shriek followed.

Ivy finally spoke up. "But John, that's going to attract the attention of…whatever's out there!"

Tony jumped in. "Maybe. But we don't have much of a choice, do we? We could be roaming in there forever, or at least until that *thing* shrieking finds us."

"Tony's right. Who knows what's out there? Everything appears blurred." John shared their concern.

The fellowship concurred.

Freddie attempted to recall the directions. "Each time it began with a right turn, but I'm not sure after that. It kept changing."

Tony spoke. "OK, let's move. Stay close together no matter what."

They proceeded into the entrance and walked cautiously down the corridor. A force closed behind them, and they no longer heard the ambient noise of the fortress. Freddie became scared at the sound of a mild shriek and ran back to try to exit, but as he reached the entrance, he felt a shock and flew back toward the others. He managed himself to his feet, but he was frazzled. Another shriek followed. This one was closer than the last.

John was nervous, as he would need to stay illuminated, which attracted the attention of the shrieks. He would need to remain as dim as possible.

"Come on, Freddie," Tony said as he ruffled his hair for motivation.

Ivy spoke. "There's only one way out now."

Freddie regained his energy to speak. "Well, technically there are an unlimited number of—"

Tony interrupted him. "We get it, Mr. Fixer. We have to stay quiet now. We don't want to attract any unnecessary attention."

They reached the end of the corridor and proceeded to make the first right. There were no shrieks. John kept his eyes barely illuminated. It seemed to be a good strategy. They soon reached an intersection and were faced with a decision: left, straight, or right.

John spoke up again. "It looks like we need to make another right turn."

They proceeded accordingly.

"Whoa! Hold on. It's shifting. We need to wait until it stops."

It would be a few moments before it stopped. John's nerves caused his eyes to inadvertently illuminate brightly.

John spoke. "Hey, guys…are you seeing what I'm seeing?"

Tony and the others became nervous as they began to hear shrieks, and they became louder.

Tony yelled, "*Your eyes!* What do you see, John? What do we do?"

John's voice matched Tony's tone. "They're coming toward us…all of them!"

"*All of who?*" Ivy asked.

The walls suddenly halted their shift.

"The forsaken!" John screamed. "To the right, *now!*"

The forsaken approached from the other corridors. "Wait! Go back! To the left corridor! They're no longer there!"

"John! We can't see anything! Help us see!" Tony was desperate.

John replied, "Come to me and grab on!"

Tony, Ivy, and Freddie did not hesitate. They latched on to his arms.

"Hold on!" John commanded. He decided the only way to proceed was to illuminate completely. He encapsulated them as he did once before, in the cavern, when the forsaken soldiers attempted to claim their lives. They were relieved that they were no longer blind to what chased them, but horrified of the monsters they saw. The shrieks came from the blurred mouths of forsaken souls who were stuck in between planes. They approached at a frightening pace. Their eyes erupted violently as they alternated between crimson and jade. It was as if there was an internal struggle of which hue would take over.

Suddenly the castle projected boulders of fire toward them. The explosions did nothing to penetrate the field surrounding the labyrinth. The explosions lit the damned souls beneath and terrified the kids further.

"Down the left corridor!" John instructed.

They backpedaled and sprinted down the corridor, which no longer enclosed the forsaken souls.

"Straight!" John continued, and they sprinted forward. "Right!" The souls maintained a terrifying pace behind them as their shrieks increased in volume. "Wait! Another shift! OK, straight! I see the castle gate!"

The damned souls had gained ground. They were one lengthy corridor away from the exit when there was an unexpected shift in the stone-walled corridors. The walls moved, and the forsaken were closed off from their trail. This was good news until several more appeared in another corridor in the opposite direction.

With her keen eyes, Ivy noticed an alternate route that was dimly lit. "Over there!"

They sprinted down the corridor and to the right. They once again had the exit in sight. They ran as hard as they could and finally reached the end and walked out of the labyrinth. In relief, they looked at one another with the same thought: *Wow. Now that was close!* It was close, but they had managed to escape.

In John's periphery, he noticed two boulders of flaming crimson blazing toward them. He gave it little thought when he pushed them back into the labyrinth. The walls shifted, and they were trapped yet again with the forsaken soldiers.

John felt that he had made the best call. They would not be able to survive the wrath of the flaming boulders. He was not sure whether he could either, but he stood a better chance without the others to feed from his energy.

He illuminated at full strength and focused on the boulders as they rapidly approached. He thrust himself forward and created a massive explosion of crimson and blue. It reached the far ends of the island country and was seen from as far as the Ice Palace.

Through the crimson that surrounded him, John could see yet another boulder hurl toward him. He remained in place and stopped it in midair. As it was suspended above the fortress, John turned his attention to one of the towers that appeared to project these balls of death, and he catapulted it forward. A huge explosion followed.

The Fire King was awake from his slumber.

XXIV: A Secret Weapon

Their heavy knocks did not capture the attention of Her Majesty. They arrived at her private prison punctually at one hour past the break of dawn as commanded, but she was not present.

"Your Majesty?" the Chief asked in his masculine voice as he pushed the door open and entered her chamber alongside William.

William looked around the familiar room. He noticed the large brewing pot and ten small cages that surrounded it. He had a brief flashback of the day they attempted to flee and solemnly thought, *We never stood a chance.* He looked closer at the cages. The heir of Sandriver lay in the corner cage, frightened as he purred. He noticed a figure within the shadows of the adjacent cage. He hadn't noticed it at first glance, as it did not move. The outline of the figure began to look familiar.

"Penelope?" William asked inquisitively.

There was no reply.

"*Penelope?*" William asked again a bit louder.

There was still no reply as the gate to Frostbite's lair creaked open. Two royal guards began to carry away the frozen body of his friend Norman.

The Ice Queen laughed as she looked at her scepter. "Well, I guess another one bites the *frost!* Ahahahaha. Halt with him at the door," she commanded the royal guards and then turned her head slowly as she spoke with a grin filled with pleasure. "Your sister *cannot* hear you."

William raced to the cage and began to yell, "Penelope! Penelope!" as he shook it. "*Penelope!*"

The shake finally captured the attention of the small figure in the corner, and it turned slowly toward William. Penelope had revealed herself. She was pale and weak. She suffered greatly, as she was unable to see or hear her surroundings.

"What have you done to her? I trusted you!" yelled William.

"You trusted *me*? You trusted your father as well, and where has that led you? I will *not* accept failure. I do not trust those who do not fear me. And *you* do not fear me *enough*! Otherwise you would not have lied to me!"

"I didn't lie! Please..." William spoke desperately.

"*Shut...up!*" she screamed as a shriek from Frostbite's lair permeated the frozen stone walls. "The fat rat told me *everything*." Her voice became somber as she walked over to the guards who waited beside Norman's frozen body. "And now...he's...gone..." She wept, and her mouth cringed for a long moment as she rubbed the ice before she broke into an uncontrollable laughter. "Ahahahahaha! Now his soul rests in my scepter along with all of the other stupid souls who have dared to cross me over the years. Guards, bring him with the others who have suffered the same fate!"

The Chief spoke up. "Your Majesty, please. They are both innocent."

The Ice Queen yelled, "Do not show sympathy for these peasants! *He* cannot replace your son!"

William looked upon the Chief, and it was all suddenly clear to him. The Chief had lost his son and tried to fill the void with his presence. He was not as coldhearted as it appeared at first. He had been forced to fulfill the many morally questionable deeds of Her Majesty in order to keep the rest of his family safe.

"My apologies, Your Majesty. It's just that…Sorry, it will not happen again," the Chief answered as his voice shook off the nerves from a moment ago.

She replied, "Of course it will not happen again!" A brief silence followed before she continued. "I *am* a fair and just queen! That has been my reputation for *many* years." She had become delusional over time.

There was another sudden shriek, this time much louder. Three successive ones followed. All were taken aback, with the exception of the Ice Queen, who remained unmoved. One final shriek from Frostbite's lair paved the way for silence.

The Chief answered as he looked at the gate entrance to Frostbite's lair, "Yes, of course you are, Your Majesty."

She continued. "I offer both of you a chance for redemption. You are to lead my army into the desert. You *must* make sure those wretched peasants do not return here. The power they carry must be destroyed!"

The Chief asked nervously, "Your Majesty, but how—"

"Do *not* interrupt me!" she yelled. "I command a great undead army, and their loyalty now lies with me. They await you in the underground. Report to Pug at once."

She had become so cold and delusional from the powerful ice enchantment that she betrayed the Fire King. The damned souls who roamed the labyrinth far away at the Forsaken Fortress just moments ago had been reformed in completion beneath the grounds of her palace. Unbeknown to her, however, she had just unintentionally saved Ivy, Tony, and Freddie. They had been desperately attempting to escape the pursuit of the forsaken within the labyrinth. Meanwhile, John unsuccessfully attempted to breach the enchanted barrier from all sides while the crimson boulders of fire launched at him continuously.

"Yes, Your Grace," the Chief replied.

"Hold out your hands, both of you," the queen said.

William and the chief nervously extended their hands. The queen extended her scepter to their hands and spoke an enchantment. "You have twenty-four hours to defeat them. If you fail, so will the beat of your heart, and so will your *precious* Penelope's, along with the remainder of both your families!" They were bound by their promise, whether they liked it or not.

"Yes, Your Majesty," they replied, nearly in unison.

"Now leave! I have afforded you a chance at redemption." The queen spoke as she pointed toward the gate that exited her chamber.

As the door of the Ice Queen's chamber slammed shut, she turned her attention to Penelope, who sat against the cage, helpless. She had no sympathy for the girl. She was the queen of ice.

"The sweet innocence of a child…that is not much of a sacrifice if you ask me," she thought aloud before she walked over to Penelope's cage and opened it. "Come here, my young one" she said to Penelope even though she could not hear. "You will not suffer much longer. Greatness requires sacrifice. *You* will soon be greatness, and many will be sacrificed. Most will fear you. We shall rule together, perhaps along with the future warrior king of the jungle." She looked at the heir as she spoke her last words.

She reached the gate to Frostbite's lair and waved her scepter to open it. She entered the lair as she helped along Penelope, who was too weak to manage herself. She dragged her feet on the floor as she struggled to maintain her balance. She was unaware of what was happening around her. As they entered, they were greeted by a mild shriek.

She placed Penelope alongside the dying phoenix dragon and spoke. "You shall both help me bring this world to new order. The dark lords shall rule no longer. I will rule the new world just as I have, fair and just.

"Aquaris, phoenix dragon of water, Terris, phoenix dragon of earth, and Aeris, phoenix dragon of wind, must all be defeated! But first you must defeat Pyro, phoenix dragon of fire, who protects *him*!"

The phoenix dragon of ice shrieked mildly as it died a bit more with each breath. The Ice Queen began to speak an ancient enchantment that she had recited several times over the past two days in order to coerce the rebirth of Frostbite. "Mostemius contik amus mosales."

There was a sudden shriek from the phoenix dragon. It was clearly in pain. Penelope could not hear the screams that exploded from her own mouth. The air that surrounded them began to form into drifting patterns. The life energy of Penelope had commenced the final stage of transfer to the phoenix dragon.

The Ice Queen held her scepter high, her eyes cold and empty. "Verasy pontai mucant fosale stocantis." Her enchantment continued along with the shrieks. The shrieks and screams were filled with agony until they ceased. Both Penelope and the dragon phoenix lay there lifeless.

The Ice Queen ceased her enchantment.

After several silent moments, the dragon phoenix suddenly opened its eyes. A burst of blinding energy surrounded Frostbite and Penelope, so bright that even the Ice Queen had to cover her eyes. Moments later, the lighting was back to normal, and before her stood

Frostbite. It was as dangerous as any creature to roam the world. The young girl no longer lay on the ground beside it.

The Ice Queen addressed the phoenix dragon. "Hello...Penelope."

The youthful shrieks permeated the walls of the Ice Palace. The phoenix dragon of ice had been reborn.

XXV: A Dark Room

The labyrinth was idle, the shrieks had ceased, and the fire no longer catapulted. They had survived relatively unscathed. As they approached the main gate, John led the others by a few paces from above. He descended as they reached the innumerable steps that led to the castle entrance. Though the dangers had subsided and made way for a sense of calm, they began their ascent with caution. After countless steps, they finally stood upon the gate. It was shut solid.

As John looked around, he was unable to see any weaknesses in the structure that could be breached. He scanned the castle a second time and noticed a shadowed figure in the largest window of the tallest tower. It was set against the backdrop of the darkest cloud in the sky.

The main gate suddenly creaked open, wide enough for the kids to slip through. Ivy had some trouble, as her bow and arrows were strapped to her back and briefly got caught; Freddie had given up with his attempts to make use of them. As they entered slowly, John attempted once again to persuade the others to wait at the entrance. He needed to do this alone. It was too risky for the others, as they did not possess the same powers Midwa had gifted him.

He felt confident as he welcomed them into the great hall, especially when he looked into Ivy's eyes, which never looked as impressed as when she returned his gaze. He was poised, proud even. He had accomplished much in a short period of time. However, as history had shown, victory did not favor the proud in these lands. And pride flowed through his blood as it once had flowed through his father's.

He explained his plan to the others and maintained his position that they would not follow. He would take care of the Fire

King alone. He suggested once again that they wait outside, but they continued to refuse.

"We're a fellowship, John," Tony insisted.

Ivy yelled, "I'm not letting you out of my sight!"

John insisted right back, "It's for your safety, guys. I can handle this. I have Midwa." After he insisted once more, the main gate slammed shut. They stood at the entrance of the great hall and looked around. The torches illuminated the hall, which exhibited its grandeur.

Heavy footsteps suddenly began to echo from afar. They could hear each one more pronounced than the last. Before long, the dark stairway at the end of the hall began to burn crimson, and a dark figure emerged. Its border burned crimson. It continued its deliberate approach and consumed all of the light in its path. The torches struggled to stay lit.

It was the Fire King.

"I can't see anything around us," whispered Tony. He hoped he would be heard only by John.

"Take the others and sneak over to the corner to your right. I'll distract him so he doesn't notice you," John whispered in reply.

John ran light-footed off to the side. He avoided immediate illumination to allow them enough time to reach the corner of safety. Soft with their steps, they reached a dark corner of the great hall, away from the crimson glow of the Fire King.

John switched on his powers and burned brightly in the opposite corner. He drew the attention of the crimson eyes, which began to approach the blue-lit corner. He had no strategy. He was unsure of how he would relieve the Fire King of his ring. He determined he would first need to exhaust him. A bright blue trail soon blazed toward the crimson-bordered shadow. John weaved around him and barely avoided the first strike before he flashed up the stairway. He stopped and overlooked the great hall from the second floor. The silence was broken only by the crackle of the crimson that blazed below.

Each waited for the other's next move. The Fire King decided. He would eliminate their strength before he dealt with the three cowards in the far corner of the hall. He lifted his arm and spoke in a foreign tongue. Something flashed toward his hand, and he placed it over his head. It was a helmet with crimson-lit horns. The Fire King ascended the steps, which had become unbearably hot in the brief moments his feet had settled upon them.

The young apprentice was nervous even though he believed that Midwa supported him from within. There was no longer an opportunity to turn back. He would soon be face-to-face with the Fire King, and he lacked a commendable strategy. As the crimson king exited the stairway and stood several yards away, John suddenly became dark. He was no longer proud and confident. He was scared, just as he had been in his dreams. He would need not only to face the Fire King, but he would need to defeat him. It was impossible. He decided to hide within the shadows.

John stood silent in the dark corner on a balcony that overlooked the great hall as he watched the Fire King walk farther away. He felt relieved, as he hoped to go unnoticed, but then he remembered that he'd promised to keep the others safe. He looked around as he tried to form a capable strategy, but it was difficult to find one as everything he could see had a faint crimson glow upon it.

He looked left and right, but nothing. He looked straight ahead. The Fire King approached as he grumbled calmly, "I can see you."

John needed to react. He illuminated almost immediately, but as soon as he did, the Fire King suddenly appeared in front of him and grabbed him by the neck. John was suspended in the air for several gasping moments as his blue glow flickered. It slowly faded as his struggles continued.

The Fire King enjoyed tormenting his victims before he exiled them to the Forsaken Realm, where they served its dark lord in purely evil ways. "*Who dares to breach my fortress?*" he asked.

John struggled to remove the searing hands. He was tossed to the upper limits of the great hall and crashed into a massive chandelier at the end of his brief flight. It rocked back and forth as his limbs dangled over the edges before it crashed hard against the surface below.

The Fire King leaped over the rail and joined John below with a loud crash of his own as the ground submitted to his weight. The ground beneath cracked as it pressed farther into the earth. He looked upon the mangled chandelier for a moment and determined the blue-lit boy was no longer a threat.

"What a shame. You did not even tell me your name," he thought aloud.

The crimson king turned his attention to the others who trembled in the distance. "You cannot hide from me. You cannot escape from me!" he yelled in their direction. He approached slowly but suddenly faded in and out, much closer with each successive appearance.

Ivy and Freddie held on to Tony as he spoke to them. "I'm sorry, guys. I wish—"

The Fire King suddenly crashed through the wall to their side. Ivy peeked through the large hole and saw the chandelier that had buried John just moments ago. It suddenly buried the crimson king. They looked back to where the mangled iron had originated from.

"Come on, guys. We don't have much time!" John gasped, his head half hung. His eyes faced them with a near-blinding light. He struggled to hold himself up, as his limbs were practically limp. Midwa did his best to feed his power to John, but he was becoming weaker and weaker himself.

They heard a commotion outside and turned back around. The chandelier had begun to levitate above the Fire King.

"Come on!" John yelled to them.

They sprinted toward the blue-lit boy. Ivy had dropped her bow. Along with Freddie, she held onto John firmly as they stood behind him, frightened. Tony tightened his fist as if he could inflict damage to the Fire King. John extended his arms and illuminated brightly as he protected them from the crimson king. He was not fearless, but he shared Tony's courage.

"Go over there!" he instructed as he pointed toward the corner opposite the stairway. "When he passes you and enters the stairway, run as fast you can and leave this dreadful place. Hurry!"

They complied immediately. Ivy retrieved her bow along the way. John watched them run to safety. He saw something in his periphery. The chandelier had been thrown back toward him. He moved out of the way just in time, but not before a sharp edge of broken glass grazed his left arm and gave him a wound that matched the one he'd already suffered on his right. He would not have time to worry, as the Fire King marched back toward the castle breach and effortlessly crushed the remainder of the wall in his path.

The kids waited impatiently behind a large statue as they counted the steps they would need to take toward safety. The Fire King advanced with ferocity in his eyes as John waited by the stairway and began to race up. He assumed the role of bait in order to lure the crimson eyes away from the others, who were buried beneath the darkness several feet away. Freddie moved a step backward, scared he would be seen, but he accidently kicked a small piece of iron debris. This immediately captured the attention of the dark king, and he directed his words toward them.

"There you are..."

John dropped from the second floor, but before his feet hit the ground, he thrust himself toward the Fire King, who faced the kids and was struck while he was vulnerable. John screamed from the heat of the burning skin before he flew away to assess what he would do next.

He needed to draw attention from the others, so he illuminated brighter and hurled anything he could lift, which included antique furniture and even a grand piano, a peace offering from Heras's predecessor. He flew high into the great hall and began to toss heavy priceless paintings. The crimson king deflected and destroyed everything with ease as it all crashed into the walls.

"Now it's my turn," the Fire King grumbled as he faded and disappeared from sight. Even with John's eyes illuminated, he was nowhere to be seen.

"Who are you?" said a voice behind him. Suddenly John was grabbed by the neck. The Fire King vanished and reappeared in front of the boy almost instantly as he still held on to his neck, which began to burn and weaken him.

"Run!" John yelled to the others.

Tony and Freddie began to sprint toward the huge breach in the wall toward freedom. Ivy did not run. As she attempted to nock the arrow in her bow, her faint visibility gave her great difficulty. She focused on John's eyes as they dimmed and then adjusted her aim three clicks to the right. She released the arrow, and it headed directly toward the crimson king's head. He caught and crushed it without a look.

"*Run!*" John yelled again, even louder as he weakened further.

Ivy attempted to catch up with Tony and Freddie, who were near the opening, but a large statue flew across the room and crashed against the breach before they could reach it and trapped them inside. The Fire King released a wicked laugh as he looked at the terrified kids, who realized they would not escape.

The crimson eyes slowly returned to John, whose eyes were open wide. John began to scream as the illumination throughout his body faded and transferred to his right hand. He concentrated the awesome power of Midwa into his fist. His fist was released toward the crimson king's iron-clad head. The glowing horned helmet cracked across its entire left side. They both began to fall rapidly and crashed into the ground. A large billow of smoke was created from the dust that had been lying there unmoved for ages.

John's eyes opened moments later. He was exhausted. He looked at the Fire King, who stood several feet away and flickered in frustration as he attempted fade in and out closer. But John had destroyed the enchantment that controlled the king's helmet. He was no longer able to cross realms at intermittent paces. He was unable to vanish and rematerialize as he pleased. John had taken away his element of surprise. The king took off the useless helmet and thrust it into a nearby wall, which broke it completely. The odds were almost even. John could once again attempt to lure him away and give the others a chance to flee.

John's energy had not yet sufficiently recharged, so he was unable to illuminate at full potential and fly up to the second floor. A traditional foot chase would take place. Quick on his feet, John would be able to outpace the hulking Fire King.

John sprinted toward the stairway and began to scale two steps at a time. The Fire King began to run just as well, but he would never catch him given the pace. The king made a risky move. He exposed himself as he removed the ring from his finger. Suddenly the torches of the castle were restored, and the light returned to the world of the living, no longer trapped within the ring. The castle's magnificence was restored. The ring was effectively a gateway to the world of the forsaken and absorbed all surrounding light in order to complete the bridge between realms. The same light fueled the king's crimson eyes when they erupted.

As the castle was lit once more, the king of the South's true identity was revealed. He was a handsome man of fair skin, quite distinguished. He looked rather noble and harmless, in fact. John ceased any further steps in his ascent as he caught a glimpse of the man.

"I'm really not so bad," the king said.

John was allured by the sincerity of his words, and he descended the steps slowly without realizing it. He was not strong enough to overcome the words of the king, which were laced with persuasion.

The king continued to speak as smooth as silk. "I am misunderstood. You can understand that, can't you...John?"

"I haven't...told you my name," John replied. He had not noticed that he was already at the feet of the king, whose eyes were no longer filled with sincerity. They were prepared for another transformation. The king would return to his alternate, terror-inducing form.

"I know all about you, bastard child of Midwa. I am finished with the games," the crimson king said as he slipped on his ring again and transformed to the beast that had haunted John in his dreams for the past several months. The great hall was once again flushed of all its light as the Fire King consumed it. He grabbed John by the neck.

John struggled to breathe. He attempted to focus his energy as he had moments ago, but he was still too weak and about to become weaker still. Something suddenly deflected off of the Fire King's head. It was a small rock. He did not flinch. Another rock deflected off of him, this time his back. Arrows struck him as well and became stuck in his beastly body, but not for long as they burned and fell off harmlessly.

Soon more followed with increasing frequency. The kids were attempting to get his attention, in hopes that he would let go of John. They wanted to give him a chance to recharge himself. It appeared to work, as the Fire King became annoyed enough to drop John and start his approach toward them. As he approached with that fear-inducing look, the kids dropped the rocks and arrows they held and began to run as far as they could.

"*Vladimir!*" yelled a familiar voice behind the Fire King.

The king replied, "No one has called me that in years. *Who are you?*"

The voice replied, "You know who I am, king slayer. You are not the rightful heir to the throne of Villanis."

The Fire King replied, "It *cannot* be…"

The voice countered, trembling with anger, "*You shall pay for what you have done!*"

Suddenly John burned as bright as he ever had. All of the energy within him flowed throughout as he levitated above the ground. With his head leaned backward, a pronounced energy began to project from his eyes and framed an image above him. It was Midwa in his true form, before he took on the appearance of John's favorite chocolate-colored rodent. Midwa was a fair-looking man himself. Ivy, Tony, and Freddie all looked upon the image with stunned eyes. They gazed upon an older version of John. Unconscious during the transfer, John was unaware of what was happening before their eyes.

"This ends now!" Midwa yelled. He then looked down to John as he spoke his final words. "I'm sorry I could not tell you…son." He then looked toward the others. "Seek out Dahlia…his elder half sister. She will explain all there is to know."

Midwa's form began to blur and could no longer be recognized. He was once again pure energy. He projected himself toward the Fire King as he once had toward the chocolate rodent. John fell limp, though conscious. The brilliant blue and crimson collided for several brutal moments as they waged war upon each other. The blue attacked from every angle before it finally found vulnerability and permeated the king through his crimson eyes. He knew that he would not be able to rejoin John, but it was the only way that John and the fellowship would succeed. They could not coexist indefinitely, as Midwa reluctantly had attempted to allude to. He would have eventually taken over John's being completely within one more day. It was time. Midwa himself was the sacrifice he had spoken of.

Piercing shrieks followed for several minutes as Midwa battled with the crimson being within the Forsaken Realm. And then there was silence, utter silence, as the beastly body of the Fire King fell limp and dropped to the floor. Stunned, John and the others walked up to the motionless body, on which the crimson slowly faded. They maintained their distance by a few paces.

John attempted to illuminate himself, but nothing happened. He tried again but felt nothing. He looked to the others and spoke as tears swelled. "My powers…Midwa…they're gone. *This* is what he meant when he said it would require sacrifice." He fell silent.

Tony spoke up after a moment of silence. "When did he say that?"

John replied hesitantly, "When I passed out after we reached the desert demon's battle-ax...I was afraid to say anything because I wasn't sure who he was referring to. But I understand now." He wiped the tears from his cheek.

Ivy hugged John to console him. "We'll find a way. We *always* do, right?

Freddie spoke anxiously. "Understand what? We still need to defeat the Ice Queen. But how can we do that *now*?"

John replied, "He said the key lies in the Fire King's ring that rests on his finger."

John looked at the ring, which still burned crimson even though the frame of the Fire King's body had all but faded to a dull crimson. Even just a normal boy again, he felt the courage to reach in to grab the ring. But it would not be so easy.

He grabbed the motionless king's huge hand and attempted to remove the ring. It was too tight. It did not budge. He pulled with all his might a second time, but nothing happened. Freddie even tried with his blade, but it quickly grew hot, forcing him to cease his efforts. John tried to illuminate once again in desperation, as he had done so many times before, but still nothing happened.

He whispered aloud, "What am I supposed to do, Midwa?" He put his head down as if he was about to weep.

Suddenly he felt a tug. As John looked up, the Fire King had grabbed his arm, with his eyes uncharacteristically bright blue. The pale Fire King whispered, "John, go to the library...Scrolls of the Guar..." The blue suddenly burned crimson, and the voice changed to a much darker tone. "You shall not..." The eyes of the Fire King were suddenly again brilliant blue. "Scroll 1894...You must recite the final paragr…" The eyes burned crimson yet again. "Release…yourself from this…*realm*!" The crimson grew deeper as he looked directly into John's eyes and locked together with them.

The floor of the great hall became wet around John's feet. Soon the entire floor was wet, and the water level rose rapidly. Water suddenly began to spew profusely from the walls. John looked at the others, who did not appear to be affected. However, the water level rose too rapidly for him to stay around, and he was forced to move away hastily from the great hall.

"Come on; we have to get to higher ground!" John yelled.

"What's the matter, John? It's just a little water. You're not scared, *are you*?" Ivy asked him in return.

"Ivy, I can't swim. You know that! And I don't have powers anymore. Come on, let's go!" John yelled.

Freddie grabbed John by the hand. "Don't worry, John. Stay! I'll show you how."

"No, it's OK, Freddie. I'll show him how," Tony said from behind. He grabbed John's head and pushed him beneath the water as it rose.

John was desperate for air and unable to breathe, a familiar feeling from a past he could not remember.

"It's not so bad, right, John?" Tony yelled with a devious grin. The muffled words reached John's ears beneath the surface. He emerged, but Ivy and Freddie joined in on the efforts, and both began to submerge him again and again.

The fleeing bubbles increased at a desperate pace.

Air continued to flee from his lungs as his arms flailed.

Time…was…slowing…

The Dreamer: Origins

There was a voice. "John, you must *focus*."

John finally fought his instincts and calmed as he closed his eyes. He no longer felt the hands that grappled the top of his head. As he opened his eyes, he was alone beneath the deep water. He swam from the depths as if it were familiar and reached the top. When he emerged from the surface, he was suddenly on solid ground. The water had vanished, along with Ivy, Tony, and Freddie.

"Ivy? Tony? Freddie?" John yelled, but there was no answer in return. He turned around, and suddenly he was no longer in the great hall. He was in the dining hall, where he saw a young woman, dressed as if she were royalty, passed out on the lengthy table. He heard a noise behind him. As he turned, again he was in a different room, a dark chamber. He heard a whisper ahead of him in the shadows and began to walk toward it cautiously. The whisper became louder. It had a familiarity to it.

The voice became clearer. "Help…me." It became progressively louder as he approached. Soon he felt as if he were next to the voice as it said, "Please…"

"How…how can I help you?" he asked into the darkness.

"Please…free me!" the voice said desperately before it shrieked and was suddenly lit.

It was the lady he had seen at the dining table. She was bound by chains and in severe pain.

"Please!" the voice shrieked.

He closed his eyes briefly in fear. When he opened them, the woman suddenly transformed to the familiar frigid figure that had caused him much suffering. The Ice Queen stood shackled before him, in agonizing pain. He could not look at her.

"Free me!" the voice screamed.

He turned away in terror. The darkness gave way to the vivid and lush colors of a fanciful garden that could exist only in the palace grounds of Buv're. John walked along a trail made entirely of gold as he looked upon the different species of flora that had been well taken care of. Many servants on either side trimmed them to perfection and made sure only the most beautiful were on display for all onlookers. He could not look down without being blinded by the sun's reflection. As he continued along the path, he noticed a woman in luxurious clothing fit for a queen. She stood under a pagoda as she overlooked a bath, which was also made of exquisite gold that only the royalty of the West could afford.

She held something in front of her that her hands struggled to tame. As he approached, he could see the short, pale arms and legs of a baby flail wildly as her face cringed above it.

Another, younger lady ran through him and up to her and screamed, "*Mother!* What have you done?"

The older woman did not address her daughter, however. She turned to John and spoke with maliciousness in her voice. "*You* were an *accident!*" Her lips trembled from the rage that filled her words.

"*No!*" John screamed as he was brought to his knees from the pain of a distant memory he could barely recall. He wept as he stared at the shiny bricks of the golden walkway beneath him.

A shadow approached and extended its smooth, fair hand, and he looked up. It was the younger lady of the two, and she was beautiful.

"You were no accident." She encouraged him to stand, and he complied. She gave him a big hug, and he began to feel better about the scarring memories that had just been presented to him. But a rush of a frigid chill began to flow through him suddenly. He stepped away from the fair lady, but she was no longer fair. It was the woman who had suffered in the chamber once again.

She yelled, "My sister did not want you! She did not deserve you!"

The Ice Queen stood before him. He screamed again as he turned and began to run away.

As he looked up during his sprint, he was suddenly in the great library of the Fire King's castle. It looked familiar. He immediately began to search for the scripture Midwa had spoken of. Unsure of where to begin his search, he began to rummage through random scrolls as he made his way from shelf to random shelf.

He then noticed some written characters on the ends of the bookshelves. They appeared foreign but had a familiarity to them for some reason. He began to read them aloud. He could not understand how he was able to read it, as the sounds did not originate from his native tongue. Something clicked, and the letters suddenly translated and appeared to him as he was accustomed to. The sounds did the same. The ancient language of his bloodline had awakened and become natural to him.

"Hesta mon Tuskannd" were the words he spoke, but to the common ear, it sounded like "Scrolls of the Philosophers."

He was on to something. He hastily made his way through the library along the ends of the bookshelves. He read aloud as he passed from one to the next, "Montukka sim kolla," "Shinka jan plonnde," and then finally "Hesta mon Midwa," or "Scrolls of the Guardian."

He ran down the aisle and read the numbers aloud, "1135...1576...1745...1891...1892..." But before he reached 1894, there were loud footsteps in the distance, and they loomed closer with each passing one.

"Where are you, *John*?" yelled the Fire King as he entered the great library.

John tensed up and leaned against the shelf quietly. He picked up the scroll labeled 1894 and began to read it in his mind so he would not make any sounds. He was halfway through it and did not feel anything happening. In fact, the Fire King appeared closer as John's shadow cast against the crimson light that the king produced.

He continued to read the final paragraph of the scroll as Midwa had instructed him to. He finished as he read the final word, "Summonis," but nothing happened. The Fire King drew closer.

There were yells in the distance. They belonged to young voices, and they attempted to instigate the Fire King. This distracted him from John, and he began to make his way toward the voices, which left the young apprentice alone in the library. The king elevated several of the bookshelves and sent them in every direction to ensure his survival. This destroyed and shattered many of them and scattered them everywhere. Some of the scrolls caught fire as they hit the few torches that barely survived the Fire King's presence.

John's foot was trapped beneath a toppled shelf, and the scroll he'd been reading was misplaced. He managed to free his foot from beneath the shelf with a lot of effort, but he lost valuable time. He began to recite the final paragraph of the torn scroll he still had in his hand. Each word now carried weight along with it.

There were nervous screams in the distance as the Fire King approached the kids. But he halted his steps as he suddenly felt himself tearing apart from within.

"No! This cannot be!" the Fire King screamed. He began a hasty return to the great library. He knew the young apprentice must have located the scroll.

The Dreamer: Origins

The scroll had been torn in the explosion and was missing the final line that John needed to recite.

John was in a dark room illuminated only slightly by a few torches that flickered in a struggle for their lives. The flickers of light allowed for only brief visibility of his surroundings. As the last of the debris fell and settled in, he could see several partially burned scrolls among the rubble of a battle that appeared to have just reached its dramatic conclusion. With his head lowered, he searched desperately for anything that resembled some meaning. He found nothing.

Flickers of Midwa faded in and out before him. John saw him in the various scenarios, almost simultaneously, as the ghosts spoke and moved about as he had seen him in his dreams. He began to hear footsteps in the distance, increasingly amplified with each step as they approached. A red silhouette finally appeared around a figure before him, veiled predominantly by the darkness of the shadows. The dark figure was beastly, with crimson eyes on the verge of erupting. John cowered. The footsteps approached and became heavier and louder. The heat emitted by the beast began to warm John's skin and soon created a mild burn. John did not have the courage to look up. He began to weep as he covered his ears, with his head sheltered between his knees. He sang a familiar lullaby: "Don't worry…It's going to be all right…"

The beast roared John's name repeatedly as he continued to whimper. He hummed the lullaby even as his lips became paralyzed; he had lost his ability to sing aloud any longer. He could not face the beast. Soon the voice transformed into a tone no different from that of a young boy, which calmed him; however, John's wrist suddenly seared as it was clenched by the firm grip of the beast. The tension that had subsided just a moment ago had returned.

"John! Wake up!"

The beast roared John's name again, but he still could not bring himself to look up. He thought of what Midwa had said: "The key is the Fire King's ring." John was not fond of riddles, but he knew that he should heed the advice of the mysterious Midwa.

John finally raised his head and looked at the Fire King's fingers. He gazed at the ring. It was difficult to miss as it spewed fire profusely. John raised his head farther and looked directly into the eyes of the Fire King. But John turned his head away as his eyes began to burn immediately from the intense heat of the Fire King's stare.

He built up the courage to look up once more. There was an explosion from within the Fire King. Midwa had escaped and would show one final act of paternal love. He incapacitated the Fire King with an all-powerful grip as the crimson lord screamed in agony, desperate to keep John from reciting the final line.

As the fires on the distant scrolls caught on and began to spread, the far corner of the library was ablaze and consuming scrolls by the shelf. Midwa afforded John an opportunity to find the remainder of the scroll before he would be taken away himself to the Forsaken Realm. John only had a brief moment to see the image of Midwa as a man before he searched desperately for the remainder of the scroll before they would all eventually catch fire.

After a frantic minute, half of the great library had been consumed by the flames. John finally found and recited it aloud: "Montik era plosintic ne znata…summonis."

Once he recited the final word, the fire king's ring loosened and fell to the ground. John ran and grabbed the ring. While it burned his hand, his will proved that mind could prevail over matter.

Midwa spoke. "Go to the master chamber on the thirteenth floor and retrieve the Ice Queen's imprisoned heart. Transport it to the Ice Palace. When you are close enough, you must free her heart, and all that was once good in the kingdom will be restored. The beat of the heart fades as she becomes darker and colder. You must"— Midwa began to fade—"hurry. I'm afraid our time together has passed. I'm sorry, John. I wish we had more time. I believe in you…"

"Wait! Just one more moment! Are you…?" But Midwa's silhouette had dissipated along with the Fire King.

"John! Wake up!" yelled a young voice.

John's eyes opened. He looked at the others as he remained in shock. "I'm sorry. I didn't mean to black out again," he said as he reflected on his final moments with Midwa. "Was I out long?"

"You did it," Tony replied.

John looked down in his palm and saw the Fire King's ring. It no longer burned. He looked up and stared at the pale body of the Fire King's true form, a threat no longer. It was an encouraging and much-needed victory for the fellowship.

XXVI: Born of the Desert

William and the Chief arrived at the entrance of the underground, where Pug waited patiently for them. As it escorted them through the network of tunnels, William refused to look at the goblin. He was still haunted by the flashbacks he'd experienced as it stared into his eyes.

They passed by the forsaken soldiers, who no longer flickered and faded as the ghosts they once appeared to be. They animated no differently than when they were once alive, though they looked no more alive than the rotten corpses they moved around as. Even the Chief struggled to come to terms with the bizarre visual.

They reached the end of the tunnel and recited the password to open the enchanted gate. William and the Chief exited first. As Pug emerged, it cued the forsaken army from within the tunnels to advance. Soon the murky jade glows illuminated the tunnels, and the soldiers began to approach the gate. Pug's eyes glowed as well, and it looked up to the Chief and signaled him to lean in. The Chief complied with what the goblin whispered into his ear and then turned his attention to William.

"They will follow us, William. You must keep your purpose in mind as we proceed. Do not forget your oath. Do not forget your little sister. Now let's move," the Chief said as he began their march toward the end of the lift.

The soldiers shrieked as the sun touched them for the first time in several years, and even covered their eyes as if they still possessed them. They emerged from the tunnels and looked no less frightening. The forsaken army had been unleashed.

Nearly one hundred soldiers followed in the Chief's wake as they shrieked fear into the wildlife of the floating jungle and caused them to scatter. William and the Chief secured themselves with the nearby mackelroy branches. The landmass began to drop. For the duration of the descent, the warriors did not appear frightening to William. He observed some as they fell over the edge to faint impacts. Others were mangled in the branches of the mackelroy trees as the pressure of the descent attempted to rip them past the trees. Still others attacked each other after they inadvertently bumped into one another. William was in dire need of the amusement. He had not had such a good laugh since he used to joke around with Jacob and Tony at the palace.

Perhaps they will bring death upon themselves before they reach the desert, William thought. But the reality was that they could not die again. As they reached the jungle lands below, they gathered, once again intact, though several remained stuck beneath the mass of land that landed upon them.

The Chief began to lead them through the villages, and screams followed shortly after as the villagers raced to their homes. The screams traveled from village to village. The news also spread throughout the channels of the leopard network. It was not long before the broadcast reached Sandriver, as he was in a huddle with the senior members of various leaps.

The warrior king had called upon countless leaps from all corners of the vast jungle to put aside their differences and join his ranks in battle. He quickly called upon the remainder of the leopards and communicated that the forsaken army would soon reach the desert. They needed to stop them if they had any hope to stop the Ice Queen and bring peace to the kingdom once more.

The army marched in the wake of the Chief. William felt no comfort as he was trailed by the murky jade glows from village to village. The injured palace guards had congregated in the streets of the town center, but it was no longer safe. They sought refuge in the Palace Pardons, as the space was large enough to fit all of them, but it had been boarded up. They could not breach the boards no matter how hard they swung their dull blades. They diverted to the homes of the villagers, but none opened their doors. It was the palace guards' turn to be terrorized. As the forsaken approached, many of them dropped to their knees, filled with the terror from the shrieks, and pleaded for mercy. As the jade eyes passed, they deemed the palace guards weak. But they were in need of the additional blades, so they began to convert them.

The Chief looked upon the palace guards as they ran in terror, but he knew his place, and more importantly his oath, which if he broke, his family would suffer. He called the undead to proceed and instructed them not to breach the homes of the innocent. They no longer moved sluggishly and attempted to convert the guards one by one. The Chief walked ahead with William and waited at the southern entrance of the jungle for them to arrive.

The forsaken army eventually arrived at the jungle, after they converted the remainder of the palace guards who had finally breached the Palace Pardons. The saloon was overrun by the soldiers, and all who sought refuge within were converted, with the exception of a few guards who managed to slip by unnoticed and sprinted their way back to the lift toward the palace.

The Chief led them through the jungle, where the unfortunate wildlife was briefly terrorized. They followed the Larris River as all life scattered from them. They marched on with a relentless demeanor and were scheduled to arrive at the border of the Desert Realm within a few hours.

Sandriver raced toward the desert with several leaders alongside their leaps. Rivalries were put aside as the Tiberian and

Sultarian leaps ran as one unit. In well under an hour, they reached the border of the Desert Realm where they had dropped off John, Ivy, Tony, and Freddie days ago. He wondered if they had been successful. He hoped they were. He halted several feet shy of the peak of the sand dune that separated the realm ahead from all others.

He turned around and gazed upon the support that had heeded his call. They stood nearly fifty strong. Sandriver growled his instructions to all of them to remain at the border and await his return. They would need to hold off the forsaken army for as long as they could without sacrificing themselves. They would need to be nimble. Sandriver turned his back to them and stared into the Desert Realm as he reflected on his past before he proceeded.

He was still in his mother's pregnant belly, mere days away from birth, when she was slain. The strike was supposed to eliminate both of them in one blow. His mother looked up at her slayer as betrayal reflected in her eyes. She knew at that point that the leopard that towered above her had also slain the king, her husband. The strike had been sloppy and gave her one last chance to express her disappointment in him. This aggravated the leopard and instigated him to strike again with malice. He struck her in the neck, a fatal blow. Life fled the queen quickly.

Though the cub was still within his mother's torn womb, an image of the queen slayer as he stood tall next to his two subordinates was burned into his memory. With a wicked look in his eyes, he'd projected his hatred into the cub's exposed eyes as his mother's blood soaked him. Her soul dissipated as it was sent from the world of the living. The slayer of kings and queens believed that he deserved to be the future king. He had earned it with all of the fierce battles he had endured. It was he, not the king, who had led the leap of warriors that protected their kingdom from outside forces.

The king and queen slayer, Krog, determined his newborn brother did not deserve such a glorious title. He had lured the queen away from the leap as he told her with conviction that they had found the remains of the former warrior king, her deceased husband. She knew the Desert Realm was dangerous, as the colossal warriors patrolled it and were able to crush anything in their path, but it was important to provide a traditional burial ceremony for the celebrated king of the past.

Krog took another swipe to finish the job. His strike was deflected by a strong force of energy. He looked at its origin. A middle-aged wizard with an ancient-looking staff stood tall above the assassinated queen in the near distance. The sweltering heat of the sun had distorted his image and left him unnoticed. As the three large leopards stared at him with ferocity, the wizard remained fearless; they did not intimidate him.

Krog and his underlings growled as they gazed at him viciously and prepared to shred him to several pieces. They paced around the wizard and surrounded him within moments. The wizard walked over cautiously and glanced down at the young heir who lay within his mother's slain corpse. He had not realized the queen bore a child within her.

The trio suddenly attacked from all sides, but before they could strike the wizard, he struck his staff upon the desert floor and created a blinding blue light. All three leopards flew backward and fell at compromised angles. They were all injured on impact and looked to be in pain. As Krog snarled at the others, he commanded them to retreat. The leopards believed they would have their revenge another day.

The wizard looked down at the blood-soaked heir. He kneeled as he glanced up to watch the leopards flee for their lives back toward the jungle. He felt bad for the helpless cub as he removed him from his mother's belly and picked him up.

He stared down at the cub as he carried him away. He attempted to wipe off the sand that the young leopard was covered in. The wizard was intrigued, as the cub had not been on the desert floor. A transformation was about to begin, and he would soon become one with the desert. He had been exposed to the enchantments of the realm as his mother's soul passed through him within the desert. He began to become no different from the desert dwellers. It was not fair, the wizard thought. He had not been given a fighting chance.

"Don't worry, young one. We will get out of here."

The cub purred in return.

The wizard grabbed his staff once again from his back and held it tightly as he recited a spell in a foreign tongue. Suddenly they were surrounded by a blue energy field as they began their journey to the western kingdom. They were suspended in another, safe realm known only to the wizard.

The wizard took in a deep breath of air and exhaled a stream of water that splashed against the innocent cub's face. The face was clear and no longer stained with blood, but it still struggled to shake off the enchantment of the Desert Realm. The sand still remained in the regions of its body it had begun to take a hold of. He took an even deeper breath and exhaled a long stream of water to rid the cub of his red stains from the rest of his body. The sand began to flow from the cub when the enchantment finally broke. The sand dissipated as it crossed the boundaries of the force field, and it was returned to the Desert Realm outside. The wizard took one last long breath and blew the water against the cub. The remainder of the sand flowed down.

The middle-aged wizard chuckled to himself as he thought aloud, "That's it. Your name will be…Sandriver. Yes, Sandriver. Now let me introduce myself. My name is Midwa. It's a pleasure to make your acquaintance." He carried the young leopard far away.

Sandriver would be raised in Buv're under Midwa's supervision until he was old enough to return to the jungle and make his rightful claim to his proverbial throne. Sandriver learned much of foreign lands and magic from the talented wizard.

Three years passed, and Sandriver had already outgrown and towered above Midwa. He was certainly larger than any of the leopards that had preceded him. No individual leopard would be able to take him down. He was ready to confront Krog.

Before Sandriver began his journey, he communicated to Midwa that he would need to overcome it on his own. This was something Midwa understood well, as honor and pride flowed through his own blood as well. Midwa transported Sandriver as far as the desert border before he took several paces backward and parted ways. The leopard, born of the desert, was not prepared for what was about to happen. He had been born in a body whose soul was about to cross into the next realm. A part of him always maintained a connection with the Desert Realm.

As Sandriver entered the desert, a rapid transformation began, one that had not been completed when he was just a cub. He grew massively. He scaled in size to the colossal desert dwellers. But he was special; he was not a slave of the desert. His eyes did not glow crimson as theirs did. He did not understand what had happened to him, but it did not matter for long. He sprinted at great lengths across the desert, ignoring the shrieks of the colossal warriors he passed who attempted to warn the others of his presence. The leopard was hungry for revenge against the one who had slain his father and mother, king and queen warriors of the jungle.

The Dreamer: Origins

As Sandriver raced through the desert, none dared to oppose his massive frame and ferocious determination. It did not take long before he neared the cliff of the dune where he would exit the realm. He reached the end and leaped in order to clear the cliff. As he crossed through, the sand dissipated and scattered back into the desert. He landed on the outside border of the desert in his normal immense profile.

It was not long before Sandriver reached the perimeter of the leap. He heard them snarl from far away. As he arrived, he saw a noticeably older Krog and his subordinates as they bullied the smaller and weaker leopards. No justice existed with this self-proclaimed king, who had stolen the throne in an act of treason.

Sandriver growled loudly, filled with rage as he stormed the camp. His attention was focused only on Krog, who had a nervous look in his eyes once he realized it was his younger brother, recognizable by his signature spotted pattern. The self-proclaimed king had not expected Sandriver to survive, let alone grow to be so massive. Krog commanded his two lead underlings who had followed in his shadows all these years to stand between them. He had forced them for many years to bloody their claws on his behalf.

Sandriver growled again as he walked forward with ferocity. Vengeance filled his eyes. Krog proceeded forward and pushed his way between his subordinates. He growled at them as he gave them commands. They would finish what they'd attempted to do several years earlier. They nervously complied and began to pace around Sandriver, whose eyes were barely removed from Krog.

One of the leopards attacked soon after. Without much effort, Sandriver turned to his left, growling, and struck the leopard down clean. The leopard limped off. Three of his ribs were crushed. The massive leopard had been kind to him, though, as he could have easily taken his life.

The other subordinate looked at Krog with fear in his eyes; he wished to retreat. However, Krog looked at him with threatening eyes. If he retreated, he would be slain by the king's claw. The leopard looked at Sandriver once more and could not bring himself to attack. It retreated with its tail between its legs. The ruthless king paced over to the loyal leopard that had been struck with fear. With two rapid strikes in succession, the leopard had been slain. Krog looked over to Sandriver, who snarled at him.

The king of the jungle was not just and would need to be dethroned. He took a pace toward Sandriver. Krog unexpectedly scratched the bed of the forest to try to instigate a sloppy attack from the vengeful leopard. Sandriver did not flinch. He was a beast that Krog would not be able to take down so easily.

Krog removed the look of battle from his face and appeared to be humbled. He was obviously overpowered, no matter how ruthless he convinced the leap he was. The king had just stepped down from his figurative throne voluntarily. Sandriver's vengeance had dissipated as he breathed away his anxiety.

Krog saw an opportunity, and he seized it. He knew he would not get another one. As Sandriver put his head down and tried to collect his thoughts on how they could coexist in the leap, Krog thrust himself forward with his claw prepared to strike sharply. Sandriver's reflexes pulled him from harm's way, almost. He had been struck in his right eye, which bled and was suddenly blinded. He swung his claws relentlessly to keep Krog away, unaware of where he swiped, as all of his attention was on the agonizing pain within his eye. The other leopards retreated in fear.

Krog paced around Sandriver. He managed to stay within his blind spot, although almost every direction was a blind spot from the shock of the strike. Krog repeatedly swiped at him and left scars all over. His spotted coat was no longer immaculate.

A courageous leopard nearby showed her disapproval by jumping toward Krog. As she swiped at him, Krog tossed her to the side and let her know that she would pay for her treasonous action. Krog continued to taunt Sandriver as he struck several more times.

The blurriness of Sandriver's functioning eye began to come into focus. He was starting to block out the pain of his blinded eye and could now see the left half of his surroundings. As he turned around, his face met another powerful strike from the claw of the king.

The wounded leopard had had enough. Krog was several paces away as he circled him. Sandriver lowered his head slightly and revealed his massive fangs. Blood streamed from his eye down the length of his face, into his mouth, and dripped from his large right fang. He licked the blood and then growled loud enough for all in the jungle to hear.

Sandriver thrust forward, directly toward Krog. Krog did not have much time to react with the unexpected speed of the massive leopard. With a quick side step, he attempted to once again attack from the blind spot, but Krog would not escape the grasp of Sandriver. He was thrown down into the ground, the impact so violent that both shoulders dislocated. He was pinned down by Sandriver, and the blood dripped from the leopard's fangs into his eyes.

As he looked up to Sandriver, Krog pleaded for mercy. The true heir to the throne looked down and felt the weight of justice tug at his conscience. Perhaps Krog could change his ways and deserved another chance. But did the queen slayer, who had looked down maliciously upon the innocent heir of the jungle as he lay helpless in his mother's corpse, deserve another chance? No, he did not. Sandriver thrust both claws at the unjust king's neck. He saw the fear in Krog's eyes, just as he could see the vengeance in his own in their reflection.

The forceful crack was followed by silence. Krog lay there motionless. He would be ruthless no more. Never again would he hurt and take advantage of the leopards of the Tiberian leap, especially the weak. Sandriver limped away from the dead self-proclaimed king and fell, exhausted. The pain had finally set in. The leopards surrounded him and bowed before him, even if he did not look like the king he would be just yet. They tended to his wounds and made sure he would heal. He would become the warrior king he was born to be.

Sandriver snapped back to the present as he gazed into the desert. He turned back and approached his brothers-in-arms. He communicated with them in their language of snarls and growls.

"The heir must be rescued at all costs. He deserves a fighting chance, as I was once given."

The massive leopard looked toward the desert. He paced slowly before he sprinted and leaped across into the Desert Realm. He transformed into a colossal desert leopard made entirely of sand and made his way swiftly across the desert. He was soon out of sight The leopards turned their attention to the jungle.

XXVII: The Palace Pardoned

"Those darn palace guards. They just can't stay away from the mead," Wilbur whispered to Gavin as the dull swords clashed against the boarded windows.

The elder men had arrived during the night, unnoticed, with Mitch and Dahlia as the guards lay in the road and nursed their injuries from the leopards. Since then, the group had been hiding behind the safety of the chairs and tables that boarded and blocked the front shutter doors and windows. It kept the Palace Pardons from being breached as they rested and gathered supplies.

Mitch was frightened of the shrieks that approached along with the screams of the villagers and palace guards. Gavin ensured them the wooden structure of the saloon was enough to keep the palace guards out but would not be able to withstand the strength of the forsaken army.

Wilbur and Gavin shared Mitch's terror. They were puzzled as they looked at Dahlia, who spoke as if the forsaken were already inside the saloon. "Stay…back. Don't come…any closer…"

Gavin limped over to her and held her in his arms. "Hey, young one. Don't worry. It's OK. We're safe in here. They're outside."

Wilbur, however, was not confident on how long they would be safe in the saloon. The shrieks became louder and the clashes of the swords more desperate. The boards that secured the windows began to give.

"Hey, Wilbur…I thought you said…!" Gavin yelled nervously.

The boards against one of the windows crashed into the saloon and allowed the light to enter. Several palace guards began to try to squeeze through simultaneously without success. Another boarded window on the opposite side was breached. More palace guards fought to get in. They soon began to flow in through the windows as they sought shelter from the forsaken.

"We need to go *now*," Gavin whispered to Wilbur and the kids.

"Follow me," Wilbur whispered in return, and they began to sneak behind the bar and down the steps toward the dungeon. They would escape through the secret door Wilbur had created many years back when he needed to smuggle illegal mead into the saloon.

The palace guards quickly accumulated as they fled from the forsaken in the streets. Some palace guards were not as lucky and were touched with the jade blade of the forsaken and converted before they could reach the window.

As the last palace guard who had not turned climbed through the window, his foot was struck by the jade blade of one of his fellow palace guards who had just turned. A forsaken soldier was suddenly present in the Palace Pardons. His eyes began to glow murky jade, and he quickly struck several palace guards, who turned within seconds. The transformation of the Palace Pardons from moments earlier was terrifying. Soon the shutters shattered, and several of the forsaken soldiers entered relentlessly. They overran the saloon and smashed it to pieces as they turned the frightened palace guards one by one.

As the group arrived at the dungeon, Wilbur raced to pull the lever that activated the secret door. The palace guard who had been shackled awoke and was finally sober. He heard his brethren upstairs cause a commotion and called to them, "Hey! They're down—"

The guard's yell was cut short as Mitch grabbed a nearby mug and smashed it against his head. He was knocked unconscious and laid out on the floor yet again. But the sound traveled.

"I heard something down there!" one of the forsaken soldiers yelled as he walked toward the back of the bar.

"Oh no!" Mitch whispered nervously.

"Don't worry. Follow me." Wilbur held open the secret door in the ordinary-looking dungeon wall. "Hurry along," he said to the others as they ran past him. He made sure to bring along the long blade he'd lifted from one of the RPG during Misty Mayhem. He shut the door just as the forsaken walked down the steps.

One of them looked down at the unfit prisoner who wore the uniform of the palace guards, but shuddered at the thought of turning him. He passed by him, approached the secret door, and said, "I smell fear…" as he looked in their direction past the wall.

The palace guard was only briefly unconscious. He woke to the sight of the forsaken and began to scream uncontrollably.

"What shall we do with this one?" one of the forsaken said as their shrieks transformed into recognizable words.

The leader of the forsaken answered, "Leave him. We have enough. Return to the man and child." The leader looked again to the secret door and slashed it with its sword. He missed the secret lever by inches. They retreated up the stairs and exited the ruined saloon.

Gavin and the group were terrified by the slash but then were relieved by the steps as they faded. Wilbur stood there frightened as he struggled to hold up the blade.

Gavin grabbed it from him and tossed it on the ground. "Come on. We're old. Let's stick to what we know, OK?"

Wilbur nodded.

"That was close," Dahlia said. She seemed to be back to normal.

"We're OK," Wilbur said as he grabbed a torch from the floor and lit it. A long tunnel was revealed. He picked up another torch and lit it with his own before he passed it over to Gavin. They each stood beside one of the kids down the tunnel as the shrieks and screams from above became fainter. They walked for several minutes before they arrived at a dead end.

"The village closest to the lift is just beyond here," Wilbur told them.

Gavin replied, "I guess you added another stop to our network, huh? I remember when we first built this underground system so many years ago. I knew the old Wilbur was still in there somewhere."

Wilbur smirked against the light of the torch as he spoke of himself. "Humph. I guess he never really left…" Then his voice became serious. "We wait here until they pass. Then we make a run for it." After several minutes, there was finally silence. "I think it's OK now."

"Are you sure?" Gavin asked.

Wilbur replied, "Only one way to find out, eh?"

Wilbur pulled the hidden lever, and the light soon entered into the dark tunnel they waited in. Their eyes hurt for a brief moment due to the rapid change from dark to light. They were surrounded by curious doe and other harmless wildlife.

"All clear," Wilbur whispered to the others, and they began to exit.

Mitch looked into the distance and saw that the last of the forsaken soldiers had passed into the village. They were alone. They began to race toward the lift. Nothing happened when they boarded.

Dahlia asked impatiently, "What do we do now?"

Gavin replied, "We wait."

XXVIII: Dissipating Reign

As Sandriver raced across the dunes, he noticed a congregation of colossal desert warriors in the distance. The general towered above the rest as he stood in the center. His eyes possessed a deeper and more volatile crimson than all the others'.

The massive sandy leopard sprinted harder. A short time passed before he reached the perimeter of the army. Sandriver approached cautiously as the warriors backed away. The general grunted to the army in an unrecognizable language.

The general stood unobstructed by his army when Sandriver finally reached the front. Krog stood as a desert demon alongside his underling that he had slain. They appeared as they had the last day he had seen them in the world of the living, the sandy texture and crimson eyes excluded.

Krog growled at the general, who then gazed upon Sandriver. The towering demon then turned his attention back toward his army and riled them up. He returned his eyes toward the desert-born leopard as he spoke to Krog in the unfamiliar language. "So the desert born that got away has returned. He will not escape from here again. My army will make sure of it."

Sandriver growled to Krog, clearly frustrated, "The North brings destruction upon all within this realm. He must command them north and defeat the forsaken army that the queen has unleashed upon us all. They mean to destroy all in their path as they attempt to stop the chosen ones. We *must* stop them!"

Krog was dismissive. "Desacles does not take orders from cowards who disobey the commands of the desert as you've done. You should have just *died* when you had the chance!"

Sandriver did not respond well to the callous words. "I am no coward!" His eyes were the only ones that did not burn crimson.

Krog refused to communicate the message to the general. He had not forgotten that Sandriver had stolen his crown. He owed his younger brother nothing.

Sandriver growled with desperation toward the general, whom Krog had just revealed to be Desacles, the keeper of the Desert Realm. Desacles looked down to Krog and watched him look upon his brother with a scathing hatred. He spoke aloud as he riled up his army once more. He then looked back down at Krog and commanded him to translate Sandriver's message, which had a sense of urgency to it. Krog complied, and Desacles laughed at what he had been told. He then instructed Krog in the foreign tongue Sandriver did not understand.

Krog turned to his brother once more and spoke the message. "We are to battle…to the death. The *winner* shall determine which direction the army marches."

"We don't have time for this, Krog. War will soon be at our feet," growled Sandriver.

Several miles away, the Chief, along with William, had led the forsaken army to the border of the Desert Realm. Most of the palace guards had joined the ranks after they experienced the touch of their enchanted jade blades. The forsaken army's numbers had swelled considerably once they breached the Palace Pardons and turned all but a few palace guards who managed to escape. The Chief believed his command forbid the forsaken to touch the villagers, but the truth was they left them alone as they did not make suitable warriors; the palace guards barely did, but their blades would be of use. The forsaken army followed instructions from their true lord.

William and the Chief were unable to proceed any farther. They hoped the forsaken army would be successful in overtaking the Desert Realm and then inhibit the efforts of the young apprentice and his fellowship who advanced with the objective to dethrone Her Majesty. They turned their backs to the desert and watched as the last of the forsaken lined up in formation and awaited further instruction from the Chief.

"On behalf of Her Majesty, Agribel, good and just queen of Belghan, go forth and destroy all in your path toward the young apprentice who means to destroy our world." The Chief hung his head in shame as if he knew he had not done the right thing. But he had sworn an oath, and it was the only thing that protected his family.

The forsaken army entered the Desert Realm and began to transform just as Sandriver had done. The sands took over their forms. As long as they remained in the realm, they would be subject to its enchantments. They began their hasty advance south across the dunes.

With vicious eyes, Krog paced around his younger but physically superior brother. He commanded his underling to do the same as he snarled, "Just like old times, eh?"

Sandriver snarled back as he turned his head cautiously, attempting to keep them both in sight, "You shall fall just the same, brother."

Krog suddenly dissipated into the winds. Sandriver was confused, and his eyes were irritated by the force of the sands. The winds suddenly stopped. Sandriver saw only the underling in front of him.

"Hello, brother," was snarled behind him. When Sandriver turned around sharply, his face was met with a fierce strike from

Krog's claw. The strike just missed his good eye as the sand grazed away.

Sandriver growled loudly, almost as loud as the cheers from the eager desert warriors who surrounded them.

Krog spoke again. "You didn't think I would easily forfeit control, did you?"

Sandriver snarled nervously as the eyes of Krog erupted crimson, "Brother?"

The voice of Krog had changed into a deeper, more ominous tone. "Your brother is but a puppet. And so shall you be once I slay you and add you to my collection. So slash this body if you wish. You will forsake your brother to face the dark lord of the Forsaken Realm himself. It's your choice, *Warrior King of the Jungle.*"

Sandriver was unsure of what to do. He had underestimated Desacles. Perhaps the forsaken army that approached would yield to the realm's keeper just as the desert warriors had. The warrior king deemed his own efforts inadequate.

"Ticktock," the voice of Desacles snarled from Krog's jaws. He dissipated even quicker and struck Sandriver violently before he appeared several paces away. "It seems you have never met an opponent you could not overpower." Desacles struck again against the rear leg of Sandriver. "Or who was swifter than yourself." Another more violent blow struck Sandriver on his other hind leg. "Or whom you couldn't outsmart." Another strike left three of Sandriver's limbs in agonizing pain as he struggled to stand. He eventually fell onto his side.

Krog stood above his brother as he once did when he was just a cub in his dying mother's womb. His eyes were no longer crimson, as Desacles had removed himself along with the crimson shackles that had remained in his eyes for so long. The keeper of the realm had granted the slayer of kings and queens temporary freedom from the crimson hold so that he could finally have his revenge against the one who had stolen his crown. It was the moment Krog had been waiting for.

Krog raised his claw as he growled and looked down upon his brother. A memory flashed across his mind, and he once again saw the cub before him. He growled again but could not strike. He just stood there, still.

"*Finish him!*" the voice of Desacles screamed from the mouth of the general. Desacles had once again possessed his eyes with crimson.

Krog lowered his striking claw and stood over Sandriver remorsefully. The anger he had nursed since his father rejected his birthright to be king seemed to have finally subsided. It appeared that he had accepted that it was not Sandriver who had done wrong by him. Perhaps Krog did not deserve the crown in the first place with his unjust morality. Perhaps his father, the slain warrior king of the jungle, had been right all along.

"*Destroy him!*" the voice of Desacles screamed again, even more agitated.

Krog lowered his claw and stood down. He retreated as he snarled to the general. He had just exiled himself.

"You *will* obey my command!" Desacles screamed once more from within the sandy frame of the general. He paced toward Krog and lifted the leopard by the neck. "You will pay with your *soul*." He then looked toward a sandpit in the distance and began to walk toward it.

Krog did not fight back. He no longer had the will to live after accepting all the wrong he had done to so many. He looked back at his younger brother as he struggled to project a snarl. "I'm…sorry…"

Sandriver looked upon Desacles as he carried Krog toward the entrance of the Forsaken Realm. He growled to himself as he watched the army encourage the keeper of the realm, who did not tolerate insubordination. The wounded leopard was alone as the forsaken army advanced from the North.

Sandriver decided to squash the old rivalry as the sand dripped from his desert-formed body as if it were blood. He struggled as he attempted to rise up to stand on his paws. It took several attempts, but he managed through the pain. As the general loomed closer to the sandpit, the will of Sandriver began to take over. The leopard pushed aside the pain and stood tall once more. Some of the cheers changed to concern, but Desacles could not hear them above the overwhelming cheers of the others, especially as he was so focused on justifiably punishing Krog.

Sandriver thrust each leg forward and leaped. He sprinted toward his brother, who was only paces away from the sandpit that would send him to the Forsaken Realm. The yells from the desert warriors started to become clearer to the keeper of the realm

Desacles saw a reflection in Krog's suddenly alert eyes as the screams finally reached his ears. Sandriver had leaped toward him with his claws extended. The keeper of the realm began to dissipate, but the claw of Sandriver struck his erupting right eye from behind before he could. The general released Krog, who fell within two paces of the sandpit. He struggled but managed to escape the relentless grip of the Forsaken Realm. Had he been one pace closer, he would have been pulled in by the magnetic grip.

The scream from the general was loud. He could not dissipate, as the crimson eye that remained flickered. Sandriver's will did not falter as he continued to attack Desacles with strike after strike. The leopard could not strike the eye that remained, however, as the keeper protected it with all his efforts.

Desacles grabbed the leopard from behind and threw him down to the desert floor. Sandriver yelped. Two of his legs had just been broken. The keeper of the realm tried to regain his composure. The broken leopard felt even more agonizing pain than moments earlier.

Finally composed, the keeper walked over to Sandriver. The crimson eye that remained continued to flicker as he drew his long sword. As he raised it above his head, he looked beyond Sandriver, who growled at him in frustration.

His army drew closer. However, they were no longer possessed by crimson eyes. Desacles commanded them to return to their formation. They did not heed his command. They no longer bent to his will.

The general became desperate as his warriors rapidly approached and surrounded him. With his blade still raised, he turned toward Sandriver. "You...*you* have destroyed *everything!*" He swung his blade down toward the courageous leopard.

"Aaaahhhhhh!" There was a yell from his left as another blade came from beneath, clashed against his own, and knocked it away from his hands. The warrior stepped forward. It was Heras, former king of Buv're, just as Sandriver remembered him from years ago, when they battled alongside each other at the Fire King's castle. No longer under the will of Desacles, Heras stood face-to-face with the towering keeper of the realm.

Heras yelled, "Vladimir has already taken away my life. You shall not take away my *honor!*"

"Heras. Do not be foolish. I do not need my powers to destroy you. I don't even need my eyes."

"You're right, Desacles," Heras replied as he raised his sword. "And you shall no longer have them."

The general jolted forward as Krog attacked from behind and clawed away the crimson eye that remained. With a swift swipe from Heras, Desacles's throat was sliced, and the sands flowed into the winds. An even swifter swipe followed from the fine king of old as he thrust his blade deep through the general's chest.

Desacles was blinded, and his reign of oppression in the Desert Realm finally came to a conclusion. As the desperate keeper stepped from side to side, he tried to regain his balance while the sand flowed profusely from him. His foot became trapped in the nearby sandpit.

He screamed as the relentless grip of the Forsaken Realm grabbed a hold of him and would not let up. It ripped his being apart while he was pulled in rapidly as the army watched on. Moments later, Desacles was finally engulfed. His reign had dissipated, along with his sands. He would need to answer to the dark lord for his failure.

Krog paced slowly toward Sandriver, who lay in pain on the desert floor and would be out of commission for the battle that was almost upon them. As he reached his younger brother, he snarled remorsefully.

The warrior king stared back at him and growled as his gasps became heavier, "I…forgive you…brother…"

Sudden gusts of wind passed over Sandriver. They revolved around him powerfully as the warriors who surrounded him were momentarily blinded. The gusts stopped and fled. Sandriver still lay on the ground but no longer bore the wounds he had just endured. He removed himself from the compromised position and stood tall as he looked to Krog.

"We must stop them, brother. They must not reach the fellowship. *They* will save us all."

Krog snarled at him in agreement. The warriors were no longer under the enchantment of Desacles and once again understood the language of the leopards. They turned toward the dunes to the North as the forsaken army marched south and came into view. They approached quickly. Heras took the command as he mounted a horse made from the sands and instructed the others to line up in formation, as he once did as king long ago. He stood alongside Sandriver and Krog. A huge battle in the Desert Realm was about to commence.

XXIX: A New Reign

Gavin, Wilbur, Mitch, and Dahlia waited in the bushes of the jungle as the few palace guards who'd managed to escape stumbled onto the lift. They began their swift ascent back to the palace grounds above.

Once the lift ceased, the dim-witted palace guards reached the gate to the tunnels. They looked at one another as if the others knew the command to open it. But they did not. They took turns as they guessed, but it was pointless.

Finally one yelled, "Oh, oh…I know, I know! Pon…*taccio!*" Suddenly the gate opened, and they entered as the guard continued to ramble on. "Hahaha, I told you I knew it!"

From the near distance, Dahlia had whispered the proper command, "Paloo Mala Tokai." She then whispered to the others, "What idiots!"

Wilbur asked, "How did you know *that?* You really must know *everything.*"

Dahlia replied with a smirk, "Not really. I overheard the Chief say it when they escorted us."

Gavin was distracted by the water exhaust that channeled through the energy field as he whispered to himself, "If only we could…Nah, *that's* not possible."

Mitch spoke up. "We need to enter before it closes. If we open it again, they will be suspicious."

They raced over to the gate before it closed, but before they reached it, there was a sudden shriek above them, unlike any they had ever heard before. A phoenix dragon's wings flapped hard and loud.

The force field had been temporarily removed to allow it to leave in search of the fellowship to destroy them. The Ice Queen had unleashed her secret weapon, which flew above them and soared indomitably across the sky.

"We have to go now!" yelled Mitch as the gate began to close. They all raced underneath.

Gavin observed the phoenix dragon become smaller and thought aloud, "What is she *up to?*"

Frostbite flew across the blue sky as aerial life scattered away in intimidation. As it huffed, the cool air of the sky transformed into frost and fell in small clusters upon the villages below. It had been at least a couple of weeks since the villagers witnessed snowfall.

With the extensive range of its vision, Frostbite searched below, far and wide, across the villages, but there was no sign of John and the fellowship. It continued forward and rapidly flew toward and past the southern perimeter of the jungle. It scanned intensely and soon picked up a familiar heat signature at the edge of the desert. It descended for closer observation.

"What do you think is going to happen out there?" William asked the Chief.

"I don't know, William," he replied.

"Will. You can call me Will. That's what Papa used to call me before he—"

The Chief interrupted. "I'm sorry about your father...Will. He was a good man, a good soldier. You know, he always talked about you, even though most did not remember you. He always bragged how talented you were, how smart you were. He believed you would make a difference one day. He really believed it. You know, he would have been in the RPG if it weren't for Her Majesty loathing him as she did. Maybe if he didn't...Anyway, he raised a fine boy. Listen, you must do what you feel is right, Will, whether it's trying to persuade John to stop his course of action or to continue on. You have to choose which path you go down, and then you have to bear the consequences. It's your choice and yours alone, even if it seems that you have only one. I fear I may have already chosen the wrong path, but it's not too late for you."

William hesitated before he replied, "But...Her Majesty, she put those curses on...What is...Aaaahhhhhh!"

The Chief turned around to see what had caused William to scream. Frostbite was approaching fast. Its wings slowed its descent just before it landed.

"What has she *done*?" yelled the Chief.

They ran away as Frostbite crashed near the desert border, clearly out of its element, as it was in pain from the heat that exuded from the sands. It flapped its wings twice more and landed on the opposite side of William and the Chief as they attempted to run away. The phoenix dragon shrieked, and they both stopped in their tracks and begged for mercy.

After another mild shriek, Frostbite approached the young boy slowly and analyzed him. It looked curious as William begged, "Please spare my life, please..."

The Chief stepped in front of William in an act of valor, but this annoyed the phoenix dragon, and it shrieked at him. When the Chief did not move, it stomped its claw forward toward him and stopped short of his feet. The Chief finally submitted to the command of the beast and stepped aside. The phoenix dragon of ice stared into William's eyes and then took a step back. It knelt down and lay on its belly. It cued William to mount its back.

"I think you had better listen to it," the Chief encouraged him.

"OK, I guess I don't really have a choice here, do I?" he said as he approached and climbed up the scales of the phoenix dragon.

"Remember, Will, you must do what you feel is the right thing to do!" the Chief yelled.

Once William mounted Frostbite, it once again stood tall. He grabbed a tight hold of the chain link around its thick neck, and the wings began to flap tirelessly back into the sky to return to the cool air and continue its search. They soared across the sky as it searched the desert far and wide for the fellowship. William focused on the linked chain as a huge battle was about to wage below in the sands.

As Heras took the command of all of the freed warriors of the desert, they were no longer under the control of Desacles, and in turn one of the dark lords. They stood by the former king's side with their swords and battle-axes raised. They looked upon the forsaken army, who still possessed murky jade eyes. The forsaken were manipulated by a powerful existence that controlled them through their jade glows. However, this jade force did not have a natural connection with the Desert Realm, and they could fall no differently than the others.

"We may not defeat the lords of darkness on this day, but we shall win this battle against their puppets. They shall be freed from the tugs of their wicked strings. We may not be able to return to the world of the living, but at least our souls shall pass to the heavens, which shall grant us the peace that we seek." Heras longed to return to his sweet Annabel. Sandriver stood at his side and looked upon him with both respect and sympathy.

The forsaken army continued to march through the sands in their colossal frames. They were no more than fifty paces away when Heras finally released a battle cry. His army, nearly one hundred strong, began to storm forward and stir up the sands from the desert floor as their huge frames crashed against them. They flattened dunes in their wake.

Sandriver and Krog led the charge. While Krog was more methodical with his approach as he bobbed and weaved around the swipes of the murky jade blades of the forsaken soldiers, Sandriver displayed his brute force as he tackled them and thrashed one after the next. Combined, they took out five of the forsaken in as many seconds. Heras's sword relieved a few of their limbs, and their sand spilled into the winds.

The battle became fiercer, and the sands began to rise up and blind all onlookers. The clashes became more desperate, especially by the forsaken, as they could not see the desert warriors who were under the command of Heras.

The desert warriors suddenly had an advantage. They were able to see the glowing jade through the strengthening sandstorms that had formed as a result of the beating of the desert. This made it easier for the warriors to thrash through the forsaken. It was not long before the last of the forsaken had been slain on the battlefield.

As the storms subsided and the sand settled back on the desert floor, Heras raised his sword in victory. They had lost few warriors in the battle. He looked at Sandriver and Krog with a smile across his sand-constructed face.

The desert-born leopard glanced at his brother and snarled at him, "That was easier than I could have expected."

Krog concurred. As Sandriver returned his gaze toward Heras, the smile disappeared. A look of worry replaced it.

Sandriver turned around and saw the gateway to the Forsaken Realm had been opened. The direction had been reversed, and the damned and forsaken souls were being catapulted outward into the

Desert Realm and transformed into sand demons. Heras commanded a retreat to a safe distance.

Several minutes later, the expulsion ceased. They were now surrounded by forces that outnumbered them tenfold. These forces burned crimson and were the soldiers of the Forsaken Realm's dark lord himself.

XXX: A Brother for a Father

They rowed the raft with increasing difficulty as the frozen oars of the sea creature had all but melted in the warming waters under the sun. They tried to row with their hands, but the progress was slow if not counterproductive.

"Do you have your powers back yet?" asked Ivy.

John tried to illuminate as he had done so many times before, but all that he could conjure now were useless sparks from his eyes and hands. "I know it's in there somewhere, but I can't bring it out. Maybe I can't do it without Midwa. But I feel like a part of him is still inside of me, even though he…"

Tony spoke up. "We sure could use your powers, John. We're never going to reach the Ice Palace, let alone the desert."

Freddie added, "Um, guys, what's that?"

Frostbite had begun its descent toward them and started to breathe iced flames from a distance.

A familiar voice screamed, "No! Stop! Don't kill them!" and the phoenix dragon halted its attack. It flapped its wings tirelessly as it suspended several feet above the fellowship. A mild shriek followed from Frostbite as it listened to William.

There was a loud explosion to the south. They all turned their attention to the Fire King's castle. A plume of fire and smoke burst from the castle gate. Suddenly the phoenix dragon of fire emerged. It was in search of the one who had stolen the ring from the Fire King. The ring had a specific heat signature that Pyro followed, as it was born of its own fire. It would seek to reclaim its link from the new potential master before he could wear it. As it was released of its servitude by the death of its former master, it had a chance to reclaim its freedom if it could prevent a new master from taking command of it.

Frostbite's instincts kicked in and sought to battle its natural-born enemy over the ages. William fell off as the phoenix dragon of ice jolted toward Pyro. Fortunately, the boy was not far from the raft when he fell, and the others were able to pull him up quickly after he swam over.

As they were sworn enemies, Pyro quickly diverted its attention from the ring and prepared for battle with Frostbite. The kids needed to continue on to the desert while the dragons kept each other occupied, but they had no way to move the raft forward. John's attempts to turn his powers back on continued to fail.

As they watched the phoenix dragons above, they witnessed the fire and ice collide relentlessly. Neither seemed to gain the advantage, as the elements effectively canceled each other out. They were coerced to resort to claw-to-claw combat. Freddie lost hope. He believed that the victor would either burn them or freeze them. He did not believe there was a happy ending. The others shared the same sentiments.

"What are we supposed to do?" Tony asked.

"We have to figure something out," John said.

William spoke up. "Guys, you have to—"

"You've said enough, William. We already know where you stand!" Ivy interrupted.

William replied, "No, you don't. What I did was…wrong. I want to help. But please, the Ice Queen, she has my little sister. If we can somehow free Frostbite from the other phoenix dragon, and somehow persuade it to return us to the Ice Palace, then we could fly past the desert. Trust me, you don't want to pass through there right now."

Freddie joined in the discussion. "And how do you suppose we do that, *genius*?" He was clearly holding a grudge against William.

John spoke up. "Freddie, relax. Let's try to figure this out together. William, how did you manage to get on the dragon without it freezing you over?"

William replied, "I really don't know. It seems to recognize me."

Tony was still upset, but he was able to put aside their differences for the time being. "Can you call upon it?"

"I don't know. I can try," William replied.

Ivy added, "Not yet, though. We can't distract it. Otherwise, it will be exposed to the other dragon's attacks."

"I have an idea." John jumped in. "It's crazy, but maybe crazy enough to work. Midwa showed me something when I...almost passed to the other side. I think if I can focus, I might be able to take control over Pyro for long enough to allow Frostbite to strike it. I'll then send myself back toward my body, and William can call the phoenix dragon of ice over. Hopefully it will still remember him."

Ivy spoke up. "John, but are you sure—"

He interrupted her. "Ivy, I believe I can do it."

She replied, "OK...I believe in you."

William looked at John. "Look, John. I just want you to know—"

John spoke up again. "We can talk about this later, OK? For now, we need to take care of this."

William nodded in agreement, with shame in his countenance.

John instructed them to back up near the edges of the raft. He began to focus without his illumination, unsure whether he would be successful even if he had told Ivy otherwise. But he needed the others to believe in him in order to believe in himself. He thought of the love of the others and their love for him as Midwa had taught him. He felt himself slowly begin to tear from his physical form. It was painful, but he continued to focus. He looked up at the phoenix dragons as they battled and tried to aim accurately, or else he would risk projecting himself into Frostbite and it being slain.

John projected himself after he lined up his aim. But the dragons once again wrestled as they knocked each other's jaws away to avoid being struck with the opposing elements from close quarters. John was close and about to enter Pyro's mind, but with a sudden twist of the wrestle, he entered Frostbite's.

He heard the voice of a young girl. "Please help me! I must free my father! The Ice Queen is forcing me to pass messages along to this dragon because it can only heed the commands of the innocent within its mind."

John's voice followed. "We don't have much time. I have to leave now!"

She replied, "*Wait!* Penelope, the name is Penelope. You have to tell my brother where I am. I have to obey Her Majesty's orders because she has threatened to forsake our father if I don't. I believe he rests in peace, so we must help him remain that way. Please help! And tell my brother that his is the only voice I can hear from within this...*place.*"

John replied with a sense of urgency, "We'll save you, Penelope. I have to go *now*. Instruct the phoenix dragon to strike when Pyro's neck is exposed!"

She asked, "*When?*"

John did not reply. He was already focused on the phoenix dragon of fire as he looked into its empty black eyes. He projected himself through the swinging claws. He could not be touched by the physical world in this form until he released himself. He entered the mind of Pyro. The phoenix dragon shrieked. John began to scream. Even the Fire King's touch did not burn with such agonizing pain.

"Leave me at once!" a muffled, screechy voice screamed painfully to him from within Pyro.

John focused his will through the pain. He took brief control of the phoenix dragon and spread its short arms wide as he leaned it back and exposed its neck.

"*Now!*" he yelled aloud, desperate for Frostbite to attack. A quick strike to the neck followed and left the phoenix dragon of fire to fall limp.

It fell quickly toward the sea as John focused once more. As it was his third consecutive attempt, he was exhausted, but he needed to return to his body before it was too late. He could potentially be stuck in the dragon phoenix until it was reborn and emerged from the sea. He was unsure of what would happen to him. He thought of Ivy and the others. He also thought of Midwa. He barely knew the wizard, but he felt as though he knew him enough to love him. They shared a connection.

His being was once again torn from where he was. With his sights set on his body, he projected himself. There was a huge splash in the sea as John's eyes opened. The others looked upon him with relief as Pyro sunk deep into the sea to reside with the creature John had destroyed.

Frostbite descended toward them as they screamed in fear.

William called, "Please, don't kill us!"

John put his hand on William's shoulder. "It's OK, William. Penelope controls it."

William looked back at him. "What? But how…?"

John replied, "I'm not sure how, but I am sure. She told me."

William was puzzled, but before he could ask any more questions, Frostbite had already begun to flap its expansive wings next to their raft. Their hair flowed in the gusts of wind that the winds created. The phoenix dragon cued William to mount it as it had once before.

He leaped onto its wing as it slowed briefly. He pleaded with it to allow the others to join so they could return to the northern kingdom. He hoped Penelope was indeed somewhere in there as John had suggested. It agreed. The fellowship joined William, and they sat along the neck of the dragon. Freddie pulled out the mackelroy branches he'd untied from the raft as it drifted apart. He tied himself to Tony, and soon they were all tied to one another. William then secured it to the chain link that circled the phoenix dragon's neck.

Their ascension began. They made their way above the sea and across the sky. They were once again over the desert. They could see some of what had begun to transpire from above, as there were pockets of visibility that the sandstorms had not yet taken over.

Was that…Sandriver? John thought as he recognized the dominating leopard. *But he was made entirely of sand.* The leopard raced back into the sandstorms as sand collided into itself violently within the Desert Realm. Hundreds of crimson eyes appeared through the hazy storms.

They approached the Ice Palace swiftly, and soon John could see no more beyond the veil of the sandstorms. They began to slow, as the force field had been raised again and blocked them so they could not enter at will. Her Majesty did not expect the phoenix dragon to return so soon. They would need to find a way to force her to lower the energy field.

There was a sudden, unbearable shriek from Frostbite. It shook the kids off balance. Fortunately, they had secured themselves with the mackelroy branch. They swung wildly as the phoenix dragon lost control of its wings.

The Ice Queen had penetrated Penelope's mind and was in the process of correcting what she had done. She had only ceased her connection with the young girl's mind for an hour as she tended to her collection of newly frozen innocents in her secret vault, which had swelled to nearly two hundred over the years.

"*What are you doing?*" she yelled to Penelope. "I gave you specific orders! If you ever want to see your father again, then you need to tell the dragon to do exactly as I have instructed! I stand now before your father and can destroy him *forever*. You have only one chance to redeem yourself and save him from the torture I will cast him to."

She replied, "But…my brother is connected to the others!"

"An acceptable loss! *Destroy them all!*" the Ice Queen yelled.

"No, it's *not*," Penelope screamed courageously.

"You *must*…you must help me. Your father will be *damned* if you do not!" the Ice Queen yelled back desperately.

"My papa's already gone. My brother is not. I will *not* sacrifice my brother to save my father." The five-year-old spoke with maturity beyond her years. "I'm sorry, Papa…" Penelope tried to regain control during their rapid descent. "Please help, Frostbite. We must save my brother. We must save all of them."

The phoenix dragon was no longer in pain and recomposed itself. It flapped its wings before it would have crashed into a village home. The scene left the mother of the family to faint in her garden, as she had gone out to see whether everything was all right.

Frostbite quickly ascended back toward the force field. Once it stabilized, the others were able to climb back up and mount it as it adjusted itself. As they searched for a way into the palace grounds, Tony noticed a familiar face just next to the edge of the waterfall. Gavin was attempting to get their attention.

"Over here!" the elder man yelled as he stood next to Wilbur, Dahlia, and Mitch. They all joined in and yelled the same.

Tony yelled, "Get closer!"

The phoenix dragon did not understand.

William yelled the same. "Get closer, Penelope!"

The phoenix dragon heeded. Indeed, Penelope was only able to hear the voice of her brother.

As they approached, Gavin yelled again, "Freeze the water! We need to block the water in and flood the palace. She'll be forced to lower the force field!"

William could not hear him, but Ivy related the instructions, as she was able to read lips. William then passed it along to his sister, who in turn instructed Frostbite.

Frostbite inhaled a deep breath and exhaled a long, freezing breath of air that froze over the exhaust. It did it once more to ensure it would not crack under the pressure of the water that would soon accumulate. It worked. The palace grounds began to flood.

However, the celebration would be short-lived for the group near the exhaust, as they needed to run to higher ground for safety in the palace. They began to hope that the Ice Queen would lower the force field in order to release the water before it flooded. It would allow the fellowship and Frostbite back in.

A loud shriek echoed behind them. The phoenix dragon of fire fast approached, filled with vengeance.

XXXI: Coup d'État

The young captives plotted their rebellion along with Katina, the adolescent Tiberian leopard. Pippy communicated with the few rodents that remained, and they advised her of a secret room that they would be able to access through the network of exhaust tunnels underground. This was their way out, and then they would overthrow the Ice Queen.

The few guards who remained had been blocked off from the dungeon. The young prisoners made their way to the network of tunnels, the first of which looked familiar, as they had been incapacitated there by the Ice Queen days ago. It was a reminder that it would not be easy. Pippy took the lead with Katina as they tracked the rodents.

They walked along the sides of the tunnel. The stone walkways prevented their feet from becoming soaked in the thick, dirty waters in the middle. They eventually reached tunnels that flowed with the clear waters that had melted from throughout the Ice Palace. These were the waters that flowed down to Lake Tarin below.

The water level began to rise. "Hurry! This way!" Pippy yelled as she followed a few rodents that had sped up.

None of the gates had been lowered, as the guards had not maintained the scheduled openings and closures during their shifts. The tunnels dimmed, and the rodents were no longer visible. Pippy grunted in frustration, but the Tiberian leopard possessed uncanny senses of smell and sound and tracked the rodents within the darkness. Katina snarled to let the rebels know where to follow.

They eventually reached a stairway that exuded an extremely cold chill. As they approached, the dimness began to transform into a light that afforded them visibility. Pippy noticed some of the palace guards' equipment laid out before the stairway entrance ahead of them, which bent around a corner and led to a bright chamber in the distance. Perhaps it was the last chamber the guards had seen.

They could not linger at the entrance any longer, as the water level continued to swell and was freezing due to the temperatures of the Ice Palace. The rate that it rose accelerated. They all filed onto the stairway and scaled the flight of steps before they exited into the chamber at the other end.

They were in awe of the chamber. Although the temperatures were well below freezing, it had a mystical bluish-white hue to it that almost glowed as it reflected against the innumerable figures spread throughout.

It was the Ice Queen's secret chamber. This was why she needed Frostbite. She could not conjure such a persistent frigid temperature like the phoenix dragon could. As the young rebels walked around the chamber, they gazed upon the figures. They were frozen.

A loud thump echoed as something crashed into the frigid floor.

"Aaaahhhhhh!" screamed one of the young girls.

"What's wrong?" Pippy asked.

Scary Carrie yelled, "It's dead! *He* pushed it over!"

Amos, clumsy as usual, had tripped into the frozen figure and knocked it over. The impact on this particularly frigid floor was enough to crack the surface.

A bright white light flew into the room from the entrance opposite from which they entered. It was absorbed by the figure that had been frozen. Its eyes suddenly opened, and the kids who surrounded it began to scream in fear. The remainder of the ice around it dissipated, and color once again returned to its pale fair skin.

"Where am I?" The figure barely spoke, as it had not felt a breath in years. She stood up as she looked at all the kids around her. She recognized one of them. *"Manny?* Manny, is that you?"

"Yes, do I know you?" Manny Petty replied.

"Do you know *me?* I sure hope so. It's me, *Mama!"* She ran up to him and gave him a big hug. His memories came flooding back. "Oh my, it's been so long since…*since you've trimmed your nails,* Manny. They're terrible! Haven't I told you…Sorry, I'm sorry…I'm just *so* glad to see you! You've grown so much!"

"I told you!" yelled Pippy to everyone else.

The Ice Queen had made sure to capture all of the mothers of the villages once they were unable to produce more captives for her. It was the only way she could ensure that the kids would never get their memories back and try to form a rebellion against her. As long as they remained frozen in this chamber, their souls remained trapped in her scepter and empowered her.

"We must free all of them! Knock them over to free their souls! We must eliminate the Ice Queen!" Pippy yelled to the sound of cheers.

The kids ran through the massive chamber, which was colder than any other in the palace. They grouped into threes around the heavy statues of frozen bodies and began to tip them over. Bright white lights began to travel into the chamber in quick succession. The bodies that were tipped over had once again absorbed their souls, and their memories were restored, freed of all the Ice Queen's enchantments. They awakened and reanimated, and several more reunions followed. Fathers, which included palace guards who had unjust charges of treason against them, also returned to life. The palace guards were no longer dim-witted and became their normal selves. They began to speak and act empathetically once again. Katina managed to find her brother, Kato, and freed him as well. She licked his face in joyous relief, as she'd feared that she had lost him for good.

The Ice Queen slammed open the door and gazed at them with hatred. "You're ruining *everything*! After all I've given you!"

The freezing water began to swell past the dungeon. It already filled the first floor of the great hall and had begun to flow around the feet of the Ice Queen as well as the young rebels and the elders who had already been freed.

"You will cease immediately! I shall incapacitate all of you, and you shall all drown!"

With her cruelest intention, she was going to drown all of them. She waved her scepter, but nothing happened, just a flicker. The power of her scepter had weakened significantly as most of the souls were freed.

"No! *What have you done?*" she screamed. "I shall freeze you one by one then!"

She began to cast spells individually, and it worked. One by one they froze, and she slowly regained her powers as their souls were once again absorbed by the scepter.

But Pippy would not allow her to regain her strength. "Charge her! She cannot stop us all!"

And so they all charged simultaneously and knocked over more frozen statues of people in the process, which added to their numbers advantage.

The Ice Queen continued to desperately freeze them one by one as they charged, but within moments, Aimless Amos had pushed her back. They would need to reconsider his nickname. She fell over, as her feet remained frozen to the ground since they had bonded with the freezing water. She now lay on her back as they stood above her and kicked and threw the shattered ice at her. She could barely move as her body continued to bond with the freezing water. The leopards emerged through the crowd and stared her down. She calmed her reckless resistance.

"Aaaahhhhhh! Mostek liftus folesi!" She had commanded the force field to be removed, and the water rapidly flowed out of the castle and briefly flooded the villages below as it passed.

"Hang on, Grandpa!" Tony yelled over to Gavin. He held him by his shirt to keep him afloat as the waters began to elevate above the top of the thick young hibich tree. Wilbur held on tightly to Mitch and Dahlia as they helped keep him afloat.

"It's starting to go down!" Mitch yelled.

They were relieved, as they had been about to drown. The water level rapidly lowered, and they descended from the tree. After they reached solid ground, Gavin kissed it with gratitude. Dahlia looked at him as if he were strange—as if they did not think the same of her.

They raced up the stairs to the main gate and knocked anxiously along with the others who had just untied themselves from Frostbite and were dropped off low enough so they would not hurt themselves. Frostbite had flown several laps around the energy field to outrace Pyro so that the kids would not get hurt in their ongoing battle.

There was no answer. Freddie spoke up. "Maybe we can pull the gate open if we combine our strength. Those guards are not the brightest and have a bad habit of not locking gates, especially with everything that's gone on these past days."

John still had not regained his powers, but it would not matter. The collective efforts of the group were able to slowly pull open the gate. A rush of water slowly flowed at first, and then the gate exploded open as they flew back. There was an abundance of freezing water released that had flooded the great hall. It flowed outside, along with one of the remaining guards, who looked to be unconscious. This helped their cause.

As they entered the great hall, a long blade leaned against John's neck as the last remaining royal guard emerged from the shadows.

"*Don't* even think about it," Ivy said as she nocked her last arrow in her bow and pointed it at his head. He forfeited his sword and tossed it away. She smiled at John as she kept a tally of who had saved each other more.

They had the advantage. Hopefully the outcome of the battle of the phoenix dragons would be to their favor. It was time to locate the Ice Queen and free everyone.

The Ice Queen shrieked from the secret chamber on the expansive second floor. She fled from the room on her ankles as her feet remained behind in the frozen water that had claimed them. She tripped over herself and tumbled down several steps, shattering pieces of herself along the way. She had never appeared so ungraceful. Her scepter fell over the rail, landed on the floor of the great hall, and rolled near her throne.

The rebels emerged from the secret chamber and chased her down the steps. They grabbed torches that lined the walls along the way. Pippy instructed Salina to escort the leopards to the Ice Queen's private prison, where they could rescue the heir of Sandriver. They raced up the steps as they left the others behind to contend with Her Majesty.

John came face-to-face with the Ice Queen as she crawled down the remaining steps toward her throne in pain. The kids and their parents emerged from the secret chamber with torches in hand. They wished to melt her away from this world for all of the suffering she had caused them. They shut the main gate to ensure she could not flee.

As she was surrounded on all sides, John spoke up, something he had failed to do several days prior. "It's over, Your Majesty."

"Why are you calling her that, John? She is the *Ice Queen*! She is as cold as ice and has no heart!" Pippy raised her voice, riling up the others behind her.

"What have you done to my baby sister?" William yelled at the queen as she continued to crawl over to her scepter.

"I did not mean to do that to her…" she said. She was in pain, still crawling.

"*Liar!*" Pippy yelled as she tossed her torch below. It landed in between the queen and her scepter.

"Please! I can change…" The queen was desperate. "I will release you all. You will have the lives you had before. But I need my scepter to do that. Please, you must believe me!"

"Do you swear to keep to your word?" John asked nervously.

"She's lying, John!" Ivy said with concern.

"We need to give her a chance to redeem herself," John replied.

"This is madness!" yelled Pippy, and soon the others were about to revolt against John as well.

"I swear! I cross my…heart. If I break my word, you can cast all of your torches upon me. Please, I am weak and in *so* much pain. I *finally* understand all of you. I've done so much wrong by you. I could never do again what I have done. I am ashamed for my actions. You must believe me…please." A tear ran down her face and froze halfway down as she knelt upon the still barely wet floor.

"John, it's a trick!" Tony yelled out. "She has no heart. You know that!"

"That's right." John spoke. "I do know that. That's why I plan to return it to her before she can retrieve her scepter. So she can *cross her heart.*"

John revealed a capsule he had been holding in the frosted hibich leaf on his back. He planned to release the Ice Queen's heart from the capsule. He grabbed the ring from his pocket and extended it to fit it into a recess in the capsule.

The Ice Queen was too quick. She leaped over the burning torch and nearly melted her upper arm entirely. She grabbed her scepter and immediately pointed it toward the capsule and froze it over. It was too cold for John to hold it. He dropped it almost immediately. Frozen over, it did not shatter, and the recess in which he needed to insert the ring was blocked. He placed the ring back in his pocket.

The Ice Queen froze the air around her nonexistent feet and melted arm and formed new ones in their place made entirely of ice. She no longer had assistance from the palace guards, as they had been overrun. Pippy and the rebels freed many of the countless captives in her secret chamber. And the phoenix dragon of ice no longer was held captive in the lair she'd constructed. She had freed it in hopes she could control it after she fused the soul of Penelope to its mind, but that plan had failed. The forsaken army she'd appropriated no longer served her. They lay in the Forsaken Realm as they originally were intended to. She had no one to control anymore. She was truly alone. It was her against the world. The Ice Queen was surrounded by vengeful eyes and became increasingly more desperate.

She looked around to the prisoners along the perimeter and waved her scepter. "Do you really think that you can overpower me? *I cannot be defeated!*" One by one she froze the surrounding prisoners.

She turned to Pippy. "I should have left you with your parents. But do not worry. I will make sure *they* pay for what you have done." After she froze her over, she did the same in quick succession to several behind the young rebel leader to block the path along the steps.

She then turned around and looked to John. "I will torment all of them before I destroy them. And they can thank you, *pauper.*"

She turned her attention to Freddie. "I will start with you, you little troublemaker. Do you know how *long* it took to fix my tower clock?"

She lifted her scepter toward him. An arrow suddenly knocked it sideways and caused an explosion of frost against a nearby wall.

"Playtime is over! I will destroy *all* of you!" The Ice Queen became stronger as she absorbed more souls to power her scepter. She turned her attention to Ivy. "Nice shot."

Ivy replied, "Fellowship forever!"

The Ice Queen hesitated. "*So…*you want your memories of your family back, *do you?*"

"Yes! *Please!*" There was nothing Ivy had wanted more for the past several years.

John yelled out, "Ivy, *no!*"

The Ice Queen replied, "Ask and you shall *receive*!" A scathing malice laced her words.

John ran toward Ivy to try to stop her, but it was too late. Ivy's memories of her parents flooded back. At first she had a smile, but as the memories flashed quickly, it was not long before it turned to a weep.

"Make it...stop!" Ivy dropped to the ground with an unnerving scream that shook the others to their core.

"How does it feel to be responsible for the pain and suffering of all of those you love?" The Ice Queen yelled to John with hatred. "I'm not finished!"

She turned her attention to Tony, who was trying to help John comfort Ivy. His fondness of her was always obvious, but he knew she only had eyes for one chosen by Midwa.

The Ice Queen addressed him. "Except maybe for you, my sweet Tony. There is yet potential in you. I will need to begin anew and will require a new chief to lead my new army. My current chief is...shall we say, *unfit for duty*. He has filled William with words of poison and derailed my plan, all because he wants to *pretend* the traitor could be the son that he lost...the *son* he exiled to save the rest of his family. I will *not* tolerate weakness!"

"I will never join you!" Tony yelled back.

"So be it," she said and froze him without hesitation.

She then faced William and spoke with malevolence in her voice. "Which brings me to you. Will you *ever* stop disappointing me? Did I ask too much of you to save your sister? No. *I did not!* And now she is gone. Without my command, your precious Penelope will be bonded with Frostbite until it is reborn, and she will then vanish— *gone!*—and it is *your* fault." With a wave of her scepter, she began to speak an enchantment in a foreign tongue that was intended to cast him away to the realm of the forsaken to face the dark lord himself. "Ashtu mak talaba hostis—"

A sudden hiss distracted her and caused her to stop the recital of the curse as she looked above. Everyone looked toward the ceiling of the palace as well.

Drops of water began to fall from the ceiling. Due to the ambient temperature of the palace, they turned into small clusters of frost by the time they reached the ground of the great hall. There was a noticeable crack that was growing quickly in the clock tower above them.

The hiss had become more intense. Soon the cracks shattered, and the clock tower descended upon them. Twenty-seven stories would be passed in a brief period of time. There was a bright crimson illumination that surrounded it. A shriek echoed as the crimson became brighter and melted the tower into pure water. Most of the water evaporated before it reached the palace floor and left only a few splashes to reach the kids.

Pyro, the phoenix dragon of fire, revealed itself as it crashed into an open space between John and the Ice Queen. It shrieked loudly as it swayed its ferocious jaws wildly and sprayed fire around the second and third floors. Everyone nearby scattered toward safety.

Composed entirely of ice, the queen was nervous. She had betrayed the Fire King, and the dragon phoenix was seeking its revenge against her in honor of its former master. It was bound by this tradition. It would also reclaim its ring so it would itself be freed from the command of whoever wielded it.

The Ice Queen raised her scepter and waved it at the phoenix dragon, but Pyro breathed its overwhelming fire toward the scepter and knocked it away. It had been melted beyond reparation. The souls it had collected had been returned to those who were frozen, both in the great hall and in the secret chamber, even the rodents of the palace. All of the prisoners, with exception of Ivy, who lay there as she still wept from the pain of her memories, were no longer incapacitated and cheered on Pyro, as it was about to eliminate the Ice Queen and all of the evil that went along with her.

The phoenix dragon was an unexpected ally. It did what they could not. However, its presence meant that Frostbite had demised, and so had Penelope along with it. The realization hit William, who was notably shook and distraught.

The Ice Queen suddenly shrieked and finally exposed a sense of vulnerability in her voice. The voice beneath the shriek was familiar as it faded in and out. "Please…*help me!*"

John was taken aback. With a flashback to the Fire King's castle, he realized it was the fair-looking lady of royalty who was bound helpless in the king's chamber. All along she had been veiled by the ice-cold surface that slowly consumed her entire being.

"*Wait!*" John yelled.

The phoenix dragon ceased his steps toward the Ice Queen and turned its long neck to John. It paced slowly around him as it shrieked. He did not move.

"If you can understand me, she's not what she appears to be! She was forced to be this way!" John yelled to Pyro.

More jeers and unpopular taunts ensued from the rebels.

John continued. "She was tricked by the Fire King!"

The phoenix dragon shrieked as it looked around at the dissatisfied kids.

"What are you doing, John? This is our only chance!" Tony yelled.

"No, it's not!" John replied. "We need to restore her heart. She's innocent! And we do not know what this dragon means to do to us when she's gone."

"How can you say that? You know what she's done to *all of us*!" Tony was frustrated with John's naivety.

"Yes, but—" John began to say before he was interrupted.

The phoenix dragon began to take a deep breath as he stared at and focused on John's pocket. The Fire King's ring glowed with crimson that burned through his pocket and had begun to sear into the chilled floor of the great hall. The dragon shrieked.

John stood there, nervous and powerless, as the dragon gazed directly into his eyes. Without Midwa, he was helpless. It would be too dangerous to project himself into it without knowledge of what to do. He could potentially kill all of the innocent people around.

Suddenly there was another shriek from above. It was Frostbite, and it blazed down as its shrieks echoed throughout. It had survived after all, though it looked to be in pain with gashes all over.

Pyro immediately flapped its wings and ascended toward Frostbite. Fire blazed upward as the frosted flames crashed into them, as it did in their previous battle above the sea. Both phoenix dragons crashed through the frozen fire and into each other as they flapped their wings recklessly and clawed each other abrasively.

They destroyed the middle floors of the Ice Palace, which began to collapse under the impact and fell into the levels below. Salina and the leopards had just rescued the heir of Sandriver and struggled to find their way down to safer ground. Salina mounted Kato, and they leaped down along the debris. Katina carried the heir within her jaws more carefully.

A massive amount of debris fell down to the lower levels of the great hall. Everyone below scattered and, ironically, sought refuge in the dungeon, even the palace guards who no longer fought for Her Majesty. The irony struck the Ice Queen as she looked around her. Everything she had worked for had begun to collapse, and there was only one person she could blame.

"*John!*" she yelled louder than she had ever done before and almost lost her voice.

She looked around the floor, desperately in search of her bow, which she had last placed beside her throne. The phoenix dragons continued to battle above and caused more debris to fall. It barely missed her. She located it under some nearby rubble and turned toward John.

"I'm going to finish what I started. This time I will not miss. Without Midwa, you are *nothing*." The Ice Queen's words cut deeply as she struggled to harness the remnants of power she still had within her, which was a fraction of her former potential, and still faded yet.

The bow began to stretch as she pulled her frozen arm backward. She slowly created a field of swirling air. It slowly frosted and transformed into the shape of an arrow. John was several paces away from the Ice Queen. There was nowhere to run, no one to help as they stood back in the distance, terrified as the phoenix dragons continued to battle above them.

The Ice Queen focused on John as she recited an enchantment. She was almost finished when Ivy rushed from the side in an attempt to disarm her.

The frigid queen noticed the young girl in her periphery and turned toward her as the ice arrow was finally prepared for launch, then whispered as she looked back to John, "I *love* a good tragedy."

"*No!*" John yelled as he had flashbacks of when Jacob fell, followed by all of the moments that he had shared with Ivy. They had come so far together, with each other, for each other. He could not afford to lose her. He could not carry that burden as well. He looked down at the floor and noticed the ring as it still seared into the palace ground. He noticed in his periphery the ice arrow was about to be launched from the bow. Immediately he leaped across the floor as he grabbed the ring and held it in his palm.

The Ice Arrow was launched.

John placed the ring on his finger.

His heart beat once, the sound of which echoed slowly throughout his mind. He blinked his eyes in order to make sure he had not imagined what he saw. His hand burned crimson as the ring spewed a lava-like liquid. He appeared to burn but was in no pain. His skin was a dark void beneath the fire. He looked at the rest of his body and saw the same. He stood up and felt taller than normal, hulking in fact.

John's heart beat a second time; the sound of which again echoed slowly throughout his mind. He looked up. Everything appeared filtered through hues of crimson and black. Darkness was prevalent as he consumed all of the light around him, which fueled the crimson that burned through him. As he looked around, he could see that everyone's soul projected as a frame around their physical forms. However, their souls displayed images of their most satisfying desires and terrifying fears. Their true selves were revealed. With this advantage, he could manipulate all that he desired.

The ice arrow traced through the air in slow motion. It appeared that he had slowed down time significantly. Everyone's voice was muffled and moved sluggishly through the dark space. He walked over toward the frosted arrow and Ivy and looked on either side of it. He could see the look of determination on Ivy's face as she rushed forward heroically to save John. On the other side was the face of the Ice Queen, which was filled with pleasure at the prospect of casting another to the world of the forsaken with her ice arrow.

Midway between the two, John grabbed a hold of the ice arrow, which dissipated in a flash with no remnants.

John's heart beat a third time; the sound of which did not echo. It appeared time had caught up, and everything moved about in a normal fashion. Screams followed from the kids and parents who surrounded him, as they were completely in the dark. Ivy stopped in her tracks and retreated. She raced to Tony and Freddie to seek safety.

"My apologies, my lord," the Ice Queen pleaded. "I did not know. I do not…"

"I am not…" John began to answer, but the urge was too great to resist. His words slipped away from his control. Soon they would not be his own. A shriek was heard from above. As he looked above, Pyro descended slowly down toward him. Frostbite was battered and was barely hanging on to the balcony of the twentieth floor after the brutal battle with the phoenix dragon of fire.

"I am not…pleased with your disobedience," John said. *What's happening to* me? he yelled to himself; however, only he could hear himself.

He looked at the Ice Queen as she pleaded. He looked closer at her soul within. He saw the image of the same young lady of royalty, bound, as she pleaded, "Please…*help me*!" repeatedly as the voice faded in and out. "*Please! Help me!*"

John looked around desperately and yelled to himself again, *What's…happening…to…me?* He noticed a reflection in a section of melting ice nearby, where several kids sought sanctuary, terrified as they realized they had been noticed. He could finally see himself as the others saw him, towering and terrifying; John had become the Fire King.

John's heartbeat began to slow once more. With each moment that passed, his heart seemed to beat even slower. Life fleeted, and he realized that it would not be much longer before he would be stuck here for an eternity. Perhaps he would make a stronger Fire King, as he did things the Fire King could not do without his horned helmet. Perhaps it was his destiny. There was much he could accomplish. With this power, he could bring the world back to goodness even.

"John..." a familiar voice echoed.

He turned around in the oblivion that was the ring's being.

"I am glad you are finally able to see me as I once was," said the voice.

"You...you look like...me," John replied.

"Yes, John. It is true...I am your father. I am sorry we could not meet earlier. I never meant to abandon you. I am sorry that I must leave you so soon. I have been hiding in the corners of this oblivion since you left the castle of Villanis, with the hope I would see you one last time."

Midwa's being had begun to fade, along with John's.

"The ring will consume any who linger. You must leave now, John. I cannot guarantee that I can defeat the ring's power from within, but I will do my best to tame it and dispel any who attempt to enter and take command. I have lived my life. I have a few regrets, but you are not one of them. Now leave! You must *not* return to this dreadful place!"

John's heart beat once; the sound of which echoed slowly throughout the oblivion.

"But...Father...it's not fair. I haven't had any time to know you!"

John's heart beat a second time; the sound of which echoed slower throughout the oblivion.

"Not much is fair, my son…You must leave now. Focus and remove the ring. Race to the capsule and restore the queen's heart. Remember your lessons. Now focus…"

John's heart beat a third time; the sound of which echoed even slower throughout the emptiness.

The crimson images that surrounded him began to fade. Light had begun to restore throughout the Ice Palace. John removed the ring. He raced toward the capsule, which was no longer frozen, as the Fire King's presence had thawed its frozen exterior.

Suddenly the phoenix dragon of fire crashed into the ground and stood between him and the capsule. It dared him to proceed. Without the ring around his finger, John was just an ordinary boy who held an extraordinary ring. He was too weak in the eyes of Pyro to deem worthy, as he could only wear it for a few moments before he gave up. The dragon shrieked and took a deep breath. It was prepared to release a raging flame of fire toward John, who had his eyes fixed on the capsule. He looked at the Ice Queen. Much of her exterior had melted; she had begun a transformation into a pool of melted ice, but it was halted when he removed the ring.

"Aaaahhhhhh!" yelled a voice from the side as it rushed the dragon's tail. It was Norman. He had finally gained some courage and began to hack at the tail with a frozen shard from the fallen debris. The phoenix dragon barely reacted at the young one who foolishly risked his life. It tossed Norman away with its tail. He flew violently across to the side and was knocked unconscious against the chilled ground.

The dragon once again turned its attention to John, who was unable to take advantage of the brief moment Norman afforded him.

Suddenly there was a war cry, "Aaaahhhhhh!" Tony began to rush the dragon as well. "The capsule, John! *Go for it!*"

The dragon was not worried. However, soon the war cries echoed and grew in number. All of the rebels stood next to each other and rushed toward the dragon. They attempted to distract it and give John one final chance to reach the capsule in order to restore the Ice Queen's heart.

As the kids attacked and annoyed the phoenix dragon, they could not overpower him, but it gave John a chance to weave under the crowd, through, and over to the capsule. He thrust himself forward and slid toward it. He barely grabbed the capsule while he continued to slide past the massive jaws of Pyro as it attempted to take a chomp out of him. During his slide, John was able to insert the ring into the capsule close enough to the Ice Queen.

There was a blinding light from the capsule as it unlocked and forced all in the room to cover their eyes. Even the phoenix dragon shrieked. The flash lasted for several seconds.

The light began to fade, and when it returned to normal, John and the others looked upon Her Majesty in her former glory. She was once again Agribel, just and fair queen of Belghan, no longer veiled by the coldness cruelly cast upon her by the Fire King. She looked around and wept. She wept for all that she had done around her. She wept as her palace was unrecognizable. She looked upon the poor kids she had imprisoned. Eyes of judgment glared at her, but the tension subsided as they saw the tenderness within her and realized that she was not the monster she had been tricked into being. She would have a chance at redemption. She would restore her kingdom to its former glory.

However, while former glory was now within reach, Pyro still stood tall above her with its judgmental eyes. She had betrayed her master, its former master. She would not have her redemption after all. The phoenix dragon leaned back as it took a deep breath. It leaned forward, about to thrust a blazing fire at Her Majesty.

The fire began to thrust from its belly and up its long neck. It would not thrust farther, however. The body of the dragon had begun to freeze over rapidly. It had been caught in its blind spot. Frostbite suddenly shrieked as it landed and continued to breathe its flames of ice against Pyro for nearly a minute. The phoenix dragon of fire had been frozen over by its bitter rival, Frostbite, in the center of the great hall. The frost it thrust would not be permanent, but it would last for several years.

The palace, while largely destroyed in areas, would eventually resemble what it once did in years past. Frostbite paced toward William, who was incredibly nervous and depressed that he could never see his sister again. The others moved out of the way. Its chilled breath dissipated quickly in the warming climate as the Ice Palace began to melt. As it stood above William, it breathed softly into his face. It lowered its snout and rubbed it against his head.

Another blinding flash followed. When it subsided, Penelope was by her older brother's side as he remembered her. Frostbite stood behind them, once again free. William gave her the biggest hug he had ever given her.

"I'm never letting go of you, baby sister," William said with a tear in his eye.

"I hope you don't mean *never*! And I'm *not* a baby anymore!" Penelope replied, slightly annoyed. "I'm a big girl!"

William hugged her tighter with a big smile. "I know, baby sister. I know."

Katina and Kato stepped forward, finally making their way down with Salina and the heir of Sandriver. She carried the heir over and asked, "Oh, can I keep him? He's so adorable. *Please!*"

Katina sneered at John as they laughed at the idea. She lived up to her nickname Stingy Salina. The leopards stepped up to John and began to lick him persistently, a great display of their gratitude.

The restored guards opened the main gate to allow the warm air outside to enter and melt the ice that remained. They all began to walk outside. Frostbite gave them a bit of a scare as it flew past them and flapped its wings wildly. It flew off to the East to rejoin the other phoenix dragons, who were still preparing for their turn in the ever-present war between good and evil. Together they would help maintain the delicate balance that was needed for more to prosper rather than suffer.

John walked along with Her Majesty into the gardens. As they looked far into the distance, they saw the sandstorms suddenly cease. One final strong gust of wind swept across the desert. The forsaken soldiers had been pulled back into their realm, while the souls that had been claimed by the realm unjustly had been freed from their torture and were allowed to move to the Realm of Peace. Their souls dissipated. The palace guards who had been claimed inappropriately stood upon the desert sands and would need to trek back north, but they could manage the distance with assistance from the mighty eagles.

The desert was no longer filled with several colossal warriors that roamed about. Only one remained. Sandriver had begun to return north. His brother had been returned to the Forsaken Realm, so he dragged along a heavy heart. He created the desert skyline as he stood alone. As the Tiberian leopard looked up, he noticed that the palace to the north had been taken over. With his keen vision, he saw his heir within the arms of a young girl, safe and sound. Reinvigorated, he began to sprint across the dunes. Soon he reached the northern perimeter of the Desert Realm and leaped as all looked upon him. He dissipated as he exited the realm. Ivy noticed with her exceptional vision that he landed unharmed and raced north in his living form. He disappeared into the jungle, but she could see the trees rustle as he passed through hastily.

"Do you see what I'm seeing, John?" Ivy asked excitedly as she stood next to him.

"Yeah. He's incredible, isn't he?" he replied.

"Yeah, almost as incredible as someone else I know," she said as she grabbed his hand.

As Tony looked on, he seemed to accept that John and Ivy would remain together. And he deserved it after all they had been through. He would find a love of his own one day.

"William? William!" a familiar voice yelled.

William turned around. "*Papa?*" It had been too long that both of them had carried a heavy heart over each other.

Tony also had his reunion, as his father and his grandfather Gavin had a group hug.

Jacob's father looked everywhere for him but was given the unfortunate news by Tony. He wept in his arms. William walked over with his father to speak with him. He spoke of Jacob honorably. It would be some time before he could tell the truth.

With a vague recollection of what she had done, the queen began to speak to John and grabbed his attention away from Ivy as they smiled to each other. "I am so, so sorry to all of you. I will spend the rest of my life fixing everything that I have done so horribly wrong. I hope my sister Annabel can find it in herself to forgive me. I wasn't myself. I understand if you can never forgive me."

John replied, "I forgive you, Your Majesty. Don't worry. We'll fix it together."

John looked around and saw many families around the palace grounds as they enjoyed their reunions. He smiled at Tony, Freddie, and Pippy in the distance, but he saved his biggest smile for Ivy. They were all tied together now by a bond that could never be broken.

XXXII: A New Beginning

The dark days that had been cast upon them had finally ended, and peace once again reigned in the kingdom. Agribel, fair queen of Belghan, held a ceremony in the month that followed to honor the fellowship as the new guardians of the North.

All was well in the kingdom once more. Villages blossomed as families were no longer subject to the cruelties of the heartless Ice Queen of old. With her heart restored, she was once again a just ruler, and her people loved and followed her willingly; however, some citizens remained skeptical after their terrible experiences of the past several years. The field of energy that surrounded the aerial palace no longer existed, and it had been lowered to reside among her people. Lake Tarin was cleared in order to avoid unnecessary flooding.

The former chief was relieved honorably from duty. He was able to return to his family in one of the more modest northwestern villages and properly grieve his lost son after all these years. William's father was appointed in his place at the former chief's recommendation. He believed William's father to be loyal and courageous to those he loved dearly, and he would serve Her Majesty in the same fashion. William would never forget the Chief.

Tony's and Jacob's fathers would be Number Two and Number Three respectively. Rob, Joey, and Norman were all present for the inauguration ceremony. William knew that his father would protect Penelope and him in his new position. That was what still mattered most to him and always would. Family protected one another at all costs. They vowed to help one another locate their families who remained in exile. A closed casket funeral was held for Jacob at the ceremony to honor his courage and leadership skills, which were exemplary for someone of such youth; his body was never found.

Mitch and William became the best of friends and often sparred together as they readied themselves to one day be royal palace guards themselves. Mitch experienced a broken heart, however, as he had not seen Dahlia since the day the kingdom was won back. He still felt a connection with her even though she claimed that she never did. Love would always remain a mystery to him.

John spent a lot of quality time with Ivy. His quirky half sister, Dahlia, had revealed his past to him, and he shared everything with Ivy. It made her care for him even more, as she felt a need to protect him. Her feelings were reciprocated, especially as she had lost her family. He vowed to her that he would search for them throughout the lands until they were found. They held out hope that her family had fled and sought refuge elsewhere. They agreed that they would begin their search in the West, where she would be able to enjoy her favorite dish, grilled poisson. Perhaps he would even build up the courage to see his mother and grandmother once again.

Sandriver had been hailed by all leaps of the North to be their warrior king. Though none would have been able to challenge him, it was the first time that the leaps put aside their rivalries and would rest and fight alongside one another. He united the leopards of the North. However, it was a role that he would not forever live to hold. He would raise his heir to take his place one day. On that day, he would be ready to pass on to the Realm of Peace and return to his former warrior queen.

Salina was disappointed that she could not keep the cub heir. She pleaded with persistence but was still denied. Others laughed because they all knew that within a year, she would already be dwarfed by the Tiberian leopard heir and could not care for it as a pet. Sandriver allowed her to name it to appease her persistence. She named him Mali, in remembrance of a small feline she once cared for before she was sent to the palace. John spent a lot of time with the cub, which would one day be to him as Sandriver was to Midwa.

One fine day, four members of the fellowship, John, Ivy, Pippy, and Tony, were playing tag in the fields. They were enjoying themselves as they once did on the lift before their adventure really began. It already seemed like ages ago. They enjoyed their newfound peace and happiness.

Ivy said to John as she tagged him, "I'm ready for another adventure." She was out of breath.

He replied, "Um…maybe we should enjoy the peace for a while." He pet Mali and picked him up. The cub had been vying for his attention for the past hour, and he finally gave in to his request.

"Hey!" Freddie yelled from the distance.

He caught all of their attentions. Tony and Pippy began to approach John and Ivy, as they figured playtime was over since they had stopped to talk.

Freddie yelled again, "My mother is cooking roasted pontaccio for dinner! You must join us. She insists!"

"I'm starving!" Pippy said excitedly. The petite girl had an insatiable appetite and never gained any weight.

Tony concurred. "I'm *famished*. I'm going. I'll go see if Gavin and Wilbur can join. I'm sure Freddie's mother won't mind. She usually cooks for an army." He laughed as he ran off.

Ivy turned to John. "I'm hungry too. Come on."

John agreed, but at that moment, Mali leaped from his arms and ran off. "I'll meet up with you. Mali's run off, *again*. He's such a rebel. It's hard to believe that he will be the warrior king of the jungle one day. I'll be right back, OK?"

John jogged through the bushes and caught the cub. He picked him up and caressed his short fur. The cub had grown quickly, and soon he would not be able to pick him up anymore. He lit his eyes for the cub, as it seemed to soothe its nerves and calm him. John finally had learned how to channel the powers of Midwa that lay deep within him, but it would be a long time before he would be able to conjure what he had several times when his master, his father, Midwa, existed within him. He would need to develop his powers in order to return the ring to safety, which meant he would need to travel to the Islands of the Phoenix Dragons eventually.

Mali jumped from his arms again and ran deeper into the jungle. The voices of his friends became fainter as they made their way to dinner.

"Hold on, Mali! You're going too quickly. Come *here*!" John said.

John continued to follow the Tiberian leopard as it ran through the lush bushes and deeper into the jungle, until he could hear the others no longer.

"Come on, Mali. It's not funny anymore. Come back!" John said, beginning to show annoyance.

He struggled through a thick bush and noticed Mali under a shaded tree; the cub tugged at something. He occasionally looked behind himself as he approached, but everyone was out of sight. He was deep in the jungle, far away from the nearest village.

John continued to approach the figure Mali was tugging at with his still-growing teeth. It appeared to be the frame of a young girl, though it was unclear in the shadows. With each step closer, the image became clearer. Soon he was only a pace away from the figure.

It was a girl, pale and weak. He knelt down and turned the head. He was looking at Dahlia.

"Dahlia…what's wrong?" he said with concern.

She struggled to speak and fought to thrust the words from her lips. "Stay…back. Don't come…any closer. Don't let her take you back again. Run…*Run!*"

Suddenly her eyes were empty, a bottomless oblivion. His surroundings quickly began to become dark. All of the light was consumed as her mouth opened like a vacuum and sucked in all around him. John was suddenly in an abyss of darkness, stuck in oblivion as shrieks echoed. He felt an intense pain as his memories were torn from him violently. He was in agony. The memories quickly dissipated as he flew violently across the darkness, unable to control himself. All of his experiences from the past weeks were torn from his memory.

And then nothing.

Beyond the rusted metal bars of his prison, John stared into the abyss of her eyes as he desperately searched for answers. Why was he being held prisoner? What had he done to deserve this? And more importantly, who was he? John had no memory of his past. All he had was the pain of the nightmares that haunted him each night without fail.

He saw nothing but pain and sorrow deep within her eyes, accompanied by an intense migraine that tore his mind apart. He could stare no longer, as his body began to numb and forced him to surrender his efforts to search for those answers.

She passed by his cell every evening as supper was thrown in; her visit was routinely accompanied by a conversation devoid of words. After she blinked her eyes once, she would often roll them into the back of her head as if to look upon the prisoners behind her. She would often exhale a humph at John in disappointment. After one final gaze at him, she reveled in a wicked, uncontrollable laughter that made him cringe.

She had earned the title of Ice Queen.

On this night, he attempted a desperate final plea with her for his freedom, a plea that fell flat as he was unable to build up the courage to utter his words beyond a whisper. "Can I please g-g-go?" The words vanished into thin air before they completed their flight to her ears, or so he thought.

She acknowledged his mumble and ceased her laughter. She turned around immediately and yelled beyond the worn teeth of her barely open mouth, "*What* did you say?"

Rumor had it among the young prisoners that her teeth were worn because she had eaten any child who attempted to flee, flesh and bone. A young prisoner nicknamed Delusional Dahlia swore that she had seen the wicked lady devour an eyeball that dangled from the tip of her ice arrow after an adrenaline-filled escape and hunt.

John mumbled, "Nothing, Your…"

There was a faint voice in his mind echoing, "Don't…let her… take you back again…"

"*Excuse me?*" the Ice Queen screamed.

"Don't…let her…take you back again…" whispered an even fainter voice that he barely heard. He tried with all his might to hold on to the words before they echoed no longer.

"Not…again, *Your Majesty*…" He began to reel in the voice. It began to become louder. The dungeon around him began to shake as the other prisoners screamed in fear. The Ice Queen began to scream as well as she raised her scepter toward him. John began to illuminate bright blue within his cell as the others looked upon him.

The Ice Queen shrieked, "Nooooooooooooooooo!"

John became brighter and brighter. He'd had the strength within himself the whole time. He just needed the courage to use it.

Suddenly the light was blinding and the shriek deafening. John felt himself fading as an enormous force rushed into him and tore him from where he stood. His memories were restored.

His eyes opened.

Mali licked his face as Ivy ran her fingers through his hair. Tony, Freddie, and Pippy stood above him as well. As he regained awareness, he sat up. He pushed Mali and Ivy's hand to the side and looked desperately around for Dahlia. He saw her leaning against a mackelroy tree, still weak, as Mitch stood above her.

He ran over to her with haste and asked, "Are you all right?"

Mitch spoke up. "She's weak, but she'll be OK. I started to twitch, so I knew she was close. I fought through it as it got stronger, and then it stopped. I knew she would not leave me. We have a connection."

Dahlia finally had the strength to look up and speak. "Thank you, Mitch..." She then looked over to John as the color in her face began to restore. "You were out for a while, but I refused to give up on you. We finally did it...brother."

Meanwhile, the great hall remained empty, with the exception of the frozen statue of Pyro, phoenix dragon of fire, which rose behind Her Majesty's throne. It had been moved from the center, as it obstructed the walkway.

A pair of eyes glistened in the shadows and slowly emerged, as no one was present. The creature slowly approached the frozen phoenix dragon and looked upon it. The creature's eyes began to glow a murky hue of jade.

"Mustasi kutnei sapuh," the voice mumbled to itself. It translated to "You belong to me now."

It then mumbled, "Verasik Monta kepo...palanka..." It translated to "I've won this round...brother..."

The glow of the phoenix dragon's eyes suddenly altered from crimson to jade as a droplet of melted ice raced down to the palace floor.